the rhythms between us

THE TOUR SERIES
BOOK 1

YOE APOLINARIO

Dedicated to twenty-year old Yoe. The new adult reader who wanted to read lesbian romance novels with Black and Latinx characters, but struggled to find them. This is for you and all the readers out there like you.

trigger warning

Trigger Warnings: Death, trauma, and stages of grief.

Dear Reader,

This novel is Women's fiction with elements of Romance. Women's Fiction does not require happily ever after, so consider yourself warned.

* * *

Spice Levels 🌶

This novel is level 3 spicy.

Level 1: Love scenes are not detailed, and more of a summary—but not closed door. These books have sexual tension and 1 intimate sex scene, usually towards the end of the book as the climax of the relationship.

Level 2: These books have ~2 descriptive intimate scenes, but mostly milder language. I feel like many romance books follow the pattern of oral in the first 50%, and traditional sex towards the end of the book. Throw in more detail, and you have a spice level 2.

Level 3: Welp, you've reached explicit intimate scenes. Spice level 3 would include more forking throughout the book and lots of detail —naughty words and all. But the key here is level 3 is still heavy on plot!

Level 4: There is a balance of plot and romance. Spice level 4 books have multiple explicit and very detailed intimate scenes that most likely don't add to the plot. Also explicit descriptive language.

Level 5: 5 Chili Peppers = erotica. There's not really a plot, but there is a lot of forking, and it's detailed, explicit, pages long, and probably kinky.

There may or may not be a cliffhanger that gets resolved in Book 2.

* Source: Spicy Levels - thespicybookblog.com

introduction

The Tour Bus

Your home-on-wheels for the next four months

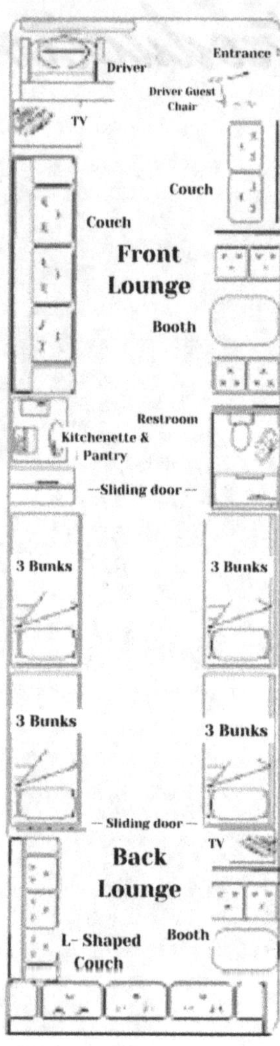

prologue

THE RESOUNDING ACHE in my head is the first thing to wake me. Pressure pounds against my temples and travels to the base of my neck and down my shoulders. I try to get up, but the pain says otherwise. After blinking a few times, I realize the darkness above me is the sky. I'm outside. Well, kind of. The roof is gone, and a mix of blood and raindrops paint my clothes. The stars twinkle back at me, almost as if God is telling me *it's okay. You're okay.*

But I'm not okay. And if I don't hear anything soon. I won't be okay. Not for the rest of my life.

I scream and scream and scream. My pleads are covered in agony. Loaded with prayer. Coated in regret. And despite all of that, she still doesn't speak. She doesn't wake up. Because she's already gone.

PANIC STARTS to trickle in the moment I turn into the dance studio parking lot. Though this is the third week of rehearsal, my anxiety is still through the roof.

"You okay, honey?"

The St. Louis drawl, in my mother's accent, soothes me from the car speaker. She's noted my abrupt silence on the receiving end of the phone call and knows exactly what's running through my mind.

"Yeah, I'm good. Just parked. Back for another day of living the dream, I guess," I say flatly.

"Yes, it *is* another day of living the dream," she begins with a stern Christian tone I know all too well. "A day God has blessed you with air in your lungs and mobility in your limbs, which are about to be put to use on the job you prayed for time and time again."

My mind flashes back through the last two years. Moving to LA with hopes of pursuing a career as a professional dancer, just to hit wall after wall.

"Thank you, but we are looking for taller dancers."

"You're amazing, but we've already filled our spots for black female dancers."

I've heard about the ways the industry does dark-skinned women dirty, but nothing could've prepared me to experience it. When dozens of knotless braids filled my scalp, casting directors informed me that the roles they were searching for were for black women with natural hair. While wearing my fro out, I was told they were looking for more urban-looking black women. The icing on the cake was at another audition where the casting director told me box braids looked too urban on me but edgy and chic on a nonblack girl. I shudder at the memories of serial auditioning. Non-stop no's. An era I don't wish to return to. At least I have that nursing degree Momma insisted I get before moving to LA, but the thought of switching careers, giving up on my dreams of having a dance career, frightens me even more.

"Do you hear me, young lady?" Momma says, dragging me down from my day dream.

"Yes, ma'am. God is good, and I am grateful to be making money doing what I love to do... but BriAnn is really testing my faith."

"Well, first baby, I can't trust no woman that changes the pronunciation of her name like that."

School girl-like giggles erupt from my chest before I can reel it in.

"I am serious. From what you told me, that lady is from Dallas, Texas. There is no way her folks chose the pronunciation 'Bri-on'. That is the biggest fabrication I've ever heard of."

"Momma..." I squeak, fighting away laughter. "While I fully

agree, that lady is a choreographer on this job and she's had a target on me since day one, for some reason, I can't figure out."

"Khloe Elizabeth Thompson."

Her voice vibrates from the car speakers, but judging by the way she recited my full name, I picture her in front of me. Hands planted on her full hips and dark, round brown eyes staring into me. Features that I inherited directly from her.

"You are a Thompson. A name built from strength and resilience. I don't know what's wrong with that woman, but you go in there and show her why you're meant to be on that stage."

"Yes, ma'am," I say in my best upbeat tone.

"Good. Now, let me get a look at you before you go inside."

I press the Facetime button, and after two rings, I am looking at my mom's pearly smile contrasting with her deep brown skin. Her dimples twinkle back at me with confidence. Her expression screaming, "You got this."

Being on this video call with Momma is like staring into a mirror. Though I inherited all her features from her face to her curvy shape, my expression still doesn't emote a quarter of her confidence. I'm still working on that part.

"Oh, baby..." Momma says, practically reading my mind. "You can endure this, and you *will* come out on top. I know things are a little crazy back at your apartment right now."

"I'd rather not think about that..."

I blink away tears before they can fall, shutting out all the chaos that awaits me in that dreadful one-bedroom apartment in North Hollywood.

"That's what I was about to say, honey. Leave those problems at the door. Don't take them into the dance studio with you. Those problems will sort themselves out eventually. I promise."

"Yes, ma'am." The tension in my shoulders unwind a bit.

"Remember to say a prayer before you start rehearsal. Pray for God's protection over your body, mind, and spirit. I've seen them videos of that boy on my TikTok. He's bad news."

"Momma, you've gotta stop doom-scrolling conspiracy videos on TikTok. Those are just internet sleuths jumping to conclusions." I pause and shake my head while a part of me wonders why my mom insists on having TikTok, anyway. "The police did an investigation, and Zion was in Europe during the time of his baby momma's car crash. He had nothing to do with it. He's not some secret drug pin or whatever the videos say. I've spent the last three weeks with him and he's been nothing but sweet and respectful, just an R&B artist I am lucky enough to book a tour with. That's all."

"I'm glad you've had good experiences. Just keep a professional distance from him. I heard he often takes a liking to his female dancers..." Momma's voice trails away. Her skepticism coating her words. "And remember, everything that glitters ain't gold."

CHAPTER TWO

THE SUN RAYS creeping around the edges of the curtain burn my eyes. Light hits every corner of my bedroom, from the olive green walls to the plush white comforter encasing my body. I rub my loose curls sprawled out around the pillow, evidence that I forgot to wear my silk bonnet to bed. I try blinking a couple of times to adjust to the early morning, but my vision responds slowly.

It must be early if my 8:00 a.m. alarm hasn't gone off yet. It's probably six, or around sev—

"Good morning, sleepyhead," a voice whispers behind me, nearly giving me a heart attack. I rarely let women sleepover after our... escapades, but this one wore me out last night.

Shit, what's her name again?

A honey-colored hand wraps around my waist, drawing me closer. I turn over, following the hand to a woman with the same honey complexion. Her freckled skin, big curly hair, and hazel eyes with specs of gold mixed with brown lies beside me. Hints of sleep shadow her face, but she's still gorgeous. Her round lips curve into a small smile as her flirtatious gaze bares into me, hurling me into flashbacks of the night before. Her gentle, yet demanding, touch exploring my body. The taste of her still left on my tongue.

Wait, what was her name? Leila? Letticia?

Shit, I have to pay more attention to the profiles I swipe right on.

"Good morning," I reply, sliding her on top of me and lining her hips to mine.

Letting my nails sink into the bottom of her ass, I circle my womanhood against hers.

A giggle leaves her lips.

"Wow, trying to go for another round? First thing in the morning?"

I've already let you break my no-sleepovers rule, so I might as well get some pussy out of it.

"What can I say?" I grind a little deeper as she tosses her head back. A soft moan escapes her throat. "I woke up *hungry*."

This time, she moans louder, and I already feel her arousal dripping onto me. That line was terrible. Waking up to this girl without so much as a guess at her name is terrible. Hell, her moan is even terrible. But this is my life. A revolving vortex of random women. It's been like this for five years since everything fell a part during my senior year of college.

"Damn, baby...I'm already wet."

"No pet names."

I slap her ass hard enough to see her skin reddening. My hand even stings from the impact, but Lorraine... or Lydia shrieks with a wild grin on her face. She wasn't kidding when she wrote "into rough play" on her profile.

"Uhhh," she moans after I send two fingers inside of her. With a heavy breath, she tries to regain her composure. "I'm sorry... as much as I would love to keep playing, I can't. I have to go to work."

"Aw, that's too bad."

I'm lying. Another round would've been fun, but I rather she leaves. I prefer my mornings to myself, especially before an eight-hour rehearsal. Whatever her name is, climbs off of me, collecting her clothing scattered across the room. My natural reaction is to help, but that goes against another rule. No sweet gestures. No matter how big or small.

Gestures = care.

Care means she feels welcomed enough to come back, and no one comes to my house twice. Doesn't matter if they've given me the best nut in the world.

"When does your tour start?" she asks while slipping on her shoes.

"Next week."

"Damn. So soon. And you have no more off days?"

"Nope."

That wasn't a lie, but like I said, no one comes to my house twice.

"That's too bad. I would've loved to see you again."

"Yup."

I let the answer hang between us, praying she gets the hint.

"Okay... well," she mutters from the living room.

Judging by lingering body language, she probably expects me to see her out. A kiss goodbye or something. I lift my arm from the comfort of my bed and wave.

"Bye, Naya."

"Bye..."

"Wow." Her expression flat lines. "Can't even remember my name. It's LaNiece!"

She turns on her heel, slamming the door behind her.

* * *

The wholesome sounds of *City Girls' Take Yo Man* blare through the speakers as I switch the car into park. Sleep pushes the backs of my eyes. I don't usually indulge in dating apps until the middle of the tour, but this rehearsal process has been... tense.

"Did you *really* just come into rehearsal with another woman's perfume on you?" Bunny says the second I walk into the studio.

I thank God for the loud warm-up music masking our conversation, but no one is here yet. Just Leah at the other side of the room, doing her pre-rehearsal pilates.

"Wouldn't you like to know?"

I stick my tongue out, sitting my bag down in my usual corner.

"Girl, I've known you since college. You probably showered, but babygirl's smell is all wrapped up in that lion's mane." Bunny wafts the tips of my curls resting by my waist, then grabs a fistful with a gentle tug. "She was like *Uhhhhhh Nayaaaa,*" she teases with a fake moan.

I nudge her arm. "Girl, you are actually crazy! You know that?"

She's unhinged, but Bunny is one of my closest friends in LA. Nine years ago, I sat behind her at Florida Atlantic University's freshman orientation as the dean delivered an "inspirational" speech. A poetic conglomerate of words meant to rally us for the semester ahead ended in half the student body asleep in the auditorium.

"And don't forget, students!" he'd boasted. "This is the beginning of your higher education. The start of your college GPA. The education for the rest of your life. This is not *Girls Gone Wild*. This—"

A giggle erupted behind me. From the same girl I'd heard scoff and blow her breath earlier in the speech. She smacked her gum and ran her long white acrylic fingernails through her perfectly laid wig, and I mean perfect—like baby soft, thirty-inch, natural brown, quality human hair. I peeped her reactions earlier and silently sang my amen in agreement. But when she giggled, the spirit traveled over, forcing me to combust into a full-forced snicker, loud enough for surrounding students to hear.

Horrified faces turned to us, their expressions screaming, "How dare you be so disrespectful?!"

"Y'all need to get y'all panties outcha asses," she challenged in a whispered announcement, then returned her gaze to me.

The whites of her deep brown eyes and pearly smiley stood out against her silky, coal-colored skin. She was stunning, regal, like she belonged to African royalty. She rolled her eyes at the surrounding students.

"What y'all *need* to be worried about is that man's toupee."

From that moment on, we were attached at the hip. Throughout school, in the dance team, we started on campus and even after graduation, when we decided to move to LA to pursue our dreams of becoming professional dancers.

Bunny plops down next to me as I slip on my knee pads. The rest of the cast trickles in one by one, offering their polite but sleepy greetings.

"I'm actually jealous you got some. My married boo hasn't been around all week. I miss that big ol' dick."

"Must you talk about male genitals so early? You trying to make me throw up?"

"I'm sorry, friend. It's just... I *need* it. I need my mouth around it!" She wraps her arms around my shoulders, trapping me into a hug. "You know? *Gawk, gawk, gawk!*" she says into my ear, accompanied by gurgling sounds.

"Bunny!" I escape her arms, giggling and clutching my stomach. "You are really crazy. You know that? I can't stand you!"

I rise from the floor, holding out my hand to her. Bunny gets up and blows a kiss in my direction. "Sis, you love me. Stop playin'."

Before I can reply, BriAnn barges into the room with a Louis Vuitton bag dangling from her wrist, an oversized, wide-brim hat, and sunglasses as dark as midnight.

"All right! Social hour is over! Let's run it from the top! Full out!" she barks while marching up to the sound system.

BriAnn.

I think the pronunciation of her name is an embellishment, she added as an adult, but it doesn't matter. BriAnn is a legend in the industry. She's toured with the likes of Anita Baker, Prince, and even Michael Jackson. BriAnn has kicked down the barriers for black women in the dance industry, booked multiple tours, brand campaigns, and even landing a few speaking roles in a movie. She is a pillar in the dance community, an inspiration, but she is... difficult to work with.

The group exchanges knowing glances as we travel to our beginning spots. I'm not surprised. This is BriAnn's usual M.O. I just wish I'd arrived early enough to properly stretch, which I would've if I wasn't gallivanting through the night with Lynette... or Lilly...

Why can't I remember that girl's name?

Seconds after setting up, BriAnn presses play. Bunny begins out the piece with a sultry walk, leading Zion's stand-in, Rob, onto the floor. A couple of counts later, the rest of us join in a rippled timing. Tiana, Rae, Me, Khloe, then Leah match Bunny's sultry walk and surround Rob as he lip-syncs into a water bottle. One by one, our hands move like ribbons in the air until they reach for Rob's chest to the bass sound in the track. Once the last dancer places her hand on his chest, Rob breaks away from the group and walks over to stage right, refusing to succumb to our luring sensual energy—the overarching theme of the entire show.

He starts the hook, and our movements transition from liquid molasses to sharp daggers. This section demands clean lines, staccato steps and the hardest part of this piece, dropping to our knees in one count and jumping back onto our feet by the next. It is one of the most athletic parts of this piece and one of the hardest, especially without a proper warm-up. With our arms straight to the side, we twist down to the floor and—whew! I have no idea how I executed the jump to my feet with these sore quads. A smile begins to take over my face until I glance into the mirror.

Everyone landed the move except Khloe. She popped up a count late and is now struggling to catch up with the group. A mistake that's nearly invisible to the regular eye but sticks out like a massive sore thumb to a dancer.

"What the fuck, Khloe?!" BriAnn roars before pausing the music.

Stillness replaces the steps in our bodies. The sound of our labored breaths blooms in the space music once was. Rage spews from BriAnn's pores. The tension palpitating throughout the studio. Here's the thing, BriAnn is a bully. Most likely because of what she endured as a black female dancer back in the day, but a bully none-theless.

Days ago, I stood by awkwardly when she tore down Rae's technical training. I gasped out loud that one time she told Leah, the only white girl on the job, that she danced like an uncooked bag of white rice. I cringed the day she smacked Tiana's phone out of her hand for texting during rehearsal. And rage rippled through me when she body-shamed Khloe, making comments like, "Maybe you could hit the counts on time if you laid off the fast food once in a while." Despite her being one of the cleanest eaters out of all of us. And with all the healthy food, Khloe has somehow managed to maintain the perfect physique. In the most platonic way I can express, she has the hips, chest and thighs people pay top dollar for.

"Khloe..." BriAnn rises from her wooden stool and launches it across the room. "Y'all leave tomorrow. Tomorrow! You've had a month to get this move, and you're still fucking up!"

She pauses. Echos from the stool's collision with the wall mixing in with our heavy breaths. BriAnn speaks again, with short venom-soaked words meant to cut.

"I. Am. Just. Sick. And. Tired." The dark shades cover her eyes, but we still feel them lasering into Khloe. "I'm tired of working with unprofessional, lazy, untalented, overweight dancers that always—"

"She's done the move before," I say with enough bass to command a small auditorium.

The words fly from my mouth before I can catch them, and BriAnn's lasers travel to me.

CHAPTER THREE

"WHAT DID YOU SAY?"

BriAnn redirects her narrowed eyes toward me, peering over her glasses.

Before today, BriAnn has never targeted me. This is my sixth tour, and by the grace of God, I've worked hard for everyone in the industry to know that Nayara Alvarez is a versatile, hard worker, so she's never attacked my dancing. And I guess my body type is muscular enough to avoid her body-shaming stabs, too. But after today, I'm not so sure I'll ever be in the green again.

Steadying my breath, I stare directly into BriAnn's sunglasses.

"I said... she's done the move before. She's done it a thousand times before. Maybe it's harder today because she's tired. *All of us* are tired. We've had *three* off days this entire month. We aren't machines. I think you need to take a second. Go outside and gather yourself." The words tsunami forward, and I let them. There's no stopping them now. "Also, the days of every working dancer being a size zero are long gone. Look around. Scroll online. Read a fucking magazine. Women of *all* shapes are embraced. Most artists *prefer* thick women now. Leave that shit back in the day *when you were a dancer.*" I say the last words with my chin to the air, mocking the very lines she starts most of her rants with.

The silence in the room is deafening. I keep my eyes ahead, but in my peripheral, I see the color draining from the rest of the dancers' faces. Their limbs are frozen. BriAnn's eyes rain down my body. She scans me from head to toe, contemplating her next move. An old Western movie stand-off wouldn't hold a penny to this scene I've created.

I lock my knees, bracing myself for all the possibilities: getting cussed in front of the entire cast, being fired from the tour before it begins, or worse, being blackballed from future gigs. Working with people like BriAnn makes me wonder how many tours I have left in me. How many times can I stand by while dancers are mistreated? Why do choreographers demand the world from their dancers? While the cost of living is inflating, why do our rates remain the same? Usually, I'm good at pushing these thoughts away, but they've started to follow me home, which explains why I got home last night and swiped right on the first pretty woman I saw. That's why I stayed up late last night, doing... *all kinds of things*...instead of resting for yet another eight-hour rehearsal. I wanted to decompress. I needed to distract my brain from dance steps, an anxious atmosphere and BriAnn's lethal mouth. The same lethal mouth that is about to get me blackballed from the industry.

Before I can continue my mental spiral, BriAnn tips her

sunglasses back over her eyes and *smiles*. A real, ear-to-ear, flash of teeth smile.

"All right, everyone," she says slowly. "Let's take a ten."

CHAPTER FOUR

BRIANN TURNS ON HER HEEL, marching to her purse. The rest of us waste no time collecting our bags and dispersing from the room. Before leaving the studio, I search for Naya, but she's already halfway into the parking lot, walking beside Bunny. One arm lugging her duffel bag and the other interlocked with Bunny's elbow.

"Hey! Naya!" I run toward them.

They spin around, a sweet expression on Bunny's face. Naya's face is unreadable, almost stoic. I pause, unsure of what to say next. The person who barely said a peep this entire month, outside of giggling with Bunny in a corner, not only stood up for me but read BriAnn for filth in the process.

"Uhm..." I stammer. "Can I talk to you?"

Bunny turns to Naya and kisses her on the cheek. "I'll catch you later, sis. Let me know if you need anything."

As Bunny walks away, I desperately search for words to fill the empty air.

"I… That was…" I take a breath. "You didn't have to do that back there. I appreciate it, though. It's been hard, and I've been feeling a lot of ways in these rehearsals, so I just wanted to say thank you."

"Don't worry about it, Khloe."

Before I can reply, both of our phones vibrate. A text message notification from the group chat hangs from the top of the screen.

Soakin' Wet Summer Tour Core Dancers

BriAnn: This break will be extended. Please come back at 2 p.m. for a full-out run-through with Zion.

I peer up to find a small grin forming in the corners of Naya's mouth. Her almond-shaped eyes are still looking into her phone. The sunlight catches every corner of her smooth mocha face, a complexion a little lighter than mine. The light rays also illuminate her moisturized neck and arms. All the bits of skin her tank top and cargo shorts do not cover seem to draw in every sun ray. I've been rehearsing with Naya for about a month, but I guess I never really noticed how stunning she actually is.

No wonder she's worked for so many artists. One time, I over-heard Rae saying this was Naya's 17th tour. With looks like that, volu-minous 3C coils all the way down to her waist, and her wicked dance skills, I can see why choreographers and artists *have* to have her. She's the total package. I hope to learn more from her on this tour. I wonder if she mentors newer dancers. Maybe I can use this tour to get closer to her, get a few lessons or advice on the industry. She looks up from her phone. That small grin fades back into a blank stare.

"I guess we have a longer break!" I blurt out.

"Yup, looks like it."

"Are you hungry? Wanna go get some brunch to kill the time?"

I don't know if I imagined it, but her face brightens. Almost as if a ghost of a smile wafts by. Then, in an instant, her expression returns to the same flat demeanor.

"Yeah. Sure."

"Cool!" I say a little too loudly. "I'll drive!"

I raise the volume on the radio to get a break from my mindless stammering. The sounds of Meg the Stallion pulse around us. I lock my eyes forward, trying not to peer over too much, while Naya sits comfortably in the seat beside me, leg crossed at the knee and scrolling through her phone.

A yawn crawls its way out of my mouth as we wait at a red light. I glance at Naya to see if she notices, but her gaze remains fixated on her phone. Seconds later, another yawn threatens to push through, and I push it away. I am so glad this is our last day of rehearsal. The long days and sleep deprivation are catching up with me. I'm counting down the days until the tour begins. The show is strenuous and might be hard to execute night after night, but I rather that than the emotional tornado funneling in my apartment and BriAnn's attitude.

"You gonna get out, or are you gonna have lunch in there?" Naya asks, tearing me away from my thoughts. We've arrived at the Broken Egg Café, and I haven't moved since I put the car in park.

"Oh, yeah!" I blink a few times.

I exit the car and follow Naya into the brunch spot, where the hostess seats us almost immediately.

"We are very busy today. I apologize for any long wait times you may experience. Your server will be right with you momentarily. Is there anything I can get you to drink in the meantime?"

Our host clasps her hands, awaiting our response. Naya gestures toward me, insisting that I order first.

"I'll have a coffee. Three French vanilla creamers and two packs of sugar, please."

"I'll have some green tea with honey."

"Coming right up," the hostess replies as she floats away.

Naya returns her focus to her phone with her scrolling thumb ready to swipe. I scan the restaurant, looking for anything to take up mental property. Pictures of animated eggs decorate the walls. Eggs with cheerful faces, sad faces and even confused faces. They were all so expressive, so cute, brightening the space with their personalities.

"What are you smiling at?" Naya asks, with her face as stiff as a statue.

"Oh! All the different eggs on the walls. They all have their own expressions, their own feelings. It's adorable."

She surveys the room, then returns to her phone.

"Yup."

"So…" I begin. Naya looks up from the phone like I interrupted her favorite television show. "Does it ever get any easier? Isn't this your gazillionth tour? Does it ever get… I don't know… Easier to cope with?"

A chuckle slips through her flat-lined mouth. I do my best to conceal my surprise.

"For starters, this is my sixth tour, nowhere near a gazillion. Second, we haven't started the tour. To me, rehearsals don't count."

"What do you mean? This definitely feels like the beginning…"

The hostess returns with our drinks and some menus. Naya pours the side of honey into her tea and stirs it softly before answering.

"I guess, technically, one could say this is the beginning. We are learning the show that we are about to perform night after night for months ahead. Everything from our social lives, love lives and hell, even laundry, is suspended in the air, forced to navigate around our crazy work schedule." She sips her tea, allowing the satisfaction to reach the corners of her eyes. "This part of the process is crazy, but I don't consider it part of the tour."

"Then when does the tour start?"

"In my eyes, the tour begins once that bus travels the country. When our feet hit the stage. The feeling of ear-piercing screaming fans invading our ears. When our work days transform from eight hours long to 'just be there at 7 p.m. in time for the show to start.' A two-hour show. That leaves ample time before and after doing whatever you desire. Sight-see, sleep, go to the gym. Whatever you want. Build the experiences tours are made of."

My eyes twinkle as she speaks, and the hope builds in my chest. A feeling I used to experience before I moved to LA. A feeling that has since been replaced with reality, bills and an astronomical cost of living. Our server arrives, sputtering like she's had enough caffeine to keep her awake for a week.

"Hello! What can I get you guys to eat?!"

"Oh! I'm sorry... I hadn't gotten a chance to look. Can you—"

"It's okay. I'll go first," Naya interrupts. "Is it possible to get an order of French toast with a side of scrambled eggs?"

"Of course! Would you like cheese on your eggs?"

"No, thank you, but I will have a mimosa."

My eyes widen before I can snatch my face back into neutral.

She shrugs.

"What? I'm celebrating our last day of rehearsal."

The server turns to me. "Perfect! And what about you?"

"I'll have a veggie egg white omelet with a side of fruit... and a mimosa as well."

"Coming right up!"

Once the server is out of sight, Naya raises an eyebrow. "Well, look who's in the festive mood now?"

"Oh. Yeah. Just trying to make the most of this break. I guess."

I rub the back of my neck, trying to ignore the nerves whirling in my stomach.

Without replying, Naya whips her phone back out and continues scrolling, her face regressing to the flat expression from earlier. My eyes fall to my lap as I twiddle my thumbs.

During rehearsals, in the rare moments I wasn't drowning in overthinking thoughts, I'd seen Bunny and Naya interact. And every single time, they'd unite in stomach-clutching laughter. Naya's smile lighting up the entire corner of the room the two occupied. Her long curls shaking and bouncing off her shoulders. Whatever got them going would last several minutes, allowing them to change the topic and rebound to the same giggles.

Why is she being so bland to me?

Maybe she's still processing what happened in rehearsal. She probably wanted to spend this break alone instead of on a lunch with a newbie dancer asking her dull questions. Based on their closeness, I'm sure she's known Bunny for quite a while. Maybe she takes a while to warm up to new people.

"So, have you ever talked back to a choreographer like that?"

She peels her eyes from the screen, staring at me blankly for what feels like thirty minutes, but is probably just a few seconds.

"Nope," she says, dipping into her phone yet again.

Fuck this.

This is like pulling teeth.

I reach into my purse, take out my phone, and begin watching a video from our rehearsal footage. A clip of the finale at the end of the show, the last routine we'd learned and the one I am the least familiar with. Since Naya can't be bothered to speak to me anyway, I figure she won't mind the music coming from my phone, so I leave my headphones tightly wound at the bottom of my purse.

Though all five female dancers are in the video, I focus on me. My lines, execution and cleanliness. I study a section of choreography that didn't seem right. The group looks okay, but I am in an entirely different rhythmic pocket from the rest of the women. Sitting in the grooves with different intention, forced movements, and I am moving a hair faster, too. I drag my finger across the screen, rewinding the footage over and over again, searching for mental notes to apply.

"That footage is from the day we learned it. Last week, Khloe," Naya states, without lifting her eyes from her phone.

"Huh?"

"That video you keep watching is from last week. Shot hours after we learned it. Whatever corrections you're obsessing over right now, I can assure you are not even a thing."

I lock my phone and put it back in my purse. Propping my elbows on the table, I bury my face into my open palms and release a low groan.

"I know it's old footage. I know. I know," I mumble, burying my face in my hands. "It's that BriAnn—"

"Hey." Naya cuts me off with a sternness reverberating through her voice.

She leans across the table and tilts my head up to meet her eyes. Before today, we've never spoken more than two words to each other. Now, we are just inches apart. Her brown eyes sear into me in a way that makes my hands sweat. Gross. At least her soft hands smell like lavender and eucalyptus.

"Don't let this one job, with one nut-case choreographer, make you question your talent. Work hard in rehearsals, take your critiques, give it your all every time, but don't ever..." She strokes her right thumb over mine. "*Ever*, let anyone question your God-given gifts. BriAnn is her own person, with her own sets of traumas and shit. Don't let her shit become your shit."

I try to speak, but nothing comes out. A part of me can't believe I'm this close to Naya.

"Thank—"

"Two mimosas, coming in hot!"

We separate, opening the space between us and allowing our server to set the drinks in front of us. Her loud words shatter the moment, but I'm grateful. Tears had already begun to burn behind my eyes. I don't want to ruin my first one-on-one with Naya by laying a trail of tears.

"Thank you..." I murmur, picking up my drink and holding it in the air.

"Don't sweat it." The ends of her mouth curve up ever so slightly. "Cheers."

Once our food arrives, we dig in, and Naya returns to the same emotionless mood from earlier. Replying to all my conversational attempts with one-word answers and barely looking up from her phone. After we finish eating, we go back to rehearsal, where Naya doesn't look in my direction for the rest of the day.

CHAPTER FIVE

EVERYONE BUZZES AROUND THE BUS, getting ready, while I sit in the front lounge of the bus, dressed and halfway through rolling a joint. Rae is in the kitchen area fixing a sandwich. It's her third one since the show ended two hours ago, but she insists on inhaling it before the club.

"Another PB&J?" Leah jokes, her floral dress flowing around her knees.

She walks up to Rae, her brown cowboy boots clicking with every step, and takes a paper plate from the cabinet.

"I'm gonna make one, too! You got a secret you're not telling me about?"

Her wavy, auburn hair lands in all different directions, matching the cute, reddish-brown freckles, which are all scrunched up, waiting for Rae's reply.

"It's the only thing that soaks up alcohol and prevents hang-overs! Grab some bread!"

Rae meticulously cuts off the crust and slices the sandwich in half. Her hip-length box braids are tossed over her shoulder as she adds the finishing touches to the sandwich. She's wearing black heels that lace to her knees and a short, black-laced dress. I've only known Rae for the duration of this job, but I quickly noticed one thing. No matter what her outfit of the day is, she's going to incorporate some sort of Japanese flair to it, proudly rocking her Blasian heritage. Tonight, she styled the little black dress with a black and red kimono that falls to her calves.

"All right!" she calls to the back of the bus while wrapping her PB&J in a napkin. "How long do you guys need?"

"Ima need about five minutes to finish the other side!" Bunny hollers from the restroom, waving around a curling iron and gesturing toward the perfectly curled hair on her left side and the small messy bun yet to be done on her right.

"Babe, the girls are leaving soon. I'm gonna call you back when we get back from the club... Okay, I love you," I hear Tiana say into her cell phone from the inside of her bunk. She'd gotten ready faster than all of us, then spent the remaining time checking in with her boyfriend at home.

"What kinda club is this, anyway? Am I letting my freak flag fly, or am I a hetero fella tonight?" DayDay asks while he reaches into his bunk for his cologne.

DayDay is the wardrobe stylist on tour and the only male on our bus.

Two days ago, we said goodbye to our lives in LA for four months and flew to North Carolina for our first show on the Soakin' Wet Summer Tour. We arrived at the venue at 2 p.m. with just enough time to load our luggage under the bus and pack a day bag with essentials. Makeup, hair products, body soap, shower shoes, and a post-show outfit. DayDay was on Zion's bus with his photographer, videographer, manager, two security guards and Zion's cousin, whose job title is a mystery to everyone. After situating ourselves in our new home on wheels, we went our separate ways. Bunny and I went to one of my favorite soul food spots, Mert's, a restaurant I'd discovered on my first tour. Some girls went sightseeing, and DayDay prepped our wardrobe for the show that night.

By the time we finished our first show that night, DayDay was sitting in the front lounge of our tour bus with his suitcases in hand and puppy-dog eyes.

"Can I move to y'all's bus? It's only been a few hours, and I already feel like I am living in a frat house. There're already dishes piled in the sink, and Zion brought ten groupies onto the bus."

The vote was unanimous, and he took the bunk above mine.

"I'm not sure what kind of club this is, boo!" I reply. "When I asked Instagram for good clubs in the area, this spot came highly recommended."

DayDay rolls his eyes and smooths out his tight purple t-button-up.

"I guess this will do for tonight, but I got some pieces in my luggage and they *will* be worn on this tour, you hear me?! Momma has a silver corset and with a matching cowboy hat that only the gays would appreciate!"

"A sliver corset? Sounds sexy babe! Make sure I'm there when you wear it."

I poke my tongue out at him and bat my eyelashes.

"Huh? A corset?"

Khloe boards the bus, hearing the tail end of our conversation.

She'd run back into the arena because she'd forgotten her phone inside.

"Is this place that fancy? Should I get my heels from under the bus?"

A hint of worry creeps into her face. A brown nylon maxi dress hugs her curves. The right side of the dress has a slit that showcases her full walnut brown thigh down to her crispy white and brown Jordans.

"It's casual, and what you're wearing is fine," I say, doing my best not to let my eyes wander her frame.

"Girl! Your dress is about to get us in for free!" DayDay adds.

The worry on her face dissipates, replaced by two deep dimples in her cheeks.

"Yeah, honey. I'm wearing heels 'cause that's my steez," Rae interjects while stuffing the last piece of the PB&J into her mouth. "If you feel more comfortable in sneakers, do you. With that body and face, you can wear a trash bag and still look beautiful."

Seeing Khloe's face light up sends a warmth to mine. I love watching women build each other up. I know it's only the first night of the tour, but I have a good feeling about this group. Everyone seems to look out for each other. They move around manically to finish getting ready, but everyone weaves through the tight spaces on the bus with ease. Nobody is a diva or a mean girl, and I am grateful. Lord knows I've done too many jobs with women like that. Each time, those work environments forced me into survival mode, where I'd either start hanging with the male dancers on the job or keep to myself entirely, solo exploring cities and showing up to work fifteen minutes before the show started. Here, I don't foresee myself transforming into a social hermit or using male dancers as my haven. There aren't even male dancers on this job.

"You gonna smoke that joint or fondle it, babe?" DayDay's judgmental eyes fall to the joint in my hands. He pulls one out of his purse and waves it in the air. "'Cause I'm gonna match you!"

"Let's go then!"

Before leaving the bus, I take one last look into the full-length mirror in the front lounge. I pull a piece of lint off of my brown cargo pants and adjust the collar on my sleeveless button-up. My hair survived the show just fine, so I don't have to freshen my curls. My makeup prevailed, too, but I wiped that off the first chance I got. I don't mind glamming my face for the stage, but I prefer being as natural as possible for everyday life. Tinted moisturizer, lip balm, and if I am feeling extra spicy, some mascara to accentuate the long lashes my Papi blessed me with. After doing one last look in the mirror, I walk toward the exit of the bus. DayDay calls to the rest of the ladies.

"We're gonna go have a smoke! Let me know when to call the Uber!"

* * *

Electronic music bounces off the walls in the club. The type of sounds you'd hear at an EDM festival or rave. I don't prefer this kind of music, but I couldn't care less. It doesn't matter what type of music the DJ plays. It doesn't matter where we go. This group is fairly new, but I quickly learn that *we* are the party.

The three rounds of shots we'd had upon arrival are trickling into my system. The nonstop dancing and delayed speech are evidence of our impending intoxication. We take over the dance floor, arms up, hips swaying, eyes closed and feeling the music. After three songs, I walk a few feet back to the bar and plop down on a stool.

"Can I get you anything?" a bartender covered in tattoos asks.

Her green eyes seem to turn colors in the club light, adapting to the pink and blue hues floating in the room. She tucks loose strands of wavy dark brown hair behind her hair and gently gnaws at her lip while awaiting my answer. I can't help but wonder what it's like to nibble on them myself.

"Yes. Can I please have some water?"

"Of course, beautiful."

Ugh. It's always so hard to tell when women like women.

Is she being nice? Or *really* nice and actually flirting?

Instead of trying to decipher, I sit back and relax. Moments later, Miss Tattoo sets a cup of water in front of me. Then, she places her ivory hands over mine, sliding a shot of tequila in between them.

"On the house, babe."

Alarm bells rang in my ears.

Definitely queer!

"Oh, for me? Thanks...what's your name?"

"Skylar."

Her eyes sink into mine.

"Skylar..." I repeat with a soft grin. Keeping my gaze fixed on her, I bring the shot to my lips and gulp it down. "Thank you, Skylar."

"Here." She slides a piece of paper across the bar. "I have to go to my other job soon but text me sometime. We should hang."

I grab the paper, snap a picture of it, and flash a grin in her direction. "Just in case I lose the paper. Nice to meet you, Skylar."

"Nice to meet you..."

"Nayara, but everyone calls me Naya."

The lights in the club switch to yellow and purple, highlighting the flush in her cheeks.

"Nice to meet you, Naya."

And in seconds, the tattooed beauty is gone, leaving me and my percolating tequila throat at the bar, watching the dancers on the floor. A dance mix of *Rihanna's We Found Love* blasts through the speakers. Bunny and Rae hold hands as they belt the lyrics in each other's faces. DayDay and Tiana model-walk up and down the dance floor like they're on a runway in Paris.

A flush of comfort washes through me as I watch their tipsy bodies sway to the music, like sipping on a warm hot chocolate on a snowy night. This group is humble, manner-able, but knows how to party, a perfect mix for a memorable tour. And the women are all drop-dead gorgeous. Naya, from about six years ago, would've had a conniption. Traveling the country with four beautiful, talented, down-to-earth women? Yeah, old me wouldn't care less that they are all straight. I would've ran through them like a 100-mile sprint. But that never ever ended well in the past, so I gave up messing with straight women. I've also made a pact with myself to never sleep with a dancer, especially on a long tour. I'd only ever had small hook-ups here and there, but I've seen how dating within the camp can change the entire dynamic of the group.

Alienation from the couple. Palpable tension invades small spaces like the dressing rooms or bus when they aren't on good terms. One time, I even had to break up an altercation between two dancers on tour. I'd been fast asleep in the hotel on an off day when I was awoken by the sound of flying objects and breaking glass next door. By the time I checked on them, tears and shards of glass were littered everywhere, and hotel security was threatening to call the police. I would never allow myself to get to that point in any relationship, but especially not in my workspace. Of course, crushes spring up, but I usually get over it by calling on every ounce of self-control I have. I distance myself from the girl. I avoid being alone with her. And no matter what, I keep conversation to a minimum, not for the entire duration of the job, but just long enough for the crush to fade or long enough to find someone to distract me. The shot I took travels through my limbs, warming my body and stirring my thoughts like a truth serum. I haven't admitted it to myself yet, but that's why I've been trying not to get close to—

"...In a hopeless place!!!" Khloe belts over the music.

She stands a couple of feet away from the group on the other side of the dance floor in an empty VIP section. With her arms stretched out, eyes closed, and her head thrown back, she continues to sing the rest of the song way louder than the music. Her brown skin looks like liquid gold under the yellow club lights. She spins in slow circles, free from all inhibitions. A sweet smile connects her dimple. I don't know when exactly, but at some point, her joy transfers to me all the way at the bar.

It's so refreshing to see Khloe like this, as opposed to the nervous mess BriAnn made her into every rehearsal. I hate the trauma this industry instills in women. The insecurities, body dysphoria, the list goes on and on. I thank God every day for my upbringing. My first lesson to prepare for this industry—my Mami. Nothing in this world can deter that Cuban woman from knowing she's the most beautiful woman in this world. She's the baddest, her family is the baddest and her kids are even badder. And anyone who doesn't agree can go *pa la pinga!*

When I was younger, Mami's boasting confidence overwhelmed me. It stood out like a sore thumb in a patriarchal American society and, even worse, in machista Cuban culture. But now, as an adult, I appreciate her. She was instilling self-worth in me. She was preparing a young Afro-Cuban girl to navigate this crazy world. A world I've seen eat women up and spit them right back out. That's why I couldn't stand by a minute longer during BriAnn's fit on that last day of rehearsal. Despite having avoided her most of the rehearsals, that's why I accepted Khloe's lunch date.

Well... it wasn't a date.

There was no way I'd allow BriAnn to tear down Khloe's appearance and talent. She needed to know how gifted her dancing is... how her beauty shone through every part of her, from her skin, her curves, those deep brown eyes and those tantalizing dimples that make my stomach flip when I stare for too long. I hate being so short and dry with her. I felt horrible shooting down her every attempt at starting a conversation at that brunch spot. But I need to establish this distance. I need this crush to fizzle out.

A crush? Naya, get a grip.

She's pretty. Most female dancers are pretty. Most are just as talented. You've done a plethora of jobs with beautiful women and were able to keep your wits about you. So... why is it taking so long to shake this?

I blink rapidly, re-centering my thoughts and breaking my gaze from Khloe before someone catches me staring. I run an exasperated hand through my hair and drop my eyes to the floor.

Whew, this might be harder than I expected.

CHAPTER SIX

THE UBER XL barely comes to a complete stop before Rae hops in the front seat yelling, "Shotgun!"

At the hands of her talented DJ skills, Whitney Houston's "I Wanna Dance With Somebody" bellow out of the car speakers, and we sing our hearts away. Once that song ends, Rae plays another hit, then another, and another, until we erupt in full-fledged car karaoke. We rumble, hit the high notes (or try to), with our chins lifted to the sky.

"Okay. We're here."

The driver lowers the music and stops in front of the arena we'd performed at earlier. The building stands desolate and quiet, a stark opposite compared to the thousands of fans buzzing around just hours ago.

"Sirrrr. Excuse me," Tiana slurs. "This is the front of the arena. Could you drop us off at the back by our tour bus?"

The driver blows out an exasperated breath. His lips fall into a flat, tight line.

"No. This is the address you put in the app. I will not go to another location. Get out."

The sternness in his voice sobers the tequila rippling through my body.

"The fuck did you just say?" Bunny calls out from the last row in the SUV.

"Ooop, I know he didn't!" DayDay's neck retracts.

Even Tiana, who'd been texting for most of the ride, shoots narrowed eyes to the rear-view mirror.

"You tryna to get a one-star review?"

"It's literally around the corner! Only fifty feet!" Leah adds.

Rae singing Beyonce lyrics with her head out of the passenger window is our only soundtrack.

"No. Get the fuck out," The driver growls, tightening his grip on the steering wheel.

The vulgarity is enough to snap Rae back into reality. She swoops her head into the car with fire in her gaze.

"Excuse me?!"

"Oh, he's lost his fucking mi—"

"Y'all," Naya says, bringing the bubbling volcano to a sizzle. "Let's just walk. It's not that far, and this asshole isn't worth it."

In seconds, everyone piles out of the SUV while spitting out their last insults.

"You are definitely getting a bad review!"

"0 stars!"

"Who hurt you?!"

"You need to save that stanky attitude for your whack ass barber, 'cause yo hairline crooked hoe!"

I clutch my stomach as laughter rumbles through me. I'd never seen a whole group roast someone so lethally, but he deserved it.

"You know what...mutha—" Bunny kicks the car's bumper as he pulls off.

"Bun, chill."

Naya places her hands on Bunny's shoulders, guiding her back to the sidewalk. The rest of the group has already moved on, starting their drunken strides to the bus. Rae continues her karaoke session. DayDay joins the impromptu concert, belting a Mariah Carey song to the top of his lungs. Tiana tries to steady her walk but still sways from side to side, probably because her fingernails are typing into her phone at Olympic speeds. Bunny and Naya walk side by side, holding hands in comfortable silence.

Being at the back of the groups allows me the perfect view of our dysfunctional tour family. Different personalities and upbringings, but somehow weave together effortlessly. Back in rehearsals, I connected with the girls at a glacial pace, but tonight was different. We drank and danced until the club closed. Bunny called my name every time I tried to leave the dance floor. Rae and I declared drunk affections like, "I just love you sooo much...so so... sooo much!"

The rare moment I caught my breath off the dance floor, Tiana appeared next to me, interlocking her elbow with mine. She admitted that she and her boyfriend were in a fight. I am the last person qualified to speak on relationship issues, but I offered the little advice I could. Though I can hear her fingernails clacking into the phone from back here, she seemed relieved during our moment in the club. She even rested her head on my shoulder. That's the epitome of cute sisterhood moments! The only person I haven't connected with was Naya. She spent more time at the bar talking to the bartender.

"All right bitches!" DayDay announces.

We finally made it to the bus, where he typed in the security code and swung the door open.

"Get your fine asses on this bus!"

Once we board, the dreamy, post-club energy evaporates. Disappears without a trace. Everyone transforms into working ants, readying themselves for bed. Using the restroom, changing into pajamas, brushing teeth and climbing into their bunks, and bringing our first night out to a close.

I take my bag out of my bunk and search for some pajamas. Earlier this morning, Bunny suggested we unpack everything we'd need for the day out of our luggage. Clean clothes, makeup, toiletries, the whole shabang.

"Finishing a two-hour show only to play Tetris with everyone's luggage under the bus and search for socks in an unlit parking lot is the worst. Pack a day bag now, before the after-show fatigue. Then repeat the process the next morning."

Advice that I regret ignoring to because the only thing I had to change into was an extra pair of black shorts and a white tank top I hadn't used in rehearsal before the show. The world's smallest clothing, which will deliver no warmth on this frigid bus. Before slipping into the restroom to change, I peek at the thermostat. 69 degrees.

Damn it.

Tonight is going to be rough.

I stare into the mirror, taking myself in. The melting show

makeup I'd revived to go out, survived the night just fine. My edges lift slightly in a few places, evidence of all the dancing from tonight, but my cornrows are still flawless. Before bringing a makeup wipe to my face, a small grin forms in the corner of my lips, causing my right dimple to stare back at me.

You're on tour, Khloe. A national tour. You had your first show in Charlotte, North Carolina, and the crowd was out of this world. After the show, you went out to a nightclub and connected with your cast mates. Rehearsals were hell, but it's smooth sailing from here. You did it.

I release a breath I wasn't aware I was holding in, then swipe my makeup away.

After washing my face and wrapping my hair in a silk scarf, I peel off my clothes and step into my cotton shorts, the cold air slapping my skin. Goosebumps travel up my arms. I shudder, throwing on the thin tank top. Tomorrow, a couple of things are in order. Real pajamas, an extra blanket, and a shower. I didn't sweat a lot, but I would've loved to clean the club air from my skin. The bus is equipped with a shower, but it squealed and sputtered tiny droplets of water upon turning it on. This must be the glamorous tour life everyone talks about. A sarcastic chuckle bounces from my shoulders.

I throw my club clothes into my bag and trade them for my toothbrush.

"Hey!" Rae knocks from outside the door. "You done? I gotta pee!"

"Just a second! I just need to brush my teeth!"

"Do that in the kitchen sink! I gotta go!"

I grab my bags and open the door to the sight of Rae's scrunched-up face, hands clutching her crotch, and her petite frame rocking from side to side. I barely clear the door when she rushes past me into the restroom. The front of the bus no longer buzzes with my coworkers. It's empty. Everyone had already retreated to their bunks for the night. Silence cascades over the space. With counter space the length of two notebooks and an even smaller sink, I'd hardly call it a kitchen, but it is on the tour bus, I guess. It sits across from a medium-sized fridge and four cabinets stocked with my bus mates' favorites. Dark chocolate, cookies, and enough bottles of red wine to last the entire tour.

I set my bags down, bringing my toothbrush to the faucet. Before I can turn on the water, a voice calls from the back lounge.

"Wait!"

Naya rushes toward me wearing a navy-blue oversized t-shirt, gray sweatpants and her long curls following behind her.

"What's wrong?" I jump back.

"Don't brush your teeth with the bus water. Here."

She reaches across me, standing a few centimeters away, her voluminous hair grazing my chest and stomach. I'm not sure why, but I hold my breath. She grabs a water bottle from the cabinet and hands it to me.

"Really?"

"Yeah, tour bus rules." She shrugs, her expression stoic and emotionless. "The water isn't all that clean. Did anyone tell you not to... poop on the bus, too?"

My eyes bulge.

"No! Why?"

"There isn't a proper sewage system, so the bus driver would have to clean it at his next stop."

"Holy shit."

Then she laughs. An ear-to-ear, pearly-toothed *laugh*. Tension overtakes my cheeks as I try to conceal the shock rippling through me.

"Holy shit is right."

Naya wipes her eyes with one last chuckle. Then she snaps back, her lips pressing together as if it never happened.

Did she really laugh that hard, or did I imagine it?

"So... Yeah." She continues. "Use a water bottle to brush your teeth on the bus."

"Oh... okay... thank you." My eyes fall to the floor, a chill running up my spin. "Ugh, I'm sleeping in a turtle neck tomorrow night."

When I look back up, I notice Naya's gaze has fallen, too, not on the floor, but to my hardened nipples cutting through this thin white tank top. She pulls her eyes back up to meet mine.

"Um...Do you want my sweater?" Her eyes wander the bus, looking for her next words. "You seem...cold."

Naya rarely ever stumbles over her words. In most of our interactions, I'm the stuttering buffoon adding *ums* and pauses between each word. Naya is always calm, collected, or emotionless, almost as if she's bored to tears. This is the first time I've ever seen her... uncomfortable?

"Oh." I glance back down and fold my arms over my chest. "Yes, please, that would be great. I forgot to pack pajamas, and this bus is frigid!"

"Yeah..." Naya relaxes into her body again, her mouth falling back into a straight line. "Tour buses are always kept cold. They say it's to fight illness from spreading, kind of like a hospital or doctor's office."

"Well damn, I feel like sleeping in this cold could actually produce sickness!"

Another shiver climbs up my spine as Naya goes to her bunk and pulls out a black, over-sized sweater.

"Here."

"Thanks."

I throw it on, and the calming scent of sandalwood swirls through my nostrils. The same scent she wore the day we had lunch.

"No problem," she replies, her expression unreadable. "Goodnight."

Before she can walk away, I reach out, lightly grabbing her forearm.

"Hey."

Naya turns back to me, her shoulders hiked from my touch.

Did I alarm her?

I drop my hand from her forearm and down to her hand, nuzzling my thumb along the top of her wrist.

"I just wanted to say thank you... for everything. Standing up for me in rehearsal, the talk you gave me afterward... all of it. You always seem to come in the nick of time... before BriAnn pushed me into a nervous breakdown, or even now, saving me from brushing my teeth with questionable water cause no one else warned me. I know we talk little, but I feel like you're looking out for me. Thank you. I appreciate it more than you know."

She wriggles her wrist away, pushing a loose curl behind her ear.

"BriAnn is a bully, and I didn't want you to catch e. coli or some-thing. No biggie. Goodnight."

This time, Naya shuffles away and climbs into her bunk before my brain can conjure up a reply, leaving me with my mouth gaping in the kitchen.

I slowly turn my attention to the sink and wet my toothbrush with the water bottle.

Why did she get so tense when I touched her? Maybe she's not one of those touchy girls. Some girls are affectionate cuddle bugs like Leah and Rae. They always hug, hold hands, and invade each other's personal space. Naya isn't really like that... except with Bunny. Maybe she's more comfortable with her because they'd known each other longer. I'd only known her for the duration of this job. It's only been a little over a month. Maybe she's just shy... But she seemed like she had *tons* to talk about with that tattooed bartender.

Whatever the reason, keeping up with Naya's mood swings is like riding a roller coaster ride, and I'm catching motion sickness. One moment, she's stoic and cold, her mouth barely curving past a flat line. Then, the next, she's attentive and nurturing. And on rarest occasions, she smiles, laughs even. A laugh that brightens the room and everyone in it. I wish I could see it more often.

CHAPTER SEVEN

UGH! *My God, are you a prepubescent boy?! Why did you look at her chest?*

Images of Khloe's plush breasts flash through my mind.

You just had to give her a sweater, Naya!

The rule is no gestures. No care. Well, is that considered a gesture? Those rules are meant for women I'm fucking. We aren't fucking, so it's not considered anything outside of a work friend helping a work friend.

Her hardened nipples burned the bottom of my vision, no matter how much I had tried to maintain eye contact—just like I do every time I'm in a dressing room with changing dancers. Open-minded dancers who are always comfortable walking around naked, completely unaware that I am a lesbian—or they just don't care. I've *never* had any issue keeping my eyes up before. I had forced myself to look into her doughy brown eyes while her perky chest tugged my attention until the pull became too much, and I ultimately gave in—

but only for a couple of seconds! Which meant nothing, 'cause the timing was not on my side, and she'd caught me in those few moments, crossing her arms in embarrassment.

I hope she didn't feel self-conscious. I pray PTSD from BriAnn's body shaming hadn't slipped into her mind. In that moment, I wanted nothing more than to uncross her arms, pull her close, and reassure her. Let Khloe know every inch of skin on her body is beautiful. No, not just beautiful, but perfect, as if crafted by a surgeon. Actually, that's incorrect. A surgeon wouldn't be able to replicate what she has. A beautiful, perfect frame that probably would have felt like Egyptian silk against me...

Ok, Naya! That's enough!

I clutch my blanket and flip onto my side. I study the tiny walls in my bunk, anything to rid Khloe of my mind. Bunny jokes, these bunks are nothing more than twin-sized coffins stacked on top of one another, but I love retreating into my bunk. My safe place. A pitch-black, ventilated place where I can succumb to slumber to the sounds of the humming engine. Right now, these walls seem a little more compact than usual.

For the next two hours, I toss and turn. Wishing to get Khloe out of my head and calm this feeling between my thighs.

The rules, *Nayara Maria*. Gotta use my full name during serious self-talk, just like Mami does when she chastises me. No coworkers. No dancers. Period.

No matter how beautiful or curvy. Or if she's asking annoying back-to-back questions that make me wanna shake her and hold her at the same time. I got this. This crush will fade. Even if a single touch to my forearm made my spine curve like a hissing cat. The subtle feeling of her fingers on my skin sending electricity to my—

Nope!

I whip my phone out and open one of my trusty dating apps. Our next show is in one of the lesbian capitals of the world, Atlanta. Surely, I can find someone to help knock Khloe out of my mind. My thumb swipes aimlessly until I land on a picture of a brown-skinned beauty with a septum piercing. Her short, curly hair, styled in effortless finger waves, shape her symmetrical face. I waste no time swiping right.

The bus is still driving through miles and miles of green trees and hills, but I've already checked my GPS. We are nearby. Unable to sleep, I climb out of my bunk, plop onto the couch in the empty front lounge, and spend hours messaging my finger-waved cutie, Imani. Sunlight tiptoes into the space as I smirk into my phone.

Imani: So what time did you say you get here, sexy?

Me: We are 40 minutes outside of the city, but I'm not gonna lie. Ima need a nap soon so I don't suck in my show tonight lol.

Imani: I don't know you like that, but something tells me you could never suck. I'm sure you're going to eat that stage up tonight.

Me: What are you up to tonight? Wanna come to the show? I can get two tickets for the standing section right in the front. Just make sure your guest is as fine as you.

Imani: Right in front of the stage? That's fancy babe! Also, all my friends are fine. No matter what though, you're still mine.

My core thrums with desire. I inhale calming breaths to bring myself back to normalcy.

Me: Sounds like a plan. The next show is only a couple of hours away in Jacksonville, so the buses won't leave until 4 a.m. We'll have time to hang or do whatever you want after the show. What's the name on your ID?

Imani: That's more than enough time to do I want...The name on my ID is Imani Franklin.

CHAPTER EIGHT

khloe

"WE KILLED THAT!" Bunny yells as we barrel into the dressing room.

Atlanta completely blew North Carolina out of the water. The big peach is the home of Zion's record label and an enormous chunk of his fanbase, so the difference was like night and day. The crowd's energy shook the entire building. Their screams traveled through our limbs, pushing our steps and providing energy during the harder routines.

Never in my life have I ever experienced an audience like that. It was monumental but also overwhelming. There were certain numbers where I felt like the energy overpowered my limbs. I started pushing too much, and movements became spastic and messy during certain sections. If any of the other cities are like this, I'm going to need to learn how to gauge my energy better.

"Anyone have any extra body soap? I left mine in the last city."

Rae is already butt naked and in her shower shoes.

"Catch!" Leah tosses a bottle toward her.

"Thanks, babe!"

I know we've only done two shows, but I am the last dancer to get undressed both times. Maybe it's residual adrenaline, but I need a second after getting off stage.

"Where are the towels? I don't see any!" Leah says, standing in her underwear with a loofa in hand.

"Oh! I think I saw some in the production office earlier!" I recall. "I'm still dressed, so I'll go grab some!"

I swing open the dressing room, step into the hallway and collide straight into someone.

"I'm sorry!"

"It's okay," Naya says dryly.

I hadn't noticed she wasn't in the dressing room with us.

"Oh! Hey, Naya! What are you doing out here?"

"I had friends in the crowd tonight, and I just wanna make sure they get into the after party all right before I go shower."

Everyone, from Zion to his management, keeps calling the get-together an afterparty, but the festivities are in Zion's second dressing room. A large arena locker room with free liquor, and bushels of weed, with his close friends and groupies from the crowd.

"Ah, I see!"

I laugh for no reason. Maybe it's because Naya barely has a heartbeat every time we speak. Maybe it's because I'm trying to fill the space with something, anything! But it just sputters out like strange, misplaced laughter, which Naya doesn't return.

"Okay...well, I just came out to grab some towels. Production forgot to put some in our room."

"Okay."

"Okay, bye!" I say as my feet lead me away.

Damn.

Conversations with a brick wall are more enthusiastic.

* * *

Casamigos, Patron, Hennessy, Jameson... all the alcohol in the world and nothing but one bottle of orange juice to mix it with. A bottle that ran out after three drinks. Because there are no mixers to dilute the drinks, most of the women in here are drunk. Stumbling, heels thrown to the side, *drunk.*

I pour a shot and meet the rest of the dancers—well, Rae and Tiana. Zion's cousin is step-touching with Leah in the middle of swaying groupies. We are all casually dressed in sweats and tour merch, with fresh faces and smells of scented soap, while the groupies sport short cocktail dresses and liters of perfume.

"Ha! Stop playing, Naya!"

A voice cackles from across the room. It comes from a brown-skinned girl with finger waves. It's probably one of Naya's friends who attended the concert tonight. She lightly smacks the tattoos on Naya's forearm while laughing at whatever she finds so funny. The other friend is Latina, with long, straight hair flowing down her back. Both of them wearing different versions of pleather and high heels.

"You play too much!"

The Latina laughs into her hand.

I sip a little of my Casamigos, accepting the burn that trickles down my throat.

"How does Naya know them?" I turn to Tiana.

I've only met Naya on this job, but I'm kind of thrown off by these friends. How is she having such a straightforward conversation with them? When I ask her a single question, she's a bag of rocks.

"No clue," she mutters, eyes barely leaving her phone. She'd been texting since the moment we entered the after-party, probably night capping with her boo. "I think she said they were some friends from college."

"Oh, they are *real* good friends." Bunny answers. "And I think they need some more alcohol. Ima help them out."

I down the rest of my drink as I watch Bunny waltz up to the bar and pour three shots. I tear my eyes away from them for a second, taking in the surrounding space. Women of all shades and sizes fill the room, speaking loudly, pouring multiple shots and dancing in the middle of the room, desperately vying for Zion's attention. And no matter how hard they try, his focus remains on his male friends, drinking, playing cards and singing along to the music.

"Hey, sexy."

A voice whispers beside me. A hand lightly taps my hand.

"Hello..." I say, trying to conceal my irritation bubbling from the tall, caramel-colored man.

"What's your name?"

"Khloe."

"A beautiful name for a beautiful female."

He grinned.

Female.

I can't exactly explain why, but men who refer to women as females always rub me the wrong way.

"Thanks."

"You know…" His green eyes flit over my body. "I know you came to the function all chill and shit, but I just wanna let you know, you not hiding nothing under all these clothes. I can see those hips through them sweats."

I choke back a gag while I laugh in his face. A hardy, wide-toothed grin.

A confused look shadows his face.

"You know…" I mock. "In order to dress comfortably, the reason *can't* be for my comfort? It *has* to be to hide my body from men?"

He stands there, unsure of what to do, so I continue.

"You are just as corny as your pickup lines. Whatever I got on my body is for *me*. My preference. My comfort. My mood."

"I didn't mean to—"

"Listen…" I place a hand on his shoulder. "Next time you do this. Take it down several notches. Ten levels down. *Hey, sexy?* You gotta be kidding me."

I'd never really been this honest with a man before, but something about the strong women I've been around lately gives me the boost. I time-travel back to all of them cussing out that Uber driver.

Before every reply, I wonder what would Bunny say? How would Rae and Tiana reply? Leah is sweet, maybe even sweeter than me, yet she still knows how to put her foot down. Despite our lack of conversation, I know Naya wouldn't entertain this idiot either.

"I'm sorry, I just—"

"Thought you would comment about seeing my body through some damn sweats, and that was gonna make me fall onto your dick? Oh, babe…" I hand him what's left of my drink. "If that was your game plan, you're gonna need more of this 'cause it's gonna be a rough night."

I walk away, leaving him a stammering mess while holding my cup. Confidence drips from my strides, but Khloe from four years ago would be so proud. The timid college girl who was afraid to shake tables tore that man to pieces.

Tiana lifts her gaze from her phone. "Who's that?"

Bunny appears from behind me. "Yeah bitch, that man is FIONE. I peeped y'all!"

"A lame that came at me sideways. Nothing to waste our breath over. Where'd Rae go?"

"I'm not sure. She took off. Said she was coming back in a couple of minutes."

"Okay, well, I need to get outta this man's eyeline. Wanna go stand with Naya and her friends?"

"Oh girl, Naya and her friends are gone, doing *other* things." Bunny smirks.

A text message pings from Tiana's pocket, snatching her attention once again.

"Like smoking?" I study the room. "But people are smoking in here. They didn't have to go do that outside."

"Oh, don't worry about it, boo. They are doing grown things."

Grown things?

The only things grown enough to make you and your friends step away are drugs.

That's it!

I had a friend in college who was into all kinds of drugs. Coke, molly, X, everything under the sun. Causing her to disappear during group outings and the effects of the drugs, leaving her moods high and low. Maybe that's why Naya is so weird with me, stoically cold one moment and struggling to hold back a smile next. The realization eases my thoughts, and my lips curve a little.

Maybe Naya doesn't hate me after all.

CHAPTER NINE

"FUCK."

Imani moans as my tongue draws up her neck. She grips the base of my neck, urging me to stay in that spot.

Her friend, Yesenia—brownie points for actually remembering this time—stands behind me. One hand cradles my left breast with her thumb rubbing over my hardened nipple. The other hand over my boxer briefs, making gentle rings over my clit.

I'd told Imani to bring a fine friend just in case Zion or his friends wanted a little eye candy. I didn't expect all of *this*. But half an hour into the after-party, Imani turned to me and said, "I get doing all this partying, but I thought I'd be doing *you*."

"Yes, of course, but I'd hate to be rude to your friend," I replied, trying to conceal my tingling groin.

"Hey, don't leave me out of the fun," Yesenia enclosed the inches between us.

I opened my mouth to reply, and then Bunny showed up with a

round of shots. My best friend and best wing woman since college. After we downed the tequila, Imani and Yesenia insisted we find somewhere private. Bunny started talking to some of Zion's friends, pretending not to notice the brewing energy.

I told myself to keep it cute. This is not only my place of work, but I'm pretty sure no one outside of Bunny even knows I'm gay. Perks of being a female dancer. All of us wear oversized ath-leisurewear. My only giveaways are my short fingernails. I'm not in the closet by any means, but the tour just started. I like to ease myself in, gain the ladies' trust, and show them I'm not some creepy lesbian trying to get sneaky peeks while they are undressing. But after Yesenia and Imani approached me with such forward energy, I was ready to risk it all. Not to mention, I was sick of watching Khloe flirt with that dull Steph Curry-look-a-like—laughing to the top of her lungs with her hand on his shoulder. I guess it doesn't matter if he needs a line-up and looks corny as hell. She is clearly enjoying herself, so I deserve the same.

This is how I end up here—lying down on a table in the middle of girls' dressing room with Imani riding my face and Yesenia gliding two fingers in and out of my wetness. Our clothes and shoes leave a trail from the door to the table. Bags of chips, snacks, and anything else on the table were swiped to the floor upon our arrival. Imani's moans ricochet off the walls, with every buck on my tongue. Loud music from Zion's party, which is only a couple of doors down, muffles it all. When we burst in here a few minutes ago, I surveyed the room for any leftover belongings between kisses and traveling hands. I had to make sure no one would be returning to this dressing room. Thank-fully, all the women lugged their bags to the bus before attending the after-party, leaving the room for this unexpected threesome.

I rest my hands on Imani's ass while I move my tongue around in all directions. Keeping my attention on her body's reactions, I settle in one syncopated rhythm, her moans intensifying.

"Yesss, Fuck. Yes, Naya."

She rocks her hips back and forth, matching my rhythm.

"Oh shit," she mutters. "I'm gonna...."

I slap her ass, digging my nails deep into her, forcing her further into my mouth until her hips buck like a wild horse. Her sweet juices run down my face, and I slurp as much as possible. Seconds after Imani unwinds, Yesenia slips her fingers out of me, gripping my hips and bringing me to her mouth.

The combination of Imani's sounds, juices, and Yesenia's skilled tongue propels me to my climax. A perfect release at the hands of two sexy ass women. I reach in between my legs, palming a chunk of Yesenia's hair, keeping her in that sweet spot as I shudder against her. When my body finally comes to a rest, she lifts her eyes to mine, batting her eyelashes with a devilish gaze and licking my pleasure from her lips.

I smile. "Your turn."

In one swift movement, I pull Yesenia up, placing her on top of me. Her slick center exactly on mine. Imani dismounts from my face and stands at the head of the table, kissing Yesenia as she rubs her clit against mine. I look around, appreciating the view. Yesenia and Imani making out, hands holding each other's necks, Yesenia's hips steadily riding back and forth, pleasuring us both and right behind Yesenia, Tiana standing frozen, eyes wide.

Wait! Tiana?!

I spring up, moving Yesenia off of me and covering my bits, though she'd already seen everything.

"Tiana!"

"I'm sorry—my charger!" she squeaks, gesturing toward a white charger sitting in the corner of the room.

Of course, I overlooked the charger when checking the room. And Tiana just had to come back for it. And she just *had* to catch me in the gayest of gay acts.

Of fucking course!

"I'm sorry! I didn't think anyone—" I yelp, but she snatches her charger and hurries out of the room.

CHAPTER TEN

I RUB the sleep from my eyes after eating another spoon of chocolate-flavored cereal. The sugary breakfast of champions. The actual plan is to venture out into Jacksonville for some real food before the show, but I gotta have a little snack first!

My phone vibrates with a text notification.

Soakin' Wet Summer Tour Core Dancers

BriAnn: Hey, ladies, I saw the footage from the show last night. Leah and Khloe look messy during the breakdown in the middle of Act 3. Naya, pull them aside and drill that section before tonight's show. Thank you.

I scrape my jaw from the floor. Footage? I wasn't aware we were being filmed every night, and I definitely didn't know BriAnn was still watching. Shivers run down my spine at the mere thought of her.

Naya: Got you. Guys, let's meet at 3 p.m. on the stage.

All right. Just enough time to finish this cereal, sight-see the streets of downtown Jacksonville, and—Before closing my phone, I notice the time.

2:37p.m.?!

Holy shit.

Curse that after-party last night and these pitch-black bunks! When the tour started, I quickly learned all the amazing reasons dancers speak so highly of bunk sleep. But the blackout curtain and windowless walls have thrown my sleep schedule to the wind.

I peek back into the bunk area. The curtain to every bunk is wide open, revealing a sea of empty beds and rumpled sheets. How was I the last one left on the bus? I heard some ladies climb into bed hours after me! Seasoned female dancers are way more familiar with tour bus life than me.

Khloe, you need to get a grip. Find some type of normalcy with this life on the road.

I inhale the rest of my cereal, throw away the plastic bowl, and spring into action.

* * *

"Let's do it again, Leah. This time, keep your knees bent and be sharper at the end of eight count."

Naya presses play. Her almond-shaped eyes hone in with laser focus on Leah's movements.

"There." Naya pauses the music. "That part is sharper. Ta-Ta Skee Boom. Not Ta-Skee Boom."

The distinct language of dancers sends warmth to my cheeks. We communicate through counts, cadences, and sound effects. A language that probably sounds insane to outside ears. I spent the past fifteen minutes coming down from the whirlwind I endured to be ready and on this stage at 3 p.m. Washing my face, getting dressed, climbing under the bus and moving around fifty-pound suitcases until I found mine, just to find some rehearsal clothes for the day. All in humid, ninety-degree weather. A crash course introduction to Jacksonville, Florida.

Naya must have sensed my disarray from a mile away because she'd taken one look at me and suggested that she work with us one at a time, starting with Leah. I don't know if I'm imagining it, but Naya seems kind of tired, too.

"Oh, don't worry about it, boo. They are doing grown things."

Bunny's explanation from the after-party resounds through my ears. Side effects of a few recreational substances, perhaps? Substances above the category of marijuana? My friend from college would wake up so dehydrated after a night of her escapades. I'd always have water bottles stowed under her bed for her. Naya isn't her usual, fresh-faced, composed self, but her skin remains still illegally flawless.

"All right Leah, keep working on the syncopation for that section. Let me see you do it, Khloe."

My body jolts at the rare occurrence. Naya addressing me directly, using my name, instead of ignoring me like an ad on television. I step out to the middle of the stage. Somehow, Naya staring back at me in this empty arena sparks more anxiety than a sold-out concert with screaming fans. Strong yet timid movements guide my limbs. I try to focus on the steps, but my mind wanders.

Am I hitting the staccato parts sharp enough? Is it too sharp and stiff? Are my thighs moving around too much in these shorts?

"Huh?" Confusion washes over Naya's face as she jogs over to the stereo to pause the music. "What are you doing?"

"Um...the breakdown in Act 3."

"Yeah, I know, but that is old choreography. BriAnn changed it the last week of rehearsals. Don't you remember?"

Nerves shoot up my spine. Moments ago, she'd addressed Leah with life in her voice and even a smile. But since with me, her expression flattens. Her monotone words make talking to a brick wall seem funner.

"Yes... I mean, I thought I was... I just—"

"The fittings!" Naya blurts out with the slightest inflection in her voice.

A piece of a regular human peeking through.

"The fittings?" I echo.

"Yes! That was the day your fitting ran longer than all of ours!" I stare blankly while revisiting that day. They assigned each dancer one hour for a fitting; however, mine took three hours because none of my options could go above my hips. Despite having sent them my sizes weeks before rehearsals began, the wardrobe team bought petite clothes.

"Yeah, my fitting took longer than everyone's..."

"That's when BriAnn changed it. She rearranged the choreo, and after you got out of the fitting, rehearsal was over, so nobody told you." She presses play and takes center stage. "This is the new section."

Realization settles in as I watch Naya dance. She follows the same rhythms I'd been doing, but certain moves are swapped out with others. A move that used to be a full-out arm swing is now a miniature elbow rotation. The 360 rotation in the middle of the choreography is now a half-turn. I must've looked like a flailing fish out of water next to everyone!

After the initial shock wears off, my eyes roam. Watching Naya's long, curly mane flows with the movement, never once getting in her face. Her sculpted, amber-brown arms hit every position with strength and precision. She's wearing black, oversized cargo shorts, but they still rest on her hips perfectly, revealing the tops of her boxer briefs. Her clothes are baggier than the rest of the cast, but somehow, her physique pokes through every time. Toned muscles from her arms to her calves, but soft curves along her chest and rear end—not as curvy as me, but still pronounced.

"Got it?" Naya says over the music, shaking me from my thoughts. I yank my focus from the lower half of her body.

"Uh. Yeah!"

She doesn't reply. Instead, she walks toward me. With cool strides, Naya doesn't stop until she's inches away from me, close enough for her scent to swirl around me. Hints of sandalwood cologne and fruity hair products, a perfect mix of earthy and sweet without an overbearing smell. Naya's eyes lock on mine, but I can feel her mind whirring. As if looking for the words to say. I glance behind her to the sight of Leah practicing on the opposite side of the stage, completely engulfed in her own world. And entirely unaware of the way my breathing is quickening. With the music still blaring from the speakers, Naya leans into my ear, close enough for her minty breath to push against my ears.

"I can teach you the new section, but you've gotta stop checking me out, Ms. Khloe Thompson."

"Oh! Uh! I'm sorry! You just look great doing the—you're an amazing dancer!"

I've heard babbling babies speak clearer than whatever word vomit coming out of my mouth. A knot forms in the pit of my stomach. A jumble of nerves, yet different from those rehearsals with BriAnn. This feeling was warm. A twist of heat sinks in my stomach. I don't really know what to call it.

Before I respond, something ghosts past her face. A hint of...is that a smile? Naya's lips curve slightly but disappear as quickly as it arrives. And that is enough to intensify the strange feeling invading my body.

CHAPTER ELEVEN

SEARING GULPS of green tea and honey trail down my throat, soothing my body from the inside out. Each heated sip distracting me from my thoughts. After that rehearsal, I ran to the first hole-in-the-wall coffee shop I could find. I had to get away. It felt like the walls in that arena were caving in. Now, I'm surrounded by walls covered in decorative faux grass, neon lights, and pictures of black musical legends. Far away from Khloe.

When BriAnn first sent that text, I was livid. I'd just left an amazing breakfast spot highly recommended by locals. With a full tummy and sleep deprivation from my *escapades* the night before, I was ten minutes away from the arena where I'd planned to get on the bus, crawl straight into my bunk and take a nap until the show tonight. But no. I had to play dance captain.

In the end, it wasn't so bad.

Leah will get better over time. BriAnn's dance style is so specific, based on southern black culture. There's only so much Leah can do with a month of rehearsals as a red-haired, freckled white girl from Idaho, but she's a hard worker. She'll find the same rhythmical pocket as the rest of the cast in no time.

Khloe, however, is a different story. BriAnn *had* to have seen her doing the old version of the choreography toward the end of rehearsals. Why didn't she say anything? I'll never know. After I taught Khloe the correct routine, she executed the steps flawlessly, like the gifted dancer I'd been watching the entire month of rehearsals. Khloe packs a different punch than most dancers. My strong suits are strength and precision. When the rest of the stage is on their last sliver of energy, I go into overdrive, pulling from reserves somewhere deep in my body. Khloe's superpowers are indi-viduality and star quality. No matter the routine, it looks like she's improvising. When there isn't a hating choreographer down her throat, the confidence she siphons from within is major. Like a new person altogether or an alter ego. Another human leading her limbs and exuding pure star quality, a specialty I'm not sure she knows she has. An ism—something that can't exactly be named. Something I pray she learns to revel in as her career progresses. Something I hope the industry doesn't steal from her.

I'm almost off into the abyss, wondering why she hadn't informed Khloe of the new choreography, but I remembered that BriAnn is a bully. Despite being a legend and a pillar in the commu-nity, she is a mean girl.

I guess this is what they mean when people say, "Don't meet your heroes."

I take another sip of the scorching tea and recollect the *other* events in that rehearsal.

The feeling of Khloe watching me so intently while I danced. The heightened feeling when she'd *continued* watching me long after I finished. The palpable heat from her eyes as they traveled my body. Or did I imagine that?

All control left my soul. Tranquil, collected, and slightly cold, Naya left the building, only to be replaced with overwhelmed Nayara. The woman with a middle-school crush. A butterflies-in-your-stomach, can't-get-her-out-of-my-mind, prepubescent crush.

The worst part is I know she feels something, too. That wasn't the first time I'd caught her surveying me. I keep conversations short and to the point, but that doesn't stop her eyes from dipping to my lips when I speak. Or the slight hitching in her breath when I'm near her. Maybe that's why I keep playing with fire. Because I know I'm not the only one with these horrendous feelings.

After a night like last night, with the type of debauchery Yesenia and Imani were up to, usually a month passes before I'm ready to slide under another warm body. So why the hell did Khloe's presence ignite my skin from several feet away?

I expel a breath, unaware I've been holding it in the first place, and down the rest of my tea, letting the warmth wash my thoughts away.

No dancers. No coworkers, Nayara.

No drama. And definitely no straight girls.

No chances of making the workspace uncomfortable.

I prop my elbows onto the table and bury my face in the palms of my hands.

I've *already* made my workspace awkward by deciding to act like a wild sorority girl. Flashbacks of Tiana's wide eyes and flushed cheeks haunt me. When I returned to the bus last night, she was already in her bunk with the curtain shut. She was also the first to wake up, so I didn't catch her in the morning either.

If they didn't know I was a lesbian, they definitely knew now.

I'm not in the closet, just private. On new jobs, I've mastered the act of withholding my sexual orientation from the female dancers until ample time has passed.

I don't know why I am so particular. Perhaps residual trauma from my performing arts high school. Once the news broke there, girls left the dressing room in droves every time I arrived.

This method is my chance of controlling the narrative. My way of letting y'all know, "Yes, I'm gay, but that doesn't mean I want *you*. Carry on."

Only thing is, everything went out the window after the show I put on for Tiana. The entire bus probably knows already. Whispered conversations are probably taking place at this moment.

What if Khloe knows?

CHAPTER TWELVE

"DOES ANYONE HAVE EYELASH GLUE?"

I scan the dressing room of ladies stationed at their own mirror vanity, with their makeup half done. Unblended contour lines, powders being whisked away and random spurts of curse words each time someone messes up. I guess this is the magical world of show business...

"I do, Khloe! Here!"

Leah tosses me a small bottle.

"Thanks! I'll give it right back."

I unscrew the bottle and carefully apply the glue to my larger-than-life stage lash. I fan the lash, waiting for the glue to dry.

Don't look, again...

I peer into the mirror and over my shoulder at the empty vanity behind me. Naya's spot. She came in with her makeup already done, set down her bags and left, but that hasn't stopped my eyes from wandering in that direction every five minutes.

It has been a couple of hours since our stage rehearsal, and we haven't spoken since. I don't know why... but I am nervous about speaking to her again.

Nayara Alvarez flusters me. Not because of her uninterested monotone responses toward me, or her short answers. It's just her.

Her deep brown, almond-shaped eyes staring back at me, the quality in her movement, evidence of her long career. And no matter what craziness is happening around us, Naya is always calm. Whether it's being rushed onto the stage, a thirty-second outfit change before the next song, or being kicked out of an Uber by a disgruntled driver, Naya is always the most zen of the group.

I glue the lash on top of my eye, fluttering my lids to ensure they are in place. Using the vanity top to steady my hand, I apply a liner around the edges of my lips.

Hm. Naya's lips are perfectly symmetrical, as if a sculptor created them from hand. I flash back to the moment those same lips were so close to my ear. Her breath sent shivers all the way down my spine.

"I can teach you the new section, but you've gotta stop checking me out, Ms. Khloe Thompson."

Checking her out?

Was I? Surely not in *that* way. That would mean I'd have to like women enough to check her out... As in, find *attraction* to one. I don't think I'm sexually attracted to Naya, but there's just something about her. An intriguing force that draws me in regardless of whether she's giving me dry one-word answers or not. I think it's because deep down, I know there's more there. Hidden stories are woven into that smile she fights so hard to keep back.

* * *

Once the stage lights hit my face, everything melts away. All the pressures of having a perfect show, BriAnn's ghost watching from a distance and… Naya, who hadn't shown up until ten minutes to walk to the stage. She'd slipped into the dressing room while everyone was distracted with last-minute madness, got dressed and waited in the hallway until it was time to walk. Once we'd arrived at the stage, I tried to wish her a good show, but she muttered, "You too." Then practically ran to her opening position.

None of that mattered now, because I was on stage with the energy of a hundred screaming fans thrashing into me. I inhale one last readying breath before we hit the choreography for the last number in Act 1. High jumps, crisp movements and lots of hair whips. The music climaxes into its finale as the strobe lights blink wildly. Then, just as the last note of the song plays, pyrotechnics placed on the corners of the stage send flames ten feet into the air.

The crowd loses it, reaching pitches in their screams I didn't think were possible. Jacksonville just might outdo Atlanta!

Adrenaline courses through our veins as we stick our ending poses. Smiles on our faces and beads of sweat running down our bodies, we wait until Zion breaks the screams with a loud "Jacksonville! How are y'all doing tonight?!"

He addresses the crowd, and we relax out of our poses, sauntering toward him. In a single file line, we strut around Zion in a circle. This is a small section, meant as a stylized exit before he sings the ballads, but it's easily one of my favorite parts of the show. Sensual, regal runway walks around the artist.

"We aren't just background dancers. We are artists in our own right. I don't care if you're walking in from the furthest back corner of the stage.

Your walk should draw me in! The way you walk on stage makes me, the viewer, decide if I want to keep watching you or not."

Ten years later, I can still hear those words from my childhood dance teacher ringing through my ears.

Before exiting the stage for a break, we complete one more walking pattern in front of Zion. Tiana passes him first, batting her eyelashes as she silks by. Rae does a little turn and winks in his direction before exiting.

"Are y'all ready for the Soakin' Wet Summer Tour?!" Zion hollers into the mic.

Now, it was my turn. I make my way toward Zion while he continues his banter.

"Oh, that's how y'all feel, Jacksonville? Y'all are bringing the vibes forreal. And guess what, you bring the vibes, I'll bring the music and—"

Just as I pass Zion, I slow my walk, sitting into each hip a little longer and trailing a hand across his chest.

"And—" he stammers as an "oooo" travels through the crowd. "I'm sorry for messing up y'all, but as you can see, Soakin' Wet Summer Tour has some of the most beautiful women in the world. Make some noise if you agree!"

The crowd's crescendo of whoops and whistles gives my confidence the small boost it needs after these past weeks. I keep my strong walk in full gear. Once I'm a couple of feet away from the wing, I stop, crossing my legs at the ankle, and do a slow, mannequin-like model rotation. I bat my lashes at Zion one last time, ready to step offstage, but I notice something.

Zion's right hand holds the mic in the front, but behind his back, his left hand fumbles at his mic pack hanging off of his pants. This mic pack that connects to his in-ear headphones, keeping him on-beat, on key, and in communication with the musical director, had somehow been unplugged during the last number. He maintains his demeanor for the audience, but his fingers move wildly behind him.

My body, unable to break from the muscle memory of rehearsals, struts away as my eyes watch in horror.

What should I do? Should I go back onstage?

Seconds after me, Leah begins her model walk toward Zion, completely unaware of the debacle behind his back. From the side of the stage, I wave my arms frantically, trying to get her attention. Maybe, at the end of her walk, she could whip around him and help plug the mic pack back in.

I should do something... I should go—

Panic threatens to settle in, but Naya cozies up behind Zion, abandoning the walking choreography altogether. She reaches over him, fanning her hands over his chest, making piercing eye contact with him and then the audience. They eat the moment up, reacting with more hoots. As she retracts her hands, she tears her gaze from the crowd and signals Bunny to start her walking pattern early.

Immediately understanding the assignment, Bunny power walks in front of Zion and starts freestyling in front of him. Hip rolls, splits, eye contact with the audience—anything to distract the audience from the mayhem occurring behind Zion's back.

Filled with tranquility and grace, which is the stark opposite of this moment, Naya's hands move around the mic pack, plastering a smile on her face while untangling Zion's knotted in-ear cords. She glances down from time to time, but mostly, never breaks her gaze from the audience. Zion rolls with the punches and offers more banter to the crowd while the ladies save the day.

"Uh oh! Looks like I got the two-for-one special! This takes me back to my first number-one single, years ago, 'Two for the Night'. Y'all wanna hear that one later?!"

The audience roars.

"Naw, Ima need y'all to make more noise than that!"

Finally, Naya undoes the last of the knot and plugs his in-ears back into his mic pack. She travels to Zion's left side, trailing her hands across his shoulders. Before leaving, she stares into him one last time. The look in her eyes communicates, "Everything is good now," and she struts off the stage. Bunny trickles off not too long after.

I heard stories about the unexpected parts of being background dancing. Helping the artist when mishaps arise. Handing off a new mic if the old one is malfunctioning. One time, I heard about a male dancer tackling a stage jumper before he'd reached the artist! But before today, that's all they were. Stories. Now, here I am on my first tour, experiencing it in real life. A moment that seemed like a half hour really lasted three minutes at most, and Naya handled it with the poise of a true professional.

After Bunny and Naya swooped in for the rescue, the rest of the ladies retreat to the dressing room for our quick break and outfit change. I was the only one left standing in the wing with my jaw scraping the floor.

"You guys...That was epic!" I congratulate them as they exit the stage.

"Wasn't it! Once I noticed what Naya was doing, I was like lemme create a diversion. We're a good team, sis!"

"I guess we are, aren't we? Since college, baby!" Naya replies with a big, toothy grin stretched across her face. A smile that is so contagious I couldn't help but match it. Like a light that shines so brightly, it's hard not to bask in its radiance. It's such a rare occurrence. I like to savor every time it happens, even if it's with Bunny and I'm just the outsider looking in.

We head back to the dressing room, and Bunny jogs ahead.

"Ima meet y'all in there. I've been holding my pee since we were doing our makeup earlier!"

And suddenly, I'm left alone with Naya.

We walk side by side, my eyes ahead and hers to the floor. An arena hallway with bass blaring through the walls has never felt so silent.

Just speak, Khloe.

"What you did back there—How you stayed so calm—I meanwhile still performing, of course. It was... It was amazing."

Okay, not the worst babble.

She peels her eyes from the floor and onto mine.

"Thank you, Khloe."

Something flashes across her face for a moment—a look that feels like she wants to say more. I open my mouth to speak, but my hand accidentally brushes against hers, probably because I'm uncoordinated, and it's hard for me to walk in a straight line, a fact I've known since trying out for the track team back in high school.

She snatches her hand away, taking the moment with it.

"Sorry," she mutters, bringing her eyes back to the floor. "Here, you go first."

She swings open the dressing room door.

"UNO! UNO OUT!"

Rae slams two cards in the center of our circle.

After the show, the girls orchestrate a game night on the bus. So we shower quicker than usual, cover up in the matching robes that Leah gifted everyone, and huddle together. We transformed the front lounge of the bus into a sea of plush pillows and fuzzy blankets.

"What?!" Khloe tosses her cards to the side.

"So you just gon' win every game?" Bunny replies.

"Yeah, let me shuffle this time!" Khloe yanks the deck from the center of us.

"Winning three times is quite the anomaly, but is it *really* when we're talking about me? Rae? The Uno champ?"

She performs her best royal wave toward us. Everyone smacks their teeth, ignoring Rae's boasting. Tiana has been invested in her phone for most of the game, but she comes up for air.

"Put some good energy into that deck, Khloe. We gotta take this girl out!"

Snickers rattle through the bus until the bus door opens and closes with a slam. DayDay runs in, huffing and puffing.

"Whew! I tried to pack up Zion's wardrobe as fast as I could! Are y'all still playing Uno?"

"Yes, I am giving everyone a chance to be beaten by me for a third time," Rae jests.

"Not this time!" Khloe chucks a couch pillow toward Rae's head, which she dodges with perfect timing.

"As you can see, DayDay, the people hate to see a winner do what they do best."

Rae smoothes her shirt and pants like a politician getting ready to make a speech. The whole bus erupts with laughter. Khloe's giggles cause her to topple over into Leah's lap, laughing until she snorts.

I love how comfortable Khole's grown with everyone in such a short time. The timid Khloe from rehearsals is slowly being shed and replaced by a boisterous, giddy woman. Her smile, accompanied by those deep-set dimples, can light up the whole bus.

Stop staring.

DayDay makes his way to the snack cabinet and pulls out a bottle of red wine.

"Rae, I'm happy for you, but I'm trying to win a glass of this first, then I'll take you off the throne."

"Hold on, lemme grab a glass!" Bunny springs up.

"Me too!" Leah adds.

While everyone buzzes with energy, Khloe tip-toes to the cabinet and pulls out a stack of red solo cups. Technically, there were no glass cups on the bus at all, but I guess everyone speaks from habit. With a mischievous grin, she slides a cup in front of DayDay.

Most of the ladies, myself included, are getting little pimples here and there from wearing heavy show makeup so often. Not Khloe. As she stands there leaning up against the counter, comfy in her PJs, robe, and satin scarf, her smooth brown skin remains as flawless as ever. Moisturized and blemish-free.

"Girl, I see yo ass standing there inching this lil' cup!" DayDay hollers.

A child-like grin spreads over Khloe's face, and she laughs like a bad middle child. Before I know it, her smile transfers to my cheeks, leaving me smiling at nothing.

Get a grip, Nayara.

"Here, Mrs. Thristy!" DayDay pours into Khloe's cup. "Hand this one to Naya since you're so eager."

My muscles tense at the sound of my name. When she hands me the cup, I pretend to relax as her fingers graze mine.

"Thanks."

"No problem."

Her dimples deepen.

I've got to get a hold of myself.

I peer into my cup for a few seconds, then gulp the entire drink down.

"Damn, sis!" Bunny snuggles next to me with her cup in hand. "Turnin' up tonight?"

"Naw..." I say with a chuckle. "I had trouble sleeping last night, so I'm making sure this wine does the job."

Bunny opens her mouth to reply, but DayDay claps his hands together.

"All right, my beautiful dancers from the Soakin' Wet Summer Tour, who wants to get smoked in Uno for real this time?!"

Three rounds of Uno games and two bottles of wine later, permanent smiles and glossy eyes dress all our faces. A rosy flush invades Leah's freckled ivory skin and Tiana's yellow honey complexion.

"Okay, these UNO games raised my blood pressure. I am breaking a lil' sweat!" Khole flips her braids over her shoulder. "Can we play two truths and a lie instead?"

A ripple of "yes" popcorns among the group.

Tiana raises her wine in the air.

"I'll go first! All right, I cuss in my sleep. I still eat McDonalds like I'm in college. And I have to swipe my bed three times before I get in it."

My eyes shoot to the right, straight into Bunny's eyes, causing laughter to explode from us. I bite my lips to conceal my own giggles, failing terribly. She'd read my mind as plain as day. I didn't know which fact was the lie, but I knew one thing. Tiana curses like a sailor in her sleep. One late night, while everyone else was asleep, Bunny and I heard it firsthand. Grunting, whispering, and yelling, Tiana blurted out all types of profanities, all while being sound asleep in her bunk. I doubled over, holding my stomach. Tears streamed down Bunny's face. Doing our best not to wake up the entire bus, we suppressed our laughs with all our might.

"What are you guys laughing at?" Leah asks.

"Yeah, y'all are being real secretive over there!" DayDay snaps.

"I'm sorry!" Bunny begins, still failing to stifle her giggling. "Tiana, you cussing in your sleep is the truth 'cause me and Naya were in tears a couple of nights ago!"

Rae's brows furrow. "What? Really? I never heard anything!"

Tiana whips her attention to Bunny, amusement with a hint of horror sprinkled over Tiana's face. "Huh?! Noooo! What did y'all hear?"

I regain my composure and say, "Honey, you said everything under the sun. I'm just thankful me and Bunny didn't wake everyone up with our laughing!"

"Damn, my boyfriend told me I don't do it as often anymore." She giggles. "I don't know what it is y'all... It's been a problem since I was a teenager."

Bunny lays a gentle hand on Tiana's shoulder. "Oh, baby girl, that is no problem! We love it over here! The only problem was that me and Naya almost peed ourselves!"

This time, laughter ripples through everyone.

"So, which one is the lie?" Rae questions.

I raise my hand like the star student in grade school. "There is no way you still eat McDonald's! This tour has barely started, and I've already noticed how clean you eat. Not to mention, I can also hear you swiping your bed three times before you get in."

"True."

Replies travel throughout the bus.

"Yeah, I saw her do that my first night here. I almost moved back to the boys' bus. Thought y'all had roaches or something!"

DayDay shudders at the memory.

"Okay, enough attention on my sleeping quirks and OCD!"

I place a reassuring hand on Tiana's knee and my other hand on my chest.

"It's okay, T! It's really fine. Everyone sleeps through it. Bunny and I only heard it 'cause we stayed up late that night. Plus, my ex used to talk in her sleep, too! I'm used to it!"

My ex... used to... in *her* sleep.

There it is.

The inevitable moment in my life where I unknowingly come out to those around me. Call it the curse of being a fem-presenting woman. I'm not a stud, and my only tomboy traits are wearing little to no makeup, sporting baggy clothes, and buying boxer briefs instead of regular women's underwear.

In the dance world, that's pretty normal attire for women. I'm not closeted or embarrassed. I just don't announce it to the world. Dancers are a no-go for me, so there aren't exes in the scene to spread the word for me. And I never voluntarily bring it up, and because of that, I always end up in *this* moment. The moment it accidentally slips in, I hope people either glaze over the details or don't care. But that rarely happens.

There's never any blatant homophobia, just little mannerisms that say, "Oh!"

Widened eyes. Stiffening necks.

Khole, who was in mid-sip, peeks over her cup, sending a chill down my spine. Bunny found out during our college days, and DayDay just has a keen gaydar, so he sniffed me out within minutes of our first rehearsal. A moment of silence passes that feels like an eternity, and I move my hand from Tiana's knee. Suddenly reminded of the after-show activities she'd discovered me partaking in a few nights ago.

Damn, I wonder if she's told any of the girls about that.

Rae breaks the silence with a round of applause.

"Uh oh! Her? Purrrr babe! That means *you* are taking us to the gay club. I prefer to shake my ass there 'cause straight men don't know how to act sometimes."

"Right! I'm down to battle the queens any night!" Bunny adds.

"Then it's decided! One of these off days, DayDay and I are gonna take y'all in our world. Now, who's next?"

A nervous chuckle escapes my mouth.

"Khloe, you go!" Leah nudges her knee.

Everyone locks onto Khloe as she downs the last sip of her wine, putting our full glasses to shame.

"Hmm."

Her round eyes scan the bus, searching for her two truths and a lie. Her white acrylic nails reflect light as she taps her fingers.

"Okay! Okay! I got it!"

Everyone leans in.

"I started dancing when I was in college. I dated a woman for two years. And this is my first tour."

Nobody moves. The bus is so silent I can practically hear the gears in everyone's brains turning, mine included. There's no way she started dancing in college. Flashbacks of her dynamic, hard-hitting style fill my brain. Khloe is only twenty-four. There's no way she harbored that kind of talent in so few years. She moves with the sureness of a seasoned veteran dancer. Surely, she's graced the stage with other artists on tour. But she is young... so this *could* be her first big tour. Dated a woman for two years? Who knows? My gaydar has never been as sharp as DayDay's.

"There's no way you started dancing in college. You're too good!" I break the brief lull in guesses.

I search her eyes for a hint of revelation. Her face remains still and stoic.

"Wrong."

"Huh?! No, that is astonishing! Most people train for ten-plus years for your type of talent!" Leah chirps.

"This can't be your first tour," Rae retorts.

"I can see you with a girlfriend, though." Bunny shrugs her shoulders.

Silence blankets the bus yet again.

Please don't let her be gay. That would make my problems so much worse.

DayDay sits quietly with one hand clasped over his face. Tiana's mentally checked out and is texting at the speed of light. Anger fuels each tap against her phone. We haven't been touring long, but it took no time for us to notice the pattern—routine arguments with her boyfriend. In random moments throughout the day, or even backstage in between numbers, Tiana is usually huffing exasperated breaths into her phone while her fingers type away. Sometimes, the texts evolve into tense, whispered phone conversations. I never know what they are fighting about, but what I do know is that when Tiana gets wrapped up in that phone, everybody minds their business.

"Honey, you have not tried kitty cats!" DayDay erupts.

Khole tries to maintain her poker face but unravels in seconds, laughing into the palms of her hands.

"How'd you know!"

"Those claws on your fingers, girl! You're not fingering anybody with those!"

Now everyone explodes into laughter.

"Isn't that what toys are for?" Tiana taps back in.

"Girl, I don't know. Care to share from experience, *Naya?*" DayDay raises his brows. He swishes around his wine like a parent waiting to catch you in a lie, and my body immediately stiffens. Shit, I thought I'd dodged this earlier, and here comes DayDay, throwing me back in the fire. At this moment, I thank God for the light brown skin concealing the heat in my cheeks.

"Yeah," I say shortly. "There are toys or other stuff women can do if they have nails."

"Not that you need those, friend!" Bunny interjects. "Those fingers used to blow minds in college! Our bedroom walls were too thin. If I didn't go to sleep with rain sounds on my headphones, I'd have to listen to your name all night. *Oh, Naya! Ohhh, Naya!*"

Giggles reverberate through the women yet again. My body was warm earlier, but it fumes into a full-blown sauna, stewing my insides.

"Okay, okay." I force a chuckle. "That's enough Bunny...Who's next?"

"I've never been with a woman before." Leah shrugs before taking a sip of her wine.

"Me either. I think women are attractive, but I am addicted to men. I mean really ad-*dick*-ted." Rae cackles.

"When I was eighteen, I dated a girl for about a year, but we agreed that we'd be better off as friends," Tiana says, then returns to her phone again.

With each addition, my soul sinks deeper and deeper. Frozen

and unsure of what to say next. Conversations like this always raise my blood pressure.

"I've never been with a woman," Khole says. "But I'd like to try it at some point in my life."

Did she just glance at me? No. There's no way. I must've imagined it.

I look at Bunny to see if she caught anything, but she is too busy shuffling the deck of UNO cards.

"Well... Uh, I have a lot of apps on my phone! Let me know if you want the names of them!" I blurt out.

Apps? Really, Naya?

"Oh. Yeah... sure!" Khloe says, running a hand over her headscarf.

"Okay, lesbihonest, moments and apps aside, I just reshuffled this UNO deck. Does anyone wanna lose one more time before I go to bed?" Rae announces.

"Honey, please!" DayDay sets his cup down and readies himself for war.

Everyone else follows suit.

I get up, dump the rest of my wine in the sink, and return to a stack of cards dealt in front of my spot. I try organizing my hand, but my mind drifts elsewhere. Khloe's words play in my ears on repeat, "I'd like to try it."

There are quite a few things I'd like to try with you.

I peek up from my cards and across the circle to Khloe, who had been trying to choose a card to put down.

This time I take her in a little more closely, my glass of wine granting me the courage to do so. Starting at her white nails, traveling up her cocoa-butter smooth arms, then to her elegant collar bone, up to the blue silk scarf protecting her cornrows, and finally, back down to her face. Her beautiful milk chocolate face. Her expressive eyes, button nose, and lush, perfectly shaped lips. I can't help but wonder what they feel like...

Khloe scans the deck in her hand and selects a blue number three card. After placing the card down, she glances up. Her knowing eyes barrel into mine, aware I've already been looking at her. Before I bury my eyes into my deck and die from embarrassment, a smirk curves the corners of Khloe's mouth.

CHAPTER FOURTEEN

"WHY WOULD you entice such violence, Leah?!"

I stomp away from my spot on the front lounge couch and yank the blinds closed. The light sears into my tired eyes, causing my temples to palpitate — Consequences of all the wine I drank last night and without a single bottle of water in sight.

"Violence? I'm trying to get ready! We have a show in a couple of hours!"

I glance at my phone and groan into my blanket.

3:45p.m.

Makeup call is at 6 pm in the venue. It was only noon when I emerged from my bunk tortilla-wrapped in my blanket and plopped on the front lounge couch. I must've dozed off.

"Here, babe."

Leah hands me a bottle of water as if she had read my mind. I gulp most of it down in one sip.

"Hey, Leah."

I wipe the last hints of sleep from my eyes.

"Why didn't you explore the city like the other girls today?"

"Aw, would you rather someone else's company, Khloe?"

She grabs her toiletry bag from the junk bunk and sets it up in front of the kitchen sink.

"No, never! I'm sorry, didn't mean it that way. I'm just curious. You're so proactive. So group-oriented. You do cute things like plan games, movie nights, buy matching robes. I feel like you've been planning pre-show brunches and handing out daily itineraries."

A grin overtakes her mouth.

"I live for stuff like that. You're right. This is only my second tour, but one thing I quickly noticed on the first tour was that people needed their alone time. The moment you say yes to a tour, everything goes up in the air—schedules, routines…" She gestures to the bus walls around us. "Personal space. While group activities are healthy and necessary for the morale of the group, so is alone time. Moments to yourself to regain a fragment of normalcy. So yeah, even if we stayed up late last night and have blacked-out bunks with no sunlight, some people make it a point to get up before the show. Even if it's just to grab a coffee at a local café around the corner. Since everyone leaves the bus, I use this space as my alone time…even if you're here walking around like a zombie."

She chuckles.

"Hey! Between these time changes and the lack of sunlight in the bunks, I could sleep all day!"

"That's amazing. Prioritize rest. Always. But make some time for fun, too. Experience cities. Explore. Make memories. Don't let any of the remedial shit distract you."

Without blantantly saying it, we both know she's talking about BriAnn.

"You're right... You are so right."

I throw the blanket off my legs, stand up, and grab my toiletry bag.

"Thanks for this talk, Leah. You have no idea how much I needed it."

I'm finally a presentable human after getting my life together inside the arena. I'd already done my show makeup, so all I had to do was return to the venue and stretch before curtains-up.

I'm ready. *This* is actually the beginning of the tour. The beginning of the end. The end of BriAnn's presence haunting me. The end of my home life in LA looming over me. It's over. I whip out my phone and type away.

Me: Hey, whatcha up to?

Those dreadful typing bubbles flicker over my screen for ten seconds that feel like ten minutes.

Am I making a mistake?

I could've messaged any of the other girls. Maybe I shouldn't have texted her...

My phone pings.

Naya: At a Ramen spot a couple of blocks down.

I bite the inside of my cheek and take the risk.

Me: Can I join you?

I pause, watching those bubbles taunt me all over again.

Naya: Sure. I'll send my location.

CHAPTER FIFTEEN

"YOU KNOW... I was a little confused when you said ramen spot."

Khloe's voice trails off. She studies the gold centerpiece on the table and the artwork hanging on the walls.

"Uh, how long do you think it took them to find the art for this place?"

Though the table blocks her legs from my view, I can still see her fingers fidgeting with her ripped denim jeans. She's paired the pants with a matching denim tube top, showcasing her smooth arms and collarbone. I'd never wear something like that, but her outfit puts my basketball shorts and Nike t-shirt combo to shame. Had I known she planned to join me for lunch, I would've put more care into my outfit.

My eyes once over the restaurant.

"What are you talking about?"

"The paintings. And pictures. Everything is black and red with gold accents. And there's at least a dozen. You'd think it was hard to find pieces with those specific traits? Or maybe someone in-house made them, you know?"

"Yeah... I guess."

She huffs a low breath and sits back in her chair. I know it's rude to allow her to meet me here and be this dry, but I have to be. I don't know Khloe too well. But something tells me if I don't put a wall between us, all hell might break loose.

Khloe's eyes watch me for a few seconds before snatching the menu off of the table. I feel bad, but it's also adorable every time she catches an attitude with me. The pouts, eye rolls, furrowed eyebrows, and she still can't warp the beauty on her face.

"So you've never had real ramen before?" I say, deciding to ease up a little.

"No." She lowers the menu. "Only instant ramen in college."

She shortens her tone to match mine and raises the menu over her face again.

"Well, no matter what spot I go to, if there's ramen with miso broth, that's all me."

"Yup." Her voice cuts from behind the menu.

"Maybe you can order another, then try mine. That way, you get to try two at the same time."

"Yup."

Okay, I definitely don't like the tables turned on me.

"Hey." I reach out, lowering the menu. "I'm sorry I'm short with you sometimes. I'm sure you've noticed. It's just that I—"

"I never would've cared that you were gay, you know."

"I—Uh..." I mutter, unsure of what to say next.

What was I going to say exactly?

I'm sorry I'm short with you because no matter how distant I am or how many women I waste my time on, my mind travels back to you.

I'm sorry, I'm dry 'cause I'm attracted to you.

Out of all the words in the world, I never expected her to utter those.

"What makes you say that?" I spit out.

"That's why you're so weird with me. You smile and joke with everyone else, but with me, you're closed off. I get it. You've known the other ladies longer, and I'm new. You didn't know how I'd react. I get it."

I blink rapidly a few times to find the words. Yes, Bunny and I have known each other since college. I'd worked a couple of short-term jobs with Rae, but I'd never met Leah and Tiana. But I guess she doesn't need to know that.

"Yeah, you're right." The lie leaves my lips effortlessly. "I just didn't know if it would make you uncomfortable, so I was being distant. I'm sorry for the way I acted."

"It's okay. But it was so damn hot and cold. It was getting hard to keep up. I'd already come to the conclusion that you do drugs or something."

"Wait. Drugs?!"

"Yeah." She snickers. "I had to make sense of it all. The distance. The bubbly personality one minute. Then, the short, curt sentences next. You disappeared with your two friends at that after-party in Zion's dressing room. And you were exhausted the next day. It was my first time seeing you with tiny bags under your eyes. I figured you were coming down from whatever drug you did that night."

I was coming down from something all right...

"I cannot believe you thought I was on drugs!"

I laugh, driving the attention away from what I actually did that night.

Khloe props her elbows on the table, burying her giggles into her hands. "I didn't know what else to think!"

"Dang, my bad, Khloe. I didn't realize I was being so rude."

Lie.

"I just didn't know how you'd react."

Double lie.

"I've had issues in the past with dancers being uncomfortable with my sexual orientation, so I try not to lead with that now."

Not entirely a lie, but it still wasn't the reason I'd been so rude to her.

"Oh no, I'm not like that." Khloe reaches out across the table with open palms. I place my hands on her and pretend my body temperature isn't skyrocketing. "I am not like that. I accept people from all walks of life!"

"Thanks, I appreciate that."

"Plus! You heard me last night. I've been thinking about exploring women. It's been on my mind for a while now, but something about this tour... about this time in my life makes me feel like the time is now. And I know exactly why."

Because there's a girl named Naya on tour who is drawn to you no matter how hard she tries not to be?

She breaks her hands from mine and spreads them across the table, leaning her upper body in as if she were whispering a master plan.

"I think you're the perfect person to help me with that!"

"Uh...how so?"

"Gay clubs on the road. Apps. Pointers on how to pick up

women. Tips on how to... uh.. be with women. I would love your help with all of it!"

"Oh! Okay!" I say a little too eagerly.

"I mean, I know you probably have a thousand better things to do with your free ti—"

"I got you, sis! Gimme your phone. Let's start now."

I open the App Store and begin typing. I feel Khloe's gaze on me. Her eyelashes blink with anticipation.

"Here."

"Damn, three of them?"

She lays a shocked hand across her neckline.

"Yeah, a lady needs her options. Femm-presenting lesbians, masc-presenting lesbians. Then there's the pansexual and non-binary babes."

"Masc-presenting? Pan-sexual?"

A grin floods my cheeks. Her confused expression brings a smile to my face every time. It's so authentic... so cute.

"Don't worry about labels. Look around, swipe right on whoever interests you. When I came out, I obsessed over labels and what to identify as. Once I let go of all that minuscule shit, I settled into me."

Her shoulders lower and I can feel her tension return to repose.

"Are you ladies ready to order?" A server with an iPad in hand interrupts.

"Yes." Khloe starts. "I'll have a...."

Her words drift far, far away. Probably alongside the better choices I should've made.

What the hell did I just agree to?

CHAPTER SIXTEEN

khloe

"UGH, THAT'S NOT IT!" I scream into the empty wing backstage.

Pre-show music rings through front of house. That's a theater term I learned for the areas open to the audience. The music taunts me and these messy steps. I peek through the curtains to the sight of hundreds of fans slowly pouring into the arena. We are still an hour and a half away from showtime, but the crowd is eager and ready. Drinks in hand and energy buzzing, they thunder over the music. Some even stand in front of their seats, twerking.

At least they are enjoying themselves. Meanwhile, I'm here, backstage, running breakdown in Act 3 for the hundredth time. And no matter how many times I practice, it isn't hitting like I want. This movement demands more sharpness, more *ism* than what I've been executing. So while the other ladies are in the dressing rooms doing their makeup, I'm on the side of the stage, breaking a full sweat.

Leah and Khloe look messy during the breakdown in the middle of Act 3.

No matter how much I try, BriAnn's words still creep in from time to time, echoing through my limbs on stage.

Okay, a few more times, then I'll go back to the dressing room.

5, 6, 7... I hit the beginning accents as sharp as I can. I focus on allowing the choreography to move through my torso. Make it more internal. Connect with the music more instead of just doing the steps. Bending my knees and feeling the floor beneath me, I change the level of my movement and—*ouch!*

"Damn it!" I sink to the floor, clutching my right ankle.

"Hey! Are you okay?!" Naya runs onto the stage.

In seconds, she's on the floor in front of me with my foot in her hands.

"Ugh. I don't know. I rolled my ankle and felt a sharp pain shoot up my leg."

Without a word, she peels off my shoe and pushes her thumbs into the bottom of my ankle.

"Be careful!" I clench my toes. "My feet get pretty warm when I dance... so—"

"So, they stink?"

She smirks.

"Not bad! But sometimes they have a little twang. You know how people's hands sweat when they get nervous? My feet sweat..."

She leans closer and *inhales*. A deep sniff from the deepest part of her lungs.

"Woah! Good lord! What died in there?!" Naya throws her head backward.

"I told you!" I snatch my foot away.

"I'm kidding, Khloe."

She laughs, reaching for my foot again.

"You play too much! What are you even doing up here so early, anyway?"

"I could ask you the same thing Miss. Practice makes perfect. I came up to check on my quick-change outfits. Make sure every piece is accounted for."

Note to self: Check quick change areas before the show starts. Naya unknowingly unlocked a new fear in me. Rushing to change in one minute or less, only to realize I am missing a glove or bra.

She continues to massage my ankle, this time switching into a soft circular motion.

"I came up here to practice..."

"I saw, but why? We'd already worked on that section."

"Yeah... but it still doesn't feel right. I feel like it could be better."

"You feel like it could be better, or do you still have the wicked witch speaking in your ear?"

I snicker at the sound of BriAnn's perfect nickname and am immediately sobered by Naya's response. It was like she'd plucked the thoughts from my head and said them aloud.

"I guess I still have the wicked witch in my ear. But can you blame me?! She picked on me for that entire month of rehearsals, then she sends critiques in the chat. I didn't even know she was watching the show!"

"Hey. Breathe." She shifts her grip from my ankle to the center of my arch, alternating her thumbs as they dig into me. "Inhale and exhale."

She mirrors me, raising her shoulders with a deep inhale and exhaling audible breaths.

"We fixed that section already, Khloe. And she has said nothing since then. Plus, I wouldn't have let you leave the stage if it still wasn't right. You kill that section. Hell, you kill the entire show. Once you sit into that star quality, you'll be unstoppable."

"Thanks... I guess I'm just trying to find myself more."

"Please do. Play. Explore. Use those brief moments in between choreo. Walking on stage, freestyle moments, poses—use all of that to experiment with different ways of moving. You'll get to know yourself quickly."

Before I reply, Naya intensifies the pressure.

"Ouch!"

"Sorry! Too much?"

"No, it's okay. There's just a lot of tension there."

"I agree. You should probably roll out your feet before and after shows. It could keep up the tension from affecting your ankle or calf."

I nod and allow a comfortable silence to fall between us. Her hands work around the top of my foot and back to my ankle like a seasoned physical therapist. She leans forward, staring at the floor, sensing the anatomy of my foot with her fingers instead of her eyes. Curl by curl, her locks fall in front of her face, until she flips them back with a soft buck of her head. The baby blue pre-show lighting cascades over her skin as if on purpose. A light cue created by production. A glow illuminating her mocha complexion.

"Where did you learn how to do this? You're great at it."

"By the middle of my second tour, my body was wrecked. Lower back pain, knee issues, you name it. If I wanted any longevity in this business. I had to discover ways to care for my body."

"Well, consider your goal achieved 'cause your hands are gifted."

"Why thank you, ma'am. Stand up and tell me how you feel."

I rise to my feet and take a couple of steps.

"So much better! Woah... Thank you! Can I pay you or buy you lunch or something?"

"You can repay me by overthinking less." She winks. "Now go decompress in the dressing room. We have an hour until the show starts."

* * *

Knees buried in my chest and a blanket wrapped around my body, I snuggle with the couch's armrest in the front lounge of the bus. After the show, I hit the showers first and beat everyone back on the bus. For the last fifteen minutes, I've been deep into my phone, swiping on The Beanery, one of the dating apps Naya installed.

This app caters to those looking for more femme-presenting women. I figure it is a good place to start since I am femme-presenting, too. I scroll by countless profiles. A white girl with tattoos all over her neck and face. A white girl who looks like America's sweetheart, Taylor Swift vibes fully intact. A black girl with long purple locks down her back. An Asian girl that was a professional hula dancer. Everyone is beautiful, no doubt, but their *about me* sections made me scroll away with vigor.

"*Looking for a good time (winky face).*"

"*I'll lick you like a lollipop.*"

"*Award winning eater.*"

And those most troubling.

"*Versatile top or bottom.*"

What does that even mean?

I swipe with rapid-fire until I land on a pair of bright blue eyes staring back at me. Her icy gaze paired with strawberry blonde hair shaved on the right side.

Elliana Vasquez.

If the last name wasn't a sign of her Latinx heritage, the multiple Colombian flags in her bio definitely give it away. Her olive skin tone pokes through the full cleavage in her crop top, but she's nowhere near as exposed as the other profiles. Elliana's pictures are pleasant. Pretty. A little on the modest side, like me. Location: Orlando, Florida. The next stop on our tour. Holding my breath, I swipe right.

Here goes nothing...

Me: Hey, what's up? I'm Khloe.

Elliana: Hey there! It's nice to meet you.

CHAPTER SEVENTEEN

"CUANDO VAS A VISITAR ME?"

When are you going to visit me?

My mother widens her eyes with her best puppy dog face. No matter how many years she's lived in the states, her Cuban accent remains as thick as ever. The sound of it is the perfect medicine when I'm missing her more than usual.

"Mami, I could've spent some time with you when the tour stopped in Atlanta or even Jacksonville. That's only a couple hours away from Augusta, *pero* you and Papi are too busy being *calleteros*."

Street runners. Party goers. Club rats. I'm not exactly sure how that directly translates to English.

Papi dips his face into the camera, wearing sunglasses, a straw hat, and coconut in his hand. The island sun has their cocoa-brown skin vibrant and full of life.

"Ya tu sabes, Nayarita! We had to celebrate! Go big for me!"

After thirty years of being undocumented, my dad was finally granted his citizenship. The years of driving without a license, working under-the-table jobs, and holding our breath every time he stepped out the door are long behind us. He became a citizen around February, but my parents continued to celebrate with a vengeance. Cruise ships, trips, and now a week's stay in Barbados, taking in the tropical paradise.

"Claro que si, Papi!" I smile into the camera. "How about we plan a family trip in September, at the end of the tour?"

"Sounds good, mija. Bueno, hablamos ahorita."

"Gracias, Mami. Te quiero."

"Nayara…" My mom's eyes pop into frame just as I am about to hang up.

"Yes, Mami?"

"Are you dating? When will we get to meet a nice young lady that makes you smile?"

"Maaaa." I groan.

"I don't mean to pry, mija. It's just that… me and your Papi want to see you happy. Living life to the fullest. Not reserved or cut off because of what *happened*."

"I am happy, Mami. I'm much better now. Promise! I am dating." Lie. Casual sex with women from random apps is the furthest from dating. "I haven't met anyone worthwhile yet."

"Okay, mi amor. I am just checking in. It's been five years… I want to make sure you aren't letting that stop you."

Hm, just like a Cuban mother to speak about hard topics vaguely.

"Thank you, Mami."

"No problema, mi reina! Que dios te bendiga. Enjoy your off day!"

I hang up and sling a plush hotel pillow over my face. The vibrations from my loud groan into the pillow reach my fingertips.

At around five this morning, we arrived at a hotel in Orlando.

"Rise and shine, ladies! The bus is parking at an off-site location thirty minutes away. Grab what you need, and I'll see you for checkout at noon tomorrow!"

With sleep heavy in our limbs, we peeled our bodies out of the bunks, grabbed our purses, phone chargers, and suitcases under the bus, then moped into the hotel lobby like a group of the walking dead.

I struggled to act like a functioning human throughout all of that, but the moment I laid down in this king-sized bed, my body refused to succumb to sleep. Now, here I am, four hours later, having watched the sunrise and scrolling into Instagram oblivion.

Taking a deep breath, I pull the pillow from my mouth but keep it over my eyes.

Inhale and exhale, Naya.

Breathe. Let this pillow block out the sun and—

The force of my phone vibrating shakes the entire nightstand.

Nope. No more phone. Let it be. Relax your mind, and you'll go to sleep in no tim—

Bzzz!

I blow a raspberry and turn onto my stomach, allowing the memory foam mattress to cradle my body differently. I sink into the mattress. The satisfaction invades my sore muscles. I ball up a corner of the soft comforter and place it in between my knees. The sounds of downtown Orlando waking up knocks at my window, but I kind of enjoy it. The cars and city buses thrumming along. Aggravated car horns blowing. Maybe that's it! The eerie silence of the early morning had been too still. That's why I couldn't fall asleep. I've grown accustomed to the constant city buzz in LA.

Ugh! I turn over to the opposite side.

Stop lying to yourself.

I released another groan. This time into the empty air of the hotel room.

Truth is, I hate Orlando. I hate all the memories this place holds. All the reminders of—

Bzzz!

"What?!" I growl, snatching my phone.

Soakin' Wet Summer Tour Core Dancers Chat

DayDay: Morning baddies and happy off day! Disney World, anybody?

Leah: Yes! PLEASE!

Rae: I can't... I'm visiting my cousin today.

Tiana: I'm down! How's noon?!

Additional messages drown the thread as my sleep-deprived eyes watch on. A ghost overseeing the group chat, but not responding. I hate Orlando, but I hate Disney World even more. I will never be caught in that theme park ever again. Too many memories. Ping after ping, everybody in the chat types ravenously to plan their day. Everyone except—

Khloe: Hey, you guys! I would love to go to Disney with y'all, but I already booked a ticket for an Everglades tour this morning!

Huh?

Without a second thought, I swipe out of the group chat and into a private conversation with Khloe.

Me: You know the Everglades is 3 hours away from Orlando, right?

Khloe: Yeah, but there's a four-hour river tour that leaves from here. Come with, if you want! There are still tickets available! I left the hotel early to grab some snacks, but the boat doesn't leave for another hour.

Shit... Anything to get the fuck out of Orlando.

Me: I'm there. Send the address.

Wondering yet again, what the hell have I just agreed to?

I throw on a white t-shirt and some basketball shorts decorated with a floral pattern, brush my teeth, and leave the hotel room.

CHAPTER EIGHTEEN

FOUR YEARS LIVING in Miami for college, a couple of miles away from the Everglades, and I was never interested in seeing it, much less taking a four-hour tour. Now I'm here years later, cutting through swampy waters on an airboat with a woman I've been trying to avoid like the plague. A woman that I can't seem to shake away. A woman who sometimes makes me want to reconsider every one of my rules.

But that'll all be over soon.

Khloe has taken the seat closest to the water, so she has the best view. Her gaze wanders like a kid in a toy factory. I took the seat on the inside, so I have a front-row view of her amazement. With every new mango tree or marsh in view, Khloe's neck cranes outward for a better view. Meanwhile, I do my best to avoid my eyes falling to her lap. The way her shorts hug her thighs tighter, sitting down.

Though it almost sends me into cardiac arrest, I'm actually

relieved Khloe told me she's interested in pursuing women. It's like a job position for a mentor role opened up right in front of my eyes. A mentor introduces her to the scene, signs her up on the apps, and offers advice when needed.

A mentor to show her the ropes, *figuratively,* of course.

A mentor to not only help her in the journey but hopefully hook her up with any semi-sane queer on the market, thus keeping her occupied and far away from me.

I've shaken off petty crushes before. Hell, when I met Bunny, she had me tripping over my words for about a week. That dark royal brown skin made me feel like I was talking to the Queen of a West African tribe. Then it simmered, like this crush will, too.

"Hey. Where'd you go?"

Khloe taps my thigh. I blink twice, sharpening the view of the marsh and murky water. The airboat slows to a leisurely pace, and the tour guide goes on about some type of bird species in the trees.

"Sorry. Zoned out for a second."

"Look!"

She gasps, pointing across the water. About thirty feet away, a massive gator lies across the grass, its snout pointed into the air. Sharp, pointed teeth hanging over the sides of its mouth. The rest of the tour attendees turn their attention to the left side of the boat.

"Ah, yes." The tour guide switches topics. "Here we have a male alligator taking in the sun rays…"

"Wait, how does she know it's a male from just looking at it?"

I lean into Khloe.

"Because males tend to be larger than the females. And judging by the size of this one, it has to be over nine feet. I have to get a picture!"

She whips out a disposable camera and leans closer to the railing. I'm not sure how much film the camera has left, but she uses five pictures on the same alligator in the *same* pose.

After a few minutes, the boat takes off.

"The Everglades is most notorious for its large population of alligators, but many do not know the other species that also inhabit this land such as the west Indian Manatee, Florida Panther and over 360 species of birds..."

"So, do you think we'll see any Florida panthers?" I murmur, trying not to disrupt the tour guide's spiel.

"Huh?"

Khloe scrunches her nose.

Leaning closer this time, I repeat myself, cursing the smell of her vanilla perfume invading my nostrils.

"Oh, probably not. Florida panthers avoid humans. They are also nocturnal, so they are probably sleeping, anyway."

Her bewildered eyes twinkle. I've never seen her so enthralled with something before. With every foot the airboat travels, her head swivels in all directions as she points out plants and wildlife, even the tour guide fails to mention.

"You see these plants?" Khloe points to a patch of mangrove trees the boat was passing. At the base of the tree are green plants with splashes of red in the center. The pointed leaves resembled the top of a pineapple. "These types of bromeliads are native to the Everglades. They aren't found anywhere else in the world—Oh! Look! You see that poking through the marsh?"

I follow her gaze, eyeing nothing but light green plants jumbled together on top of the water.

"Uh.. no."

"Here."

She sits back and gestures for me to lean over her lap for a better view. I try to focus on whatever she's trying to get me to see instead of how soft her legs are when they make contact with my forearms.

"Look a little closer."

Seconds later, I see it. A set of round eyes stare back at me. An alligator is studying the boat as we pass by, using the marsh as cover.

"How'd you even see that?"

I shift back into my personal space.

"Good vision. I guess! Aw, look at that one! How cute!"

This time, she leans over my body toward the right side of the boat. That damned vanilla scent draws me in, yet again. I turn to see another gator on a patch of land with its leathery skin basking in the sun. This time, with its mouth gaped open and its eyes closed.

"It looks like it's smiling," I note.

"Doesn't she! How adorable!"

Never thought to describe a gator, or any reptilian for that matter, as adorable, but leave it to Khloe.

I raise my hand to get the guide's attention.

"Why do they lay in the sun like that?"

"It helps them control their body temperature!" Khloe blurts out before the guide can utter a single word.

"Well, look who knows their gator facts!" The guide spits out. "Maybe you should lead the rest of the tour."

"Er... Sorry. No, go ahead. Got too excited, I guess."

An embarrassed smile spreads across her cheeks.

She hates me, Khloe mouths.

I inch closer. "It's not your fault. You're doing a way better job than her."

Tiny snickers rattle through us, which come to a screeching halt when the tour guide shoots us a death stare.

"Why do you know so much about the Everglades, anyway? Aren't you from St. Louis?" I whisper to her, careful not to further disrupt the tour guide.

"Yeah, but my mom had this book about the Everglades. It was huge, like a textbook, with pictures and everything. I think she bought it to decorate the coffee table, but I read it a lot as a kid. Whenever our power went out, which was a lot, I'd cocoon myself in a corner with a book and a flashlight. I've probably read that whole textbook ten times. I don't know... I just became infatuated with the Everglades. The land. The animals. The abundance of life here, it's magical. And I've never been this close to it, so I couldn't pass up on this opportunity."

"Yup. It's official. You're a nerd."

"Asshole!"

She smacks my arm playfully.

"I kid, I kid." I throw up my hands in surrender. "It's refreshing to see how interested you are in this. Honestly, it's refreshing to be talking about anything outside of dance. Keep that. Little things like that help you maintain your sanity in this industry. Little bits of your heart that you hold dear to you, outside of this dance shit."

"Thank you." For a second, her eyes seem to glisten, but she blinks it away. "Every time we talk, I feel a little lighter.. I just wanna let you know, I appreciate you for that. The other women include me in petty conversations about celebrity gossip and hot guys of the week, but you talk about the things that actually matter. You pour into me."

She pauses.

I try to mask the way my insides leap when she places her hand on my thigh, her glossy white nails twinkling at me.

"Thank you, Naya."

CHAPTER NINETEEN

FOR THE NEXT FEW HOURS, Naya and I talk about a bit of everything in between random moments of me geeking over another Everglades fact. And with every wide-eyed discovery or shrieked, "Omg, look!"

Naya never seems the slightest bit annoyed or bored.

"I think there's only about half an hour left of the tour. Are you sure you don't want to switch seats with me for a better look?"

I offered my seat once before, but she politely declined.

"I'm good. I promise. Honestly, I'm still shook that you got me on a boat to begin with."

"Oh..." I tease. "Is the great Naya afraid of the water?"

"Kinda." She chuckles. "I just respect the bodies of water."

"So, you don't trust boats?"

"I do. But..." She pauses as if deciding to continue or not. "My parents were rafters, so boats, oceans, rivers... we stay clear of large bodies of water."

"Rafters?"

"Cuban refugees that escaped the island on a raft. They left in the middle of the night in a ten-person raft with twenty people. My mom was pregnant with my sister, too."

Any hint of a joke I had left evaporates, only to be replaced with horror.

"Oh, my goodness. I'm so sorry. I didn't mean to pry."

"It's okay. They made the journey in three days. That's short compared to other stories. Some rafters end up in a random current that leaves them stranded in the middle of the ocean for much longer, or worse, capsized in a storm. When they reached Miami beach, they were hungry, and a little dehydrated, but that was about it. Their story ended luckier than most, but they still reminisce about those three days in the ocean a lot. Waves large enough to take down their boat, pitch-black darkness at night, and the deafening spurts of silence when the sea and sky stood still."

I shudder at the thought of being at sea, floating to God knows where. Circumstances so bad, the thought of possibly dying at sea seems better.

"Wow. I can't even imagine, Naya."

"So yeah." She breaks into a strained laugh. "Oceans, lakes, rivers, pretty much any body of water Mother Nature created has been a 'no' for me."

Before replying, I take her in just a second longer. The closed-off, emotionless Naya that I'd grown used to, softens a bit, right before my eyes.

"Wait, so why'd you agree to take this airboat tour with me?"

Her eyes flicker off to the distance for a second.

"I'm not really a fan of Orlando, especially Disney. I liked the idea of getting away."

Our words plateau between us. Announcements from the tour guide drone in the background. The clouds swell with different sunset colors over the river. The golden hour lighting causes the tattoos on her arms to glimmer. Both of us stare off toward the left side of the boat, leaving Naya as nothing more than a shadow in my peripheral. I can't fully see her, but I can feel some of her long curls grazing past my right arm. A ticklish, almost bothersome feeling four hours ago, now felt comforting. Reassuring.

"Hey..." I turn to her. "I know bodies of water may not be the easiest activity or topics of conversation for your family, but from what I heard, it sounds like your family has a strong connection to it. You said it yourself: a sea that strands people and takes the lives of many somehow guides *your* family to the States. Allowed them to set roots here for you and your sister. Maybe your lineage is more connected to mother nature's water than you know..."

My words trail away because I'm not exactly sure how to finish that thought. Naya's eyes scan my face, taken aback by what I'd said. Hell, I surprised myself. I've only known words like that to leave my mother's mouth.

"It's kind of crazy that you said that because my family follows an Afro-Cuban religion, introduced to the island by Africans during the slave trade," Naya says with an exhale. "In the faith, there are hundreds of Orishas, or deities, that you pray to, but there's one that is assigned to you. One that has chosen your life or even lineage. My family's Orisha is Yemaya, the deity of creation, water, moon, motherhood, and protection. Since I was little, we prayed to her, dedicated our altars to her, and gave her offerings on specific days in the faith. I'd like to think she guided my parents' boat to Miami that night... Sorry. I've never really told anyone about this before. You probably think I'm crazy." She halts the dreamy tone in her voice. "I know it's kind of weird. Deities, altars, offerings—I promise it's not demonic or anything."

Laughter escapes from the pit of my belly, which travels over to Naya. The giggles ease her nerves.

Is this the first time I've seen her actually nervous about something?

"Demonic? What? That's light years from what I was thinking!"

"Sorry. That's the stereotype we get from Christians or Catholics... I don't know if you're religious—"

"Oh yeah, I'm Christian. Vacation bible school, church choir, the whole nine. If a teen boy came to service with a trendy lip piercing, my mother was the first to ask, 'Little boy, explain this metal in your face. Is this the devil's work?'"

Naya cringes.

"But when I went to college I saw more, learned more. I realized God created lots of different, beautiful people on this earth. People with diverse backgrounds and beliefs. Plus, some of the most 'Christian' people I've met are top-grade sinners in the good book. Religion aside, I think there's room for human error in everything. Even my mother has calmed down in her older years. Now, she'll call me quoting Buddhist texts and questioning some of our own teachings."

"Buddhist texts? That's cool of her to be so open. I know someone like that. When I came out at fifteen, it was... interesting. My parents tried to be as supportive as they could, but deep down, they were disappointed. Swore up and down our family doesn't have those types of people. My mother struggled more than everyone else until one of our neighbors, Mrs. Shirley, an older Christian woman from Mississippi, pulled my mom aside. Mrs. Shirley is the only person I'd heard scold my mom, outside of my grandma. She insisted my mom drop any preconceived notions and love her child because family is everything—the Lord loves everyone. Since that day, my mother's cold exterior defrosted. She's been nothing but supportive ever since. Sometimes too supportive—always pestering me about my love life."

"Pestering? How long have you been single?"

"About five years…"

Another expression brushes past her face, but I can't read it.

"Damn, and you have found no one? What does that mean for me?"

The strange expression on Naya's face dissipates, and a smile takes its place.

"There are amazing women out there. Promise. It's my choice to be single. I'm just chillin' right now, waiting for the right moment."

She stares off toward the water.

"Right moment like what?" I ask, leaning closer to her.

"Like when aliens invade and decide I'm their new ruler," she replies with mischievous in the corners of her mouth.

"Oh! You're such an ass!"

I smack her leg.

"My bad. I couldn't pass up an opportunity to mess with you."

"All right ladies and gentlemen," the tour guide announces. The airboat slowly lines up with the dock. "Thank you for joining me on this excursion of the Everglades. The gift shop is on the left of the dock, and I hope you all have a great night."

I step off the boat, reaching a hand out to help Naya.

"Thanks. I'll order the Uber back to the hotel."

"Back to the hotel?" I try to ignore the twinge of disappointment in my chest. "You're not hungry?"

"Oh, I'm starving. I just didn't know if you wanted some alone time or not."

"Miss Naya Alvarez…" I interweave my arm at her elbow. "We are friends now. You won't get rid of me that easily!"

CHAPTER TWENTY

I'VE NEVER TOLD anyone about my family's faith before. Through all the years I've known Bunny, she still has no clue. It just never came up. Or maybe my childhood memories don't allow such vulnerability.

All the neighborhood kids made fun of our altar to Yemaya. Their parents gossiped, saying we practice witchcraft. A teacher even made it a point to reiterate that in her class, *God rules all*. Mind you, we believe in God, too. I tried to set the record straight, but nothing worked.

Gotta love small towns in the South.

"All we do is tend to the altar. Rituals on New Year and the solstice that aren't meant for nothing more than luck and prosperity. We celebrate our ancestors and pay homage to those who came before us," I pleaded, but no one listened.

Kids will be kids.

Even if some of those kids grew to be adults who pay for an overpriced retreat led by a hipster teaching the same practices. Everything dwindled by the time I reached middle school, but the memories still poke at me from time to time. Still, my religious upbringing didn't faze Khloe in the slightest. She is accepting, even a little intrigued. Unknowingly silencing away those childhood bullies.

My skin buzzes whenever she touches me, even for a split second. My knees almost buckle every time she invades my personal space. And I swear that sweet vanilla smell lingers even when she's not around, but the crush is waning. I think. Now, I can talk to Khloe like a normal human without my eyes drifting to those adorable dimples every time she smiles. I can control my emotions without randomly shifting into a secretly smitten, closed-off weirdo. And because of this, I've been able to look past her doughy eyes and learn about some of her other quirks, like the fact that she's a nerd. A walking Everglades encyclopedia... even though it was kind of nice to see.

"I think it's on this right corner, sir," Khloe says to the Uber driver, tugging me back into reality. "I'm so excited to try this spot. It went viral on TikTok a couple of months ago, and I've been watching their slo-mo noodle videos ever since."

"I'm sorry. Come again? Slo-mo noodle videos?"

"Yes!" She exasperates. "Dripping sauce, glimmering spices, moist noodles..."

"Moist... Noodles..."

I stare blankly until we both break out into laughter.

"We've arrived."

The driver points to a beige building with a large oak tree beside it. A red light-up sign titled My Thai Cuisine marked the estab-lishment.

"I'm telling you!" Khloe exits the car. "This place is gonna be bomb!"

"Right... Judging from videos on the internet," I tease.

Seconds upon walking into the restaurant, a loud but sweet voice startles us.

"Welcome to My Thai!" A short Asian woman yells from the back of the restaurant as she walks toward us. "Table for two? Come, follow me!"

We can barely let out a nod before we're barreling through the tables behind her. Dozens of workers buzz around the room. Different conversations overflow from each table. The restaurant isn't overcrowded, but I don't see many empty tables. Hmm, maybe this place is actually worth trying.

"Thank you," we say in unison as we sit down.

"Your server will be right with you," the hostess replies before disappearing into the room.

"What are you gonna get?" Khloe's eyes pop up over the menu.

"Dang, I picked up the menu two seconds ago!"

"Right!" She giggles. "Sorry, I'm just amped! I've been following this restaurant for a while now. I can't believe this tour... dance brought me here... and the Everglades.."

"You are overly deserving of all the places dance will take you."

Khloe's expression softens, turning tender and raw, and then she blinks the emotions back.

"I've looked at their menu at least five times. I wanna try their Pad See Ewe, Crying Tiger—Oh! Maybe, their Tom Kha soup!"

"Sounds good. I'll probably just get the shrimp fried rice."

I slowly set down the menu.

"Just shrimp fried rice?!" Her brown eyes widen. "You just came to this award-winning place, and that's what you're gonna get?!"

"Yup. It's the only way to ensure that what I get is good. It's hard to mess up shrimp fried rice."

"Naya!"

The sound of the sweet, well-mannered Khloe Thompson chastising *me* brings a menacing smirk to my mouth. She balls her hands into soft fists and pretends to slam them on the table.

"You introduced me to ramen outside of a Styrofoam cup. It's time for me to return the favor!"

"Fine." I roll my eyes. "Order for me. I'll have whatever you think I should try."

An excited screech bursts out of her.

"Okay!"

* * *

The waistband of my pants pushes up against my stomach as I struggle to finish the last few bites of my Pad Thai. Meanwhile, Khloe has already cleared her plate and is ordering a dessert.

Hyped, viral restaurant or not, she wasn't wrong. This place was definitely worth trying.

"Lemme get the mango sticky rice. That's my favorite!—Oh wait! You guys have Khanom Tako?! Wait, I might get that instead..."

The server sighs, looking around and tapping her foot, but Khloe doesn't seem to notice. She's in her own world.

"Sorry."

Khloe turns to me, matching the soft smile I unknowingly have.

"No worries. Take your time. I don't have room for dessert, anyway."

Her shoulders relax as she asks the server about the type of milk in one item. I can literally see the spark ignite in her eyes when the woman replies, "Coconut condensed milk."

The spark grows into the rest of her face.

"Okay!" Khloe exhales as the server walks away. "Whew, that was one of the toughest decisions of my life!"

"What did you decide on?"

"I ordered three desserts..." She says sheepishly. "I'm not gonna eat them all! I just wanted to try them, and I wanna take them back to the bus for the girls to try!"

"Naw, let's eat them all. Fuck those girls!" I joke.

A vacant air passes over her face, her mouth falling flat.

"Sorry," she stammers. "I lied. I definitely didn't plan on taking anything back."

"I figured. You practically yelled the lie at me."

I chuckle. Khloe buries her face into her hands, joining my laughter.

"Ugh. It's been a bad habit since I was younger. I would lie about how much I ate so no one could bring it up when they talked about my weight."

"Well, I don't know how many people are fixing their mouths to talk about your weight now, but they can suck several dicks."

"Naya!"

She forces a whisper and glances at the surrounding tables.

"I'm serious. You literally have a shape people pay for or do squats until their knees click. I don't know who these people are, but I can reassure you I am not one of them."

Khloe hesitates, her eyes searching my face. "Thanks... I'm sorry. I feel like every time we hang out, it turns into a therapy session for me."

"Don't be sorry. And hey, you aren't the only one. I've never told anyone about my family's faith and my coming out story in one day. Hell, I've never told any friends about my family's faith at all. So—"

"Wait, nobody?!"

She props her elbows onto the table, leaning closer to me.

"Not a soul."

"Wow... I must be one special bitch!"

"You are," I say *way* too quickly.

What the actual fuck, Naya?!

"You're special, too!" She continues with an airy light, countering the serious tone I regrettably introduced. "Not only are you one of the most phenomenal dancers I've ever seen, but you are also super down to earth. Not a hint of ego in sight. Yeah, you're a sarcastic ass sometimes, but I love your sense of humor."

"Thanks—"

"Three desserts for the two beautiful ladies!" our server shouts.

She'll never know how thankful I am for her interruption. I was one minute away from the blush tearing through my brown cheeks.

"Ooo! You have to try these!" Khloe exclaims, eyes wide on the array of dishes between us.

Sweets are arranged in shapes and colors I'm not familiar with. My mind nearly talks me out of it, but Khloe pushes a spoon topped with a mango and a creamy swirl of I don't know what in front of my face.

"It's delicious!"

I look up from the spoon to find that she's already chewing her first bite. Eyes bright and satisfied as hums poke through her mouth. I try not to focus on the fact that she doesn't mind me eating off her spoon, leaning forward, and taking a taste. In seconds, a sweet vanilla-like flavor invaded my taste buds. A doughy yet firm mass in the middle that tastes similar to rice pudding. Then, a dash of tart from the pineapple swoops in to balance everything.

"Ladies and gentlemen." Naya's eyes are closed. "I would say it's a hit!"

Khloe pretends to announce to the surrounding people.

"Huh? My bad." I open my eyes and wipe the corner of my mouth. "This is bomb! What is it called?"

"Honestly, I don't remember. I went back and forth with the server for so long I lost track. We'll have to ask when she comes back."

"Well, whatever it is. It's bomb!"

"If you think that's good, you should try this one!"

I hadn't noticed, but Khloe picked up the unused spoon and dug into the next dessert, delighted satisfaction invading her face. Instead of waiting for me to clean off the food left on my spoon, Khloe scoops her spoon back into the dessert and brings it to my lips.

"Open up."

Sharing a spoon twice and feeding me? Yeah, there's no need to make this any gayer.

I drop my jaw slightly and let my eyes fall to the spoon so we aren't making eye contact. Before my spiraling thoughts take over, the chocolaty, coffee, milky taste of whatever I ate brings me back to reality.

"Woah..."

"Right?!"

Crumb-filled plates are riddled across the table. I sit back in the booth with my hands tucked into the waistband of my pants. Sleep preying on my eyelids. I don't know how in the world I made room for those sweets after my meal. While I'm in a food coma, Khloe sits up as straight as an honor roll student, sipping the last of her Thai iced tea.

"Thanks for bringing me here," I mumble. "I might not eat for another two days, but it was well worth it."

"Thank you for all of today. I thought I was going to be on solo adventures today, but I'm glad you came."

"Yeah. Yeah. It's not *so* bad spending time with you." I smirk.

"Hey!" She chucks a balled-up napkin at my head. "For real, though. Today was fine and... I'm glad I have you here. I want to ask you something."

As if my stomach muscles aren't tight enough, the rest of my body seizes.

Khloe's eyes fall down to her lap and her teeth sink into her bottom lip. I hate seeing her so nervous. Something about it makes me want to hold her until the anxiety dwindles.

Platonic friendship, Naya.

Okay, I know I *just* said I could talk to her like a regular human, but that might not be true yet. Something about Khloe is just so enticing—overwhelming in the best possible way.

And you know what? I've decided to live in it for a little. What's the harm in looking? Spending time with a beautiful person? It's not like I'm gonna make a move on her. It'll be a pleasant distraction from work. Plus, the more I learn about her, the more she'll become a "regular" woman. Someone who is normal and dorky instead of the flawless vixen her shape presents to the world. The more I learn about her, the more these feelings will subside. Then, maybe one of her dating apps will come through? Or one of mine? Welcomed dates that'll distract me from *whatever* these feelings are. A perfect plan.

"Don't be nervous."

I position my elbows on the table and bend closer to her.

"All right!" Khloe claps her hands together. "I'm just gonna spit it out. I'm going on a date tonight, and I need your help."

Damn, that date sure came quick.

CHAPTER TWENTY-ONE

"SORRY, I was rushing while getting ready for the boat tour this morning."

Embarrassment prickles my cheeks. I toss the mountain of clothes from the desk chair and onto my bed. When we arrive in my hotel room, I insist Naya sit on my bed, but she refuses to do so in her "outside Everglades clothes."

Once I clear what feels like the 100th article of clothing, she takes a seat, assuming her regular sitting position. I haven't known her for long, but I've grown accustomed to Naya's seated posture. Relaxed and free of tension. Knees separate and taking up space around her. Hands either collected softly in her lap or swiping through her phone. This time, she's scrolling through Instagram videos as I shift around the room like a nervous wreck.

"Do you mind if I hop in the shower real quick?"

"Not at all," Naya replies, barely looking away from her phone.

Moments later, I return from the bathroom with my skin still damp but draped in a long white hotel robe.

"So, what do you need help with?" Naya says before I can completely step out of the restroom.

I hope I haven't kept her waiting for too long.

"For starters. I don't know what I am gonna wear."

"No idea? Well, you just tossed a hundred options onto your bed," she taunts.

"Most of that pile are skimpy dresses, short-shorts and crop tops small enough to be a bra. I can't wear any of that!"

I walk to the other end of the room and drop to the floor to fumble through my open suitcase.

"Or... Should I wear something like that? I don't wanna appear a prude or anything."

"You're going on a date with someone you met off an app. That's the exact opposite of prudish behavior. Wear whatever you feel most comfortable in. Where are y'all going anyway?"

"Some jazz lounge."

"Oh! A jazz lounge?"

Naya's highbrows shoot up.

"Yeah. Why? Hold on, why'd you say it like that? Is that code for something? Is she taking me somewhere else?"

"Tsk. Tsk." Naya sucks teeth and shakes her head from side to side. "Oh Khloe, I'm afraid you've figured it out. Jazz club is actually code for a sex club."

"A sex club?!"

"Yeah. A big, nude lesbian sex club. And you know what they say about the ones in Orlando? Only ten-inch Mickey Mouse shaped strap-ons allowed."

My eyes fall from my sockets and roll halfway out of the room. I throw up my hands and march toward my phone on the desk.

"That's it. I'm canceling."

"Khloe."

Naya grabs my wrist inches before it touches my phone. The soft touch stops me dead in my tracks, soothing me instantly.

"I am just messing with you. Mickey Mouse shaped strap-ons? Did you *really* believe that?"

"Ugh!" I haul my limbs back over to the bed and collapse face down on top of the mountain of clothes. "I don't know what to believe, Naya. I've never done this before."

I hear Naya get up and walk around the room, but I keep groaning into the clothes.

"I'm in way over my head. Women?! Am I for real? I've barely scratched the surface with men. What are we supposed to talk about? Is she gonna get up when she finds out I've never actually been with a woman? Do I drink? Should I stay sober to avoid making an ass out of myself? Wait...Who pays for the drinks?! This is a disaster."

Naya nudges my leg. "Go to the bathroom."

I lift my face from the clothes to the sight of her standing by the bed with a pair of my heels in her hand.

"What are you——?"

"There are three outfit options hanging on the shower rod. Pick your favorite and see if you like it with these shoes."

"Um...Thanks," I murmur, grabbing the shoes and closing the bathroom door behind me. "Oh wow! Thank you!" I yell the second I lay my eyes on the outfits.

No.

The word outfit doesn't give it justice.

She put together *looks*. Slacks partnered with a corset, form-fitting dress and a loose skirt option, too. Layers, accessories, and even different lipstick colors assigned to specific looks. She assembled combinations from my suitcase I had yet to discover in minutes!

I wriggle in and out of the clothes at the speed of light, trying options one, two, three, then back to two, revisiting one, then finally landing on lucky number three. A coral dress that stops in the middle of my calves and hugs every curve and dip in my body. A flawless look when combined with the heels and lipstick.

"Are you okay in there?" Naya calls out.

"Yeah! Sorry! I had trouble making a choice. But I'm almost ready!" I crack the bathroom door open and tip-toe out. "How do I look?"

Naya sits in the desk chair, her wide eyes scanning over my frame, and then she clears her throat.

"You look good, friend."

I can't pinpoint why the word friend made my mood simmer, but the look on Naya's face warms cheeks.

"Styled by Naya!" I present my hands like I'm giving a presentation.

"Stop, I just threw some clothes together. It's all about the person in them. Your date is gonna lose her mind."

"Right. Hey, I still need to finish my makeup. Do you mind waiting a little longer before you leave?"

"No," she says flatly.

"Oh... Okay. Nevermin—You know what? I'm not falling for your shit this time!"

I pick a pillow up from the bed and throw it at her head.

"You caught me!" She grins. "Of course, I can see you off. Gotta take care of my gay-bies."

"Speaking of baby gays, how do I do this?"

"Do what?"

"You know." I exhale, sitting on the pile of clothes on my bed. "The date. The conversation. The bill. The end of the night. Oh my goodness, what if she wants me to go back to her place? I don't think I'm ready for that."

I bury my head in my hands.

Naya rises from the desk chair and takes a seat on the floor in front of me. There's no use inviting her to sit on my bed, because I know she'll refuse. I keep my head in my hands but tighten my legs closed to avoid flashing her.

She reaches out, peeling my hands from my face. A dance that occurs far too often between us.

"Khloe. You are spiraling. The date is like any other date you've gone on with a guy. Getting to know one another. Conversation. Pertaining to the bill, well she asked you out, right? I believe she should cover it, but if she doesn't, just pay for your half and take a mental note. As you date more women, you'll develop your opinion on who should pay for the date." Her thumbs rub small circles on the tops of my hands, unwinding all the tension from my shoulders. "And as far as the end of the night, that is whatever *you* want it to be. And if you choose to go all the way, have her come back here—a very public hotel room in a busy part of town, with dancers in other rooms that don't play about your safety. As a matter of fact, if you choose to bring her back, text me every step of the way. From entering to the send off. And if you sense anything out of the ordinary, please call me. I'll be over here in a second. As a matter of fact, here's my room key, just in case of an emergency."

I'm not sure when, but the tension left my shoulders. A soft grin curves my lips while that familiar warmth overcomes my cheeks.

"I don't think I'll be bringing anyone to my hotel anytime soon, but I appreciate you. Thanks for always looking out for me."

CHAPTER TWENTY-TWO

naya

I FED her to the lesbian wolves on a silver platter. Good. Great. Outstanding. Just phenomenal. I styled Khloe in a dress that molds to every God-given curve on her body, accompanied by a pair of heels that elongate her shea butter smooth legs to the ends of the earth.

I pace around my hotel room, searching for something to keep me busy, but I've already reorganized my suitcase twice and cleaned my sneakers.

Ah, a bath. That'll do it.

I turn on the hot water and pour in enough Epsom salt to make an elephant float. I dim the lights and light my favorite sandalwood candle, a must when touring. That or anything else that can make a hotel feel more like home.

I should've told her to wear a trash bag. The biggest, baggiest trash bag and dirty rehearsal shoes. But an alternative outfit wouldn't have made a difference. Khloe could make a rehearsal shirt look like a million bucks. A million-dollar outfit paired with a million-dollar face.

This is necessary, Naya.

The sooner she gets into someone's bed, the sooner I'll stop wanting to get her into mine. Khloe doesn't seem like a serial dater anyhow. She'll probably fall in love with the first okay contender on the app. She'd probably be head over heels in love. Distracted, turned out, and far away from me. After all, there's nothing like your first queer love.

Though it's only been a couple of hours, I still feel the strain that shot through my back when Khloe's date pulled up in front of the hotel.

Why did she pick Miss Shaved Head, anyway?

They'd only started messaging last night. What could she have said to make Khloe think *a date* was the right idea? That girl probably texts "cuz" instead of "cause" or "luv" instead of "love"—like come on now!

I joggle my head, hoping to change these thoughts. Miss Shaved Head is actually very attractive, so I had to resort to trashing her texting methods, something I know nothing about. In different circumstances, I probably would've swiped right myself. In different circumstances, I also wouldn't be pacing around like a jealous girlfriend at home.

I peel off my clothes and throw my hair up into a messy bun. Inch by inch, I submerge my limbs into the steamy tub. A little too hot, just the way I like it. My shoulders release as an exhale escapes my lungs. I lay my head back, closing my eyes and praying this bath eases my mind.

I steady my breathing.

Inhale images of white sand beaches, and exhale the memory of Khloe in that dress.

Inhale the vision of my body floating in ocean waves, and exhale the taunting smirk in Miss Shaved Head's pictures.

Inhale tranquility, and exhale the overwhelming idea of what Shaved Head and Khloe could be doing right now.

Are they a few drinks in? Is she grazing Khloe's fingers as they stand next to one another? Or resting her hands on Khloe's knee while talking? Or are they up to *more*? Khloe may seem like a nervous wreck sometimes, but something tells me she has a bold side to her. A side that throws all caution to the wind and dives head first in—*oh fuck this.*

I sit up so abruptly that some bath water sloshes out of the tub and onto the floor. I leave wet footprints behind as I step out of the tub, throwing a towel around my body and walking into the bedroom to grab my phone.

"What's up, babe?"

Bunny answers the FaceTime after the first couple of rings. Whether it's her usual boisterous tone or the soft, nurturing side most don't get to hear, the sound of her voice grounds me every time. She is in a restroom identical to the one I'd just ran out of with half a gray charcoal face mask on. I throw myself onto the bed, still wrapped in the plush white towel.

"Nothing much. Sorry, are you busy?"

"Girl, come on, now. Where am I going looking like this?"

She props the phone up on the bathroom sink and continues applying the rest of the clay to her cheeks. I sink into the bed a little more.

"I don't know where you would go lookin' like that, but you could be on the phone with a certain someone."

"As a matter of fact," Bunny gushes. "We came back from Disney about three hours ago, and I *just* got off the phone with him."

"Oh, y'all were boo'd up for real!"

"It was magical, Naya. He said he really misses me. He's even planning to visit one of the shows and spend time with me. I don't know when, though, we had to get off of the phone 'cause he pulled up to his house."

Code for his house with his *wife and kids* inside. On the outside, I keep a supportive smile on my face, but I know how this story ends. I love Bunny and would support her through hell and back, but she's traveled this path more than once.

Rodney separated from his wife and is waiting for her to sign the divorce papers.

Theo is recently divorced, but continued living in the same house as his ex-wife to save money.

Then there was Clay. Single and never married, but he had four kids and two baby mommas he still slept with.

Bunny is an amazing person and deserves to find love, but she has a weakness for unavailable, lying-ass men. It infuriates me to watch her get her heart broken, but I'll be there for her no matter what. At least this time, Demario is honest about being married with kids. He says he's planning to leave his wife, so I pray this time actually works out.

"... home made food and a candlelit dinner—Naya, are you listening?!" Bunny says, pulling me from my overprotective thoughts.

"Of course! Sounds cute!"

"You're such a liar! Anyway, how was your day? Did you really go on a boat tour... of the Everglades... *with gators?*"

A chuckle escapes my chest. "Yes. Surprisingly enough, I did, and it was way better than I thought it was gonna be."

"I'm glad, friend. How are you doing, though? For real? I know Orlando and Disney hold a lot of memories for you. I just wanna make sure—"

"I'm good. I don't really want to talk about it, Bun."

"Okay, I understand. The most important question is, what's your room number 'cause the new season of Love in Paradise just dropped, and I heard it is juicy!"

There goes my best friend, doing what she does best. Being there for me, even if she isn't saying it outright. An immaculate support system, but an annoying sister that forces me to watch reality dating shows.

"Ugh! How many episodes, Bunny?"

"There's fifteen, but we can just watch the first five!"

She tries to flash a convincing smile, but her clay mask is completely dry and freezing her facial expressions.

"I'm sick of you! Room 1523."

khloe

"YOU SURE YOU don't want me to walk you to your room?" Elliana bats her long eyelashes at me as she pulls up to the hotel. "No funny business, I promise. I want to make sure you are safe."

A coy grin invades my face before I can stop it. I appreciate her honesty; it was one highlight of our date. She's twenty-six years old and broke up with her girlfriend of seven years a few months ago. She explained that she had signed up for the apps because the dating scene had changed drastically since she was nineteen, and she was still learning how to navigate it. Because of that, she also wasn't interested in random hookups, at least not yet. She made me feel comfortable enough to confess that this was my first date with a woman, and she didn't flinch.

"Thank you, Elliana. I'm okay, though." A spark of courage invades my limbs, and I place my hand on her thigh, feeling the soft skin leading up to her black pencil skirt. "I really enjoyed my time with you tonight. Maybe we can hang tomorrow? I have my show, but I don't have to be at the arena until 5:00 p.m. for hair and makeup. Wanna get some lunch?"

"Of course, just let me move some clients around."

"What? No! I wouldn't want you to change your schedule for me. Plus, isn't that barber-suicide?"

"Barber-huh?" Elliana bursts into laughter.

"I don't know! People take their haircuts very seriously! Just don't want you making any clients mad."

"Oh, trust me. You're worth it." She flits her blue eyes at me, melting away my insides. I'd almost forgotten about my thumb making soft circles into her thigh. We sit in a comfortable silence, taking each other in until my inner courage strikes again, and I ask, "Can I kiss you?"

* * *

I fast-walk into the elevator. Despite tapping the fifteenth-floor button at the speed of light, the door doesn't close until a few long seconds later. I rock back and forth while a sea of butterflies flutter around in my stomach. Elliana's peppermint lip balm is still fresh on my lips. The feeling of my hands gripping her waist is still palpitating through my fingertips.

Damn, what was Naya's room number? This can't wait till the morning. I have to stop by and tell her the news!

I pull out the room key she gave me earlier and read the number written on the sleeve. Her room is at the end of the hallway, furthest away from the elevator, but this time, I arrive in what feels like ten long strides. I wave the key in front of the door and waltz in.

"Naya! I kissed her! Me! I took the chance and I—Oh, I'm sorry!"

I freeze at the sight of Bunny and Naya on the bed. Bunny sitting up with her back against the headboard, stroking Naya's curls as she lays in her lap, sound asleep. The entire room is dark except for the movie playing on the television.

"It's okay." Bunny conceals a chuckle. Cautious not to wake Naya, she raises her eyebrows and whispers, "Sounds like someone had a good night."

"Uh...Well...Yes. Sorry. I didn't mean to interrupt." I step back toward the door, trying to ignore the fact that Bunny is in bed with just a sports bra on.

"It's okay, gir—"

"Have a good night!" And in seconds, I exit the room and practically sprint to the elevator.

My suitcases thrash against the sides of the narrow elevator door. My stumbling feet trip over the wheels. I align the wheels enough to roll halfway out, but then the thirty-pound duffel bag hanging from my shoulder slides to my elbow, tugging my body weight to the floor. I will never understand why so many hotels still have carpet floors. Centuries-old stale carpet that serves as nothing more than a real-life obstacle course for guests entering with more than one bag.

"Need help?" DayDay's arm reaches into the elevator, grabbing a suitcase.

"Thank you 'cause your girl was struggling!"

"Where are your bags?" I ask as he leads the way to our bus parked outside of the hotel.

He holds the door open, allowing me to pass first. I mentally kiss my room goodbye: the huge bathtub, king-sized bed, and the well-needed alone time. DayDay and the ladies are great, but I was feeling a little cooped up sharing a bus with everyone. I guess that's one thing people mean when they say touring can be hard.

"I loaded my bags onto the bus early this morning. I wanted to have a little time to shop before checkout time."

"Is that where you got this fit? 'Cause if so, I'm gonna need you to see if they have one in my size!"

I gesture to the oversized denim overalls gracing his limbs.

"Yes, ma'am! Put your bags down." He opens the storage compartment under the bus. "And we can walk to the boutique where I bought them!"

I toss my bags in and glance at my phone.

"Oh, I don't think I'll have time. I've got a...a date in half an hour."

"You're seeing her, again?" a voice calls out from behind us.

I turn to find Naya waiting patiently to stow her bags. She looks tired. Her eyes are swollen a bit from lack of sleep, and she's wearing a wrinkled sweat suit. Her clothes are usually always ironed to perfection.

"Oooo a date?" DayDay squeals, completely unaware of Naya's out-of-the-ordinary appearance. "Seeing *her... again*?"

"Uh. Yeah. I'm having lunch with her today. The date went well last night..." Flashbacks of me barging into Naya's room flood my mind, and I immediately shake them away. "So I asked her out again."

"Wowwwww." DayDay gawks.

"Nice," Naya says.

DayDay stores Naya's luggage next to mine and shuts the

compartment. "Baby girl wasn't playing when she said she wanted to try women! She got right to business!"

"I couldn't have done it without Naya. She set me up on the apps and picked out my outfit."

"Well, aren't you the best gay fairy godmother?"

DayDay cranes his neck to Naya, and she daps him up.

"Gotta look after the baby gays, right?"

CHAPTER TWENTY-FOUR

THE BUS SWELLS with energy as we ride to the venue. It's only fifteen minutes away from the hotel, but it feels like hours.

Or, I guess it feels like that because of the night I had. The second Bunny walked into my hotel room, I broke. Fell apart at the seams, collapsing into her arms and releasing sobs I'd been holding in since we arrived in Orlando. Bunny sprang into action immediately, rubbing my back and carrying my hollow body to the bed.

Anxious sweat drips down my spine, reminiscing about all the things I screamed into the pillow while Bunny rubbed my back.

Why did God do it?

Why would he do such a thing?

Why her and not me?

Why God? Why?

Screams so piercing, my throat is paying for it this morning. I screamed into the pillow until Bunny moved the pillow onto her lap, where I screamed some more. The screams turned into sobs, and the sobs turned into sniffles until I fell asleep, probably because she was stroking my hair the entire time, soothing me like she has many times in the past. Bunny is the only reason I got any sleep and made it to the bus on time this morning. When I woke up fifteen minutes before bus call, Bunny had already packed my suitcases and filled my duffel bag with the necessities for show day. She'd even left my toiletries out so I could at least brush my teeth and wash my face before checking out. Best of all, she did everything without a single mention of last night. I love my best friend. She just gets it. As soon as she stepped on the bus and laid eyes on me, she went straight to the kitchen to make me some tea.

I still feel like shit. Plus, hearing DayDay, Leah and Tiana blab about their Disney trip makes me want to bang my head against the wall. Rae is sitting in the corner of the front lounge, smiling into her phone. At least she's being quiet.

"Ugh...it was magical! I'm glad we did that yester—Wait, where's Khloe? Did she miss bus call?" Leah questions.

"No, honey. She'll be meeting us at the venue later. She's got her *own* plans."

DayDay shoots me a knowing look and sips from his water bottle.

"Whew! Thank the lord!" Leah settles into the couch again. "I can't tell you how many times I missed bus call on my first tour!"

"Right!" Tiana adds. "During the European leg of my first tour, I woke up hungover in my hotel room two hours after bus call. When I called the tour manager, he told me to 'figure' it out. So, I ended up at a train station in Barcelona bawling my eyes out because I couldn't read the signs, and I couldn't figure out how to get to Portugal for our next show. Thankfully, a bilingual college student stopped to help, but the trauma remains. I haven't missed another bus call since!"

"One time, I missed bus call, but instead of traveling to the next city over, we were going to the airport to get on a flight to Australia. Not only did I miss bus call, I missed the flight and had to come out of pocket for another ticket to Australia!" DayDay shares.

"My wallet hurts thinking about buying a plane ticket to the next town over. Australia would've done me in! And lost in Spain? Oh, sugar, I would've been crying right along with ya 'cause my Spanish is terrible!" Leah shares with her sweet Nashville draw. In the middle of her laughter, she spots Bunny handing me a cup of tea and plopping down next to me.

"Naya, honey. You gettin' sick?"

"Yeah. I woke up with my throat a little scratchy. I might be coming down with something." I lie. "Make sure y'all are taking extra vitamins this week."

CHAPTER TWENTY-FIVE

"ARE you sure you don't want me to stop by and see you off after the show?"

Elliana's striking eyes tear into me. I throw my purse over my shoulder and grip the car-door handle.

"I would love that, but we are leaving right after the show..." I lie straight through my teeth. "Wouldn't want you to drive up here again just for a couple of seconds."

"For you, it's worth it. I wish I could stay for the show and watch you in your element."

Her gaze intensifies.

"Me too! But they don't give us any extra tickets," I lie again.

"It's all good, babe. Hit me if you ever come back to Orlando. I've really enjoyed my time with you."

She draws into me despite my body being halfway out of the car. I lean back into her and dip my head until our lips collide. The smell of her peppermint lip balm swirling around our lips in between kisses. Our tongues tango slightly as my hands trail along her legs. She palms the back of my neck, intensifying the kiss. Suddenly, a wave of awareness pulls me back down. I can't help but wonder what this looks like from outside of the car. I hope none of my cast mates just so happen to be walking into the arena right now. A vision of the shock on Leah or Tiana's face invades my brain. Dropped jaws, widened eyes and piping hot tea to gossip about with others. I really hope Naya doesn't see this.

Why didn't I have Elliana drop me off further away?

"It's a shame you aren't staying longer," Elliana says, releasing her hand from my neck and dragging it along my arm. The longing in her touch communicates she wants more. Meanwhile, I hadn't even realized the kiss was over. My mind had wandered so far and the first date jitters right along with it, only to be replaced with reality. I feel no connection. There is no electric spark between us, at least not on my end. There's no magic.

Shower shoes. Sweatpants. T-shirt. Underwear. Toiletries. Check.

I rummage through my duffel bag, adding all the items I'd mistakenly left in my luggage this morning. I had been so excited about my second date with Elliana that I packed like a mad woman. When I opened my bag, the only thing in there was a shirt, a headscarf, and two eye shadow palettes. The evidence of a baby gay *so* eager to go on her second date she'd failed to adequately pack for work.

After twenty minutes of playing Tetris with everyone else's

luggage in the storage compartment under the bus and finally reaching mine, I grab the rest of my essentials.

Now it's 6:30 p.m., and instead of being halfway through my makeup, I am still on the bus getting ready to go into the venue.

Ugh, just forget it!

I stuff the remaining items in my bag, throw a jacket on and start fast-walking off the bus. My fingers fumble with the jacket zipper so sporadically that I don't hear someone enter the bus until we smack right into each other, knocking me flat on my ass. My duffel bag items and unfamiliar makeup raining all over the bus lounge.

"Oh shit! My bad! I'm so sorry. I didn't see you."

Naya reaches her hand out to help me up.

"No, I'm sorry. I was rushing and not looking where I was goi— Damn, you beat your face today!"

The precise application of foundation and bronzer snatches the words out of my mouth. Swirls of brown eye shadow and specks of honey-gold glitter extenuate her almond-shaped eyes. Naya is usually a lash, liner, and lip gloss type of girl. Her skin is so free of blemishes, I'm pretty sure she hardly wears foundation either. Except for tonight. She's pretty without makeup, but how she beat her face highlights her features beautifully. I force my eyes elsewhere, suddenly feeling embarrassed. Then, I turn my attention back to the floor.

"And now all of your makeup is on the floor."

"Don't worry about that," she says, kneeling down to pick up her mascara and concealer off of the floor. I dip down to help.

"Here." I pass her a compact of setting powder that rolled toward the bunks.

"Thanks."

Our fingers brush for a split second and heat thrums where we'd made contact. Once we finish picking up all of the makeup off the floor, I spring up and throw my duffel bag back over my shoulder.

"Well, I should get to the venue and do my face, too. I pray for a quarter of your speed and skills."

"I can do your makeup if you'd like."

"Really? I don't want to impede your personal time before the show."

"Khloe, stop. My face is already done, and I don't do much to my hair, anyway. All I need is twenty minutes to stretch before the show."

I take in the loose, bouncy coils framing her face like a lion's mane. A balanced mix of volume and curl definition that is unfair to humankind. If I didn't share a bus with her, I wouldn't believe she *actually* woke up like this.

Naya points to the couch in the back lounge of the bus.

"Come on. The light is better back here."

I follow her and sit down on the couch. She sets her makeup bag on the table and empties it like a surgeon preparing for an operation. I'd helped pick everything up moments ago when I knocked the bag out of her hand, but only now am I really seeing how much makeup Naya has. Four eye shadow palettes, a sea of miniature highlighters, a heap of brushes, all kinds of eyelashes and three bottles of foundation. I flit my eyes back to the bottles and read the brand. Fenty. Dang, for someone who doesn't wear makeup daily, she sure has a lot of it—and good quality, too!

"I use this one in the winter, when I get extra light-skinned like my grandma." She picks up the lighter foundation, noticing how it caught my attention. "Otherwise, I use this one the most," she says, pointing to a bottle that matches her mocha skin perfectly. Then she picks up the last bottle, a rich, God diva chocolate tone. "I mix drops of this one with my bronzer, but today, I'll finally use it for real. On you."

"Oh," I stammer.

"Unless you want me to use yours. I'm sure you'd prefer that."

I think about the cheap drugstore foundation in my duffel bag.

"No, I don't mind at all. Do your magic."

"Okay. I wouldn't call it magic, but I can do a little something in fifteen minutes."

Naya chuckles. She pulls out a stool from under the table and sets it in front of me.

"Close your eyes."

Naya aims a beauty blender at my cheekbone. She dabs the foundation into my skin, and suddenly, this spacious back lounge feels smaller and smaller. Naya sits about an arm's length away, but leans in closer to focus. She trades the beauty blender for concealer and then powder. And every so often, our legs brush, sending tiny electric bolts through my skin. I scoot to the edge of the couch and part my knees.

"You can scoot closer if you tire of leaning so far forward."

She stills for a split second, then pushes the stool toward me.

I *would* hate for her to strain her back, especially before a show, but another part of me is at play. A game of some sort. Toying with the same adrenaline that led me to initiate that kiss with Elliana. The rush in my blood lifted my hand to the back of her neck as our lips collided. A flicker of bravery that arrives seldom in my life. I feel it bubbling from the depths of my core.

Naya opens an eye shadow palette with the same brown and

honey colors on her face. She picks up a brush from the table and dips it into a beige base. She peers up at me through her full stage lashes.

"Do you mind if I use some of the same colors I used on myself?"

"Not at all. Twinsies unite!"

What, Khloe?! Twinsies.

I close my eyes and inch my face closer. Naya pauses for a second, then applies the shadows to my eyelids. We fall into a comfortable silence as she finishes working with the shadows and moves on to my eyebrows. I usually hate silence. From when I wake up in the morning, to the moment my head hits the pillow at night, something is playing in the background. Podcasts, music, ambient spa sounds, it doesn't matter as long as it's not quiet. Silence can be deafening, especially for a person whose brain moves as fast as mine. But right now, I don't mind the lack of sound. Something about Naya causes that quirk to fade away for a moment.

Maybe it's her placid demeanor. It should be impossible for a person to be this serene all the time. We are barely into the tour, but I've already witnessed an array of emotions from the other women. Leah has a soft heart and will cry about anything involving puppies or babies. Tiana and Rae are professional, while on the clock, but as soon as we step off that stage, their personalities shine through. Bunny is sweet and welcoming in a big sister type of way, but the moment she feels crossed, her temper breaks the ceiling. I can't say anything like that about Naya. I've only ever seen her cool, calm and collected.

I think back to the moment I walked into her room last night. The way her body laid in the bed was... different. Her limbs seemed to have been sinking into the bed. Relaxed in a way I haven't seen before. Her head falling deeper and deeper into Bunny's lap as she stroked her hair. My brain almost spirals about what Bunny and Naya were doing in that bed, but a shiver runs up my spine, jolting me from my thoughts.

"You good?" Naya pauses.

"Yeah, sorry. Just kind of tired."

"Oh, the second date went that well?" She says with an unfamiliar inflection filling her voice.

"No. I mean, yeah, but not *that* well." I reply pertaining to whatever deeper meaning she'd hinted at. "She was nice and easy to talk to. Respectful, too. I kissed her at the end of our first date."

"*You* kissed her?" Naya's eyes bulge then snap back in seconds, then she continues applying soft swipes of highlighter on my cheekbones.

"Yeah, I don't know what came over me. I was feeling ballsy at the moment. At first, the attraction was there, but after our second kiss today, the spark was gone. I think it was just the thrill from kissing a woman for the first time."

"Thrill?" She jests. "Hmph, the baby gay has a wild side to her."

"Shut up!" I smack her knee. "I would hardly call a kiss wild, but I'm glad I got it over with. Hopefully, my future dates will be easier now. Less nerve-wracking."

"Future dates? Oh, she's a professional. I guess you don't need me to hold your hand anymore."

"Hold my hand? Never. You are more than welcome to pick out my outfit again, though!"

"Whatever you need, I got you. Close your eyes." She points setting spray toward my face.

"Damn, you're done *already*?"

"Yup, a quickie with quality." Naya presents me to the mirror like she's on a game show. I look into the mirror and steer my mind from the possible innuendo woven into her words.

"Woah. You really snapped, Naya!" My jaw drops. She matched my skin tone exactly. Concealer and foundation blended to perfection. Lip liner drawn directly on my lip line, instead of over it, just how I like it.

"Some people like their eyebrows sharp and dark, almost painted on. You filled mine with light brown and brushed them upward. How'd you know the way I prefer my eyebrows?"

"I've seen them every night before the show, Khloe." She flashes a cool grin. "I pay attention to detail."

And suddenly, that warm feeling returns to my cheeks.

CHAPTER TWENTY-SIX

"WHAT'S HAPPENIN' Orlando?!" Zion hollers into the mic. The crowd roars as we hold poses in our designated spots sprawled out across the stage. Though it may be undetectable by the audience, our chests heave up and down. I hold one spot in the front, putting me closest to the crowd's shenanigans. The screaming women professing their love. Purposeful hands reaching toward Zion as if one swipe on his abs could absolve them of all their problems. And my favorite, the handwritten fan signs.

Me on Zion.

Marry me.

Do unspeakable things to me.

My boyfriend broke up with me, and I came by myself.

I'll be your dime piece. A phrase alluding to one of his hits. *Are you my dime piece?*

Blue light masks the stage, leaving the dancers as silhouettes. The opening songs aren't the hardest, but they always get my heart going. In reality, I think holding these poses while Zion spiels with the audience is more difficult than the entire opening.

"Right side, make some noise!"

He strides over to stage right, pointing his mic toward the crowd, a bright spotlight following him. Their screams pour into the mic and blast from the speakers.

"Okay, okay. I see y'all. But I think the left side can do better. Ain't that right?!"

Zion moves to stage left, his hand cupped over his ear to hear the crowd. By this point, my arms are pulsating with pain, eager to move on in the show. Then, I finally hear those fateful words come out of Zion's mouth. A signal to us and the musical director.

"Are y'all ready?"

A resounding bass thrums through the arena. And with every bass, we switch into another dynamic pose.

"For the..." bass.

"Soakin'" bass.

"Wet." bass.

"Summer tour?!"

A series of sounds layer on top of the bass, signaling us to move on to the next part of our choreography, a ripple melting into a pose on the floor. First Leah, then Bunny, Me, Tiana, Rae, and Khloe. The ending pose is on the floor with my left arm outstretched and my right arm bent by the side, both palms facing the floor as my right knee hikes up. Allowing my muscle memory to take over, my body continues the choreography on autopilot as my eyes wander toward stage left, where Khloe is. The stage lights are still dim, but I can still spot details of her makeup from here. Pride boasts within my chest, allowing me to hit the next piece of choreography with a little more attack than usual. I've never longed to be a makeup artist, but I welcome the reassurance of my gifts outside of dance.

I did pretty well on my face, but Khloe's came out like a masterpiece. Not bad for a student at YouTube University. All those hours of tutorials and product reviews finally paying off. But it's hard to mess up a face like Khloe's. I could've stepped outside and thrown actual dirt on her cheeks, but somehow, it would still look like *something*. It's hard to mess up those features.

Her eyes stayed closed while I did her makeup, but a part of me worried she felt my gaze roam. I'd never been *that* close to her for longer than a minute. I prayed that she didn't sense me exploring every detail, like the trail of tiny beauty marks on the side of her nose.

I had tried to conceal the relief in my voice when she said there was no spark with Miss Shaved Head, but horror quickly settled in when I realized that was the first date of many. What if there's a spark with the next woman?

That's what you want, Nayara.

The worst part was lightly resting my left thumb on her chin and fingers on the base of her neck to steady her head, then trying to follow the shape of her lips with liner. Looking at the full god-given shape that outlines her impeccable smile. The dips and curves that I swear drew me in the longer I traced them. I wondered what it would be like to—

"Earth to Naya!" Tiana calls out as she struts past me, finishing out the phrase and exiting into the wing.

I had kept doing the phrase, but stationary. Damn it! I'd missed the cue to leave the stage. I guess that muscle memory wasn't all the way intact after all.

The quick-change tent isn't as spacious as our dressing room, but it gets the job done. The tent allows us to change a couple of feet from the stage and race back on two songs later versus high tailing twenty feet and an elevator ride down, putting us at risk of missing our cue. Our active muscles steam as we peel our costumes off. Everyone is on a mission to change swiftly, but that doesn't stop us from our usual mid-show dialog.

"This Orlando crowd did not come to play with us!"

"Did y'all see that one lady on the left side throw her bra on stage?"

"Yes, I saw that big ass double D bra! I had thrown it right before we hit the second verse 'cause it was directly on my spot!"

The group snickers as they disrobe and zip up the pieces to our next costume. Cherry red lingerie that ties into Act 2, the bedroom scene. The moment where Zion, who has been trying not to succumb to the siren-like energy of his female dancers, falls short. We lure him back to the double king-size bed, on the stage, and perform choreography. The first time BriAnn explained Act 2 in rehearsal, my face fell flat on the floor. There were too many variables. The bed. Women in lingerie. Zion—a man? I don't mind doing suggestive choreography with male dancers—For obvious reasons, I prefer it over women.

But there are no men on this tour. And there's no partnering, just a moment of freestyle where everyone spreads out on the bed. The outro of the song plays while everyone performs suggestive movements of their own choosing. I can only see two dancers from my peripheral. Tiana is in a split, stretching forward and grazing her hands down her leg. Bunny is on her knees in a deep backbend while her hands roam over her chest. And using the headboard to steady me as much as possible, I chose a low squat where I wind my hips in small circles and run my hands through my hair.

It's steamy, but an individual steam. No partnering. The first dress rehearsal, a week before the show, sent me home with an ache between my legs, but I quickly got over it. Now, I perform the number and move around backstage with ease. As long as I keep my eyes off of a *certain* dancer.

"Did anyone bring edge control?"

"I got you!"

"Does Zion sound hoarse tonight?"

"I hear a little congestion. It's probably all those dressing room functions after every show!" Everyone balances small talk while zipping garments, adjusting hairstyles, pulling up lace stockings, and whatever else this two-song change permits.

"Can you hook the back of my bra?" Rae steps toward me just as I am leaving the tent.

Our costumes aren't regular one-hook bra sets. They are eccentric, strappy ensembles with three hooks in the meeting in the center of our backs. I figured out my method early on, hook the bra, then slide it on like a sports bra, careful not to let my sweat twist and turn the lace into oblivion. Everyone else is still fine-tuning their quick-change methods. Because Rae has the longest nails of the group, it's significantly harder.

"Of course," I reply.

She turns around and takes a few steps toward me, her ass on full display in a black lace thong. Round, firm, muscular 'cause she never misses a day at the gym but still has the right amount of jiggle. And even with Rae's ass just centimeters away, I feel nothing. Just hours ago, I practically gasped for air while doing Khloe's makeup, and she was fully dressed.

God, please don't ever let Khloe ask me to hook her bra, I won't be able to handle it.

I finish up the last hook and tap her shoulder.

"All set."

"Thanks, babe!" Rae says as she makes it back to the only full-length mirror in the tent, where all the ladies are trying to complete their finishing touches.

Dear God, it's me again. Don't ever let Khloe call me babe. Even when I successfully friend-zone her. I definitely won't be able to handle that.

khloe

MY SUITCASES CLUMSILY thump against the wall as I drag my limbs to my hotel room. I will never understand why so many hotels across the country have carpeted hallways. No matter how bougie this Miami hotel was downstairs, with its crystal chandeliers and pristine marble tiles, they still committed this horrendous act upstairs. Thick, gold, and burgundy carpet with enough friction to make me feel like I'm hauling bags through quicksand! It doesn't help that the bus driver woke all of us up at 8 a.m. so we could check in, and he could go park the bus off-site.

After finally making it to the end of the hallway, I wave my key card and step inside the room. Ease drapes my body as I set my eyes on the plush queen bed in the center of the room.

We have two off days in Miami... Maybe I can see what the apps offer here...Put this bed to—

Baby steps, Khloe! You just had your first girl kiss two days ago! Let's not get ahead of ourselves.

I make a left to find a spacious gray marble shower accompanied by an even larger bathtub. A bathtub! I've seen enough. The closets and other spaces in the room will be explored later. I turn back toward my luggage, lay it down and unzip it to find my bath bombs and Epson salt. The essentials.

First order of business, a nice, long, hot, ba—

My jaw drops to the floor. I hadn't noticed earlier because that queen bed caught my attention, but on the other side is a steel balcony overlooking the most perfect ocean view. Soft, crystal blue waves crashing against the white sand. The sun sparkling over the water just right. The most serene display of nature since I started this job. Rehearsals for a month. Eight hours, six days a week, inside of a dance studio with all-black walls. A week of back-to-back shows in multiple cities I remember little about. On an action-packed tour that leaves little time for leisure activities. Besides my Everglades tour, I don't remember what I did in North Carolina, Atlanta, or Jacksonville. The only memories I have are of the inside of the arenas and surrounding food establishments, and even that is seeping from my memory.

"Thank God for these off days," I mutter, unpacking some items from my suitcase: underwear, pajamas, and my toiletry bag. My bag is still pristine from Naya's organizational magic, and perhaps with a touch of OCD. She'd folded my clothes at the speed of light *and* styled three bomb outfits! On the bus, she's always the person to start a cleaning spree. First thing in the morning or in the middle of our nightly glass of wine, she springs up and starts organizing the shoes in the bunk area, wiping down counters, disinfecting handles, the whole sha-bang. Usually, the rest of the ladies follow suit, making Naya's cleaning episode even quicker. I'm the type of girl that lets messes grow before tidying up. I am more courteous in shared spaces like the bus, but I let it rip in the comfort of my own environment. Dirty clothes, clean clothes, hair products, shoes and jackets are everywhere. Something I wish Naya hadn't seen the night she came to my hotel room. Hopefully, I will leave this tour with new habits.

I zip up my bag and walk back to the restroom to draw a bath.

A bath, food delivery and a nap in my queen bed—the perfect plan.

Surprisingly, tour bus sleep has been immaculate. Something about the humming engine and the bus driver's road skills gently rock me to sleep every night. And the best part is the curtain outside the bunk, blocking any ounce of light from my slumber. I love the snug nature of the bunk. Bunny says it's like being back in the womb—cut off from the entire world. I agree, but I also look forward to sprawling out without smacking the bunk walls in the middle of the night.

I pour a generous amount of Epson salt into the bath while the water rises. Once it reaches a perfect height, I slip out of my clothes, wrap my braids up and lower my body into the tub, allowing my head to rest on the makeshift pillow I made from a rolled-up hand towel. Eyes closed and achy joints floating, I relax and massage my temples to rid myself of the wine headache I earned last night.

I've gotta stop throwing back so much wine after the shows.

One glass is fine, but most nights, I nearly take down a bottle all by myself. Thankfully, none of the girls have noticed, or they don't care 'cause production will restock it at the top of each week. Meanwhile, I still can't believe I have access to something like a bus grocery list funded by someone else. Just to think, months ago, the sheer mention of the words grocery store made hives sprout on the back of my neck. My wallet decaying in my pocket and bank account screaming like a tea kettle every time I'd made it to the front of the cashier. Not only does Zion's production team fund the list, but the limit doesn't exist! We ordered snacks, wine, fruit, candles, cereal—hell, we even asked for an air fryer and a hot plate. And they granted our request. Most mornings, Leah makes egg whites and spinach. And no matter what after-show food the tour manager orders, DayDay cooks up some frozen dinosaur chicken nuggets in the air fryer.

I'm sure gonna miss that grocery list when this tour is over.

Closing my eyes and practicing some of the yoga breathing exercises Leah taught me, my muscles relax even more. Until the sound of my phone vibrating forces my eyes to open. It's been about a week since we left LA, but every time my phone rings, I can't help but think it's a piece of home haunting me.

Chill, Khloe.

I dry my hands and unlock my phone.

Soakin' Wet Summer Dancers Chat

Leah: Good morning, ladies! I've rented a small boat today, so we can have a girls' day (plus DayDay) on the water! Meet downstairs at 11 a.m. for pickup!

Out of everyone, Leah is the most group-oriented in the bunch. She spearheaded the first wine and movie night that set the tone for the first week of the tour. During rehearsals, she started *get-to-know-you* conversations that tore us away from our phones. And here she is now, planning another group activity. My eyes shoot to the top of my phone. 9:15a.m.

Ugh… I guess I won't be meeting that queen bed until later

today. Is this the tour life people talk about? Shows, partying, alcohol, and crushes?

All right, focus, Khloe. No crushes, just experiences. A break from the stress of back-to-back auditions. Slowing down from the constant LA hustle. A weekly check to ease the impending anxiety of bills each month. Not to mention all the other stuff I have going on at home. This is my break from it all. My first tour. A goal I prayed for. The beginning of my career, and I have to make the most of it! A cup of coffee will fix this fatigue!

I open the drain to the tub, hoping all my uneasy thoughts go down with the water.

CHAPTER TWENTY-EIGHT

I PULL on some beige cargo shorts to go over my peach, two-piece bathing suit and stare into the full-length hotel mirror. Despite having thrown it into a messy bun two minutes ago, I undo my hair and let it flow down my back.

I glance at the phone.

10:50 a.m.

Okay, cool. Ten minutes before it's time to meet downstairs. Leave it to Leah to plan a day event, even though we haven't gotten a wink of sleep last night. But hey, is there any other way to spend a day off in Miami?

A text message notification stops me in the middle of putting my phone away.

Soakin' Wet Summer Dancers Chat

Leah: Hey guys! Looks like Zion found out about my boat plans. He reimbursed me, upgraded our rental to a yacht, and invited the whole crew! See you guys soon!

I rub my temples, convinced my fatigue made me imagine the words on my phone. I was ready for a chill boat situation with the girls, but a yacht party?

This is tour life, Naya. You're not new to this.

This is the tour cycle, or at least the one I've experienced throughout my career.

Rehearsals: full of focus, budding excitement, with a hint of stress because the show is ever-changing. Choreography is altered, deleted, and then thrown back into the show again. Eight-hour rehearsals, six days a week, leaving you with just enough energy to order takeout, do some laundry and clean your house, only if you're lucky. After weeks of regular rehearsals, you upgrade to production rehearsals a week before the tour begins. That's the first time other departments are involved.

Rehearsals extended from eight hours to twelve long, grueling hours to give everyone time to do their jobs. Now, the lighting department gets to work with physical bodies in real-time instead of imagining what it would look like from videos. Creative directors get to see the production on an actual stage instead of a dance studio and ultimately decide what works and doesn't. This is usually the hardest part of the job for me. The part of the process where I question my chosen career path. Why did I choose a profession where my body is my instrument? An instrument that is sore, tired, and overworked.

Then, the tour begins. Rehearsals are over, and you are free. Unless there's any sickness or injuries, the show remains the same. Outside of shows, our bodies have more time to recover. Rest should be at the forefront of everyone's minds, but this is also the most free time we've had for weeks, so group activities and partying become the focus: museums, sightseeing, or renting a boat in Miami with plenty of drinks in every activity. This is where everyone gets to know one another more personally. The overall atmosphere is group-oriented.

Then, there's the last part of the tour, what I like to call The Great Decline. Activities aren't as group-oriented as they used to be. Smaller groups of two or three explore the cities instead of everyone together. Some people spend more time with themselves on free days. Others don't show up until thirty minutes before the show. The morale of the crew is lower. Performing the same choreography month after month makes it harder to find inspiration. The lifestyle catches up to our bodies, causing sickness and injury. And during the last couple of weeks, a cloud of uneasiness forms over the crew, reminding us we are about to be thrown back into the world of free-lancing, auditioning, and fickle income. Though I, too, fear returning to the roller coaster of freelance dancing, I welcome the end of tour with open arms, looking forward to something new.

On my last tour, I started the job in The Great Decline. All I wanted was for the tour to end. That was an entirely unfamiliar environment, though. Everyone, from the cast, crew and artist, was predominately white. Not the progressive, actively anti-racist type of white like Leah, but the tone-deaf, "I don't see color, my neighbor is black" type of white. One day, I'd hear someone lecturing about how systemic racism doesn't exist, and another day, I'd be listening to someone tell me he would've voted for Obama for a third term if they could. That tour put me through the longest game of mental Olympics I'd ever experienced. The Soakin' Wet Summer tour is my redemption. Another chance to travel and dance, this time with a black artist and a predominately black crew, and maybe for the last time, 'cause to be honest, I don't know how much more of these I have left in me.

Another message tears my attention away.

Leah: I heard some of his celebrity friends are coming too, so I hope you gals are ready!

Whew, now I am definitely gonna need some caffeine.

I grab my things and head out the door.

The elevator pings a little too loud as it passes each floor. Fluorescent lights assault my tired eyes, but my sunglasses save the day. When the elevator reaches the lobby, I step out, searching for the cafe I passed when we checked in earlier. I scan the left side of the lobby while my body takes a couple of steps to the right until—I collide with another person.

"Oh, my goodness, I'm so sorry, ma'am."

I search the floor to see if I knocked anything out of the woman's arms.

"It's okay, Naya."

The stranger flashes a smile.

My eyes shoot up to find Khloe standing in front of me, suppressing her laughter. With each chuckle, she dips her head slightly, which puts her baby hairs on full display. Perfect swirls and swoops lead to the design of cornrows on her head. And they should be. She's serious about wearing that scarf after the show. I wish I shared the same discipline with my bonnet.

With everything in me, I divert my gaze from the yellow bathing suit and wrap-around skirt that perfectly cradles her curves. One side of the skirt sits higher on her right hip, revealing her entire leg from the hip down. Her thick and athletic legs...

Stop staring and say something!

"Well, look who's bumping into me again!"

"Excuse me?! You bumped into me, Nayara Alvarez."

Don't say my full name. With perfect Spanish pronunciation. My body, once tired, springs awake.

"Oh, we're doing full names, Miss Khloe Thompson? Well, I suppose I might be at fault this time, but not entirely. I think the sleep deprivation is getting to me... I like your bathing suit, girl! So cute! I think I have the same one back home."

Nerves push that babbling lie straight through my teeth.

You don't have that bathing suit, but she doesn't know that. Be cute, be friendly. Be a girl's girl, Naya.

A friendly, uninterested girl's girl.

"Sleep deprivation? You were the first to go to your bunk after the show last night!"

She noticed?

Pushing those thoughts away, I place a wide hand over my chest.

"You caught me! I think the show days are catching up with me."

"My muscles agree with that." Khloe snorts. "Wanna get some coffee before Leah rushes us into this Uber?"

"Yeah, that's what I was looking for before you smacked into me."

A mischievous grin stretches across my face.

* * *

The menu only has about six items, but I read it over and over again. Anything to avoid my eyes veering over to Khloe's frame standing in line ahead of me.

"So..." She begins. "I've been messaging another girl from one of the apps."

Damn, already?

"Wanna see her?"

She extends her phone toward me.

Be a girl's girl, Naya.

I ignore the split second our fingers touch while she passes me the phone. Then I stare at the brown girl with a fully shaved head but enough hair left to dye baby lavender. Tattoos run from her wrists to her neck, making the ones on my forearms look like child's play. And to make matters worse, her stunning hazel eyes are staring back at me. Hazel fucking eyes. Are you kidding me?

"She's cute!" I say a little too loudly. "Went from half-shaved head to full-shaved head, I see. Someone's got a type."

"No, I don't! Well, I guess I don't really know yet. This is only my second match..."

Her words trail off into silence, and I can already sense what's happening.

"Don't overthink it, Khloe. I was joking. Like whoever you like."

The small furrow in her brow relaxes.

"Do you have a type?"

Her round eyes blink with curiosity.

"My main preference is black women, but I dabble from time to time."

"Oh! Do you meet most women on apps? Sorry if I'm asking too many questions."

"I don't mind the questions."

I really just wanna get out of this line because your cleavage has been tugging my eye line for too long.

"Half and half. But I only use the apps if I'm on tour. When I'm back in LA, I deactivate the accounts."

"She said 'I got hoes in different area codes!'" Khloe snickers until the barista clears his throat, completely unamused with our banter.

"Oh... um, can I have an iced mocha latte?"

"No, not at all! I just use them to meet people outside of the tour I'm on at the time. I like to keep my work and personal life separate. The tour bubble puts everyone in such close proximity, hookups, tourmances and all kinds of drama spread like wildfire. Nothing like that has ever happened to me, but on my first tour, I saw the flames all around me. So since then, I vowed to never shit where I sleep. It complicates everything."

A puzzled look shadows her face as she hands the barista her credit card.

"Out of all the tours, which one was the longest?"

She steps aside as I take her place in line.

"I'll have a small green tea with honey." I slide a five-dollar bill across the counter and bring my eyes back to Khloe's.

"A year and a half."

"A year and a half? On the road?!" Her eyes widen.

"Yup, and the shortest was two months."

"And out of all those tours, you've never had a tourmance?"

Her string of questions spark laughter from my cheeks.

"I'm sorry. I'm really grilling you," she retracts.

"It's okay," I say, coming up for air between giggles. "No tourmances, hook-ups or nothing. I don't date dancers. It is too small of a community. There's been a few crew or band members, but that's still too close to home."

"That's dating. No hook-ups? Or sexual tension even?"

"Of course, I've experienced a little crush or tension, but that's where my trusty apps come in handy."

An expression that I can't read washes over her face.

"We have an iced mocha latte and a green tea!" the barista announces, jolting me from my thoughts.

"Yes, thank you!" I grab my drink and hand Khloe hers. "Come on, Leah is probably sending search parties by now."

When the Uber XL pulls up, I practically glue myself between DayDay and Bunny. I'd had enough of Khloe's perfectly glossed lips asking me questions.

There's no way I'll end up sitting next to her in the car, too. Keeping my blood pressure down was difficult earlier, but I'm proud of myself. In one quick conversation, I established boundaries. Well, not directly toward Khloe, but specific enough for her to understand that I don't date dancers. On top of that, I downloaded the apps for her. I said Miss Shaved Head number two was cute. Now, she can date freely and never wonder if we're a possibility. Not that she gave me any vibes like that... or at least I don't think she has. Either way, now she can find another lesbian to interview. Hookup, befriend or interview, I don't care as long as the spotlight is off me.

Yeah, one point for me. I wish younger Naya could look at me now. The days of fake gay women and heartbreaks are far behind me. Those women were bi-curious and closeted, treating me like a dirty secret on a drunk Friday night. I fell victim to those women as if my life depended on it. Gone are the days of being someone's experiment. Not to mention, I still have to uphold my no-dating coworkers rule. I survived five tours, and there's no way I'm breaking that streak now.

A pole dancer from Letti's tour several years ago playfully referred to herself as Mrs. Alvarez because I was her wife. A coke bottle-shaped woman with finger waves like Nia Long stole lingering touches across my skin every chance she could.

On the tour before that, there was a female dancer who straight up told me, "What do I have to do to get into bed with you?" one drunken night after the show.

Despite my rejection, she kept that same energy throughout the entire tour. I'd stayed strong, but there were nights when her prolonged eye contact and double D chest almost took me to the point of no return.

When I was twenty-six, I toured with a teenage boy band, and one of their mothers, a very fine thirty-five-year-old woman with an entrancing beauty mark above her full lips, used to hunt me down after shows like prey stalking their kill. Had I met her outside work, I would've served myself like a charcuterie board.

All temptation in the world, and I've never buckled. Why is it so hard this tim—

"Hey, you good?" Bunny nudges my shoulder. "Why are you staring out the window like you're doing math?"

"Oh, me? I'm good, just a little tired." I raise my tea. "But no worries. This is about to get me right."

As I finish my sentence, I glimpse Bunny's eyes. Not the glass protection she puts on for everyone else, but the real person behind them. The hilarious and vibrant woman who also deals with real life from time to time. Something tells me this is one of those times.

"What about you? What's going on?"

I clutch her hand and interlace our fingers, thankful for this level of platonic intimacy we'd developed during our college years.

"I'm all right." She lays her head on my shoulder. "It is just my momma… She had an episode today and was doing what she does best."

Bunny's mother has bipolar disorder. She does well most days, but when she has episodes, hurtful words shoot from her mouth, impaling anyone nearby, usually Bunny.

"I know it's easier said than done, but you can't take the things she does personally, especially when she's in that state. She still loves you. She's just not herself during those moments."

"Ugh, I'm trying, friend, but it's hard. She said she's tired of watching me waste my life away with this dance shit. As if this shit isn't the very thing paying for her medication and her apartment."

I squeeze her hand and rub my thumb back and forth.

"You are an amazing daughter. God blessed her with a strong daughter to watch over her, but you're also human. Get spicy with her! Establish those boundaries."

"No, I could never disrespect my momma." Bunny slumps into her shoulders. "Nigerians do not play that."

"I'm not saying go crazy on her. But when my abuelo was dealing with dementia and cussing us out every day, I had to let him know. 'Hey, do you want your ass wiped or not? Okay, then! Be nice to me!'"

Giggles pour into Bunny's smile. "Girl, you are crazy! Okay, okay. I see what you mean."

"Excuse me!" DayDay clasps his hands like a schoolteacher. "I'm not trying to interrupt this little love fest y'all got going on, but it's time to bring up the mood."

The rest of the car had fallen asleep during the lengthy car ride. The driver parks the car in front of a massive brown dock leading to an even larger white and blue boat. A multi-deck boat with a pool, couches and a DJ on the top deck two-stepping to Afrobeats. Zion didn't rent a yacht. This man reserved an entire cruise ship! A crowd of about seventy-five people line up on the dock, waiting to board. And judging by the name brands in that line, the crowd are most likely friends of Zion. DayDay unclasps his hands and opens them in presentation style.

"Ladies, the daddies have arrived. The rich zaddies. Take advantage. Naya, I'm pretty sure there's a mami or two for you, too. So, let's wake it up, perk the tatas and get ready to make some memories!"

"Is that a basketball player?!" Rae chirps.

"I don't know, but do you guys see Alayna James?! I adore her music!" Leah announces.

Excitement brews among us as we grab our purses and pile out of the car. Leah's long, red hair cascades over her green bathing suit top and mesh pants. Besides a little mascara, she has no makeup on, so her freckles and green eyes are more pronounced than usual. Rae's hip-length box braids swing from side to side as she exits the car. She's wearing a fire-truck red bathing suit with a matching black and red kimono on top. Bunny exits the car, flipping her 42-inch Brazilian-wave hair in the breeze. The sun illuminates her dark brown skin.

"Babe, I can't right now. I just got to the dock. Ima call you when I get back to the hotel," Tiana says, finishing the phone call she'd gotten seconds before pulling up. She gets out of the car, running a frustrated hand through her dirty blonde curls. She tucks the phone into her short Daisy Duke jeans, rolls her eyes and exhales.

"All right, y'all. I'm sorry. I'm present now."

"Good, 'cause today is not the day to be bickering with your man. The yacht is for fun!" DayDay says as he climbs out of the backseat in his colorful swim shorts and white tank top.

"Exactly!"

"Period!" The ladies echo.

"Y'all are right. He is not about to stress me out today!" Tiana retorts while playfully twerking.

This is our first daytime outing as a group. The first time outside of a makeshift after-party in Zion's arena dressing room. Gorgeous female dancers and a handsome DayDay. I don't know who Zion invited, but they are about to drool.

As soon as my feet touch the dock, I take a deep breath. The salty sea air expands my lungs with peace. Since the Everglades tour, I've been thinking more and more about my parents' arrival to the United States. Trekking through choppy ocean waters in hopes of a better life. A story that hasn't crossed my mind in some years. A story that hasn't seen the light of day, yet poured from my lips in that muggy Florida swamp. Effortless and free from the concrete wall I'd built around it. Somehow Khloe did that. I've been thinking about what she said about my family's connection to water. The ocean can be ferocious and unforgiving, but for some reason, guided my parents' boat here safe and sound. Maybe there is an unseeable tether to my family and mother nature's water.

"Naya, you coming, or are you gonna stay on the dock and stare?" Khloe tugs at my fingers. Though we'd spoken back at the hotel, I felt like I was looking at her for the first time all over again. Her bubbly brown eyes and inviting dimples stall all the words trying to leave my mouth.

"My bad. I zoned out. Now, let's get on this boat before Leah and DayDay yell at us."

I take a couple of steps toward the majestic yacht at the end of the dock. A relaxed smile spreads across Khloe's face as she catches up with me. She interlaces her hand with mine, and the pit of my stomach turns to mush.

"Let's go."

CHAPTER TWENTY-NINE

WHY DID Naya get so stiff when I grabbed her hand? She held Bunny's hand the same way in the Uber moments ago, and they've been friends since college, so what's the—unless they aren't really friends.

My brain performs mental gymnastics while Naya and I board the boat, hand in hand. I try to remain as relaxed as possible. 'Cause it is normal for us to hold hands. As two platonic coworkers... Right?

We turn the first corner and enter a large lounge with blue and purple lighting and an all-white illuminated dance floor. Dozens of bodies dressed in name brands way outside of my pay grade sway to the music. The DJ is upstairs on the top deck, but his music syncs with the speakers all over the boat. Next to the dance floor stands a long bar where the stagehands and band are catching up, laughing and ordering drinks.

"Let's do a round of shots!" the bass player booms over the music.

"Okay!"

"Say less!"

"Dark or light?"

I wave my free hand around to greet them. "Don't forget us!"

"Heyyyy!" They greet us.

"What's up!"

"Nice to see y'all!"

Because of everybody's boisterous energy, Bunny's body language sticks out like a sore thumb. She's standing painfully still, staring at me and Naya. Her gaze locks onto our hands, then bounces back and forth between us. Am I doing too much?

"Here! This is tequila." A band member says, holding a shot in front of me. I break away from Naya's hand and unnecessarily grab the shot glass with two hands. Anything to stop Bunny's studying eyes. The band member hands an identical shot to Naya and turns to the rest of the crew.

"To an amazing week of shows, memorable off days and an even more memorable tour!" The group cheers.

Among all the excitement, Naya wiggles through the group, and right in front of the bartender.

"Excuse me, can I get a lime?" I overhear. Just as she had moments ago, I move through the crowd and stand right next to her.

"Can I get a lime too?" I say. Then Rae and Tiana's voices come from behind us.

"Oh! Me too!"

"Me three!"

Once the bartender distributes the limes, everyone holds their shots high.

"To the baddest bitches on tour!" Rae bellows. We clink our glasses. "Eye contact! Or seven years of bad sex!"

DayDay sucks his teeth. "Y'all better look into these pupils. I'm not risking that for nobody!"

Tiana clinks her shot with DayDay's with searing eye contact. "Never!"

"Y'all are crazy." Naya chuckles.

Her smile is infectious. When you look at it, you can't help but feel good. It's also... really cute.

Khloe, what are you doing?

I tear my gaze away and inhale my shot, allowing the burning sensation to numb my thoughts. I bite down on the lime in my hand, this time trying to use the tart flavor to distract me. The rest of the crew downs their shots and places their glasses back on the bar. When Naya puts her glass down, the bartender peers up through her short, blonde locs. Her marble-like hazel eyes study Naya like a predator in the wild.

"You know," she says quietly enough for nobody to hear.

Nobody outside of my eavesdropping ears. She slides another shot of tequila directly into Naya's hands.

"Whether you give eye contact during a toast or not, I'm sure sex with you is never bad."

Her words leave a buzzing energy between them. The bartender gently rubs her thumb over Naya's hand.

The residual burn from my shot, lime juice and my saliva combusts inside of my throat. No matter how hard I fight it, coughs escape from my throat, loud and hard.

"Uh oh, you okay girl?!" DayDay pats my back.

Then, he leans into my ear until his mouth is centimeters away.

"Never seen a lesbian takedown before, huh?"

Eyes wide and residual coughs thrumming my chest, I grab his arm and lead him away.

"You saw that, right?! Everyone else was so oblivious!"

I splay a hand over my chest.

"The gays can be a little secretive, like whispering Goldilocs over there, but honey, I see everything."

"Is that really how it happens? That forward?"

All I knew so far was messaging on an app.

DayDay signals another bartender.

"Two margaritas, please!"

He sets some money on the bar, then turns his attention back to me.

"Not all the time. It depends on the person. But in this life, straight or gay, you gotta put your bid in. Let 'em know."

"That's wild. If a guy approached me like that, I would vomit into that shot glass."

For some reason, though, watching Goldilocs and Naya isn't cringey. It's intriguing...

DayDay starts talking about hooking up with a straight guy in a supply closet last Halloween, but I can't hear any of the details. My mind is elsewhere. I peek over his shoulder. Naya rests her elbows on the bar as she leans in, this time holding Goldilocs' hands. Naya's eyes scan her frame like... like she's hungry. A polite yet primitive gaze that makes me feel like I shouldn't be looking. Still, a part of me wonders what it would feel like for Naya to look at me that way.

"...After getting off the phone with his wife, he dropped his pants, and I went to town on him babyyy!"

DayDay throws his head back, laughing.

I join his laughter, trying to piece together what he'd just said.

"You are crazy DayDay!"

I look back over his shoulder just in time to see Goldilocs handing Naya her phone.

Damn, they are exchanging numbers. Already?

"All right people!" DayDay announces to the group. "Let's move this party to the top deck and get into the pool!"

Everyone hoots in agreement and makes their way upstairs.

A crystal blue pool and Jacuzzi sit in the center of the top deck, filled with beautiful women. Not regular pretty, but video vixen, you-have-to-be-a-model type of women wading in the waist-deep water. Someone must've sent a mass text or email before the party because most of the women are wearing similar bathing suits. Thin string bikinis barely cover their bodies. Their perfect, surgically crafted bodies. I fight the urge to glance down at my bathing suit. I stop myself from reaching toward the back of my thighs and counting the cellulite dimples. And as much as I try to resist, thoughts of comparison creep in.

Stop it, Khloe.

You are just as deserving as all the women in here.

Even if their clothes are worth three months of my rent. It doesn't matter if they have the means to fix any unfavorable quality on their body. I am just as pretty, just as deserving. If fifteen-year-old Khloe could see me now, partying with rappers, producers, and athletes, she'd be blown to pieces.

This boat with multiple decks, an open bar and a pool definitely beats playing in the water hose every summer. Hell, if Khloe from three months ago knew what awaited her, she'd be blown to bits, but she was dealing with too much.

Men with expensive sunglasses, elaborate grillz, and large gold chains are sprinkled all over the deck. Some ogle the women in the pool. Others wave money to bet on their card games. And though there were few of them, some men grace the dance floor while the DJ spins everything from Hip Hop to Reggae. Zion two steps in the center of the dance floor holding two champagne bottles.

I appreciate the atmosphere the music provides, but something else grabs my attention on the top deck. On the opposite side of the DJ is another bar, this time with a fruit stand operated by a tan Hispanic man in a straw hat. Keeping my eyes on the prize ahead, I walk toward the bar as my fingers fumble around my purse for money.

"Drinks with fresh fruit? I'm in!"

"You sure, babe? Should we order some food first?" Leah points toward a small buffet section I'd overlooked.

"Yeah, I'm hungry," Rae adds.

Though she swore off boyfriend drama on the dock, Tiana is sucked back into her phone once again with her fingers wildly typing. She pauses, taking a break from the screen.

"Me too. I need something fried and unhealthy."

"I'll stop there after the food. Unless y'all wanna drag me off this boat in an hour, I need to get some food in my belly," Bunny adds.

"Y'allllll," I interject, allowing my St. Louis drawl to take over. "There's no line right now. We can get another drink and sip on it while we wait in that buffet line."

Silence blankets the ladies. Bunny and Leah lock elbows as they turn on their heels and go straight toward the buffet. Tiana glances up from her phone.

"Sorry, girl, I'm hungry, but the bar isn't far. We can still see you. Holla 'stranger-danger' if something happens."

Rae is already two steps behind Bunny and Leah.

"I'll go with you, sis," Naya says.

"Thank you! I know these are all Zion's friends, and the bar is not far, but I still didn't wanna go alone. You feel me?"

"Oh, I know exactly what you mean. And to be frank, fuck if they're his friends. They could be his abuela for all I care. I don't trust industry environments."

Relief drains from my chest. "I'm so glad you understand. Some of my friends in LA say I'm paranoid."

She hooks her elbow into mine with me as we make our way to the fruit station.

"Better paranoid and safe than reckless and sorry. A few years ago, I did a tour with this artist that we never saw during off-days. He was sweet and kept to himself, but his cousin was always around. Frederick, but everybody called him Freddy. He was the life of every party, telling jokes, doing crazy dances, making the female dancers laugh until they cried 'cause he'd wear our show heels and pretend to do the choreography."

"Heels?! Okay! I love a black man that's comfortable in his sexuality!"

I hold my hands up, praising a stranger named Freddy.

"Me too. Most of the women did. In retrospect, I feel like that's one of his tactics to make women comfortable, and honey, did he fool us. During one of the after-show parties, I was posted up against a wall with sunglasses on. At this point, we were at the end of the tour, so I wasn't drinking as much—"

"Posted up. Sunglasses. And Sober? You saw everything crystal clear that night."

"Crystal clear?!" Naya leans in, close enough for me to feel her breath on my ear. "Girl, I saw Freddy spike the punch bowl the entire party was drinking out of."

My hands clutch her forearms while a gasp escapes from my lungs.

"Was everyone okay?!"

"Yeah, thank God. Most of the female dancers were on the same vibe as me—drinking very little or not at all. When the guys weren't looking, a lot of the girls made mocktails and fake shots just to make it look like they were drinking. One girl had enough punch to mess her up, but I ensured she got back to her hotel room safely. The second I saw her stumbling, I'd catch her and turn the stumbles into a slow dance between us. Because I'm gay, most of the guys assumed I was claiming her, so Freddy backed off. Instead, he passed us while we were slow dancing and gave me a nod of approval."

My jaw must've been gaped open for a while, 'cause Naya broke out into a fit of laughter.

"Be careful before a fly goes in there!"

I blink a couple of times, coming down from the shock of her story.

"I'm sorry. I just can't believe shit like this really happens. People warn women about these things, and you hear about it from the female rappers or singers, but it's shocking that female dancers have to deal with this, too."

"It took me years to get over the initial rage of it all... Hold on."

She places a gentle hand on my shoulder, then turns her attention to the man at the fruit station.

"Con permiso, puedo coger un tragito con maracuya y rum?"

The Spanish flows from her lips with ease.

"What kind of fruit do you want in your drink?"

"I don't know...Is that passion fruit you're getting?" I divert my eyes to the man chopping in front of us.

"Only the best fruit known to man."

"Then I'll get that, but I want tequila with mine."

Naya nods her head and turns back to the man.

"Y ella vas a coger los mismo pero con tequila."

With each additional Spanish word, a familiar swirling sensation invades my stomach. Maybe this should be my last drink. I reminisce about the shots we'd taken on the first level. I should probably follow the rest of the crew and get some food after this. When the man hands us our drinks, I take a sip. A perfect mix of sweet, tangy and tart, blessing my taste buds. The aftertaste of tequila lingers but isn't overpowering. This is one of the best drinks I've had in a while! Naya and I clink our cups, and I take another sip.

Yeah...I don't think this is gonna be my last drink.

CHAPTER THIRTY

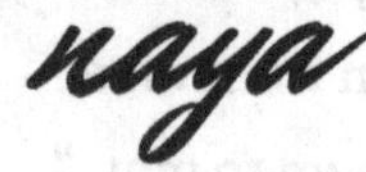

SUSHI, Indian curry, tacos, lobster mac-n-cheese bites and much more decorate the buffet tables. The opportunities are endless. After much indecision, I decide on two rolls of sushi, and we join the rest of the girls seated at a round table. The last open seats sit directly across from one another. So, while I inhale my sushi rolls, I have the perfect view of Khloe demolishing lobster mac-n-cheese bites.

I loathe the idea of possibly making eye contact with Khloe while eating, but I rather sit across from her than sit next to her. The drinks are starting to catch up with me, and I can't risk our legs accidentally brushing against each other.

I had agreed to accompany her to the bar so she won't be alone, but I can no longer ignore the draw I feel towards her. Despite the boundaries I've set, something is still there. Something about her presence, her energy, wraps me in. When she speaks to me, I feel like she's staring right through me, and it makes my stomach feel hallow.

"Where's DayDay?" Leah asks before biting into her sushi roll. "He's been gone for quite a bit."

Bunny drizzles barbecue sauce over her French-fries. "Oh, I haven't seen that baby since he made googly eyes at that fine Spanish daddy on the dance floor downstairs!"

"The one with the long, wavy hair?" Rae questions. "Damn, I thought his fine ass was Asian!"

"Oh crap, I thought he was a white guy with a tan..." Leah snickers.

"Shoot, I don't know! What I do know is that DayDay is probably somewhere finding out as we speak!"

Bunny laughs into the French fry in her hand.

Khloe and I giggle as we stuff our faces. Tiana nibbles on a slice of pizza with her left hand while typing into her phone with the right. Then, a new text interrupts her initial message. Seconds after glancing at the words, her eyes blink with rage.

"What the hell does he mean by that?!" Tiana blurts out.

She wipes her eating hand and picks up her phone, this time typing even quicker.

Rae reaches toward Tiana, rubbing her shoulder.

"Babe, remember when you said you weren't gonna let your man stress you out on this boat?"

Tiana slams the phone down, drops her head in her hands, and massages her scalp.

"It's just so hard, sis. When I booked this job, he was so excited for me, but since I left LA, he's been picking fights left and right!"

"He's probably feeling a little insecure because of the type of people we're around," Khloe says with bits of breading stuck in the corner of her mouth. "Zion is literally an R&B sex symbol. Not to mention, most of his homies are handsome, too."

Somewhere deep down, Khloe talking about Zion's good-looking friends stings a little.

Snap out of it, Nayara.

"That doesn't matter! Two years ago, I went on tour with a teenage pop artist. Bubblegum personality, clean-ass music, and polite white women everywhere. That didn't stop my ex from accusing me of cheating or entertaining men every two days. Insecure men don't need a reason." Rae swirls a sushi roll in soy sauce. She pops the roll into her mouth and continues, "So after about a month of him accusing me, I gave him a reason to accuse me!"

The table explodes into laughter. Even Tiana catches a case of the giggles.

"You're crazy, girl."

"Wait," Khloe says in the middle of sipping her drink. Bits of food cling to the corner of her mouth. She looks so... adorable. I resist the urge to reach out and brush the crumbs away with my thumb. "So, you cheated on him?" Khloe asks, breaking my thoughts.

"Hell yeah! First, I started smashing road booties! *Then*, I broke up with him! There was no way he was about to prematurely give me high blood pressure and ruin my tour experience. He thought I was fucking off? I showed him what fucking off looked like, for real!"

With wide smiles, some ladies threw their heads back, others clapped, and a few clutched their stomachs.

I struggle to keep the last piece of sushi steady between my chopsticks as I question, "Road booties?"

"Yes, some road booty! Booties belonging to fine daddies all across these beautiful states! Athlete booty, dating app booty, single dad booty... Oh! There was one guy who worked at the airport. I call him sky lounge booty!"

"Single dad booty is actually a thing!" Bunny adds. "They wanna treat you well because they have kids and a conscience, but they don't want anything serious *because* they got kids! So, they'll smash your lights out but won't pressure you into a relationship!"

"No, ma'am." Rae holds a chopstick in the air. "I used to mess with this single dad, and I had to cut him loose. After a few days, he was talking about his child meeting a wonderful mother-figure like me. Hellllll naw! I did not sign up to be a step momma!" Rae explains.

They are a little unhinged, but I absolutely love being in the company of these women. Since high school, I've been the only lesbian in most of my friend groups, so I'm used to it. I've tried to have more gay friends, but I always end up on too many tipsy nights where they'd try to make out with me. Studs, femmes, and stems, it never fails. A couple of shots later, they get all touchy and start staring at my lips while I'm speaking. Straight women don't give me that stress. They talk about men most of the day and read them for filth (a part I enjoy a little too much), then go about their day.

My phone vibrating from inside of my Fanny Pak, forces me to take a break from my plate.

Jean: I go on a thirty-minute break in about five minutes. Can I steal you away from your friends?

Jean? Who is—Flashbacks of the caramel-brown woman with hazel eyes and blonde locs flood my memory.

My name is Jeannette, but everyone calls me Jean...

Me: Of course. Just let me know where.

I lock my phone screen and look up to find Bunny staring straight at me.

"I know that smirk. Got a text from Goldilocs?"

I stand up and push in my chair, failing to hide the giddy smile on my face.

"That's none of your business. I'll catch y'all later. I have something to do."

"More like people to do!"

Bunny applauds. My cheeks flush while "oh's" spread through the table.

"Hot mama!" Leah fans herself.

"Oh wow. That took no time... Have fun," Khloe practically whispers.

"She's not going to a water park, Khloe... Or is she?!" Rae cackles, joining Bunny's applause.

Tiana peers up from her phone and sighs. "Well, at least somebody is having fun."

"Girl, we are having fun. You're the only one that isn't. I'm about to take that phone!" Rae snaps and turns her attention back to Naya. "Live your life, babe, and make me proud!"

"All right, now that my business is thoroughly broadcasted, I'll see y'all later. Love you guys."

Before I can finish pushing my chair in, a tall, muscular man with chocolate brown skin slips into my seat.

"Forgive me for intruding, ladies," he says through big, moisturized lips. "I wanted to return to the dance floor, but I couldn't give up the opportunity to sit in front of the most beautiful woman on this yacht."

The women stir as everyone cranes their attention to Khloe, who is sitting silent, her lips slightly parted and the same crumbs on the corners of her mouth.

"Excuse my friend," Bunny interjects as she throws a napkin into Khloe's lap, gesturing to wipe her mouth. "My friend isn't used to handsome brothers like yourself coming at her respectfully."

Once again, my best friend wins the award for best wingman.

Mr. Handsome man shifts in his seat to get more comfortable.

"Not used to it? That's because those guys are boys. They don't know when they're among a real queen."

I clench my jaw to stop my food from coming back up.

A real queen? Surely, Khloe sees right through his corny—

"Oh really? Well, how 'bout you show me how a queen should be treated?"

Khloe props her elbows on the table and leans forward, allowing her cleavage to be on full display.

"It would be my honor. What are you drinking tonig—"

The rest of his sentence never reaches my ears because I walk away, desperately trying to ignore this strange feeling invading my body. I can't find the words to describe this feeling. All I know is I couldn't watch Khloe flirt with such a lame guy a second longer. Even if he has huge muscles, a perfect smile, and dozens of chains around his neck. He probably attends rich yacht parties often. He probably goes home to a multi-million dollar mansion or a penthouse downtown. He could probably buy her the world. She probably loves guys like that. A text message notification jolted me from my thoughts.

Jean: Meet me by the garden on the first floor.

A Garden? Damn, what else does this yacht have?

* * *

A young man in uniform greets me as soon as I enter the first floor. "Hello, ma'am, welcome to the Spa at Sea. Are you interested in a massage? Facial treatment? How about a sea salt body scrub?"

I open my mouth to reply, but a voice calls out behind him.

"Eric, she's with me! We'll be in the garden!"

Toward the back of the spa, Jean peeks her head through a door leading outside.

"This way, Naya."

The familiar way she says my name as if we'd known each other for months, brings a smile to my cheeks. I thank the young man at the front and meet Jean. But nothing could've prepared me for what I see when she leads me through a door. Exotic flowers of all shapes, colors, and sizes line the walls and floors. Green vines invade all the empty spaces the flowers don't occupy. A sweet yet earthy smell swirls through my nostrils. The glass walls and ceiling overlook the ocean, allowing the perfect amount of sunlight to pour in from every direction.

"Oh, my..." I try to speak, but the view renders me speechless.

"You like it? This is my favorite spot on the yacht. I spend every break here, even if it's just ten minutes. Come."

She takes my hand and leads me further into the garden until we arrive at a yellow bench surrounded by a sea of white orchids. She sits down and pats the space next to her.

God, I love forward women.

The bench has enough room to seat four, but I match her forwardness and nuzzle beside her, allowing our thighs to touch. Once I'm comfortable, she raises her leg and rests it on top of my thigh. I lay a hand on her knee and rub my thumb back and forth over her work slacks.

"So, how long have you lived in Miami?"

"I'm born and raised... But Naya, can I be frank with you?"

"Of course."

In one swift motion, she grabs my hand and drags it further up her thigh, directly to her center. Heat radiates through her pants and warms my hand. An identical heat buds in the deepest part of my core.

"My break is short, and you are on tour. What if we skip the cordiality and fast forward to the part where your fingers are inside me?"

God, I loveee forward women.

Forward *lesbian* women. No guessing. No newly gay women or experiments. No over analyzing each expression and conversation searching for gay innuendos. Just straight shooting. And I'll shoot back every time.

I bring my lips to her ear, pressing the pads of my index and middle finger against her. Moving my fingers in a soft round motion.

"Your wish is my command. But..." I lean away, retracting my hand.

A small gasp escapes her lungs.

"Why'd you stop?"

"Because, as sexy as this is, I don't feel comfortable fucking you in this humongous garden. Got anywhere a little more private?"

A smirk forms in the corner of Jean's mouth. "Follow me."

With a timid pulse thrumming between my legs, I follow her back into the spa, where she addresses the young man who welcomed me earlier.

"Which massage room is free for the next half hour?"

He rolls his eyes.

"Room three. No longer than a half hour, Jean. I'm serious! And put the bedding in the washing machine!"

We are already halfway down the hall when she responds, "Got you!"

The door barely closes behind us before our mouths invade each other. Searching, tasting, nibbling, taking full advantage of the little time we have. My hands cup her perfectly round ass while her left hand grips the back of my head. Taking a quick break from our kiss, I unbutton her pants as she pulls off her work shirt and tosses it to the side. Letting our mouths reclaim each other, we continue our kiss with more intensity.

I push my body against hers until her back meets the massage bed. She slowly leans back until I'm hovering over her. I break away for a moment to study her marble gaze searing into me. A gaze that adds more moisture to the pool already forming in my core.

The looping spa music playing in the background fades to black when I bring my lips to her neck. The only thing I hear is a wonderful soundtrack of Jean's moans and gasps for air. My left hand curves around her lower back, yanking her closer to me. Starting from her bottom lip, I trace my right hand down her neck, along her stomach, and finally to her thong, which is soaked.

"What do you want?" I whisper into her ear before nibbling her earlobe.

A loud moan roars through her throat.

"Fuck me. Pleaseee."

Pushing her thong to the side, I enter her with two fingers, slowly moving in and out, savoring her warm walls.

"Like this?"

"Yesss," she whispers in between moans.

I wonder what Khloe sounds like when she moans. Is it soft and right up against the ear, or does it rattle the room?

What, Nayara?

Snapping out of it, I added a third finger, increasing my speed and pressing her body against mine. Jean doesn't even seem to notice my wandering mind because her moans intensify. No matter how loud Jean is, I struggle to mute the thoughts invading my head.

Was Khloe still upstairs talking to Mr. Handsome Man? Would this be their same fate on this boat?

My lips travel from Jean's neck to her mouth. Tongues intertwining, I kiss her harder, searching for anything to erase Khloe from my brain.

"I'm about to come," she rasps against my mouth.

Perfect.

I bring my focus back to my right hand. This time using my thumb to draw soft circles over her clit. Moments later, she cries out with her body trembling on my fingers. I bite into my bottom lip, admiring her jolting limbs. I bring my fingers to my mouth, taking a sample of her sweet juices.

"Mmm. Wanna know how good you taste?"

She props herself up on her elbows with a devious grin.

"No, ma'am. I wanna know what *you* taste like."

CHAPTER THIRTY-ONE

TRAP MUSIC BLARES through the speakers while the entire cast is on the dance floor. The band, dancers, tour manager, and everyone except Tiana, Leah, and me. We're sitting at the bar listening to Tiana vent. She slams her phone onto the bar and slides it toward Leah.

"Take this away from me, 'cause I'm two seconds from booking a flight back home to look at him in his stupid face!"

"Aw, babe..." Leah rubs Tiana's hand. "Did you tell him we are the only ones at the bar?"

"Of course I did. He just doesn't care. He said that doesn't stop me from entertaining dudes from afar. What the hell does that even mean?"

I stare down at the napkin in my hand, my thoughts drowning the rest of Leah and Tiana's conversation. I've read the writing on the napkin so many times I can recite its contents from memory. Derrick 555-235-5210, followed by a heart. The bold man from the buffet had a name. He was kind of corny with all his real queen talk, but it's been a while since someone pursued me. It is refreshing. And he's handsome as hell. Not to mention that perfect smile. But no matter how many pros outweigh my mental list of cons, I can't bring myself to text him.

Come on, Khloe.

You don't have to marry the guy. This is your time to have a little fun, maybe even get on the same level as Naya and—

Ugh!

I bury my forehead in the palm of my hand. No matter how hard I've tried to distract myself, my mind keeps wondering what Naya and Goldilocs are doing. Well, they are obviously doing each other, *right?*

Why else would she run off to meet the hazel-eyed vixen? I mean, I can't blame her; it should be illegal to look that good in work clothes. A vision of Goldiloc's figure out of her bartending attire makes me shudder. God, she's perfect. Do lesbians really move that fast? What was that joke about the second date and the U-Haul? Will Naya be dating her in a couple of days?

Khloe, stop.

I glance down to find the napkin with Derrick's number is crumpled. I push it to the side and signal the bartender.

"Excuse me, can I have a shot of tequila?"

"Coming right up."

A few minutes later, the shot appears in front of me. I gulp it down in seconds. The burning sensation momentarily takes over the tornado in my head. Then, the idea appears like a light bulb. The apps! Maybe there's someone I can meet up with when I get off of this boat. I pull out my phone and open one of the many apps Naya downloaded, BQ. Black Queers. An app specifically tailored to the black queer community. I usually only date black men, so that means I would date black women too, right?

I inhale a nervous breath and exhale. Yes. Black queer women. Let's start there.

I try to scroll, but a pop-up blocks my view.

Would you like to narrow your search?

I look up from the screen and into the crowd of people around me, searching for the meaning of that question. Narrow my search? What do they mean? What's more specific than queer black women? Surely, they don't mean light-skinned and dark-skinned. Not in this day and age.

I select the yes option, but a sea of search filters open, all of which I have no idea what they mean.

Femme, butch, stem, stud, female-presenting, non-binary, power bottom femme, versatile stud, the list went on and on. I read the words repeatedly, hoping to find their meaning. What category does Naya fit in? That's the one I need to pick. I can't tell if it's the choppy waters or the tequila sneaking up on me, but a hint of nausea rushes to the pit of my stomach.

Okay, forget it.

I push the button titled *no filters* and return to the search.

A list of profile pictures fill my screen. Another pop-up drops.

Swipe left to pass. Swipe right if you're interested. Winky face.

What does that mean?

Is this an app for sex or dating?

Stop overthinking.

Just swipe left or right. Simple.

Out of the twenty profiles I look at, I swipe right once. Once for a girl with sweet eyes and a mocha complexion. Bria. A pretty fresh face, with little makeup on, just a little foundation and mascara. In one of her pictures, she sports an oversized T-shirt and cargo shorts with a fly pair of Jordans. In another picture, she shows some of her hourglass figure, in a crop top and jogger pants. She isn't completely girly, but she isn't too masculine, either. She sits somewhere in the middle. A tomboy, kind of like...Naya.

Damn it.

I close the app and open another one, The Beanery. I silently giggle at the dirty innuendo as I explore the profiles. This app was for queers of all backgrounds. That's it. Maybe I should explore non-black women. Anything as far away as Naya as possible. I scroll and scroll...and scroll some more. A Filipino girl with a stunning facial structure and abnormally perfect breasts. A sporty white girl with a snapback and toned biceps on full display in her tank top. There was even a Middle Eastern girl whose username was Israeli_Princess. She looked like something straight out of a magazine, strikingly gorgeous. Most of those women are, yet I can't bring myself to swipe right on any of them right now. Somehow, my brain finds a way to compare the women to Naya.

"Oooo, this is my song!" Tiana hollers as the sounds of *Missy Elliot's One Minute Man* rain through the speakers. "Let's dance, y'all, I'm tired of wasting my time on this yacht! Let's dance!"

We rise from the bar stools and grab our belongings. Dancing. Having fun. Anything to distract me from thinking about—just as we are about to leave, Goldilocs reappears behind the bar. She pulls her shirt down and washes her hands at the sink while asking another patron for their order. I glance back at the entrance of the club to find Naya standing in the doorway, looking as cool, calm, and collected as ever. She spots the rest of the crew and snakes through the dance floor to meet them. I look back at the bar to find Goldilocs mixing a drink with ease.

Is this what after-quickie energy looks like? This nonchalant?

Memories from my own sexcapades flash through me. The most I did with my college boyfriend was steal kisses in the guest bedroom when he invited me to his mom's house for Christmas. Sex on a yacht is level 28 in comparison.

Okay. You don't know if they had sex, Khloe. Why are you so fixated on it?

They could've been talking or playing Scrabble or whatever it is lesbians do when they meet. Whatever it was, Naya probably looked gorgeous doing it…

Okay. That's enough.

"I'll meet y'all on the floor!" I call out to Tiana and Leah, who are already several steps ahead of me. "I'm going to order another shot!"

Goldilocs is on the opposite end of the bar, but I scoot a few more inches away to ensure I catch the attention of her coworker instead.

"Excuse me! Can I get another round of tequila?"

The burn sets fire down my throat as I gulp down the alcohol.

"Thank you!"

I get up and slide a tip toward the bartender. Woah. The feeling in my knees feels like the boat is going through choppy waters again.

Our bodies sway on the dance floor. The cast recites the ending lyrics of a Cardi B song. Everyone else seems to move easily, but I can't shake the feeling of the boat shifting beneath my feet. Fighting currents, wave after wave. I stumble a little with every couple of moves, bend my knees more, and switch up the groove, hoping nobody notices. I fight the sea motions for two more songs, and then something catches my eye. The disco ball in the center of the floor looks radiant, even more so than when we'd arrived. Its rays of light beam through the club, decorating the walls and reflecting off the bodies gyrating to the music. It even looks a little fuzzy, as if lint is around each light ray. Keeping the groove in my hips, I follow a fuzzy ray of blue light from the disco ball to—

Wow...she looks...wow.

Right there, in the path of that fuzzy light, Naya is laughing with Bunny as she pretends to belly dance to the sounds of *Hips Don't Lie by Shakira*. Together, the two attempt the motions from the music videos, but the thing is, Naya isn't pretending. She's good, really fucking good. The blue light beams onto her body, highlighting all the right places. She waves her arms up like a sorceress. She continues winding her hips, then rotates. A full display of her curves. When I finally break my gaze, I realize no one is watching. Everyone is engulfed in their own world. Their own dancing. Their own sidebar conversations. I am the only one under her spell. Naya breaks out of belly dancing and starts rapping to Wycleaf's section of the song like she is Wycleaf, holding an imaginary mic in her hands. That tomboy is alive and well, but she embraces her womanhood, too. And that's sexy as hell.

With newfound confidence coming from God knows where, I walk up to her, stopping just arms-length away and mirroring how she's swaying her hips. Her eyes widen for a split second when they meet mine, but she quickly adjusts her face and flashes a sweet grin.

I rock my hips from side to side while staring straight into her eyes. She tears her gaze away and starts singing the song lyrics to others around us. But no one hears her. Everyone remains wrapped up in their world. I inch forward, closing the space between us a little more. I'm not sure if it's the dancing or tequila, but my body hums with warmth. Naya switches her groove into a two-step, rocking her body from side to side, step touching, and—wait, why is she moving that way? She uses the two-step to move backward and recreate the distance between us in one swift movement. Not far enough to feel awkward, but just enough feet to disconnect the energy between us.

Unsure how to hide the disappointment on my face, I start singing the lyrics and clapping. I increase the intensity of my dance moves, too. The perfect cover-up to act like I wish to have more dancing space too. No matter how large I made my dance moves or how much alcohol I've ingested to distract me, I can't ignore this feeling anymore.

I want to be in Naya's space.

I want her to touch me. Even if it's just a brush of the hand.

I want her to look at me the same way she'd been looking at Goldilocs earlier.

I want to stand centimeters away from those cocoa butter-soft lips.

My mind flashes back to the interaction between her and Goldilocs earlier...I need to bolder. I need to establish what I want.

Her.

CHAPTER THIRTY-TWO

NO MATTER how many ways I alter my dancing or how many retracting steps I take, I feel it. The fire. Electric strikes. The laser coming from Khloe's fixated gaze on me.

Why does she keep invading my space?

The worse question is, why do I like it?

My head is fighting hard to think logically.

The rules, Nayara. Your rules. To save you from messy drama and heartb—

Oh my lord.

Khloe steps toward me, completely closing the air between us. As if that didn't do enough damage, she places her hands on my waist and positions her right leg in between mine. With just enough pressure to make my skin catch fire, she squeezes my waist and leads my body into a swirly side-to-side movement with hers.

I let her take control as my eyes wander all over her body. Her abs beaming in the light. Her thick thighs brush up against me ever so slightly, making me want more.

And...

Ugh, I can't take this!

Her chest is just centimeters away from mine. If I so much as take a deep breath, my breasts will graze hers. If I bend down a little, I could probably get a taste. I envision my tongue running from her neck, down her collarbone and to her breast. Taking a small piece of her bikini top between my teeth and moving the fabric to the side to see what's behind... To taste what's behind...

Khloe halts my daydream because she ends her side-to-side movements, pulls my waist to hers, performing full body rolls against the front of my body. With each roll, our bodies make contact. Our chests, down to the center of our stomachs, until the body roll finishes with her pelvis brushing against mine. Her center is directly on mine. With each roll, she increases the pressure little by little, adding more moisture to the pool forming in my bikini. Thank God for the thickness of these cargo shorts. I'd just left Jean a couple of minutes ago! Usually, it takes at least half an hour for me to get aroused again. What is Khloe doing to me?

This has to be the worst it can get. I can feel her breath hitting my collarbone. Her hands keep slipping from my waist and closer to my hips. I just need to stay calm, separate and...

Khloe, who has been looking down at our moving bodies, glances up at me with a smirk and—

Fuck.

That dimple will be the death of me. It's too much. The body rolling. My hips ignite from her touch. And how dare she place her center perfectly on mine? Through clothes? But when she smirks with those dimples staring back at me, I almost climax on the dance floor.

I grab her hands and throw them from my hips, a little harder than I intended.

"Whew, I need some water! Worked up a sweat!"

I cut through the crowd and straight to the bar, leaving Khloe on the dance floor. I'm too embarrassed to look back.

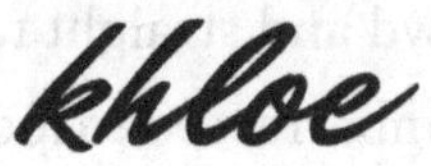

THE SUN BEAMS down my back, along with beads of sweat. There's plenty of shade by the jacuzzi, so most of the boat attendees have traveled over there to flee the sun. Too many people. Too many energies. My volatile energy needs as much space as possible. So here I am, in the pool, alone, directly in the sun.

There are other places I could've gone, but after Naya left me on the dance floor, my brain went into overdrive. All I could think about was running to the restroom to wipe up the fluids threatening to seep through my bathing suit bottoms. After cleaning up, the inferno pulsating through my body led me straight to the pool, which was miraculously still cool despite the unforgiving sun.

You came on way too strong, Khloe.

No wonder she ran away. You basically tried to dry hump her on a yacht full of people. Well, how else was I supposed to stand out from Goldilocs? Not all of us can do wonders with a sexy gaze and a soft hand rub!

Doesn't matter, you could've been more composed. Instead of being a bi-curious horn dog.

My mind travels back to us on the dance floor. The way our bodies moved in sync. The flames beneath my skin every time different parts of our body made contact. I've never been that aroused *and* fully clothed. Even after collecting myself and dipping into this pool, my core still murmurs with a heartbeat.

I've had sexual tension with men. I've thoroughly enjoyed sex with men. But whatever happened earlier... That was more than tension. That was different. It was energy. An electric rhythm. Electric and out of control, like no matter how close Naya was to me, I wanted to be closer. I wanted our clothes to melt away, to feel nothing but skin between us. I wanted to touch every inch of her. That feeling overtook me and any ounce of self-control I had left.

But this is your time to explore, Khloe. To be free. This is what you wanted. This is what you talked about before going on tour.

Yes... but not with a woman who doesn't date coworkers! She already told you. She signed you up for the apps, for heavens' sake. Naya looked at that bartender with an intensity I'd never seen before, another side. An intoxicating, primal side that she whips out when it's time to pursue women. A side that she's never shown you. Not during the tour. And definitely not during rehearsals. I'd put myself in her vicinity during most of that month of rehearsals. She kept it professional no matter how many forced questions I'd asked her. She never noticed. Fast forward to today. She ran away like something was chasing her.

Well, maybe my attempt was too public. She seemed kind of embarrassed when Bunny aired out her business about meeting Goldilocs. Perhaps she's a private lover.

There's only one way to find out...

"Excuse me, ma'am, would you like to order a drink?"

A server appears at the edge of the pool.

"Yes, can I order two more shots of tequila?"

CHAPTER THIRTY-FOUR

BUNNY, Tiana and Rae hang their heads out of the car windows while belting out the lyrics to *Sweet Tooth by The City Girls*. Rae claps her hands to the syncopated beat. Bunny and Tiana take turns bouncing lyrics back and forth.

The Uber driver raises the volume to fuel the mobile concert. I take a breath for the first time in about an hour. My body settles into the seat as I enjoy the mobile concert, thankful to be far away from that boat. How I ended up hooking up with Jean while struggling to get Khloe off my mind—only to end up body-rolling with Khloe moments later is beyond me. Something I would've never thought possible a month ago during rehearsals. That is enough action for me to go to my hotel room and never come out.

When we left the boat, Uber XLs were nowhere in sight, so Khloe and DayDay separated and ordered their own car. That had to have been God, the universe, and guardian angels looking after me because there is no way I could've survived another moment near

Khloe. Those suggestive facial expressions, that taunting dimple, and her perfectly crafted figure. I don't want to see her in a bathing suit ever again. I already steer clear of her during costume changes in the middle of the show. I hope to disappear altogether next time I am in a dressing room with Khloe.

We pull up to an empty hotel. Either we are here early, or Khloe and DayDay beat us. Regardless, I am thankful not to have laid eyes on her.

I hug all the ladies goodbye, allowing them to stroll drunkenly toward the elevator as a group. Instead of following them, I make a quick right into the hotel restaurant. After the day I'd had, I need the greasiest food on the menu.

I slide my tip across the counter and grab my to-go food.

"Thank you so much. Have a good day."

Taking a few steps out of the restaurant, my hand explores the brown paper bag, hoping to taste at least one fry before I get up to my room and go in. Scarf down the food, take a bath, maybe read a few pages of my book, and get some sleep.

The perfect plan.

"Shit!"

A crashing noise and whispered curse word echo from around the corner. Once I round the corner and discover the cause of the noises, the handful of fries in my mouth almost fall to the floor.

Khloe is standing in front of the elevator, bent over, picking up everything that fell out of her purse, the source of the crashing sound moments before. Tiny receipts, lip gloss, credit cards, perfume, and cash riddle the floor around her as she struggles to grab it all. Her hands ramble against the items, but the mess stays the same. Her wrinkled skirt sits over-rotated and discombobulated around her body. The slit that once sat at the top of her thigh was now positioned in the back, and exposing her entire ass hanging out of her bathing suit bottoms.

Stuffing the fries back into my mouth, I hurry to her. In one swift motion, I grab the waistline of her skirt and tug it to the right, just enough to cover her rear end. I whip around to the front of her and reach for any items she hasn't picked up yet.

"Here, Khloe... I got you."

Despite having touched her to rotate her skirt, she hadn't noticed. She pulls her eyes from the floor only after I speak, acknowledging my presence.

"Naya!" she squeaks a little loudly.

She adjusts her bathing suit top and runs a hand along her baby hairs to make sure they are still intact, all while maintaining a consistent sway from side to side.

"What brings...you ...herreee?" she slurs.

"Oh, nothing crazy, I was hunting elephants and decided maybe it was time to turn it in and go up to my room."

"You're... sillllly." She attempts to nudge my shoulder, but the movement causes her to stumble to the side. I reach for her arms to steady her balance.

"And you're drunk. Can I walk you to your room?"

Her head sinks into her shoulders with shame.

"Yeah...um.. you can walk me to my room. I'm sorry if I am being sloppyyy."

"Hey, you are fine. All you did was drop your purse. What floor are you on?"

"Sixxxteen."

Is this a cruel joke? Why didn't I notice we were on the same floor when we checked in this morning?

When the elevator doors open, Khloe steps off, composing herself as best as possible until she arrives at room number 1608. Okay. At least we aren't neighbors. My room, 1637, is at the other end of the hall.

"All right..." I lean in the opposite direction. "I just wanted to make sure you made it to your room safely. Have a good—"

"Fuck! I can't find my room key."

"It's okay, we can go back downstai—Are you okay?"

Khloe's small side-to-side sway somehow develops into a full-fledged, cross-legged, pee-pee dance.

"Do you have to pee?" I chuckle.

"Yes! And it's not funny!"

"My room is down the hall. You can use my bathroom and then go downstairs and get another key."

"Ugh!" She groans while holding her crotch. "What room number?"

"1637."

She takes off in a light jog, leaving me in front of her room, eyes wide and mouth gaped.

"Wait! You need my room key!" I run to catch up with her.

The second I unlock my door, she bulldozes past me and straight into the restroom, slamming the door behind her.

"I'm sorry! I'm so embarrassed!" her muffled voice rings through the walls.

"It's okay! Don't be!"

I take the rest of my fries out of the to-go bag and sit on the foot of my bed. They'd cooled down but are still hitting the spot! A balanced amount of crispy and salty woven into each bite. Ambient sounds of the toilet flushing and Khloe washing her hands fill the silent room.

"Shit! Sorry!" The sound of clattering objects accompanies Khloe's profanity.

"I knocked down some of your hair products!"

"It's all good, boo!"

Her clumsiness warms the smile, spreading across my cheeks.

Moments later, the door swings open, and Khloe steps out with a wide grin of relief.

"Thank you so much! I thought I wasn't gonna make it—Oooo! Can I have a fry?"

Before I can answer, she plops beside me and palms a handful of fries. She stuffs them into her mouth without a care in the world. Completely unaware that the outside of our thighs are touching because of how close she sat next to me.

"Hmmm." She moans. A real moan. A sound that rattles through my body and straight to my core. "These are perfect! Crispy, but not burned. Thick, but not potato wedges. Salty, but without hypertension knocking at your doorstep."

"What are you? A fry connoisseur?" I tease.

She swats my shoulder. "Shut up! Not an expert, but I know my fries! I know what's good and what's trash. Now, lemme have more!"

"Nope!" I lean back, switching the bag to the hand furthest from her and lifting it toward the ceiling. "You are not killing off my fries. You gotta get your own, ma'am!" I stick my tongue out, taunting her.

"Come on! Those are award-winning fries!" She inches closer, reaching her arm across my body and toward the bag.

"You need to take your connoisseur tail downstairs and get your own!"

She extends her arm further until her bottom foot slides out from under her, causing her to lose her balance and fall forward. The impact launches the bag of fries into the air, causing them to rain all over the floor. This would usually upset me, but something else was too busy overtaking my mind.

Khloe has fallen so hard she lands right on top of me. Her forearms, which by the grace of God have caught her fall, keeping us from head-butting, rest by my sides. Our bodies lay flat against each other. Our stomachs, chests, everything tightly pressing together. My body buzzes beneath her, but her face tugs the most of my attention.

Her face is just centimeters away from me. So close I can feel her unsteady breath graze my lips. I thought I struggled when we danced on the yacht earlier, but this, whatever *this* is, is stealing every ounce of breath I have left.

Khloe's eyes search mine. A look that is both empty and full of something else. Her eyes flit to my lips, then back up to my eyes. Our bodies are still, but that pulse I felt earlier returns with a vengeance. The strange yet familiar rhythm beats under my skin. The feeling of her warm skin against mine, her breasts grazing mine even with bathing suit tops in the way, sends shivers through my spine.

I have to go. *She* has to go. We have to leave this room now.

"Shit, I'm sorry." I lift onto my elbows against her body weight. "I play too much."

She leans down and places a soft kiss on my lips.

"Khloe..." I break away. "Hold..."

Those are the only words I get out. Khloe pushes my upper body back onto the bed, deepening the kiss.

Forget breathing. All the oxygen evaporates from the room. The walls are closing in around us. My restraint holds on by a thread. But I don't give a damn. I kiss her back. Her soft, full lips crash against mine. Her tongue explores mine, and I welcome it. In one swift motion, her hands slide down to my hips, pulling them to hers. Pressing her center against mine. Gentle at first, then again with intensity. Grinding against me as I press back, playing a sweet, yet dangerous game.

"Wait. Stop." I raise our bodies back to a sitting position. "You've had a lot to drink. I don't want you to do anything you are going to regret in the morning."

Plus, you're different. I can't mindlessly fuck you on a drunk night. If this ever happens, I want to be stone-cold sober, with hours to spare. I want to take my time and explore every part of you, from the curves on your body to that intoxicating dimple.

"Oh, my goodness." Khloe hops up from the bed, smoothing her skirt. "I am so sorry. I didn't mean to..."

"Don't overthink it. It was a moment, and we can forget it ever happened. Or whatever you'd like to—"

She bolts out of my hotel room, leaving me, my whirling hormones, and the French fries on the floor in silence.

CHAPTER THIRTY-FIVE

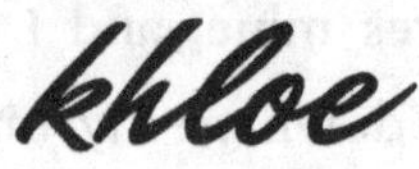

I DON'T KNOW what time it is. The only thing I can be sure of
is this insistent sunlight pounding through my eyelids. I try scanning the room around me, but see nothing but stark white sheets,
hunter-green hotel carpet, and half-zipped luggage staring back at
me. Why is my mouth so dry? Why am I still wearing this bathing
suit? And where the hell is my silk scarf?

In seconds, scraps of last night flood into my brain. The yacht.
Multiple fatal shots of Tequila. And... oh no. Naya. I bury my eyes in
the palms of my hands, praying it was all a nightmare.

Khloe, how could you? Why on earth did you make a pass at her
like that?! She's already made her stance very clear. She does not
pursue dancers. She signed you up for dating apps *herself*! Hell, she
practically undressed that bartender with her eyes last night before
they disappeared to ... *Ugh!* I don't even want to know. What I need
to know—what I need to get through my brain is that Nayara

Alvarez does not want me. She couldn't wait to push me off her during that dumb kiss. It probably repulsed her.

"Okay," I announce to the empty hotel room. "I need to get it together. I've been unraveling since I left for the tour... or maybe before then—Whatever! The point is, you."

I turn to the right and study my reflection in the decorative mirror.

God, I hope my neighbors can't hear me talking to myself.

"You, Khloe Thompson, need to reel it in. You need to focus on your job. The job that jump-started your career. The job you desperately prayed for. You will not spend this precious experience trailing after a woman who isn't remotely interested."

Before uttering my ultimate affirmation, my eyes sink deeper into the mirror. I need to commit this entire moment to memory. Yesterday's clothes on my body. The smell that accompanies this crusty wardrobe. The cotton mouth assaulting my tongue and throat. And the most terrifying, the crippling embarrassment that is about to wrack my nerves when I see Naya again.

"Khloe. You don't even know if you like women. You've been on two dates. Don't blow up your professional life acting like you're on some wild college spring break. This is work."

Although my butt is falling asleep, I am appreciative that Rae came over to redo my cornrows. After a much-needed shower, food, liters of water and tidying my hotel room, I finally feel like a normal human being. Well, as long as I never step foot near a bottle of tequila ever again. Rae tugs a section of hair tighter than the rest.

She's a little heavy-handed, but the convenience of this setup outweighs all the cons.

Thank God I ended up on tour with a coworker who can braid. Lord knows the pickings are thin in some of these cities. On top of the horrible hangover, my cornrows looked like I was doing head spins on the hotel carpet last night! Fuzzy and raggedy. Just like my behavio—

"Girl, will you stop moving?!" Rae bellows.

"I'm sorry! All those shots are still affecting my motor skills!"

"Hold it together, Ms. Blame-it-on-the-alcohol. I just need to finish two more braids, and then I'll be done. Are you sure you don't want to come to the movies with me and Leah?"

They are going to see a cutesy rom-com hand-picked by Leah. A genre right up my alley. Meet cute, enemy-to-lovers trope, riddled with the perfect amount of humor along the way, or at least that's what it seemed like from the trailer.

Rae hasn't mentioned Naya in these plans, but I can't leave room for any surprises. Earlier, I had already made a risky run to the lobby Café. I carried as many bottles of water and electrolytes as my arms could manage. I'd managed not to run into her then, but will I be so lucky next time? It is probably best to face my issues head-on, but today, my primary focus is returning my blood-alcohol level to a sane level and mustering up the strength to face Naya *tomorrow*.

What will happen next time we meet? How will she respond? What do I say?

I'm sorry I kissed you. I'll clean up the fries I spilled in your room... but you must've already cleaned it up.

All the shots last night... made me act on my attraction toward you.

No.

All the shots last night made me act unladylike.

Unladylike?! That's something my grandmother would say!

She hasn't responded to the group chat about the movie, but what if she meets everyone there later? I imagine Naya arriving at the movie theater just as we've already sat down, leaving her to occupy the only vacant seat next to me.

"Thanks again for the invitation, but I need to hydrate and eat carbs. I am taking the day to rest. I'm not even sure if I'll leave the room."

"I understand! Pro-tip: Order delivery food, call the front desk and request that hotel staff bring it up to your room because you are 'under the weather'. Usually, they are very strict about guests meeting their food deliveries in the lobby, but they care more about the cleanliness of their establishment!"

"Oh! That's a great idea! I will do exactly that."

And successfully avoid Naya.

CHAPTER THIRTY-SIX

NO MATTER how many times I try, I can't stop my eyes from floating over to Khloe's makeup chair. I apply concealer, then look. Glue eyelashes on, then look. Close my eyes to dab eye shadow on my lids, peek up in between dabs, and look again.

Khloe has been avoiding me for three days. Three show days. Three cities: Tampa, New Orleans and Houston. There's no hotel to hibernate in. We've been sharing dressing rooms, retiring to the same tour bus at night, yet she's still alluding me like a pro. It's almost as if she planted a tracker on me that beeps whenever I'm near. She hasn't done her makeup in the dressing room in days. For the past three shows, she's arrived thirty minutes to showtime, with her edges laid and a stage-ready face, leaving her with just enough time to get dressed and head to the stage.

In the show, there are certain moments we share. Fragments of time when we are about to start a routine, finish a difficult one, or walk by each other to switch formations. Usually, we exchange silly faces or smiles during these moments. Brief flashes of connection I share with all the cast. It's one of my favorite parts of touring, the camaraderie you build with your fellow dancers on stage. The knowing glances, veiled jokes and the secret language only the dancers comprehend. The same language signaled Bunny and me to help Zion with his mic pack several shows ago.

With Khloe, that camaraderie has been nonexistent. She avoids me like the plague. When we pass one another on stage, her eyes focus ahead. Moments we'd usually exchange a smile or silly face, she cranes her neck to another dancer instead. She even keeps the act up off stage, practically running to showers after the show, being the first to leave the venue, board the bus and crawl into her bunk for the night.

She isn't the only one always missing. Rae has also been arriving in the dressing room thirty minutes before the show. While Khloe shows up stage ready, Rae appears as the exact opposite, bulldozing into the dressing room with a bare face, hair fuzzy as if she hadn't wrapped her hair the night before, and hectic energy buzzing like she'd just ran a marathon. Each time someone asks where she's been, she chirps, "Went to see some friends!" while struggling to slap some lashes on.

Tiana does the usual during glam time, having a tense, whispered conversation with her boyfriend on the phone in the dressing room corner. Or her nails are angrily texting into the phone in between makeup applications.

Bunny and her man have been in good standing, so she has been doing her glam with Bluetooth headphones snug in her ears and using her sweet, sexy voice to talk to him before the show. She's more present after the show, but that's probably because he's at home with his family by that time.

Leah is still as pleasant as ever, but her buzzing pre-show energy has dwindled a bit. It's really early in the tour for the energy to shift like this. Usually, this type of shift doesn't happen until halfway through the tour.

We are barely three weeks in.

Like clockwork, Khloe floats into the dressing room with stiff shoulders, her attention focused on her makeup chair.

"Hey, y'all," she murmurs to the room.

Everyone mumbles their response and returns to their tasks, everyone except me. I rotate and watch Khloe as she sets her bag down and unwraps her hair. She adds one more spray to her edges and setting spray onto her face. No matter what she does, her eyes avoid me at all costs. After finishing her final touches, she treads over in my direction. And just when I think she's finally going to acknowledge me, she strides right past me and turns on the sink next to my chair.

"Hey, Khloe," I say through a forced smile.

"Hey," she mutters with shifty eyes.

"How are you doing?"

"Good."

I pause, wondering if I should force any more of this enriching conversation, but Rae bursts through the door. Hair undone, a face bare and her sporadic energy tunneling like a tornado. Just like clockwork.

I lay inside my bunk, staring into the complete darkness, as the bus barrels down the highway. It's 6 a.m. and I'm still waiting for sleep to grace my body. Because Dallas is only a four-hour drive from Houston, our bus call was 3 a.m., leaving Zion with enough time to have another party in his dressing room. I went to see if Zion's entourage had invited any pretty women to distract me, but as usual, they were there for Zion, and Zion only. They batted their long lashes at him, laughed too loudly at his jokes, and twerked with extra vigor in his eye line.

I have a theory that Zion actually has after show dressing room parties to raise the chances of his homies getting lucky. He rarely ever gets close to the groupies. They scatter around the dressing room, vying for his attention, but he usually stays on the couch smoking or playing cards with his friends. And as of late, he's been leaving the parties early. He entertains everyone for about an hour, then disappears from the dressing room altogether, leaving the groupies to turn their attention to his friends instead.

Bunny had entered the dressing room party, grabbed a drink, and walked straight to the bus. Leah and DayDay didn't go at all. They snuggled up on the bus and watched Mean Girls in the back lounge. Rae was at the party for about half an hour, then said she was going to go meet up with her cousin who lives nearby. Tiana came to the party with her phone tucked away in her purse. She never took it out! Never sent a text or nothing! But after I saw her down four shots and talk to any man looking at her for longer than two seconds, I figured her intentions were elsewhere. She giggled and flirted with some guys in between drunken slurs. After stumbling and trying to pour another drink, I walked up to her with a knowing look.

"Maybe it's time to get back on the bus."

A flash of sadness fell over her eyes before she agreed. I accompanied her to the bus and returned to the party, where I spent the rest of my time playing spades with Zion's friends and watching women hang on their arms. Khloe never made it to the party or any of the previous nights.

I had got through three shows with Khloe's strange behavior, but I almost lost it after the Houston show. She'd dropped something from her bag coming out of the bathroom after the show, probably from trying to rush to the bus like a bat out of hell. She stood before me, wrapped in a towel, freshly showered and free of stage makeup. Meanwhile, I was still in my show costume, stage sweat still glistening on my skin. All I wanted was some toilet tissue so I could start taking off my makeup. As I walked toward the restroom, Khloe popped out, practically jogging past me. As she skirted by me, a t-shirt fell from her bag, so I reached out and tapped her arm. A light, fingertip-grazing touch. But Khloe's body jumped like someone tried to mug her in an alleyway. Knees buckling, eyes widening and all.

"You dropped this," I say, handing her the shirt.

After the initial shock dwindled, she snatched the shirt and speeds off. Strange behavior is one thing, but acting afraid of me is another.

It was a kiss.

A damn kiss.

"Ladies! And DayDay!!" I hear our tour manager yell outside of our bunks.

I don't even feel the bus come to a stop, much less hear our tour manager board. We poke our heads out of bunks like sleep-deprived groundhogs.

"I have good news and bad news." She pauses for a second, taking in our blank stares. "Good news is we've arrived in Dallas, and the hotel rooms are ready for check-in. Bad news is every decent hotel in the city is at capacity because of the Cowboys game down the street, so for this city—and this city only, you all will share rooms."

A string of groans trickle through the bus, mine being the loudest. I haven't experienced this since my first tour. We had shared hotels for the entire three months. No personal space, no privacy and most importantly, no bachelorette pad to bring women to. And when we realized the rest of the crew—sound department, lighting, stage assemblers and production received *their* own rooms, we raised hell. We petitioned the Dancers' Union and won. It is now unacceptable for any touring jobs to enforce shared rooms. So, after this little announcement, I'll be making a very passionate call to my—

"We have already contacted your agents and added a $500 bump to your paychecks this week for the inconvenience."

"Well shit, can we buddy up in any other cities?!" Bunny bellows.

"I'm afraid not, as this will not be a regular occurrence." The tour manager chortles. "Anyway, the bus will be parked at an off-site location about fifteen minutes away, so grab whatever you need for the off day. You'll check out at noon tomorrow. I've already assigned pairs for the rooms. Please listen for your name: Leah and Rae, Tiana and Bunny, and Naya and Khloe. DayDay, you'll be rooming with Mike from the lighting department.

The rest of her words trail off. My thoughts suspend, and I'm pretty sure my chest concaves.

I whirl my neck to look back at Khloe, who's already shut the curtain to her bunk and is rummaging around inside.

Maybe I should ask Bunny to switch?

Wrong. She'll know something is up immediately. If Khloe is this weird about a kiss nobody knows about, she might quit this job altogether if she hears Bunny teasing me about it.

It's okay, Naya.

It's just one off day.

One day. We check out the next day and off to the next city.

CHAPTER THIRTY-SEVEN

THE HOTEL GUESTS on the ninth floor probably think Khloe is a six-foot linebacker. Because the force she's using to drag both of her oversized suitcases down the hallway makes her bags thump into the walls with each step.

I had offered to help, but Khloe muttered, "It's okay."

She nearly ran to the room while I followed a few feet behind. We finally arrive at our room, the last room in the hallway, furthest from the elevator and my greatest pet peeve.

"You can take whichever bed you want."

I gesture to the two queen beds in the moderate hotel room.

"Mhm."

Thank God she buries her face in her open luggage because I can't control the eye roll that leaves me. Is she *really* going to go all day without speaking?

I unzip my luggage at my side of the room and take out my toiletry bag. Usually, I'd go straight to sleep after pulling an all-nighter, but Khloe's weird mood hits my body like an espresso shot. I grab clean clothes, undergarments, and my hair products. With the wonderful smells of sweat, weed, and a cocktail of all the dancers' perfumes having cemented into my curls over the past few days, I am in dire need of some TLC. So I barrel into the restroom, praying Khloe's strange energy remains on the outside. If only it could be that easy.

No matter how much I try to focus on my hair, shampooing, detangling, and conditioning, thoughts of Khloe trickle in.

I should've talked to her sooner. The day after the kiss. Seconds after. When she ran out of my room that night, I should've chased after her, nipped this in the bud, because look at us now, sharing a hotel room, uneasy energy whirling in all directions.

About thirty minutes later, I'm sitting in the office chair putting on sneakers when Khloe exits the bathroom wrapped in her towel.

"Where are you going?" she asks, with more acknowledgment than the past four days.

"I'm having trouble going to sleep, so I'm gonna go downstairs and eat breakfast. See if the food settles me."

"Oh…" A wave of disappointment flashes over her face. "Me too."

"Well, you know, you don't *have* to sit with me. I'm pretty sure there will be plenty of empty tables."

"Yeah. Of course."

"I guess I'll see you downstairs."

"Mhm."

If she says that one more time, I think I will explode. I turn on my heel and exit the room. When I arrive at the breakfast buffet, I load my plate with food, hoping to get Khloe off my mind. With no care for presentation, I pile eggs, pancakes, bacon and hash browns on the plate. I place the plate on the closest table and go back to the fruit bar.

As I fill my bowl with an assortment of fruits, someone else arrives at breakfast. I glance up to see Khloe, standing in the middle of the seating area, staring at me with—*is that fear?* Her brows furrow, matching the tension in her hiked shoulders. Her body language is palpable. She takes slow, timid steps toward the buffet as if the boogeyman himself is getting food.

You know what? Fuck this.

I throw the entire fruit bowl into the bin of dirty dishes at the end of the buffet and storm out. My breath pulsates with my rage as I tread one foot in front of the other. Once I'm outside, I fumble through my purse until I find half of the joint I smoked last night.

I position the joint at my lips, light the end, and draw in a sharp breath.

Being awkward is one thing, but acting scared is outlandish.

Khloe stares at me as if she's seen a ghost. As if we weren't together moments prior. I've done nothing to make her afraid of me.

What the hell is her problem?

I finish the joint in what feels like seconds and make my way back up to the room. The silent elevator echoes the sound of my tapping right foot. It's like the joint hasn't calmed me one bit. When I throw the door to the room open, Khloe is inside. She freezes, halfway tucked into bed.

"What did I do to you?" I ask a little too loud as I march toward her.

"Nothing."

"Your behavior is far from nothing. Get up!"

I yank the covers off of her legs, already feeling a cloud of regret in the back of my mind. I never wanted this conversation to be so forceful, but tranquil Naya is gone. This is hurt Naya. Nayara, from high school, caught kissing a girl under the bleachers, only for that girl to tell the entire school that I coerced her. Nayara, who had to watch the same lying ass girl act scared of her for the rest of the school year. Hurt Naya also doesn't care about these skin-tight pajama shorts and her braless chest in this see-through white tank top. Hurt Naya needs answers.

"What are you doing?!"

"No, Khloe, what are *you* doing? What is up with you? Yeah, we kissed. One alcohol-induced kiss. I tried to talk to you about it, but you ran out of my room at the speed of light. I gave you space while you avoided me this whole week. Space is one thing, but acting scared—looking like you've seen an abusive ex or something? That's overkill and, honestly, a trigger for me."

"I am scared," she says, barely audible.

"What?"

"I said I am scared!" she says with more volume, this time rising to her feet.

Tears wallow in the corners of her eyes but don't break through. Silence falls between us, and all I can hear is the sound of her breath hitching like she's trying to hold in a sob. No matter how hard I try to fight it, seeing this side of her softens me.

"Scared of what?"

"Drunk or not, I think I still would've kissed you. It sounds crazy, but I don't know. I've got these *feelings*..."

Her voice breaks a little, making me regret snatching those sheets off her even more.

"What kind of feelings?"

"I don't know. I'm just drawn to you. No matter what I do—the dates, the partying, that man practically throwing himself at me on that boat... I can't bring myself to let loose, explore, pursue hookups I know hold no future."

"Why not?" I ask, unsure if I'm prepared for her response.

Then she just says it.

"Because I want to pursue a future with you."

She stands firmly with her voice, carrying each word. If my mind weren't tumbling into an abyss, I would acknowledge how proud I am of her, too. This is the same woman who had stammered to oblivion a couple of weeks ago just to ask how long I'd been dancing.

"I'm not saying I want to be your girlfriend or anything like that. My life is kind of messy... and I don't even know if you're the serious dating type." She continues after my lack of response. "I just don't care about these people on these apps. When they talk about where they grew up, I wonder about *your* childhood. When they approach me and their eyes study me suggestively, I think about what it would feel like for *you* to look at me that way. Yeah, I was excited about kissing Eli 'cause I'd never kissed a girl before. But it took milliseconds into the kiss to wonder what it feels like to kiss *you*, Nayara."

Don't you dare do that.

I was listening. I was ready. Preparing to deaden everything. Deny my attraction to her. Never admit that my thoughts drift back to her no matter what beautiful woman stands before me. She'd already been chipping away at my armor with every word spilling from her mouth, but Khloe Thompson saying my full name, always considerate enough to do so with correct pronunciation, unwinds me every time.

Her words drown out for a moment before I return to reality.

"But I'm almost always a pile of nerves, and I don't even know if I'm your type. I look nothing like Goldilocs. Or whatever her name is. I'm sorry. I just had to distance myself for a second. It was rude but—"

"Can I?"

"What?"

Confusion scrunches her face. Her expression could crumple like a paper ball and still take my breath away.

"Can I kiss you?"

I enclose the space between us. If I take a deep breath, my chest will graze hers. The firm stance she took earlier softens, and her shoulders relax with an unsteady breath. Khloe's eyes flit down to my lips, then back up to my eyes.

"Please."

CHAPTER THIRTY-EIGHT

SPARKS CRACKLE through my limbs as our lips collide. Naya's hands cradle the base of my neck, her thumbs drawing soft circles onto my cheek. My body relaxes into Naya's, but fear glues my hands to my sides. A recipe of shock, excitement, and fear taking control.

"Do you want me to stop?" Naya whispers.

My overthinking will not ruin this. I refuse to be the reason the very moment I daydream about comes to an end.

"No." I take her hands and reset them on my waist. "We are not stopping."

I wrap my arms around her neck and sink back into her, this time parting my lips. Hints of fruit invade my mouth as her tongue explores mine, most likely from the watermelon-flavored gum I've seen her chew so often. Naya's sandalwood cologne encompasses the surrounding air. The exact smell I've been working so hard to avoid now undoes me. Our tongues dance around with ease as if we've done this a million times before. Her hands are dormant on my waist, immobile, almost as if she is still trying to be respectful. But I don't want her to respect me. Not now. I know for a fact Naya is respectful. I've seen it in the way her eyes laser into mine when we speak instead of roaming over my body like I'm a piece of steak. Hell, she put an end to our first kiss because of my alcohol intake. She's so tender with me. I know it. I love it. But fuck that. I want her to handle me. I want to know her ravenous side.

Palming a fistful of her soft curls, I press my body into hers. I suck on her bottom lip and bite down gently. A low moan escapes Naya, forcing life into her hands. She lowers them onto my ass, digging her nails as she pushes her hips into mine. The electricity in my body amplifies, traveling straight to my center, loathing the clothes in our way.

If I want more, I am going to have to be the one to say it. Demand it. Confident and steady. If there's any uncertainty in my voice, Naya will put an end to all of this. Sit me down. Talk. Ask if I'm ready, blah blah blah.

"Naya." My lips break away, but our bodies stay as one. Her almond eyes peering into me.

"Yes?"

"I want you."

"Are you sure?"

Her concerned eyes search into mine.

"Naya, I want you to fuck me."

CHAPTER THIRTY-NINE

NAYA LAYS me on the bed, steadying her body with her left hand and hooking her right arm in the small of my back to ensure a soft landing. Trailing light kisses down my neck, she uses the same arm to raise my hips to hers.

I wonder if she can feel the moisture seeping through my shorts, but those thoughts cease because she removes her hand from my back and cups my breast. Naya draws small circles over my pebbled nipples, threatening to slice through my tank top, and sending waves of pleasure to my core. When she pinches ever so slightly, I throw my head back, and my hips buck. With everything in me, I fight back the urge to climax right then and there.

"Woah." Naya squeezes harder, allowing her eyes to observe my jolting body. Her sweet almond gaze changes into something else. Something hungry. "Not yet, Khloe. We've barely started."

A giggle escapes me.

"I'm sorry. I've been daydreaming about this for a while. Excuse me if I'm a little eager, Nayara."

It was as if my words were a green light, signaling her to move forward. Because the moment her name leaves my lips, she rips my tank top, taking my nipple in her mouth. A loud moan crashes through me. For a second, I wonder if it's too loud, but I don't care. With every lick and swipe of her tongue, the throb in my core intensifies.

Keeping her mouth glued to my breast, her hands travel all over my body, trailing my stomach, squeezing my thighs, clutching my ass, and gripping my hips. Firm but soft. Searching. Claiming. Taking ownership of every inch of skin I've wanted her to have since the beginning. She brings her hand to the waistband of my pajama shorts, fumbling with the elastic. I hoist my hips up so she can slide the shorts down, but Naya pauses, looking directly into my eyes.

"What happened?" I say through labored breaths.

"Nothing. You are just... absolutely beautiful. You weren't the only one daydreaming about this. Forgive me, but I'm trying not to rush this moment. I want to savor it, savor you."

I can't explain the rush of warmth that rushes from my stomach to my cheeks. It isn't lust. It's something else. I dot soft kisses up her neck, along her cheek, and to her lips.

"I don't wanna rush either. But just know, there will be plenty of other times to savor."

What did I just say?

And just like that, I admit I want this to happen again and again and again. We are barely fifteen minutes into our first time, and I am already aware of the drug I've introduced into my life. The drug I am going to crave for weeks to come.

Something flashes over Naya's eyes as if she's read my mind. Then she presses her fingers on my core. My body seizes as she presses firmly.

"Ms. Thompson, I'm afraid you've soaked your shorts."

Naya circles the pads of skilled fingers on my clit.

"This is how wet you make me, Nayara. I can't control it."

Naya tugs my shorts to the side and slides two fingers into me, moving at a gentle pace, in and out. My moans scatter along the walls. I can't take this. The teasing. The slow pace. I am about to explode. Sensing my rise to climax, Naya stops. She brings her fingers to her lips.

"Damn, all of this is for me?"

"Yes," I rasp.

She keeps her eyes locked on me and takes both fingers into her mouth. I almost unravel right then and there.

"Damn, you taste good. Can I taste more?"

"It's yours, Naya. Taste how much you want whenever you wa—."

Before I can utter another word, Naya yanks my shorts to my ankles, and I wriggle out of them. The second I part my knees, she tastes me. Soft and tender. Exploring every part of my clit. It's all becoming too much. My body trembles, but I fight it off. Holding on with the ounce of restraint I have left.

"Nayaaraaa."

As if my call was a signal for more, Naya deepens herself into me. She tightens her grip on my hips, forcing me further into her mouth. Her nails dig into my skin slightly. A tinge of pain that only intensifies the pleasure. A pain that I know I'm going to crave again. Tongue flicking, teeth nibbling, and—what? Pleasure crashes through me when I peer down to find her softly sucking on my clit. Eyes searing into mine.

"Naya." I rasp. "I can't... I'm gonna—"

"Come for me, baby," she mumbles against my center.

The vibrations from her throat wreck me. Forcing my hips to buck wildly back and forth against her mouth. Her nails dig deeper. Her tongue slashes in patterns I'd never thought possible. Foreign sounds escape my throat and bounce off the hotel room walls. I shouldn't be so loud, but I don't give a damn right now. I don't care about anything because the only thing I can focus on is the way Naya is unwinding me at the seams, like a balloon losing air, sputtering out of control until landing on the ground lifeless.

When I lift my head again, Naya's eyes are still on me. A wide grin as she wipes me from her face. The sight makes my body convulse all over again. Naya lands kisses from my center, up my stomach, chest, and neck until she reaches my lips, where I taste myself on her tongue.

CHAPTER FORTY

I LAY ON MY BACK, arms folded behind my head. The decorative hotel room ceiling tile taunts me. After all the resisting, avoidance, darting my eyes in the opposite direction when her bubbly gaze passes me, or playing it cool—all of it went to the wind last night, and my self-imposed tour rules right along with it.

Five tours. I'd survived five tours without sleeping with a coworker. Sylvia's suggestive eye contact. Kim getting all touchy, grazing her fingers across my hands and legs each time she spoke to me. Stefanie smacking my ass every time we got off stage. And that's just the beginning of my experiences. During one tour in South America, Diane Walters, one of the highest revered dancers in our industry, and very straight, looked at me dead in my eyes and said, "You know, Naya, I feel like you'd fuck me until I couldn't speak English anymore. And I'm tryna to test out the theory."

And no matter how hard my pants jumped, I'd maintained control.

I'd survived all that, yet every ounce of my restraint crumbled last night. I don't know who that was with Khloe last night. Why the hell was I so timid? Me? Nayara Alvarez.

Is this okay?

Are you sure you want this?

Can I touch you here?

I'm all for consent, clear permission to be intimate, but I'm more of a do-you-want-to-spend-the-night-with-me? Let's-find-some-place-quiet. You-want-it-fast-or-slow? Type of girl. I might as well have been giving Khloe a whole questionnaire last night! What am I? A prepubescent baby gay?

Judging by a couple of exasperated yeses she gave me, I'm sure Khloe is over my display of manners, especially for someone as aroused as she was. My stomach turns when I think about how drenched she was... for me. I was too enthralled to give a damn about the volume of her moans, sounds I pray none of our cast mates heard.

"Hmm," Khloe mumbles next to me, freezing my body.

I almost forget that she is sound asleep next to me. But how could I forget? Her vanilla scent has engulfed the air between us. Each time she stirs, her cocoa butter legs brush against mine. And best of all, her soft snoring has been the soundtrack to this room for the last two hours. A cute version of white noise, I'll be sure to tease her about later.

As I turn my attention to her, Khloe's eyes peel open.

"Morning," she rubs sleep from her eyes. "You seem up. Did you nap at all?"

Nope.

"Yeah, I woke up a couple of minutes ago, just in time to hear you sleep-talking."

"I do not sleep talk!" She nudges me from under the covers. "Or do I? What did I say?"

"You were calling someone's name. Mumbling at first, but then it got clearer."

She leans into me. An expression I can't exactly place washing over her.

"Who's name?"

"Something with a D... Di, no Don." I snap my fingers. "Oh, I remember, it was Deez."

"Deez?"

"Deez nuts!"

Okay, I really might be a prepubescent baby gay, but she makes it too easy to mess with her!

"You know what?" She grabs an extra pillow from the headboard and whacks it into my face. "You are such an ass! And that's an old ass joke!"

I return the gesture by hurling the pillow across the room, flipping my body on top of hers. I interlock my legs and arms so she can't move and position my fingers directly into her armpits.

"What'd you say?" I squint menacingly.

"Naya..." She fidgets. "Don't you dare."

"Huh?" I wiggle my index fingers ever so slightly, sending her body into a spastic jolt.

"I'm ticklish! Stop!" Khloe's laughter echoes through the room. She throws her chin back, grinning from ear to ear.

"Really?" I wiggle my fingers again. "I would have never guessed."

"You play all day!"

"Who, little ol' me?"

"Yes, you, Nayara!" She attempts to wiggle out of my hold but fails again. "You know what? Why don't you play with this instead?"

Khloe lifts her hips to mine, somehow landing in the most perfect spot and forcing a groan to rumble my throat. Her smile, once playful and joyous, transforms into a sly smirk, tantalizing and sinister. She lowers her hips and raises them again. I return the gesture, applying the same pressure.

"I could play *this* game all day."

* * *

"You know you can't bring a kitten on tour, right?" I say, but Khloe is already several feet ahead of me, practically running to the doors of Dearly Loved Cat Rescue. After our second round of... escapades this morning, we got some food, but instead of returning to the hotel, Khloe insisted we come here.

"I know I can't! And there are no kittens here!"

She holds the door open and signals me to walk in. A receptionist says we are welcome to look around and to let her know if we need anything.

Then Khloe continues, "This shelter is one of the largest in Dallas. This girl on TikTok said it was the second largest in all of Texas, and it's specifically for adult cats. The cutie poos-poos that are often looked over because everyone prefers kittens."

"Cutie poos-poos?"

"Yes, like this little guy right here!"

She puts her palm up against a glass wall. Behind it sits a

medium-sized cage with an orange cat inside, sound asleep and balled up next to a blanket. The label on the cage reads Sir Mittens. Seconds after Khloe places her hand on the glass, Sir Mittens wakes up and stretches his paws out toward Khloe.

"Oh, aren't you just the cutest?"

The cat meows as if he understood her words. Now that he's up, I can see the white marble swirls in his coat.

"He is kind of cute."

"Kind of?"

"Just look at his wittle face!"

Khloe continues talking about Sir Mitten's handsome cutie-patootie face for a few moments, and then we move on, walking further into the shelter and stopping to talk to more cats along the way. It's like watching her on that Everglades tour all over again. Cheerful. Bright. Free from nerves and any uneasy energy related to the Soakin' Wet Summer Tour. I like this Khloe. I wonder how many people get to see her. It's cool to be the person she reveals this side to.

At the end of the hallway, we reach the last glass wall, but instead of a cage, there's a room riddled with toys and cat houses. There's a sign on the door with a picture of Garfield that reads: Want a playdate? Ask the receptionist to let some of us meet you!

"Naya!" Khloe gasps.

Already sensing where this is going, I ask, "So, who should I tell the receptionist to bring out? Sir Mittens and..."

Khloe has cat hair all over her. A few strands have also made their way to my clothing, but Khloe's chest and thighs bear traces of Sir Mittens, Mew, King Fluffington, and Binx. I've enjoyed our time in the playroom, but I spent most of it taunting the felines with laser toys and cat nip. Khloe has been full-on hugging and baby-cradling each little pootie-tootie. I never knew the possibility of so many pet names until today. Khloe's full of them. At the beginning of the play-date, we were side by side on a wooden bench, but it took no time for her to follow Mew to the floor. He's one of the more cuddly of the bunch. While the rest chased the laser toy with me, Mew stuck to her and pooled in her lap, cuddling and purring. Now, Khloe has him cradled in her arms like a baby, and he seems to be in heaven. When we first left the hotel, Khloe's choice to wear a skin-tight unitard stressed me out. I was overstimulated and ready to take her back to bed for round three. But now, watching this scene unfold, I cannot care less about what she has on. Watching her in her element, in utter bliss, is all I need.

Just when I think this couldn't get any cuter, Mew stretches his paw out and rests it along Khloe's collarbone.

"Oh! Did you see that?" Her eyes fling to mine, catching me already staring at her.

Fix your face, Naya. I'd been staring for so long that I probably looked like a lovesick puppy. That wouldn't be right, though. That would imply that I am in lo—

"Are we gonna talk about last night?" Khloe says.

I'm thankful she tore me from those thoughts before I completed that sentence.

"You mean last night and this morning?"

A sheepish closed-mouth smile forms on her face, leaving her dimples on full display. She sets Mew down and rejoins me on the bench.

"How are you feeling?" I ask, unsure of how to begin this conversation.

I'm usually great at the morning after talks, but this time, it's tougher. With every passing second, Khloe's bubbly brown eyes staring into me hurl all my usual responses into a jumbled mess.

"I'm feeling fine. Surprised… a little confused, but overall proud of myself."

"Proud of your first lesbian conquest?" I joke.

"No!" She chuckles. "Well, yes. I've never been so honest about my feelings before. I mean, you did demand an answer for my weird behavior, but at another point in my life, I would've denied everything and made you feel crazy."

"I appreciate your honesty, but even if you lied, I think I would've sensed something was up. I knew you had a little…energy toward me."

"Really?! No way! How?"

"For one, Khloe, your eyes drop to my lips when I talk to you. I've seen how you interact and hang with the rest of the cast, but you are especially attentive to me. Confiding in me, inviting me places with you, touching me a little longer than normal. I was holding the verdict out, ready to classify it all as regular friend behavior, but that first kiss confirmed my suspicions."

"Ugh, that first kiss. I'm sorry about that. I didn't even know if you wanted to do that."

"Don't be sorry." I shrug. "I think it's safe to say I was *more* than okay with the kiss."

A nervous giggle escapes her lips. She picks up Mew, who's circling her legs and sits him on her lap.

"That's true. That's true. Well, you also had a few telling signs yourself, Ms. Alvarez."

"Oh really? Enlighten me Ms. Thompson."

"I'm not sure if you're aware, but you do some looking yourself. Mostly, you're very respectful. No matter what I'm wearing, you always look straight into my eyes, but there were split seconds where your control faltered, and your eyes would fall to my chest. Or I'd turn around, and your eyes lifted from my ass, then to my eyes. It always heightened my body temperature, and I couldn't pinpoint why at first. I developed pretty early as a teen, so I'm used to long stares and people looking at me like I'm a piece of meat. Usually, it makes me feel filthy, sending shudders down my spine. But with you, I felt a tinge of disappointment each time you looked away."

My eyes drop to my hands, clasped and tense on my lap.

"I apologize for that. One thing I believe most women understand is discomfort from being gawked at. Because of what I've experienced as a woman and 'one of the guys,' in groups of men, I vowed never to prey on women unless I'm getting clear energy."

"Hey." Khloe places a hand over mine. "Don't be sorry. Like I said, I didn't mind at all. I was actually trying to figure out how to signal that I wanted more, then Goldilocs gave me an entire masterclass."

Chuckles shake my shoulders. "Excuse me? Who is Goldilocs? Are you talking about Jean from the yacht?"

"Yes." Khloe throws her hands over her face. "I'd never been *so* emotionally confused in my life. A part of me was jealous that she took no time to grab your attention. Another part couldn't look away 'cause I felt like I needed to take notes or something. Then, when she took you away to God knows where. I wanted to jump ship all together!"

"Not jump ship!" I laugh, trying to control the grin spreading across my face and the twinge of embarrassment gracing my cheeks. "Wanna know the only thing I remember from that boat party?"

"What?"

"Mister Cool Guy with a chain swooping in on you. Stepping in front of me like I didn't exist, in order to get to you. And the worst part was I couldn't get my mind off it while I was with Goldi—I mean, Jean."

Khloe throws her head back in a full fit of belly laughter, an infectious mood that travels to me, too.

"This is absolutely crazy. We are crazy." Her smile rests while her eyes wander off for a couple of seconds, acknowledging the other cats in the playroom. "But you know, it's a relief to know that I wasn't alone in those hectic thoughts. It's even more relieving to be talking about all of this with you... in the middle of cat shelter. I know we haven't known each other for long, Naya, but you make it easy to talk to you... about the hard stuff, the uncomfortable parts of life a lot of dancers skip 'cause it's encouraged to be overly chipper in this industry."

"And that is one of the many bullshit parts of working in this industry, unfortunately. But I assure you, I'm here for all the talks. Anything you need."

I place my hand on her knee and offer a gentle squeeze.

Khloe lowers her hand onto mine and returns the squeezes.

We talk for a few minutes longer before the receptionist comes in and announces our time in the playroom has ended. We talk about other moments leading up to last night—stolen glances, prolonged touches, the whole nine. But during the entire talk, we fail to discuss the most important matter: what happens now?

khloe

"DOUBLE CHECK and make sure you have all of your belongings," the Uber driver announces as we pull up to the hotel. We thank him in unison. While I'm fumbling to pull the strap of my purse over my shoulder, I spot Rae wheeling three suitcases into the front lobby. With each step she takes, her knees clash with one of the large bags.

"Rae!" I call out. "Hold up! Let us help you!"

We catch up to her, grabbing a bag each. After securing the luggage and seeing her from the front, I *really* see Rae. The messy bun of fuzzy box braids on the top of her head, her gray sweat suit dotted with light sweat stains, and her face... She still has last night's show makeup on.

"Girl, why do you still have show makeup on?" I question.

Rae's eyes widen for a second. "Oh, honey. I had a night last night. Went out with some old friends from college. You know how that goes. They still act like they're still in college."

"Ain't that the truth?" Naya replies, way less concerned with Rae's story than I am.

"Wait, so you went out after the show and stayed out the whole night? After the show, you showered and left the dressing room first. When we got on the bus, I saw that your bunk curtain was closed, so I thought you went to sleep early!"

I chuckle, but Rae doesn't even flinch. The silence forces more words from my mouth.

"Wait, so you just got here from Houston?"

Naya clears her throat.

"The drive is only about three and a half hours … so my friend and her boyfriend dropped me off just now," Rae stammers.

Naya clears her throat again, bringing my attention to her.

"You need some water?" I ask.

"Naw, I'm good. I think I might be coming down with something. My throat has been feeling a little scratchy since this morning. Let's get these bags in for Rae so I can get some medicine."

"Wait, what have y'all been up to today? And why do you have animal hair all over you?"

Rae's eyes scan us up and down.

My inner thighs clench thinking about my whereabouts this morning—the places Naya's fingers and tongue were so delightfully placed.

"Uh, cats! Cat pound. I mean animal shelter."

Smooth. Real smooth, Khloe.

"Khloe is a TikTok fiend and found a shelter that lets you play with the adult cats that are least likely to be adopted," Naya adds.

Rae's questioning eyebrows relax while the corners of her mouth curve.

"That's really random, but cool. You see, I need to get into stuff like that instead of all this partying."

We stop at the front desk in the lobby and park the bags beside her.

"We'll definitely let you know next time! See you later. Get some rest!"

Naya leads the way to the elevator, presses our floor and leans up against the wall. I practically skip behind her, my intuition jumping, begging for the elevator doors to close quicker. When they finally do, my neck swivels to Naya.

"Why did Rae seem so skiddish?"

I lower my voice just in case the elevator carries sound.

"The better question is, why did you give her the third degree?"

Naya stands up straight, wraps one arm behind her back and grabs her chin with her free hand.

"Um, yes, hello. My name is Khloe The Spy, Khloe Drew, and where were you last night at around the 12:30am bus call?"

"Oh, you got jokes!"

"Hell yeah, and you're the funniest one because as soon as Rae returned the question, you word-vomited... Miss Cat Pound."

"It caught me off guard!"

I nudge her shoulders as the elevator doors open.

"She was probably doing her own thing last night," Naya starts once we are back in the confines of our hotel room. "Maybe met up with a guy or something. Remember that time she talked about a random man from Tampa who sent her money to get her nails done? I wouldn't be surprised if she has a few of those sprinkled across the states."

"Oh."

A tinge of shame heats my cheeks. I guess I did grill her. Maybe that isn't the wisest thing to do, especially now that I have a secret of my own. Wait, are we keeping this to ourselves? Whatever *this* is. I should probably ask, just in case Naya says something.

"You don't have to worry about me telling anyone," Naya says once we arrive at the hotel room.

"What? How'd you—?"

"Khloe, your face said it all." She chuckles and holds the door open for me to walk in. "We can keep this private. It's cool with me. Plus, it'll be one less thing for Bunny to grill me about."

"Right... Cool."

I force a smile, though I'm unsure what to make of the Bunny comment.

Our phones buzz in unison, ensuring that my thoughts cease.

Soakin' Wet Summer Tour Core Dancers Chat

Leah: Hey guys! I'm with DayDay doing some shopping, and we are planning to see that new Marvel movie today! Y'all wanna come?!

Rae: Aw, that sounds awesome, sis, but I'm gonna stay in and rest tonight.

Judging from what I saw earlier, it made sense that Rae wanted to stay in. My fingers freeze over my screen, unsure of how to respond. Silence falls between Naya and me. I should probably go out with the group. Avoid any suspicions. But the truth is, I need at least one full day to process. One day with myself before I face the rest of the girls.

Me: I'm gonna stay in, too. I think a bug is going around.

Tiana: I'm down. Let me know a time.

Bunny: Me too.

Naya: I have some friends here I'm gonna meet up with tonight. Thanks for the invite! Let me know how the movie is.

"You have plans tonight?"

I do my best to mask the disappointment in my words.

"Yeah, I had planned to have a solo movie night at the hotel, with chips, greasy delivery food and with some random girl I slept with last night."

"Oh, really? Some girl?" I step toward her, enclosing the space between us. "You don't know her name? What a shame."

In one swift movement, Naya picks me up, wrapping my legs around her waist.

"Naya!"

She ignores my shriek and walks toward my bed. The bed I laid in for seconds last night before realizing I wouldn't be sleeping in it at all. The sheets were still crisp and hardly disrupted. Meanwhile, Naya's bed is a rumpled mess of sheets. Pillows out of place, and the mattress on a slight diagonal. Evidence of our actions.

"The only shame here is that I'm not sure if I'll ever get the chance to inconspicuously share a hotel room with her again." Naya throws me onto the bed and climbs over me. She props herself on her elbow while her eyes study my face, fire radiating from her as she takes me in.

"This booking fiasco was the best mistake this tour could've made, and I'm taking advantage of it."

* * *

Ending credits scroll down the screen, but Naya remains as attentive as ever.

"This is where they show all the cute bloopers!" she chirps.

She's sitting at the desk at the other end of the hotel room, steadily rocking back and forth while finishing a bag of kettle popcorn. Because of her no eating-in-the-bed rule, I opted out of snacking to remain snuggled up under the sheets, which proved to be the best decision because I had the perfect view of the movie and a wide-eyed Naya.

"You know, when we met, I never would've pegged you as someone that loved *Bring It On this* much."

"The sequels are touch and go, but the first movie is a classic— an early 2000s masterpiece! Easily one of the most quotable of our lifetimes."

Excitement drips from Naya's words.

"Okay. I sat quietly while you anticipated all the big scenes and mumbled lines under your breath, but this is where I draw the line, Ms. Alvarez. Most quotable? What about Mean Girls, Friday, White Chicks—Hell, I'll even take Hocus Pocus, but Bring It On? You're buggin'!"

Naya ignores me, then cracks up at one of the last bloopers. Something tells me she's already seen it before.

"I'm buggin'?! Naw, you wildin'! White girl drama, black girl drama, highlighting appropriation before it was a 'woke' topic, *and* women in skirts? It's got everything we need!"

She throws the kettle corn bag onto the table and rises from the desk. Shoulders high and a plastered ear-to-ear smile, Naya claps her hands and recites a cheer from the movie. Word for word, arm placements in sync until she ends the show with a herkie.

"Boo! Tomato! Tomato!" I jest, throwing a pillow in her direction.

"Oh, really?" Her hands slowly clasp over a pillow at the end of the other bed. "You don't wanna play this game with me."

I take hold of another pillow, eyeing her carefully. "I think I do, Nayara."

As if my saying her name was the equivalent to an announcer yelling, "On your marks, get set, go!" we fly toward one another. Pillows flying, limbs bracing, and hair swinging with each blow. It's utter chaos. She takes a big swing, aiming for my right arm. I dodge the attack and deliver a blow to her left thigh. Naya stumbles back, and I seize the moment to land a blow to her leg again. Just when I think I have the advantage, she wonks me right on the top of my head, sending me to the floor. I flip my eyes up to the sight of her standing over me, a smug smirk curving the corner of her lip.

"Gotcha." Naya winks.

I'm on my knees, but I use every bit of my strength to hurl my pillow into her. The force propels her backward a couple of inches behind the bed, where she trips over something beside my luggage I can't see.

"Ahhh!" she yells, falling onto her rear end.

"Shit! Are you okay?!"

Once I crawl over to her, I see the cause of the fall. A stack of books I pulled out of my luggage while I was searching for clothes this morning. Back when all I could think about was how I'd survive a room with her.

"I'm good, just a little confused, though." Naya blows a curl out of her face.

Here we are, on the floor beside the bed, amongst strewn pillows and the bed sheets Naya grabbed to ease her fall. I reach out and tuck another stray curl behind her ear.

"Why?"

"Because I need to know why you have a miniature library next to your suitcase."

"Oh, shut up!" I playfully smack her leg, trying to ignore how soft her skin is against my fingers. "It's just a couple of books!"

"A couple of—Khloe, I tripped over one, two…eight books! Eight—wait a minute, what kind of old English books are these?"

"They aren't old English! They are historical romance novels."

"Khloe." Naya's eyes flat line, her expression calling bullshit. She points at the cover of the book on top of the stack. "This woman's dress looks like it's from the 1600s. And this man with flowy blonde hair, he is a classic Disney male love interest douche bag."

"The story takes place in the 1800s. His name is Prince Aaron, and he's not a Disney douche or whatever you said. He's arranged to marry another affluent royal but ends up falling for his handmaiden instead."

"1600s or 1800s. It is still old as dust." Naya rolls her eyes. "I just can't believe that's your preferred genre—sounds no different from the *telanovelas* my grandma used to watch when I was younger."

"Well, what do you like to read since you have so much to say?"

I snatch my book from her hands, doing my best to hide the tinge of embarrassment tickling my cheeks.

"I like nonfiction, mostly self-help and memoirs."

She sits up, but we remain on the floor with balled-up limbs, leaning in toward each other like two teenagers having a sleepover.

"Typical."

I spit out before I can rein it in.

"What do you mean by that?" Naya says sternly.

"Nothing serious. I'm sorry." I take a breath. "It's just… It's hard for me to find similar book interests among dancers. They always lean toward those genres, while I've always loved fiction."

"Why?"

"Well, I could ask you the same thing."

I can feel my blood heating. People say Virgos don't like to be questioned. I can't help but wonder if that's the truth.

"Fiction is nothing but made-up stories." Naya begins with an even tone. "And historical fiction? That's just a bunch of over-policed, sexually deprived women finding love in a society where men are praised for doing the bare minimum."

"And has-been celebrities usually write memoirs looking for a quick check. Leaving the work poorly written and self-centered."

"Yes. That can be true, but I specifically like memoirs about influential black women: actors, writers, and producers. It doesn't matter which industry they are in because they all have one thing in common. They devote years, most times decades, to their work before someone 'discovers' them. Usually, white people. For example, after Love Craft Country, mainstream magazines deemed Journey Smollett, Breakout Artist of the Year. That woman has been acting since she was a little girl."

"Damn. And our auntie Angela Basset deserves way more Oscars."

"That's what I'm talking about. Years of work, little to no recognition. It's inspirational to read about the resilience these women have. And as far as self-help goes, who doesn't want to be a better human, emotionally or financially?"

I stare at her blankly, replaying the words she'd just said.

"Why do you prefer historical fiction?" she asks, breaking the silence.

"There aren't too many sex scenes. If there are, they aren't vulgar. There is no naming of genitals or dirty talk. Things are more masked. The author might describe a woman's wetness as a warmth between her legs and a man's erection as his desire, instead of the blunt vernacular used by our generation. They write less about the sexual act and spend more time on the tension leading up to it. It's refreshing."

"Okay, Khloe Shakespeare." She picks up a stray pillow and tosses it at me. I take hold of it midair and nuzzle the plush onto my lap.

"I see what you mean. But why not incorporate a little nonfiction from time to time?"

I pause for a second, wondering how I should answer Naya's question. Honest words? Or should I raise the guard that I use with the rest of the cast? I scan the messy hotel room again, taking in the bed we'd broken in this morning.

We've already surpassed one boundary. Hell, what's another gonna do?

"Nonfiction is real. Too real. Fiction can be whatever your heart desires. Whatever you need at the moment, and most often, I need the escape."

THE SOOTHING SOUNDS of *WAP by Cardi B and Meg the Stallion* grace our dressing room. All of us are at our own vanity, deeply engrossed in our glam routine.

Because of the way the vanities line the circular room, they allow the center of the room to be a makeshift dance floor for DayDay, who is twerking on all fours. His shift, if one could even describe any job in the entertainment industry as such, usually begins thirty minutes before showtime when Zion gets dressed, leaving him with ample time, which he spends twerking and singing in our dressing room.

I section off and apply product to my hair. Bunny is laying her wig with the expertise of a seasoned cosmetologist. One of the many talents dancers often pick up in this line of work. Sometimes, we are the makeup artists, models, hair stylists, nail technicians and more, so if you don't pick up at least one of those skills, you're left at the hands of whoever the job provides. This tour didn't hire a glam team, so it helps that we all know how to fend for ourselves. Bunny was good at wig application in college, but since we moved to LA, a city where people want your first-born son in exchange for the service, Bunny took matters into her own hands, getting better and better with each try. Now, she has a side hustle laying dancers' wigs down for events and auditions.

Tiana is doing her makeup but has spent the last twenty minutes on her under-eye concealer alone. A task that demands five minutes at most. In a perfect world, she'd be breezing through the process, but she keeps picking up her phone every couple of minutes to text. And judging by the volume of her acrylic nails hitting the screen and the small furrow in her eyebrows, those texts are going straight to her man. During the first week of tour, the group was very involved in her relationship issues, offering advice and solace as much as possible, but now, everyone keeps to themselves. Minding their business while Tiana's relationship issues hinder her ability to be present on this tour.

"Bunny, please!" Leah pleads from her vanity.

"Hell naw! I gave you the aux before our last show. You had me singing Taylor Swift in my sleep that night! Keep that white girl music in ya headphones!"

"Two songs! That's all I ask!"

"Hold up!" Khloe interjects.

Because our vanity mirrors are right across from one another, I have a clear view of her and the one lash strip she's applied. With one eye batting like a butterfly and the other bare, she continues, "Not too much on T-Swift! That's my girl!"

"Her Reputation album was bumpin'," Rae adds.

She hasn't started her makeup yet because she's been swooping her edges, but she looks way more refreshed than yesterday. The wonders of water and sleep.

"So, y'all are just gonna ignore 'Love Story' T-Swift?" DayDay pauses his twerk session.

"Or 'Look what you made me do?'" Leah continues.

I glance away from the reflection of fresh curls and the small bun of what's left on the top of my head. "The woman can write her ass off."

"Ugh! Fine!" Bunny rolls her eyes and passes the speaker to Leah. "Here, but none of that shit after 2012. I only like her country songs."

"Hm, that's very specific knowledge about 'white girl music' Bunny..."

A wide-tooth smile invades Leah's freckled cheeks.

"Girl, whatever!"

Bunny fails to hide the grin creeping into her, too.

The conversation continues, but it fades to the sound of my blow dryer. I flip my head forward and perform the up-and-down motion I'd learned from a YouTube tutorial. Years ago, a hair routine was the bane of my existence. I was more of a wash-and-go type of girl, but once I witnessed the results of diffuser-set curls, I changed my ways. I position the instrument in the different parts of my head, my curls shifting with each movement. A few movements of the diffuser later, I spot a set of brown eyes peering through my curls and straight into my eyes.

Khloe has got to stop looking at me. If no one is going to suspect us, we need to act chill. I was already a babbling idiot when Bunny asked me which friends I met up with yesterday. It's going to be way harder to hide this if we are making googly eyes at each other all day.

I throw my hair back and lift my head. Through my mirror, I can see that Khloe is no longer looking at me. She's carefully applying her brown liner to her lips. Those full, perfectly symmetrical, warm—

"Who is it?" Bunny yells when we hear a knock at the door.

"Zion. Y'all decent?"

Wide glances ping-pong throughout the room. We never see Zion before the show. We'd grown accustomed to seeing him moments before the first track in the set list plays. I've never given too much thought to what he does on show days. Production keeps him separated from us, so the only pre-show responsibility I'm aware of is the meet-and-greet an hour and a half before show time.

"Yeah, we're cool."

DayDay opens the door, answering with his best masc voice. "What's good?"

Zion cranes his head in.

"Rae, can we rehearse real quick? I text BriAnn about needing help with the choreography in Act 2, but she told me to ask you."

"Oh, um. Yeah!" Rae's eyes bounce from side to side. "She sent me a text about that earlier! I'll be right there!"

In seconds, she packs up her makeup bag and is out of the room.

Poor baby. Most shows she arrives thirty minutes before curtains up and rushes all the way through her glam. On the one day she's early, Zion hijacks her time with a last-minute rehearsal. Technically, I'm the dance captain and that duty should fall on me, but if BriAnn delegated the task to Rae, I won't argue with that. Plus, I prefer not to have my pre-show routine intruded upon.

Now that I'm done with my hair, I empty my makeup bag onto my vanity. My show makeup is very minimal, so I take no time. A little concealer, mascara, a touch of bronzer and a little lip liner-gloss combo. Most female dancers may consider this look bare minimum or natural, but my mother sees it as a runway model look. Light years away from the tomboy who hated tinted moisturizer in high school.

"Forty-five minutes to showtime!" The stage manager yells from the outside of the dressing door.

"Thank you!" We all reply in unison.

"Y'all wanna do this TikTok challenge real quick?" Leah asks.

Everyone hums with excitement.

"I think I'm gonna head up to the stage early, stretch a little and get changed there," Khloe adds, sending a knowing glance in my direction.

"I'll go with you," I reply, unsure of my true intentions.

It's only been a couple of hours since we checked out of the hotel room, and I can already feel my skin buzzing around, tingling every half hour. An internal alarm clock wondering how far Khloe is and how much longer till I feel her skin on mine, again....

I am pretty sure I'll remember that hotel in Downtown Dallas for the rest of my life. The place of my demise. Where my devout rule flew to the wind. The room Khloe and I crossed a line that is going to change the trajectory of this tour, no matter what.

"You sure? Don't wanna make TikTok videos?" Khloe chuckles.

"As much as I would love to, I'm a little sore from my workout yesterday. I should take more time to warm up today." I grab my Act One outfit and small stage bag packed with the essentials like powder, setting spray and a miniature fan.

"Boo! Y'all suck! Go take care of your bodies or whatever."

DayDay rolls his neck back to the tripod and ring light Leah unfolded in the middle of the dressing room.

* * *

I set prep my pants and unwind my shoelaces for the quick change in Act Three. Technically, that's wardrobe's job, but I prefer doing it myself. This way, I can be sure everything is in its right place at showtime. Ever since the debacle from my second tour, a show where the wardrobe team forgot to set my pants for a quick change, causing me to miss the routine entirely, one could say I have trust issues.

"So, what happens now?" Khloe asks, standing by her chair in the quick-change tent. I'm thankful for the loud pre-show music carrying through the space, granting us a veil of privacy. Plus, there's usually no one near the stage. All the stagehands use this time as a break before the show begins.

"What do you mean?" I ask, knowing exactly what the hell she means. Usually, I'm the one leading tough conversations. When did the roles reverse?

"Us."

"Well, I'm not trying to marry you or anything."

It comes out more curt than I expected.

Khloe grimaces.

"I mean, not that I wouldn't want to. You're great. I just don't think I'll ever get married."

Geez, look who's word vomiting now.

"What I am trying to say is that nothing has to happen if you don't want to. I'm letting you take free rein of this. If you want to put this behind us and act like it never happened, I'm down. If you wanna get back on the apps, I'm not gonna act like a raging, jealous bitch. We are not together, and I do not own you. And if you wanna keep messing around, no strings attached... I'm down for that, too."

"No strings?" Khloe's expression perks up. "Are you sure you can do that?"

"Baby girl, I haven't been in a serious relationship in over five years. I am the definition of no strings. The question is, are you sure *you* can do that?"

She doesn't need to know why I haven't pursued a relationship in so long.

That's a Pandora's box I'd rather weld shut forever.

"Oh, most definitely. My love life was a mess before this tour, has been for a while. I don't need to jump into anything serious." She straightens her posture and salutes. "Plus, as a baby gay, I think it is my duty to explore women freely, no string in sight."

"Okay, Sargent Queer." I mimic her salute. "May you have bountiful exploration in this journey with me and whatever beauty you swipe right on. However, before you do so, there's a more serious matter we must discuss."

"What?" A serious expression falls over Khloe's face, and she lowers her saluting hand.

"Those talons on your fingers." I gesture toward her white, acrylic nails. "Unless you go on dates with a bag of toys, you gotta take those off. No one likes a pillow princess!"

I tease, but Khloe is *far* from a pillow princess. I've dealt with a few lesbians that starfish on the bed waiting for me to do all the work.

Last night, she rode me like a pro. A seasoned lesbian. Matching our centers up perfectly and rolling her hips at exquisite rhythms. She hasn't tried to finger or taste me yet, but if I'm being honest, I haven't given her much time to. Something about watching her come over and over again was enough for me yesterday.

"Talons?!"

Instead of answering, I bunch up my hands in front of my chest and tiptoe around the tent like a dinosaur.

"You're such a dick!"

"And all you're gonna give off to your new dates is 'I want dick' unless you take them off."

I stick my tongue out.

"Fine. I'll go to the salon tomorrow."

Khloe takes a step closer to me and, out of nowhere, places the pads of her pointer and index finger directly on my center. Despite my sweatpants being in the way, her touch ricochets through my body.

"You keep mentioning all these dates, but I'm not ready for that yet. I need to practice."

She moves her fingers in slow, daunting circles, nearly forcing my knees to buckle. A low hum vibrates from her throat.

"You know... make sure I know what I'm doing."

Yup, *far* from a pillow princess.

I draw in a sharp breath. "Uh, hmmmm. You can practice with me."

I barely get the words out because Khloe speeds up, toying with every ounce of control I have left.

"Can I?"

She leans in, her soft breath against my ear. I can't believe she's unwinding me at the seams like this backstage. I would never be this reckless—well, I would, but not when trying to keep this a secret.

Khloe presses her fingers harder against me. My body jolts, and I part my legs a little more.

"Yes."

In one swift movement, Khloe slides her hand thru the waistband of my sweats, boxers and directly on my clit, launching an uncontrollable moan from my lips. A guttural sound I didn't intend to be so loud, but prayed the pre-show music cascaded.

"Shhh." Khloe places her other index finger on my lips, then slowly glides it into my mouth. My tongue dances with her, matching the sorcery she's doing between my legs. "Gotta stay quiet, Naya."

"I'm trying..." I arch my back, and my eyes roll back.

"For someone that doesn't like talons, you seem to enjoy this."

A devilish grin bends the corners of her mouth, her dimples taunting yet again. She doesn't kiss me or anything. She just stands in front of me, watching, surveying with low, hungry eyes. With hooded eyes studying me, she switches the rhythm again and this time, my knees actually buckle.

"Hold on." She grabs the small of my back to keep me from melting onto the floor. "I want you to come. Here. Standing in front of me."

"Khloe..."

"Come for me."

The music fades around us. Echoed bass sounds thrum from the speakers. I bite my bottom lip to stop the scream from climbing up my throat. My core convulses a little, and then it intensifies.

"Momma, hold on a second! Imma just grab my show shoes from the backstage tent. It's a little loud!"

Khloe and I glance at each other, eyes wide. She slips her hand out of my pants and moves over to her assigned chair. When Bunny walks in, Khloe is pretending to arrange her Act Two costume, and I'm on the floor with my legs extended as if I was stretching this whole time and not about to climax all over Khloe's hand.

"Oh, hey, y'all," Bunny says casually.

"Hey."

"What's up?"

"I need to start stretching before the show like you, Naya."

"Let's make it a pre-show ritual, B! An hour before every show, let's meet backstage to stretch out forreal."

If she doesn't say yes, I fear my new pre-show ritual could be fucking Khloe in arenas across the country.

"I'm down!"

She grabs her show shoes, which are inches away from me. I pray she doesn't feel how flushed my body is. The heat percolating from my pores.

"Next show, though. Imma go finish talking to my momma."

"Okay, sis! Tell her I said hi!"

And just like that, Bunny's gone.

Khloe has unfolded and refolded her Act Two pants about five times. And my clit is throbbing.

"Maybe we can finish our stretching session later."

Khloe peers up at me through her lashes.

"Yeah, of course," I say cooly, knowing for a fact I'm gonna take me and my right hand to the bathroom to handle this immediately.

CHAPTER FORTY-THREE

THE SYNCOPATED bass drums of the last song in Act One vibrate through the speakers. My body performs the choreography almost on autopilot. With each additional show, the stress of remembering the choreography drifts further and further away. I thought all this was impossible a couple of weeks ago.

Retaining these demanding routines. Back-to-back shows. Reaching a point where I feel so comfortable in the movement, I am more present on stage. I notice everything, like Zion's alternative run in the second song. A screaming fan throwing her bra onto the stage. A fight broke out at the top of the show, which came to a quick end thanks to Zion's security team. I perform floor work, knee slides and staccato arm movements, all while watching one of the security guards carry a woman out on his shoulders. Despite all the madness, she still locks eyes with Zion and screams one last "I love you!" before being escorted out of the building.

I pass Rae during the last formation change of this song; her face is still untouched and sweat-free. What a blessing. I have to hold a mini fan and reapply setting powder every time we get a break. We decline into the last pose of this act, and Zion finishes the song with one last run into the mic. He travels from note to note with such ease. I knew a professional singer in college. She was a psychology major but toured with a viral choir on the weekends. The care in which she tended to her voice was Olympian level. Every time I saw her, she drank tea drenched with honey or held a travel-sized humidifier to her mouth. She also didn't drink or smoke to avoid drying out her vocal cords.

I'm not sure if Zion has any vocal care regimen, but the only thing that coats his vocal cords after shows are shots of tequila and blunts. Yet somehow, he sounds flawless every night. I am truly blessed to be on stage with a talent like his. Zion stays on stage, reciting a couple of lines of banter with the audience. The rest of us exit the stage, sassy, cute walks at first, then sprinting into the quick change like Usain Bolt as soon as the audience is out of sight.

Chests heaving and bodies sweating, we pack into the tent.

"Y'all seen that girl get rocked during the first number?!" Bunny yells over the stage music pouring into the tent.

She wiggles out of her shorts and flings them into the laundry basket.

"See it? I think I heard that punch over the music!"

Tiana peels her top off.

Leah laughs, already halfway dressed in her next costume.

Jokes, laughter, frantic limbs rushing to change and I can't focus on any of it. My body is changing, but my brain slows to a glacial pace at the sight in front of me. Naya, in nothing but her show thong. She's turned away from the group, as usual, out of respect, but her choice leaves me with a front-row view of her muscular shape and plump ass. My thighs clench, not only at the sight but at the memory of what we were doing in this very tent a couple of hours ago.

I'd seized control. She hadn't even touched me. Yet, desire dripped down my inner thigh. Playing in her silky juices, feeling her body shake against my fingers, almost made me come right then and there. All that energy crackling between us, evaporating the moment Bunny almost caught us. I ran back onto the tour bus and changed my underwear, with not an ounce of sexual tension left, only shock. I've never had sex in a public place before. If one could call a tent backstage public. Last night in the hotel, Naya ran the show. Fingering and tasting me until I was blue in the face, gripping the sheets and screaming her name till my throat was hoarse. I rode her a little, but that was it. It's not that I didn't want to do anything. I just wasn't sure how. Cut to a few hours later, my fingertips are winding in her sweet juices. How did I get here?

"You good, girl?" Leah asks.

After the initial shock of Naya changing, my eyes had fallen to the floor to avoid getting caught staring. Hands slowly pulling the costume for Act Two over my hips. Changing my shoes. Towel wiping sweat from my lower back. All while fantasizing about what could still happen in this backstage tent, perhaps in the next city. *No, Khloe. Naya already told you we have to be more careful.*

"Oh, shit, I'm good!" I laugh it off. "Sorry, I'm just moving slower today. A little tired, you know?"

"I totally understand! I'm dragging a little too, today. But why are you still tired? Couldn't sleep?"

An image of Naya with a fistful of my braids in her hand, tugging my head back while I ride her, flashes through my mind. Naya, fully dressed now and touching up her hair, stiffens at the question.

"Yeah, I had trouble sleeping. I think these late-night shows are messing with my sleeping schedule."

"Knock knock!" Our stage manager calls from outside of the tent. Literally saved by the bell.

"Yes?" Naya calls out.

"Any of you gals ready yet? Zion wants to do a little merch give-away before act two starts. I've got three guns loaded and ready to go."

We are a third of the way into the tour, but one thing I'm learning is that it wouldn't be a Zion show if there wasn't at least one unexpected event. Naya eyes the tent to see who's ready and willing to go with her. I just finished getting my clothes and shoes on, I still have to check my makeup in the mirror. The dressing rooms under the stage are always spacious. Individual vanities and absolute luxury for us. The backstage tent, however, is merely a conglomeration of a couple chairs inches away from each other, costumes and one full-length mirror with shitty lighting. I'm kind of thankful some ladies will leave the tent early so I can touch up my face without dancing around them. I am also thankful for this break from Naya.

"I'm done getting ready!" Tiana says.

"Me too!" Leah shakes her red curls one last time.

"All right, y'all come out with me," Naya replies, then turns her attention to the man waiting outside. "I've got three!"

Moments later, I am sitting in front of the mirror, reapplying the last bit of powder to my face. Bunny is texting, smiling ear to ear into her phone, and Rae is downing an energy drink.

"Before we get into these other songs, I got a question. Who wants some free merch?!" Zion announces.

The pitch of screaming women in the crowd is enough to shatter glass.

"Oh, y'all are ready forreal! I'm gonna bring out some of my favorite dancers to help me. Ladies!"

The crowd roars again, this time with even more vigor. I pack up my makeup bag, store it under my chair, and head out of the tent. From the wing of the stage, I can see Leah, Tiana, and Naya with large cannon guns shooting balled-up shirts into the audience. They all look like big ass kids during field day, but Naya is the biggest kid of them all.

She ducks, runs low to the floor between shots, and even army crawls like a secret agent. The blue stage lights radiate off of her skin and wide, pearly smile. With each step, her curls bounce up and down. Turning the concert stage into a t-shirt shooting battlefield. She pretends to aim the cannon at Zion, who dodges, weaves and even gets behind Leah, using her as a human shield. In between giggles, Naya redirects her attention to the audience and sends her last shirt into the air. I love seeing this side of Naya. It appears in spurts, but it is night and day compared to her usual demeanor—the chill girl that is never really affected by the stresses of tour or life, for that matter. She approaches everything with such ease. A tranquil characteristic I wish to have more of. It's easy for her, though. She doesn't have the shit show I do waiting for me back in LA. She isn't avoiding her home life *and* navigating through her sexuality. Whatever my sexuality is.

"Can they hurry this shit up?" Bunny says from behind me.

I jump in surprise. How long was she there? Was I staring at Naya? Did she notice?

"Right," I reply, trying to appear as calm as possible. "They were supposed to just go out there and shoot a couple of shirts. Now they are out there playing call of duty."

"They need to call of duty they asses onto Act Two 'cause my man is in the audience tonight, and I'm trying to spend some time with him before bus call!"

"Your man?!" I squeal. "How long have y'all been together?"

"A couple of months. Almost a year, I think. You know, I don't really be keeping track of all that stuff." Bunny trips over her words in a way I've never seen before.

"Oh, I totally get what you mean. Is he coming to any of the other shows?"

An expression I can't place falls over her face.

"Maybe. I don't know. He's gonna try, depending on his... schedule."

I open my mouth to reply, but we are bum-rushed by Leah, Tiana, and Naya running off stage, breathing heavily and giggling like schoolgirls. They hand the cannons off to the stage manager and take their positions in the wings, preparing the top of Act Two. I turn to reply to Bunny, but she's already gone to the other side of the stage.

* * *

Leah, Rae and I are snuggled under the covers, waiting for DayDay and Naya to reboard the bus after their smoke.

"Here you go, babes!" Leah hands us individual packs of Korean face masks.

"Before you sit back down," I plead. "Do you have that hook contraption with you or is it under the bus?"

Leah has all types of gadgets for body care: foot rollers, muscle creams and one of my favorites, a three-foot hook. The curved end sinks into your shoulder blade, while the other end allows you to tug down and increase the pressure, easing any knot of all tension.

"Of course, babe!"

Leah walks over to her bunk and whips the contraption out.

"Excuse me." Rae struggles to maintain her laughter. "Why do you have that thing in your bunk?"

Her snickers travel to us. Rae has to adjust her bonnet because the force of her laughter makes a loose braid fall free.

"Laugh now, but don't knock it till you try it! Imagine waking up with a little kink in your neck, then, bam!"

"Leah..." I peep in between giggles. "I can't deal with you! Now, get out of the bunk area and close the door behind you before you wake Tiana!"

"Oh, shit!" Leah says in a forced whisper, closing the sliding door behind her. "Well... is she even sleeping?"

"Hell no!" Rae joins the hushed tone. "You know she's in there, clacking away, sending angry texts to her man!"

"Shut up!" I smack her arm, though I completely agree.

"What?!"

The moment we'd left the arena, the group planned this movie night. Tiana immediately retracted. Said she'd take a rain check and join us next time. But the truth is, whether she's physically with us or not, her mind is elsewhere, enveloped in a world only she and her boyfriend occupy. Bunny is also in boyfriend world, letting us know she'll be having a late dinner with him after the show. But the difference is Bunny seems happy. A visible twinkle in her eye when she speaks about him. An audible flutter from the butterflies in her tummy. Night and day compared to Tiana's permanent frown and labored sighs when she's messaging her man.

"Why are y'all whispering?!" DayDay hollers from the entrance, making us all jump.

Naya follows behind him with a smirk on her lips.

"No reason!" Rae squeaks.

I lower my head, digging the hook tool into my shoulder. Leah switches her direction to the unopened wine bottle on top of the kitchen counter.

"Wine, anyone?"

"Please." Everyone says almost in unison.

After everyone fills their cups and claims their snack of choice, we return to the couch. I assume the same arrangement with Rae and Leah on one couch while Naya sits with DayDay on the other. Before I know it, the intro music to *White Chicks* is blessing the bus speakers. I quickly learn that I am not the only fan in the group because all of us take turns reciting lines with the actors. DayDay takes the title of super fan by the way he not only remembers lines but also reenacts certain mannerisms performed by actors. Not too long into the movie, Leah snuggles closer into me, intertwining her leg with mine and locking elbows. Rae sits on the other side, Leah twirling one of her red curls.

If I had paid attention sooner, I could've noticed Naya was lesbian way before that fateful two truths and a lie game. Every time the ladies cuddle and invade each other's space in the best girly sleepover style, Naya maintains her distance. Well, except for that night, I went to her room after my date... and Bunny was *in bed* with her. Marlon Wayans' voice booming from the screen drowns away. A sinking feeling tugs at my abdomen as my mind slowly drifts elsewhere.

How close are they, exactly?

I think back to the yacht party. The tender way Naya held Bunny's hand in the Uber. The way they were cuddling in Naya's hotel room. Bunny has a man now, but were they involved before? Because I don't think I've seen them be that close since. Everyone bursts into laughter at a scene in the movie, forcing a break from my thoughts.

"Naw, the first time I saw this, I laughed at them, saying they got their knees done for days!" Rae sips from her glass.

"No, I almost peed myself when one friend said the comment about her lips going from Cameron Diaz to Jay Z! The Wayans did an amazing job of highlighting microaggressions in a comedic way. A lot of white people hated this movie, but that's just 'cause we were the butt of the joke for once." Leah giggles, her glass of wine already making its way through her rose-colored cheeks.

That short sentence is one of the many reasons I love Leah so much. My phone pings, breaking my attention. Because of how close she is to me, Leah feels it, too. We glance down, but I shift my attention back to the movie. Then it pings again. And again.

"Well damn! Aren't you popular? Answer it, honey!"

Leah unwinds her leg from mine to give me room to dig into my pocket. As my fingers wrap around my phone, a shudder runs through my spine.

Please, Lord, don't let it be *him*.

"You matched with someone? And she's messaged you three times?!" Leah announces over my shoulder.

The tension in my chest releases.

It is alarming that this stranger messaged me so many times on the app, but I couldn't care less right now, as long as it isn't...

"Oh, lemme see her! Is she cute?" Rae climbs over Leah and snatches the phone from my hand. "Is she cute?"

In seconds, they are scrolling through the profile.

"Oh, she's hot!"

"Yamilet? Such a pretty name!"

Naya's eyes shoot from the movie to us. At this moment, I'm especially thankful for the melanin masking the blush in my cheeks.

"Girl, she lives in Tulsa! Did you plan this?" Leah asks.

I take a long swig of my wine before replying.

"No, when Naya helped me download the apps, we set them to align with the tour schedule."

"So, you're about to match with a bad bitch in every city?" Rae cackles.

"Maybe!"

I struggle to mask the nerves peeking through my laughter.

With a sinister look, Rae types into my phone.

"Well, looks like you have a brunch date with her tomorrow!"

"What?" I ask, though I heard her loud and clear.

"Aw, how cute! Please let us know how it goes," Leah adds.

My eyes cut to Naya, looking for a way out, and then she replies, "Yeah, Khloe. Have fun!"

Have fun?

khloe

A LOUD KNOCK rumbles the bus door, pulling our attention from the movie. DayDay, Naya and I are the only ones left in the front lounge of the bus after Leah excused herself to her bunk halfway through the movie. The knock is heavy, rhythmic, but slow and off-beat all at once. Like me, during those two weeks my mom forced me to take drumming lessons as a kid.

"Who is it?" I ask, but Naya is already at the door.

"Aye, what's up?! You good?!" Naya puts a bass in her voice that would make anyone think twice.

"Oppeeeeen upppp." A voice slurs from outside. "It's me, Rae!"

When Naya lets Rae in, she stumbles onto the bus.

Fifteen minutes into the movie, Rae went to grab something she'd left in the arena dressing room. Then, she'd sent a text saying she was gonna chill at Zion's dressing room function. By the looks of her buckling knees, the handful of braids hanging out of her crooked bonnet, and the smell of Hennessy in her breath, she did everything, but chill.

"Oh lawd. Somebody get this girl a bottle of water. Hell, maybe some milk, too." DayDay shakes his head.

I spring up, grabbing a cold bottle from the fridge.

"Oh, only mizu, please. I don't do stuff to require me needing milk."

Rae tries to stand straight but reaches out to Naya to steady herself.

"I'm sorry. Mi-who?" DayDay snorts. "Uh uh, I know this drunk baby didn't just start speaking Japanese!"

"Who?"

Rae looks around the front lounge for other people, then snickers into her hand, making the rest of us share in her laughter.

"Sis, do you want a PB&J or headache medicine?" I ask.

"Nooo. Just hand me another bottle of water and some crackers. I have electrolyte packets in my bunk that are ready to do magiiic."

"If that's all you need, I got you, boo. I was just about to take these old bones to bed. Come on, I'll walk you. Wouldn't want you hurting yourself by getting into that top bunk." DayDay presents an elbow. They take a few steps and stop at the door leading to the bunks.

"Goodnight." DayDay smiles.

"Night!"

"Y'all heard from Bunny? We have ten minutes till bus call, and she still isn't back." His brows furrow.

"I texted her," Naya starts. "Her Uber is five minutes away."

"Perf. Well, I love you gyals."

And just like that. Naya and I are the only two left, sitting across from each other.

I hear the familiar lines playing from the film. On the outside, I pretend to focus on the comedic scenes, but on the inside, my head is spinning. A nauseating concoction from three glasses of wine and the unexpected date I have tomorrow. A date Naya told me to "have fun" on.

A part of me wonders how she goes along with this so easily. Meanwhile, my brain is doing backflips.

"Are you really cool with me going on a date?" I say, breaking the ice.

I can practically feel my limbs calcify with every passing second.

"Why wouldn't I be?"

"Oh, um," I say, remembering how thin the door separating the bunks from the front lounge is. "No reason. Still a baby gay, so I wasn't sure if she was up to your standard."

Naya rises from the couch, walks over to me, leans over, steadying her weight on my knees and leans into my ear. With each word, her breath brushes against my earlobe.

"I don't own you, Khloe. You should explore what's out there... Just don't give it all away. Save me some."

As if under a spell, my neck gravitates toward her, wishing she'd kiss and bite, just like the other night. Feral. Primal. The perfect mix of gentle and ferocious. But she doesn't.

Naya stands back up, reestablishing the distance between us, and says, "So, have fun."

The skin she'd touched is still prickling, traveling straight to my core. I try to speak, but nothing comes out, just air Naya stole from my chest. A smirk stretches across her lips. She knows exactly what she's doing to me. Her eyes flit over me, traveling across my legs, rounding around my hips, exploring my hardening nipples threatening to cut through my t-shirt, then to my lips. The throb between my legs intensifies so much that I have to cross my legs.

"Aw," Naya says, gesturing to my womanhood, then licking her lips. "Wish I could help with that."

I think a small moan escapes my lips, but I can't tell because all I hear is the front door of the bus slam, followed by heavy footsteps up the stairs.

"Hey, y'all."

Bunny acknowledges us but keeps her eyes on the floor. She crosses her arms with sunken shoulders, holding tight at the elbows. I know that position all too well. She's not cold. She's keeping herself from breaking down.

"Friend, what happened?" Naya springs to action, wrapping her arms around her. Bunny immediately bursts into tears. I join them, trying to rub comforting circles on her back.

"He doesn't want to be with me!" Bunny hollers into Naya's shirt in between sobs. "He said he's not leaving his wife! Why am I not good enough? Why can't I find a man that wants me? Like *really* wants me?!"

"Aw babe..."

Naya squeezes tighter and kisses the top of Bunny's head. Her arms take over the space on Bunny's back I was rubbing, so I slowly break away.

"Khloe, could you give us some privacy?"

"Oh. Of course. I'm sorry. I was going to sleep, anyway. Goodnight, y'all."

I don't know how much time is passing—well, that's untrue

'cause I've glanced at my phone every two minutes. I guess I mean I don't know *what* they've been up to this entire time. Bunny's sobs stopped bleeding through the walls about twenty minutes ago, so either her crying has grown silent, or she has stopped altogether. Naya is probably giving Bunny one of her award-winning talks. Lord knows I've benefited from a few of those.

After what feels like a thousand more glances into my phone, an hour has passed by. A familiar sinking feeling in my stomach returns, one that I notice appearing anytime I think of Bunny and Naya for too long.

What are they doing?

What is the depth of their relationship?

I think back to a lesbian roommate I had in college freshman year. She often joked about the community.

"It's like being best friends with your ex, and occasionally making out is a requirement for us."

"If we have five close friends, we've hooked up with at least three of them."

"If you aren't dreaming about adopting a cat together after the first date, is it even real love?"

All stereotypes, but at this moment, waiting up for Naya like an obsessed teenager, I can't help but wonder if they are true. My mind also travels back to our afternoon at the cat shelter, but I can't even go there right now 'cause Naya might be in the next room... *busy*.

CHAPTER FORTY-FIVE

SOFT SNIFFLES ESCAPE Bunny's nose. She's not sobbing anymore, but I can feel her unsteady breath in my lap. I rub her arm back and forth, just as she did for me all those nights in college—during my lowest point.

Every breakdown, panic attack and nightmare, Bunny was there with a fuzzy blanket, tea and endless support. Bunny is a big reason why I could pull myself out of that space, so I am committed to being there for her anytime she needs the favor returned.

"I know I'm a good person and an even better partner. Beautiful, caring, and more than deserving," Bunny utters.

"Damn right." I give a gentle squeeze to her arm.

"But I wouldn't be honest if I didn't admit how hard it is to maintain my self-confidence when *these* are my dating experiences. These are the type of men that find me. Unstable, pathological liars —or worse, married. Men that treat me like the center of their universe behind closed doors but never want to love me in the open."

"That man is a fool, Bunny. A fool for not seeing the gem he had in front of him and an even bigger fool for stepping out on his marriage. That is the first indication of his stance on commitments."

"I know. I know, but when we met, he told me they were separated and getting a divorce! After a few months, I noticed there was no update on the process. He'd take phone calls in secret. We could only meet after 11 p.m. when she goes to sleep. Then, he made it seem like I was the reason we couldn't be together."

"Excuse me?" I say, struggling to keep my tone even.

"He started talking about how unorthodox my lifestyle is and how he couldn't see himself in it. 'How are you supposed to settle down if you travel for months at a time? How are you supposed to have a family? Raise kids?' Shit, I'm already well aware of this as a thirty-year-old woman! He just—I'm tired of falling for this shit, Naya. I'm exhausted."

"Friend... I am so sorry."

In this moment, I am so thankful that Bunny is facing away from me while lying in my lap because her words sting my eyes before I can control them. Though our wishes are a little different in that I don't want to settle down or have a family, we still battle issues because of this chosen career path.

Reassurance in a job depends on the health of our bodies. Dance jobs can vanish in an instant, leaving us unemployed. What happens if I injure myself? I have to pray the artist's camp offers substantial workers' compensation, a luxury not guaranteed in live stage jobs, just television dance gigs.

In a freelance career, stability doesn't exist, as you can be fired or hired in the blink of an eye. Going on a six-month tour in the winter? None of that matters if the artist cancels the tour a week before the first city. No one cares if you've declined other opportunities for said canceled tour. There is no compensation. No protection. Dancers have to figure it out and find the next job.

Work, life and social balance in a career that can take you on the road for months or years at a time, making it almost impossible to maintain proper relationships. Without the wonders of social media and FaceTime, life at home passes you by. Weddings. Graduations. All of it. When my niece was born, I scrolled through countless pictures of my entire family at the hospital in pure merriment. Meanwhile, I was on tour halfway across the country, wishing nothing more than to be there.

Bunny and I possess different goals, but they orbit the same question. When you don't want to dance anymore, what's next? What's a normal life for us? There was once a time when I wanted nothing more than a normal life. I was ready to drop it all. Move somewhere outside of the city, get a house with land and maybe open a dance studio. Have a family with *her*... But everything changed. That dream died, and that version of Naya went along with it.

"Friend?" Bunny sits up and faces me.

"What's up?"

"Your tear hit my shoulder." She reaches for my cheekbone, swiping away tears I didn't even know were there.

"Shit, my bad. Your words kinda got me."

"Are you sure?" She squeezes my hand. "Or are you thinking about Mahalia?"

The sound of her name teleports me back to that night. The chilly rain. Spinning lights. And the piercing sounds of her screams.

"Naya." Bunny's voice tugs me from my thoughts. "You know, if you ever wanna talk. I'm here for you, just like senior year. And I know the anniversary is comi—"

"I'm good, Bunny. Promise."

She opens her mouth to say something, but I give her the look.

The telepathic communication we created years ago that states, "Don't push anymore. Not now."

The same look that Bunny gives me when she talks about her red flag-ridden male love interests. And the same look I shot at her when I'd started running through women like I was trying to win some competition.

"All right." Bunny sits up beside me. "Do you want anything from the fridge? I need a bottle of water before I go to bed. I think I had a little too much to drink tonight—back when a bitch thought she scored a husband."

That's my friend, making everything into a dark joke before the dust settles.

We bust out laughing.

"Sure, sis. Can you do me a favor and grab one for Rae? Just slide it into her bunk on your way back here. Something tells me she had way more to drink than you."

"Where did she go? I thought she was watching the movie with y'all?"

"She was but realized she'd left something inside the arena and left to go get it. Then she ended up at Zion's dressing room party, and you know how that goes! I had to tap out last time 'cause that one homie of his likes to call shot o'clock every fifteen minutes!"

"The little short one? With the raspy voice? That man sounds like he smokes Backwoods for breakfast, lunch and dinner!"

"Yo, you are really crazy!"

I laugh into the palms of my hands.

"Ha! My bad. My bad. In all seriousness, though, Rae might have taken a field trip, too, 'cause Zion canceled the party after thirty minutes."

"Huh?" My neck retracts inward.

"I called his photographer 'cause I was trying to get him to send me some photos of me from tonight. I wanted to gift them to my man for—nevermind. Anyway, I insisted he do so after the party ended, but he told me the party barely started before Zion shut it down."

"Why did he shut it down?"

"No clue. The photographer said Zion just unplugged the speaker and told everyone to get out. He was probably having a little episode. You know that man has a temper!"

"Oh, I see."

"I'll slip that water into her bunk, though. At least one of us turned up tonight!"

Bunny slips out of the back lounge and shuts the door behind her. I remain still. Limbs frozen with my thoughts. The question percolates in the back of my mind.

"Where did Rae go tonight?"

MY KEY CARD unlocks the room, revealing yet another drab corporate hotel. The redundant earth tones, stark white sheets, and granite bathroom vanities from the last city. It doesn't matter what city we're in. All these hotels look alike. At least the mid-morning sun offers stunning natural light.

After rolling my luggage in, I grab my fuzzy blanket, sandalwood-scented candle, and smart light bulb, capable of changing into any color of the rainbow. I know we only have one day off, but I need to make this hotel feel a little more like home. That's one of the first lessons I learned from touring. Bring pieces of home with me on the road, and I won't miss home too bad. I morph these bland hotel rooms to my needs. Just as I finish screwing in my lightbulb and setting a dark purple hue to the room, my phone vibrates.

Khloe: So we're finally in Philly...

Me: So???

Khloe: You play so damn much! You said the break would be over when we arrived in Philly! Let's hang! What do you wanna do?

It's been a little over a week since I almost sat Khloe on my face in the middle of the front lounge on the bus. I'd thought I was doing the teasing, the one in control of the situation, but in reality, I was the one hanging on by a thread. Playing a game I had no clue would affect me just as much, if not more. I can't help the spell this woman has cast on me. The more time I spend with her, the more I learn her mannerisms, like how her eyes fall to my shape when I walk in and out of rooms. I hear her breath hitch slightly when I enclose the space between us. If Bunny hadn't walked in when she did, I think I would've lost control and broken my other rule. No sex on the bus. I did it years ago with a random hookup on my first tour, but I'm trying to be more considerate as I near my thirties. Not only was I seconds away from defiling the bus, but I also cried over my best friend's shoulder moments later while I was supposed to be consoling her. That number of emotional Olympics led me to one conclusion: I have to recenter.

So the very next morning, when we woke up parked behind the arena in Tulsa, Ohio, I sent Khloe a text.

Me: Let's keep our distance for a few days so we don't tip off the cast. Take a break, ya know. This will also give you some time to explore.

Khloe: That makes perfect sense. So when do you think this break will be over, Ms. Alvarez?

Me: Hm, how about when we hit Philly?

Khloe: Sounds good to me!

Me: Cool, enjoy that date tonight. (Winky Face)

Now here we are. A little over a week and a few cities later, and it hasn't been easy.

We snuck a few prolonged touches and lingering eye contact, but when the cast had a group outing in Memphis and Khloe arrived in a tight pleather unitard, I nearly gasped loud enough for the entire crew to hear. I even started spending less time in the dressing room and completing my glam on the bus before the show, anything to regulate my body temperature around her. But all of that is over now. I can't help the smirk in the corner of my mouth as I respond.

Me: What do I wanna do? You.

Typing bubbles flicker on the screen for a few moments before her response drops down.

Khloe: What's your room number?

The second I open the door, our bodies clash. Mouths dancing. Tongues tangled. Clothes fall to the floor, leaving me in my sports bra and briefs, Khloe in her thong and lace bra. Our hands frantically cascade over one another, gripping, searching and squeezing, desperate for all we've been starved of. Khloe grips the back of my head as I trace kisses up her neck. I draw my tongue from her sweet collarbone and all the way to her ear lobe, where I nibble slightly. I let my hands slide down her back and to the bottom of her perfectly plump ass. When I squeeze, allowing my nails to sink in slightly, she releases a moan that sends electricity straight to my pelvis. Khloe nudges my body into the foot of the bed, where she presses me back and straddles her legs over me.

"I'd like to finish what I started, Ms. Alvarez."

She sits up, legs draped over both sides of my body. The underwear between us doesn't stand a chance because I can already feel they are warm with our juices.

"What are you talking about, Ms. Thompson?" I raise my hips into hers, right onto her center.

"Mmm." Her head falls back as she rocks back and forth on me.

I bite my bottom lip to avoid the feral sound that had nearly escaped.

Then Khloe recollects herself and stares at me.

"What I started in the dressing room... This time.." She flashes her hand to me. "With no talons."

The memory comes flooding back, sending a shudder through my body.

"Please do."

Given the green light, Khloe leans forward into my ear, kissing, licking and tugging. She props herself up on her left elbow and slides her hand under the small of my back. Meanwhile, her other hand travels to—

"Uhh!"

The moan I'd bitten back earlier forces its way through because Khloe's fingers find my clit, applying the award-winning pressure. She graces my womanhood with the familiarity of someone who has known it for years.

"I can feel how wet you are through these draws. Is all that for me?" she rasps against my ear.

"Yes, baby," I reply, ignoring the tinge of panic in my chest. I don't do pet names. Not since Mahalia.

Before my mind spirals any further, Khloe glides her hand inside the waistband of my underwear and slips one finger inside me. My walls pound around her as an even louder moan rattles the hotel room. I should probably be a little quieter 'cause we just checked in, and I still don't know who my neighbors are.

"Damn, you feel so nice and warm. Wait, lemme get a taste." Khloe's hooded eyes sear into mine. She lifts her finger to her lips and takes it into her mouth. Slow and deep. Her full lips encase it all. "Hmm. Yummy."

"All yours, babe."

What am I saying? Granted, I didn't have any hookups or dates during our week break. Maybe I'm just pent-up.

Don't overthink it, Naya. This is just bedroom talk.

Khloe slides her hand back into my underwear, this time filling me with two fingers. Sliding in and out, first slowly, then picking up the pace. A scream blares from my mouth before I can reel it in. My hips meet her hand, bucking and riding to the same rhythm. Khloe watches intently, licking her lips with satisfaction.

This isn't the same Khloe who was terrified of asking BriAnn to use the restroom during rehearsals. Not the same girl who stumbles over her words when she's nervous. This Khloe is assertive, dominant and definitely not acting like a baby gay. She's moving like an experienced, full-fledged lesbian, pulling me apart at the seams. I don't even let my mind wonder why Khloe is so good at this. And what *she* may have been up to during our week break. I just grab the sides of her face and bring our lips together once again. Kissing and nibbling while Khloe speeds up the pace of her fingers.

"Uhhh. Khloe. I'm gonna—"

"Come for me, baby. Come all over my fingers, Nayara."

And just like every other time, hearing my name leave her lips sends me to the heavens. My body convulses against her as I cry out.

"Yes, baby. That's it. Give it all to me."

"It's yours, baby. All yours," I whisper.

As my quivering lessens, Khloe softly kisses my neck, face, and lips. Then a devious smile spreads across my face.

"All right, Ms. Thompson. It's your turn."

khloe

CITY LIGHTS from downtown Philly pour into Naya's hotel room. It's 4 a.m. and the only sound I hear is the air conditioning. Our fun began around noon and gave birth to the pattern that overtook the entire off day. Sex, cuddles, room service, TV and repeat. A dance that leaves me starved, satisfied and depleted of all energy all at once.

By the time 11 p.m. rolled around, we were exhausted. Earlier, one of the girls messaged the group chat about visiting Liberty Bell, but Naya and I never answered. We looked at the message and, without words, ignored it. I stayed intertwined in Naya's limbs, my head resting on her chest, feeling the soft rise and fall of her breath. That is until I woke up in the middle of the night to use the restroom. I've been scrolling through TikTok since. When the fifteenth cooking tutorial comes across my screen, Naya stirs beside me. I tense a little as she mutters something under her breath, and then she turns over and settles back into the sheets. A rogue curl has slipped from the inside of her bonnet and is sprawled out across her pillow. She tucks her arms neatly under the covers as her face peeks over the top. Regal and calm. The complete opposite of my open mouth, sprawled arms, and snore-ridden slumber. Even in sleep, Naya maintains composure. I set my phone down, ready to join her in such a relaxed state, but a text message drops down my phone screen.

Spam likely: When are we gonna talk about this?

My chest tightens, kidnapping my breath along with it. I took the advice I overheard my mother give women in the family for years.

"Don't want him to hit you up? Change that number in your phone. *Don't answer. Trash. Spam.* Whatever label you want! As long as you look at that number and do not answer!"

I never thought I'd be the one having to take her advice, but since we've hit the road, I've swiped away from countless Spam Likely messages. My eyes dart back and forth between Naya and the screen.

Maybe it's time I finally nip this in the bud.

"Hello. Khloe? Finally, you answer."

Mike answers on the first ring. I slip into the restroom and cut on the fan to drown out the sound of my voice.

"Hey."

"Why have you been ignoring my calls and texts?"

"I think you know why, Michael." The sound of his full name sounds foreign, leaving my lips.

"I've been trying to talk to you about that, Khloz."

That pet name used to make me giggle. I would poke fun at him because it sounded like he was saying clothes. Now, when I hear that name, I feel sick to my stomach.

"You wanna talk? Let's talk about your sorry-ass choices. Let's talk about the way you gallivanted overseas, putting your dick wherever it fit. Oh! I know! Let's talk about how shit followed you home. Let's talk about—actually, fuck that. Talk to your damn self. Let *me* enjoy my first tour. Let me do something without your ghost lurking in the background."

Rage stings the back of my eyes.

"Khloz, please."

"No. Let me be."

"You're fucking Zion, aren't you?"

My hand flies over my mouth to control the laughter seeping through my fingers.

"You've got to be fucking kidding me, Michael. Goodnight."

I hang up and grip the edge of the bathroom sink to steady my wobbling knees. I stare into the reflection ahead of me, but all I can see are the memories I've been desperate to forget. When I imagined speaking to Mike again, I pictured more chaos, more tears—salt poured over my fresh wounds.

But it was nothing like that.

Being away for this long altered something in me. Experiencing my first tour with one of the biggest R&B artists in the world. Traveling the country. Meeting amazing women and—and then there's Naya.

My eyes widen, and I tighten my hold on the counter. I turn on the faucet and splash cold water into my face. The residual drops hitting my bonnet and t-shirt don't bother me. I need the blast back into reality.

Is Naya the only reason I'm not locked in my hotel room on the off-days, mourning the travesty waiting at home for me? What happens if this thing between us ends? She's already broken her no-dating-coworkers rule with me, so that means this situation-ship must have a time limit. And when that limit runs out, where will that leave me?

"Hey, you good?"

Naya softly knocks on the other side of the door. I check my phone. Shit, it's been twenty minutes since I hung up on Mike.

"Yeah." I plaster on my best smile and open the door to the sight of a sleepy Naya rubbing her eyes. "Got up to pee and got carried away picking at blackheads."

"Lies." She steps past me and plops onto the toilet. My joints freeze over. "Your skin is practically flawless. If you found black-heads, they must be microscopic."

She smirks at me before a yawn overtakes her. The ice in my limbs thaws as I make my way out of the restroom and back onto the bed.

"I rarely get them. Just a couple of days before my period."

"Word. I'm supposed to be getting mine soon, too. Lemme know if you need anything. I'll make sure they stock the bus with all the best snacks."

She washes her hands and sneaks a little wink at me through the mirror. When she looks away to dry her hands, I exhale a hidden breath I'd been holding in since hanging up the phone. While Naya dabs lotion on her hands, I pull the covers back and tap the mattress.

"Come to bed."

* * *

The clock is ridiculing me. Naya fell asleep moments after wrapping her arms around me. Forty-five minutes later, I'm still here, eyes wide open, staring at downtown Philly. That phone call served as a stark reminder; this tour bubble won't protect me forever. My phone buzzes from the nightstand, but it's faced down. It's probably another text message from Mike, but I won't know for sure until tomorrow. He's already taken too much of peace tonight. I will not allow him to steal anymore.

"Hmm," Naya mumbles behind me.

Her arm tightens around my waist, then relaxes with the rest of her body. I reach down, interlock my fingers with hers and nestle into her. Though it's been about three months, I still remember the day I left LA. The shouting, tear-stained clothing, slamming the front door behind me, driving around with beady eyes peering into my rear-view mirror to ensure I wasn't being followed.

I've been running.

Avoiding everything I have to face, eventually. That's another reason BriAnn's bullying made me so nervous. I was terrified that she'd actually fire me. Not only ripping my dreams of touring from my fingertips but also forcing me to return to that dreadful apartment in North Hollywood.

"No..." Naya mutters behind me.

"Huh?" I glance back to find her eyes still closed shut. Her body shifting around in search of comfort.

"It's raining..."

This time, Naya's body jolts, sending me into a fit of concealed laughter. I try to reel it in, so I don't wake her, but this is gold. Who would've thought Nayara Alvarez talks in her sleep? And raining? What is she, the weatherman?

"Naya," I say in a gentle, singsong voice. "It's not raining, but it was cloudy today."

"The rain—no." Her body twitches again, this time a little stronger. "I got you…"

"I got you, too, babe."

I snicker.

She twitches and tightens her grip around my waist. I feel her body temperature against my back. She's warm, yet cold at the same time—and wet. Her body spazzes again, more violently. She's having a nightmare.

"No!"

She yells this time, squeezing me tighter.

"Naya!" I grip her arm and shake. "It's just a bad dream!"

"I got you! I got you! I got you!" she screams into the air.

"Nayara!"

I whip around, shaking her shoulders with all my might. Her bloodshot eyes pry open as she screams.

"Mahalia!"

CHAPTER FORTY-EIGHT

"NAYA! WAKE UP! NAYA!"

The voice pounding into my dream grows louder and louder. Then suddenly, everything disappears, the rain, the blood spattered all over me and—

"Naya!"

My vision clears, and all I see is Khloe hovering over me with a petrified look on her face.

"What happened?" I sit up, instantly feeling the cool hotel air hitting my drenched t-shirt.

"You were having a bad dream... You kind of scared me."

"I'm so sorry, babe." I clasp her hand and land a soft kiss. "It probably wasn't too bad 'cause I can't even remember what it was about."

The lie slides from my mouth like baby oil. Slippery and quick— couldn't stop it if I had tried.

"You kept saying no, and your body was practically convulsing. I think it was raining in the dream because you said something about that, too."

"Oh, Khloe." I spring up from the bed and peel off my shirt. "Sorry for the sweaty hug! Sometimes, I get hot under hotel comforters. Too thick, ya know? But I'm sorry again. It was probably a thunderstorm dream. Thunderstorms are pretty regular in Augusta. I've always hated them."

An unreadable expression drapes over Khloe's face. She takes a moment, her eyes blinking slowly as if calculating her next words. Then she says it.

"Naya, who is Mahalia?"

"Oh!"

I fast-walk to the restroom and cut the shower water on. Hopefully, if I give my limbs a task, Khloe won't see them tremble.

I force a chuckle.

"My bad. Gonna shower real quick to knock this sweat off... Uh! So what'd you ask me? Oh! Mahalia?! Uh, I don't know! Why do you ask?"

"You kept screaming her name, Naya. *Loud.*"

Once again, I force a laugh.

"Mahalia? Girl, the only Mahalia I know is from that zombie series on HBO I told you about. Remember?"

"Yeah, I recall you telling me about the show, but I'm not that into shows with a lot of blood or gore. Remember?"

"Of course, I do! And you know what? I should probably take a break from those types of shows myself 'cause look at me— screaming Ma—that girl's name, a character that got turned into a zombie a few episodes ago."

I slide the rest of my clothes off and step into the shower, keeping the bathroom door open so Khloe can still hear me.

"It was such an impactful episode. She was the only black character on the show, so when she turned into a zombie, the internet lost it. Black twitter went up that night!"

"Oh," Khloe croaks.

I can almost feel her discomfort through the shower curtain.

"Okay... Maybe you *should* take a break from that show."

"You're completely right! Well, hey, I'm sorry for waking you! Don't let me be the reason you miss out on sleep! Check-out is at eleven, and we have a show tomorrow—or tonight, I guess! Haha!"

I could eat this bar of soap right now. Anything to stop more dumb shit from leaving my mouth.

"Okay, well... Goodnight. See you in a couple of hours."

"See you soon!"

I peer around the shower curtain and blow her a kiss. Once Khloe rolls over, I close the curtain and turn the water temperature to the hottest setting possible. Anything to stop my body from shaking. I sink to the floor and clutch my knees into my chest. My eyes sting, and I can't determine if it's from the water's temperature or the salt in my tears. I bite my lip to hold back the sobs pushing against them, and now I regret not closing the bathroom door earlier.

Five years later.

Five years later, the pain is still fresh. Nightmares haunt me. Screaming until my voice gives out. The images permeated in my mind.

Five years later, no matter how much growth I think I've accomplished, I'm always dragged back to square one, especially on the anniversary week.

CHAPTER FORTY-NINE

THE SILENCE in this elevator is deafening. Nothing but whirs from the machine and pings as we pass each floor. Oversized suitcases are by our sides, sweatsuit sets coddle our bodies, and everything left unsaid last night lingers between us.

After Naya hopped into the shower last night, I stayed awake for a bit, periodically checking the time. By the time she got out, sleep had overtaken me, so I'm not sure how long she was in there. But two things are for sure. One, Naya showered for at least thirty minutes before I dozed off. Two, nobody holes up in the shower for more than half an hour after having a night terror because they are *okay*. Another thing I did while counting the minutes was dive head-first into a Google search spiral.

I googled *Mahalia HBO*.

Nothing.

I narrowed the search to *Mahalia, zombie show, HBO* and still, the search came up empty.

Who is Mahalia? Why was Naya having a night terror about her? And most importantly, why are you obsessing over it, Khloe?

"You can go ahead," Naya croaks when the elevator doors open.

Her voice sounds hoarse, the only evidence from last night. Well, that and the glimpse of bags under her eyes. I thank God for the extra dose of melanin he blessed me with, otherwise, the bags under my eyes would be on full display.

When we arrive at the bus parked outside the hotel, everyone's energy is yet another reminder of the sleep I did not get last night. Leah is in a flowy sundress, singing *Love on Top* by Beyonce with DayDay. He stores their luggage in the storage compartment and commits to the infamous high note. Leah almost falls out from laughter, throwing her head back.

"Hey, y'all!"

"Mornin'!"

"Happy show day!" Bunny, Rae and Tiana are halfway onto the bus and poking their heads out of the door. They are also the dictionary definition of fresh-faced and well-rested.

"Morning," we mutter with our best poker face.

Everyone trickles onto the bus, and Naya throws her suitcases into the storage.

"Get on the bus. I'll stow your luggage for you," Naya says, keeping her attention on the bag in her hands.

"Really? No, it's okay, my bags are kind of heavy."

"You're good." This time, her voice cuts a little sharper. "I got it."

"Oh. Um, okay."

And with that, I'm on the bus.

Everyone is buzzing about their afternoon at Liberty Bell. They stared at the monument for five minutes, then rolled into a bar nearby. Apparently, Leah's drinks gave her enough liquid courage to not only flirt with the bartender but give him a wink on their way out. According to Bunny and DayDay's standards, the wink was atrocious. Worth nothing more than an F, or maybe a D+. Rae says though the wink was not so great, Leah's flirting game was impeccable. Tiana said she'd been too preoccupied with her boyfriend's fight of the day to notice.

"What did you end up doing last night?" Bunny asks.

I'd been doing such a great job as a wallflower, listening but never drawing too much attention. My efforts are thwarted because now I can feel everyone's curious gaze on me.

"I just chilled in the room yesterday. Ordered room service... I thought I was coming down with something, so I just wanted to rest."

"I feel you," Tiana adds. "Naya must be fighting the same thing. She doesn't look so hot."

"I don't know what Naya did yesterday!" I blurt out, regret immediately lining my cheeks.

"Well, of course you don't. You were cooped up all day yesterday."

Then, as if we conjured her up ourselves, Naya walks onto the bus. Lifeless strides coat her steps. She doesn't acknowledge anybody in the front lounge. Instead, she beelines straight for the bunks and shuts the door behind her.

"Yup, definitely sick," Tiana concludes.

"That was me last week."

Rae checks herself out in her phone camera.

"Something might be going around." Leah places a hand on her heart. "Poor thing."

I fade into the background, thankful for the shift in conversation.

"Ima go check on her." Bunny rises from the couch and disappears behind the door.

All it takes is DayDay talking about the new Victoria Monet music video for the group's focus to shift yet again. They all take turns sharing their favorite moments from the video. Leah reenacts some of the choreography, and Rae goes on a tangent about how Sean Bankhead is the top choreographer of our generation. Everyone buzzes with energy. Springy and active, but I remain motionless. Fatigue cemented into my muscles, and all the possibilities of what's happening in the back of the bus encompass my thoughts.

* * *

It's been an hour since the bus parked at the venue. DayDay has gone inside the arena to prep Zion's wardrobe and the rest of the cast is God knows where. When everyone strayed in different directions, I stayed on the bus, cleaning, wiping stuff down, watching Netflix, making a PB&J, and anything else to pass the time until Bunny and Naya emerge from the back of the bus.

White noise from the engine pads the entire space, so I can't tell if they are talking quietly or not talking at all. Are they in the back lounge? Or the bunk area? And if they aren't talking, what are they doing?

Stop, Khloe.

In the middle of folding a throw blanket for the tenth time, I shake my head, an audible breath leaving my lips. Allowing the blanket to slip from my grip, I will my shoulders to loosen. I toss the blanket onto the couch and head straight to the door leading to the back of the bus. My fingers float in front of the knob, then I go for it.

Just as I step into the bunk area, I see the back of Bunny's head climbing down from her bunk. Her hair is fuzzy as if she were lying down without a bonnet or a scarf. Then I realize. That's not her bunk she's climbing out of. It's *Naya's*.

My eyes dart into the dark space. All I can see is a comforter cocooning Naya's body and a few stray curls poking out of the top.

When Bunny turns around, she nearly jumps out of her skin. "Oh shit! You scared me, girl!" She keeps a low tone, careful not to disturb Naya.

"Sorry. Just wanted to take a little nap before the show."

"Um... I crawled in to see if Naya needed any medication or anything. She isn't feeling too well," Bunny notices my inquiring glances into the bunk.

"Oh. Okay. Well, see you later."

Before she can even finish slipping on her shoes, I'm in my bunk, tucked into the covers. I *can't* think about the fact that Naya isn't sick. I *can't* focus on why she was so distant this morning. And I *definitely can't* admit that my suspicions might be true. Naya and Bunny are closer than friends.

Nope, I am going to sleep.

CHAPTER FIFTY

FOR THE REST of the night, Naya is distant. Her mind is suspended in a secret place she's denied me access to. Physically present but mentally elsewhere. In the dressing room before the show, during the show, and even now, on the bus during the group's drink and movie nightcap.

During one of the quick-changes backstage, I tried to make a joke about one of the fan signs in the audience that read, "I'll suck the black off that dick, Zion!" Vulgar, I know, but it doesn't hold a candle to some of the other signs I've seen fans hold in the audience. I directed my words toward Naya, but only the rest of the girls reacted. Naya kept her gaze glued to the laces on her shoes and mumbled, "That's funny."

I tried my hand at random small talk a few more times—the massive size of this arena, the tattered seam on my costume from overuse, and even the cold after-show food production supplied us with—and each time, Naya replied with short answers, if she replied at all.

Now, as the sounds of Martin float from the television, weaving in and out of the girls' and DayDay's conversation, I sit cuddled up beside Rae and Tiana, nursing my cup of wine and pretending to care about how rare it is to have skilled makeup artists on set.

"One time I did a couple of episodes of this major scripted series —one my momma even watches." Rae takes a dramatic sip of her wine. "Everyone in the makeup team was trash, from the young to the old. One of those girls made me so bright, I might as well have been Casper the Friendly Ghost!"

On a normal night, a comment like that would have launched my head back with laughter, but tonight, only a chuckle pokes through. A soft flash of teeth, just to have a reason to glance toward the other end of the front lounge and see what Naya was up to. She sits on the furthest end of the couch, her eyes glued to the TV. To everyone else, Naya seems fixated on this episode of Martin, but I'm the only one can tell that her eyes are blank, free of any connection to the scenes playing before her. Bunny would probably know, too, but she went to her bunk as soon as we boarded the bus. She was also acting a little strange during the show tonight, not anywhere near as dry as Naya, but not her usual boisterous self. What's up with them?

"Bitch, is that a hickey on your chest?" Tiana squeals.

"Ooop!" DayDay and Leah peep, practically in sync.

I almost break my neck to look down at my chest, only to realize I have the world's highest crew neck t-shirt on. I glance up to the sight of Rae covering her heated face and her robe ajar, revealing a tiny bralette and a quarter-sized purple hickey above her cleavage.

"Damn it! I thought I was in the clear after no one noticed at the show tonight!"

"Those are some of the fastest, quick-changes I've done in my entire career. Nobody got time to look at your titties!" Tiana snickers.

Rae holds her hands up in surrender. "I met up with an old college friend last night."

Leah whistles. "At least someone had a good off day!"

Tiana points. "Wait, are those teeth marks above it?!"

"Damn, I'm overdue for a dick appointment like that." DayDay raises his cup of wine in salute.

"Yeah!" I force out to say something, anything to act like I'm present in the moment and like my mind isn't currently on an Alvarez roller coaster. "Me too!"

DayDay side-eyes me in a way I can't exactly put my finger on, but before I can investigate any further, I hear the door to the bunk area shut and spot Naya's vacant seat. I spring up and disappear to the bunk area, too. A quick look into Naya's bunk and the dimmed light pouring under the door in front of me lets me know she's in the back lounge.

"Hey," I murmur, closing the door behind me.

"Sup?" Naya sits on the couch, not even lifting a centimeter from the phone on her lap.

Who the hell is this person in front of me?

"Are you okay? No—I'm going to rephrase my question. What's wrong? You've been distant all day. Did I do something?"

"I've been dealing with some personal stuff, but I'm good."

She glances up, only to continue scrolling through her phone seconds later.

"You know…" I keep my arms tight by side and pinch the sides of my legs to brace myself. Anything to keep my voice from cracking. "I consider myself to be pretty…close to you, so if you ever need to talk, I'm here for you."

"I'm good, thanks," Naya spits out immediately after I finish. "I don't really want to talk. Actually, I think I need some distance for a few days."

"Distance from me?" I pinch my thighs hard enough to feel the sting travel. I blink away the water threatening to cloud my vision.

"Yeah, Khloe. Just for a couple of weeks. I need to be with myself for a litt—."

"And Bunny?!"

The words escape my mouth before I can stop them.

"What?" Naya finally yanks her eyes from that stupid phone and stares straight at me.

"Bunny," I begin, no longer unable to fight back the tears. "I can tell you've been dealing with something, and I've also noticed Bunny is the only person you'll let in."

Naya's stoic expression softens. Water wells around her eyes for a couple of seconds, then she blinks it away.

"You don't understand…"

"There's a lot about y'all's relationship I don't *understand!*" This time, razors line my words. Insecure thoughts spew from my mouth. This is not how I imagined having this conversation.

"Understand?" She raises her voice to a strained whisper, minding the thin wall the back lounge shares with the bunk area. "You wanna know what I don't understand? I don't understand what would possess you to say you need a dick appointment, too, in front of the woman you've been fucking for the last month!"

"I had to add to the conversation somehow! We are still keeping this thing private!"

"Private or secret? Private or an experiment to play with until you get off tour? 'Add' to conversations, book dick appointments and take secret phone calls in the restroom with Michael all you want. I'm good off that."

Hearing his name leave her lips sends a shock down my spine. I grip the side of the couch to keep my knees from buckling.

"No... wait. You don't get it."

"No. I actually do get it. I can smell fake gays like you from a mile away. But you know what? It's my fault, 'cause I ignored every sign, broke my personal rules, and pursued... whatever the fuck this is."

"Pursued?! Every time we get an inch closer, you're quick to bring up the dating apps and other women. You practically push me to date other people!"

"Other *women*. Not people, women. The very thing you said you wanted to explore at the beginning of this damn tour. I wanted you to have that experience. Yes, getting to be with you intimately is nice, but I had to make sure I wasn't robbing you of your own experiences. I had to make sure I didn't—you know what? I'm done."

Before I can fix my mouth to respond, Naya slips past me and out the door, leaving me alone in the empty back lounge. The humming engine takes the place our voices once were.

* * *

At first, I wondered how long this could last. How long could Naya and I realistically go without speaking? We are sharing a bus, sleeping in bunks separated by a couple of feet, and dancing in the same show. But two weeks flew by, and I am thoroughly aware of how two people can act like the other doesn't exist in a tight living arrangement.

Two weeks of stolen glances on stage and in group settings. Replying with tight, one-word answers. Occasionally, we are forced to speak to each other, like when we had to decide who would escort Zion's guest performer off stage. I don't know if anyone else can sense our strange energy, but they act like they don't. Like now, during glam in the dressing room, where Naya's empty chair has become a regular part of the equation. We've all grown accustomed to Naya being MIA before the show, only to stroll in fifteen minutes before stage with a full face of makeup and fresh curls.

"Hey, do you have eyelash glue I can borrow?" Tiana turns to me with warrior streaks of concealer and bronzer all over her face. "I can't find mine."

"Yeah, sis. I got you!"

As she grabs the glue from my hand, her eyes fall to the floor, blinking away—are those tears?

"T..." Bunny's speaker plays music loud enough to mask our words, but I whisper just in case, careful not to alert the other women. "What's wrong?"

"My boyfriend is in the audience tonight."

"Correct me if I'm wrong, but isn't that a good thing? I know he's ..." I clear my throat. "Difficult sometimes, but he finally gets to see you shine on stage. The outcome of all the hard work and long hours bred."

"Yeah, but what if he doesn't like the show? What if he has an issue with one of the parts?" She quickly swipes a stray tear and dabs the foundation to cover up the evidence.

"I mean, the show is very sensual, and they refer to us as 'Zion's girls' for most of it, but you don't actually partner with Zion—just Bunny and Leah."

"Yeah, you're right..."

"Hey." I take hold of her hand. "Your man came to support you. He's going to be so proud of you. Live in that."

The corner of her lips curve upward.

"Thanks, Khloe. You're right. He hasn't seen me dance on stage in almost a year, so he'll love this."

I give her hand a gentle squeeze, and we go back to doing our makeup. After applying the finishing touches to my T-zone, I feel grateful that my conversation with Tiana went smoothly. I'm relieved that her pre-show nerves have eased, but to be completely honest, I didn't believe a word that came out of my mouth. I don't know—is it Larry? Terry? Damn it. I don't know Tiana's boyfriend from a can of paint, but I do know that he's been stressing her out since the first day of the tour. Who knows if he'll like the show or hate it? Regardless, Tiana deserves to perform without those thoughts in the back of her mind.

"Thirty minutes to showtime, ladies!" the stage manager calls from outside the dressing room.

"Thank you, thirty!" we all reply in unison.

naya

"ZION! ZION! ZION!"

The audience chants until the stage trembles beneath me. The outro to the final song fades away. We stick our ending poses, smiles wide, and labored breaths spilling from our chests. I inhale in the warm feeling of the stage lights and take it all in.

I am finally creeping out of the slump that's overcome me these past two weeks. After much prayer, crying spells, talks with Bunny and phone calls with Mami, I've decided one thing. I need to go to therapy. This is the fifth anniversary of Mahalia's death, my college sweetheart, soulmate and the woman I knew for a fact I was going to spend the rest of my life with. Five years later, I am nowhere near better. I'm still running. Full speed, stride after stride, hurling myself away from healing and genuine connections. An issue I've been able to overlook for years until I met Khloe.

Harboring this trauma, allowing it to fester and plant roots within me, is poisonous. And I witnessed firsthand how that poison can affect those around me. It shattered Khloe. Destroyed her in front of my eyes. My sweet, sweet Khloe. The one person I've let in since then. The only person to be patient with me outside of Bunny. There hasn't been a woman I've cared for this deeply since Mahalia. Not just care for, but love. No matter how many times I've tried to stop it or push her away. I have fallen in love with Khloe Thompson and I owe her a huge apology.

That's also on the top of my list.

"Thank you, Seattle, for all the love you've shown me tonight! Every time I pull up, y'all show out!"

The audience roars in reply.

Our clumped ending formation sits toward the far end of stage right while Zion stands on the opposite end, stage left.

"Before they leave, I want y'all to give an enormous round of applause to my beautiful dancers!"

With that cue, we break our ending pose and perform our final bow. A few of us give a few waves and air kisses to the audience. As we walk off stage, Zion regards us one last time.

"They are some of the baddest in the industry, and on stage with ya boy! Aren't I lucky?!"

He blows a kiss in our direction as we walk away. As much as playing the usual male eye candy role grinds my gears, I don't mind it on this tour. Off stage, Zion is polite and well-mannered. His eyes never roam while speaking to us, and he never says any of the misogynistic one-liners he uses during the show. Zion keeps that character strictly for the stage. In reality, I don't see him much off-stage. Unless he's throwing an after party, or off-day hangout, he keeps to himself and his entourage.

"He loves the show!" Tiana squeaks in the backstage tent.

"Who?" Bunny asks.

The rest of us clean up our personal items with open ears. Wardrobe is already removing costume pieces from our stations at the speed of light.

"My boyfriend! He came to the show tonight. I was a little nervous, but he messaged me at the beginning of the second act. 'You are doing amazing, baby! I love to see you do your thing! Keep killing it!'"

"Aw, that is so sweet!" Leah says.

"That's adorable! We love *supportive* boyfriends!" I add.

I'm not the biggest fan of Tiana's boyfriend because all he seems to be good at is starting arguments, but I'm overjoyed to see my sis on the high.

"Oh girl, what y'all doing after the show? Bus call is at 3 a.m tonight, and it's only 11:45 p.m. That's just enough time to get a hotel for some quickie action!" Rae snickers. "That's what I would do! Or hell, once we finish showering, our dressing room in the arena will be empty!"

"The arena dressing room?"

Leah's mouth drops in shock, like the sweet Disney princess she is.

"Scandalous!"

Khloe's dimple deepens with her smirk. When she feels my gaze on her, I look away.

I *need* to talk to her first thing tomorrow.

We have an off-day, and I'll spend the entire day pouring my heart out to her in the confines of my hotel room if that means I can win her back.

"Rae, don't fill that girl's head with that freaky shit!" Bunny smacks Rae's arm.

"I mean, it wouldn't be the first time one of us got some action in the dressing room after the show. Right, Naya?" Tiana chirps.

My skin grows hot at the sound of my name. I feel Khloe going rigid in the corner of my eye, and then she tries to relax and act normal, taking off her show shoes.

"Huh?" is the only word that leaves my mouth.

Questioning eyes barrel into me.

"Don't act all modest now!" Tiana begins. "Naya got the most game out of all of us. 'Cause one night I came back to the dressing room to get a charger, and she had not one but two women in there! Doing unspeakably freaky activities!"

"Two?!"

"Damn, I feel like a virgin after hearing that."

"Big daddy, Naya!"

Everyone's responses fade into white noise. I keep my eyes forward, careful not to look in Khloe's direction, but I can still see her in the periphery. Now, she's grabbing her belongings at a quicker pace.

"I didn't even know you were gay at the time, so you have to imagine my surprise!" Tiana continues.

I force a chuckle, attempting to ease the moment. "That was at the beginning of tour... I was doing too much."

"Well, I would love to continue this conversation, but I gotta beat y'all to the showers so I can get to my man quicker! Tonight, I wanna do *too much*." Tiana flips her hair and slips out of the backstage tent, simmering the spotlight she placed on me.

"I'll walk with you, T," Khloe says, following behind her.

The rest of the cast remains in the tent, grabbing our things and situating our wardrobe at a normal speed. I mean, Tiana has an excuse, but Khloe... If I were her, I wouldn't want to risk the possibility of being left alone with me, either. Maybe I'll apologize to her tonight instead of waiting for the off-day tomorrow. There's no need to drag this out any further.

"You gonna head back to the dressing room or stay in here all night?" Bunny nudges me.

"My bad, I zoned out. Let's go."

We exit the backstage area and turn down the hallway. That's when I hear the commotion. Yelling. Female voices. A man's voice. Two men's voices? Followed by cracking sounds that can only be landing punches.

"What the—?"

Without a word, Bunny and I jog toward the noises.

"Baby, no! Laurence, stop!"

Tiana's scream trails from the dressing room. Once we finally turn the corner, the source of the noise unfolds before me. A man I've never seen before swinging at Zion. He lands a fist into Zion's side, which Zion returns with a blow to his jaw. Judging by the way Tiana continues to scream the man's name, this has to be her boyfriend. How did he get backstage and all the way to Zion's dressing room?

Tiana tugs his shoulder. He turns around and pushes Tiana with all his might. The force is enough to send her flying into the concrete wall behind her.

I step further into the dressing with my right fist clenched.

"Aye! Hold the fuck—!"

Before I can finish my words, Khloe emerges into the scene with a... *a folding chair* raised above her head.

"Don't you ever put your fucking hands on her!" she screams before driving the chair directly into the man's back. The impact forces him to collapse on the floor. She raises the chair above her head again, but four bodyguards sprint into the dressing room and tackle the stranger. In seconds, three of them drag Laurence out of the dressing room while the other tends to Zion.

"That's what the fuck I'm talking about!" Bunny grabs Khloe's shoulder and lowers the chair. I head toward Tiana, who's holding the back of her head.

"Come on, sis, let's find the tour manager. We need to get you to the ER to have your head checked out." I add.

"What the fuck is wrong with him? He said he saw Zion blow a kiss to me and only me on stage. He's convinced we've been messing around since the beginning of the tour. You see, Naya! I do nothing but stay on the phone with his insecure ass! I do nothing but reassure him and give him all my damn time. And now he does this dumb shit!"

"Don't worry about that right now. You'll deal with him later. Right now, your health comes first, sis."

CHAPTER FIFTY-TWO

RESTING my body against the outside of the bus, I pull a long drag of my joint. Because of the night's events, the tour manager pushed the bus call from 3 a.m. to 5 a.m. Tiana returned from the hospital about thirty minutes ago. The doctors diagnosed her with a mild concussion and prescribed three days of bed rest. Besides a bruised rib, Zion is fine and has decided not to press charges. Judging by the way he and his entourage kept recounting and acting out the events, the fight actually seemed to have left him invigorated.

Now, everyone is on the bus showered, draped in robes and judging from the giggles I can hear pouring from inside, probably watching a comedy. Everyone except Rae. Once everything died down, she left for drinks with a friend and said she'd return before the bus call. I swear that girl knows someone in every city.

I put out the end of the joint with the sole of my sneaker, but the sound of a slamming bus door snatches my attention. Khloe is walking toward me. Timid yet confident strides guide her steps.

Her steps come to a halt in front of me. "We need to talk."

"Talk about divine timing! I actually planned on talking to you tomorrow on our day off, especially after you turned into a pro-wrestler."

Khloe's eyebrows furrow as she folds her arms across her chest. "Jokes? Really, Naya?"

"Okay, you're right." I study the concrete floor between us, searching for the right words to say, but there aren't any. I have to rip the band-aid off. Dive in head first.

"I'm sorry. I am deeply sorry for the way I treated you."

She opens her mouth to say something, but I cut her off. If I don't say it now, I might not ever.

"Five years ago, the love of my life died in a car accident two weeks before I planned to propose to her. I was in the car, too. I told her we should probably wait for the rain to lighten up, but she insisted. I offered to drive, but she insisted. I screamed her name while the car spun out of control. I screamed when the car made impact with other cars and finally the barrier wall in the middle of the freeway. I screamed until my voice was hoarse, holding her in my arms, begging for her to come back to me, but she never did. Her body was limp. Warm but cold in my—"

"Hey." Khloe's tight embrace breaks me from my rambling. Only once her solid frame sits against my body do I realize I've been trembling.

"I'm sorry for rambling. I've never told anyone before."

She squeezes tighter, and that vanilla scent I've longed for these past two weeks wraps me like a warm blanket.

"Don't be sorry. I knew something was up, but I had no idea. So that's who Mahalia is?"

I flinch at the sound of her name leaving Khloe's lips, then remind myself of the necessary growth ahead. The journey of healing I need to embark on if I want any type of future with Khloe. She doesn't hesitate to reach out to cradle my face between her hands, the pad of her thumb rubbing my cheek back and forth.

"Yeah. I'm sorry for lying about that, too. The anniversary of her death was around the time of our fight. Usually, I am a mess for the entire month leading up to the date. Over drinking, partying, and hooking up with randoms, but as the month approached, I didn't feel the need to act out. I thought I was *finally* getting better. That is until the week of the anniversary arrived. I'm so sorry for how I lashed out at you and how cold I was."

"Nayara, you are grieving. Yes, it was five years ago, but you never fully allowed yourself to heal. So, it only makes sense that these stages of grief push through in unpredictable ways. Honestly, I'm proud of you for even telling me."

"I had to. I don't know when or how it happened, but you're the only person I've let this close since Mahalia. Bunny was my roommate at the time, so she witnessed everything firsthand. Me coming home drenched with clumps of mud and blood on my clothes. The panic attacks during the day. The night terrors holding my sleep hostage. That's really what drew us closer. And that's why she was in my bunk with me that day and in my hotel room that other night. I'm not sure if you realize, but I don't talk about my feelings a lot—"

"Oh really? I couldn't even tell!" Sarcasm drips from her words. The menacing smirk on her face launches a hearty chuckle from my core.

"Okay, okay. Obviously, I don't talk about my feelings, so whenever I'm feeling down, I call Bunny to just sit with me in silence or hold me for a little."

"You know..." Khloe encloses the space between us and drops her hands to mine, giving a gentle squeeze. "I'm really good at sitting in silence or cuddling—not to intrude on your bond with Bunny—which I'm sorry for being jealous of. That was not cool of me."

"And it wasn't cool to be standoffish with you out of the blue and spend all my time with Bunny. And while I'm here, I'm also sorry for calling you a fake gay. I was projecting my insecurities onto you."

"It's an insecurity that makes sense. At this moment, I'm not into men, yet I've never been with women, either. I can understand, but I am wondering if I will ever turn back. I can't predict the future, but let me reassure you. Nayara Alvarez. You have ambushed every thought in my head from the moment you cussed BriAnn out in rehearsal. Everything, from your talent, easy-going but endearing personality, and your tenderness with me. I don't know why, but it has a hold on me. I don't see myself breaking free from it soon."

I wrap my arms around her waist and pull her in, bringing my lips inches from hers.

"Good 'cause I'm not letting go of you anytime soon."

When our lips collide, I feel everything: the desperation in our bodies, the sexual tension, the way I've longed for this woman's touch and, most importantly, the unwavering safety I feel with her. Our tongues search wildly. Breaths hitching in syncopation. Her hands slide up my sides and into the base of my neck. Weaving her fingers into the root of my curls, she tugs and presses into me even more.

"Damn, Leah!" a strained whisper comes from the bus window above us. "Get off my foot!"

We break away. Milliseconds after glancing at the window, four silhouetted heads dip out of sight.

"We saw you guys." I chuckle.

"And heard you…" A sheepish smile curves across Khloe's face.

"I'm sorry!" Leah emerges first. The rest trickle in after. "I peeked out the window to check on you guys and saw how close y'all were standing so I…"

"Watched the show?" I cut in.

"Then, the rest of us joined her… Sorry, guys." An abashed grin washes over Tiana's face.

"Shouldn't you be resting?" I tease.

"How much did you hear?" Khloe pinches the bridge of her nose while shaking her head.

"Enough…" Leah sinks into her shoulders.

The humiliating realization makes me wince.

"If you ever wanna talk, we got you, babe!" Leah holds up her cup of wine.

"Yeah… I'm sorry about your loss, sis." Tiana fixes her hands into the shape of a heart and pushes it against the window's screen. "My cousin owns a mental health practice in LA with over twenty thera-pists on staff, twelve of which being black women and four black Latina women. Let me know if you want that info."

"You already know I love you. I'm so proud of you, sis." Bunny clutches her heart.

I grimace at the thought of the entire cast knowing about my trauma, but everybody's support makes the back of my eyes sting with tears. Good tears. Bunny's eyes dart back and forth between Khloe and me.

"Khloe, you must be something special to get a stubborn hoe like Naya to open up. I'm glad you'll be around to knock some sense into her, too. And for the record, I *do not* want that hoe. I *needs* dick in my life."

Giggles travel among the women. I flick off my best friend, then grab Khloe's hand.

"This is cute or whatever!" DayDay's voice travels from the front lounge. "Sorry, gals, there's no more room left by the window, so I couldn't eavesdrop like the rest of these so-called spies, but I didn't need to, anyway. I already knew."

"What?!" Khloe and I shout in unison, our eyes bulging from our skulls.

DayDay walks up to the window like a lawyer giving a closing statement.

"Hello, my name is Darrion Smith. Some people call me DayDay. I'm on a tour where the tour manager prefers to book hotels by last name. It's nice to meet you, Miss Thompson, or should I say, neighbor?"

"Oh, shit."

The words leave us in unison once again.

Everyone's jaw practically drops under the bus.

"Oh, shit is right." DayDay laughs. "Or should I say, Oh, Naayaaaaa! Oh, Khloeeeee! Y'all be so damn loud!"

The rest of the bus joins in with their own sex sounds. Now, I'm the one pinching the bridge of my nose while Khloe has her face buried in her hands.

"I didn't...witness it like DayDay, but I had a feeling." Tiana shoots a knowing side-eye.

"Okay. I've had about enough of y'all." I hold up my hands to make it all stop. "How'd *you* know?"

"It's kind of obvious! You guys make googly eyes at each other all day." Bunny chuckles.

"True." Leah sips her wine.

"Oh yeah, major googly eyes," Tiana adds.

"Yeah! We all felt that shit!" Bunny taps the window screen. "Now, get y'all asses on this bus so we can celebrate!"

Everyone squeaks in agreement. I take hold of Khloe's hand, bringing her knuckles to my lips. A shadow of her dimples emerges with each kiss to her soft hand. The rest of the bus leaves the window, readying themselves for a toast to Kaya, Nloe, or whatever relationship name I heard Leah concocting. I'm not sure. They could backflip on that bus for all I care, and I still wouldn't be able to break my gaze from the woman before me.

The woman who is no longer the meek, mild-tempered dancer I met in rehearsals. That sweetie is still somewhere in there, but she's stepped aside for another side to take the reins. Someone powerful, passionate, and, after the way I saw her wielding that folding chair around, outright ferocious. A woman who not only stepped into her own on her first tour but pulled me out of my vortex in the process.

CHAPTER FIFTY-THREE

THE LAST TWO Weeks of Tour

I press the handheld vacuum against the corner of the couch and wall, patiently waiting for that satisfying crackling sound. Though I'd only boarded the bus twenty minutes ago, I cleaned the restroom, wiped down the counters, disinfected the doorknobs, and organized the cabinets.

I move to the hallway in the middle of the bunk space and continue the cleaning frenzy there. This morning, Rae sent a text from an urgent care room letting us know she has the flu and will be out for an unknown number of shows. Everyone left the bus in a frenzy hours ago, determined to explore San Francisco as much as possible before our 3 p.m. rehearsal. I'm not sure where they are now, but we've got forty-five minutes before rehearsal. So, I crank up the vacuum to the highest mode. I have been feeling more attached to my home on wheels these past few days. The space that witnessed the monumental changes in my life. Here and in most of the hotels across the nation.

"Damn, could you clean any louder?" Naya swings open the door to the back lounge with a teasing smirk.

"I'm sorry, Naya! I thought you'd be taking your session some-where in the arena!" Embarrassment creeps into my shoulders as I fumble with the off switch.

"You're good, baby. I just finished up." Naya steps forward, wrapping her arms around my waist. She plants a soft kiss on my cheek. And to think, just two months ago, we would've been doing this in secret.

"How was the session?"

"Good. I think Dr. Streeter and I are really making headway. Before therapy, I could barely think of Mahalia without breaking down, much less say her name."

"And look at you now. I am so proud, Naya. Therapy sessions by day and choreographer by night? You are overachieving on all fronts." I drop my hands below her waist, squeezing her ass and aligning her with my hips in the perfect spot.

"And I do mean.. on *all* fronts."

"Babe." Her voice is coated in restraint, but her hips say otherwise.

"What? We've got two weeks to christen this bus. I'm surprised we haven't done so already."

"Because I try to respect the public places I share with people." Naya's lips land on my neck before she puts a little space between us. Despite the inches of self-control, I can still feel desire rippling from her.

"Plus, I am not a choreographer. BriAnn told me to rearrange the formations and fill Rae's 4-8 counts with something else. Fixing formations is life-size sudoku, and I'll probably have everyone party dance around Zion in the section that's usually Rae's solo."

I ignore the tingle in my smile from the sudoku comment and continue.

"Why don't you take the opportunity to implement some of your own choreography? I've seen your college dance team videos. Your choreography took them to the championships!"

"I knew I liked you, Khloe!" Bunny's voice carries from the bus door as she walks toward us. "'Cause every time I'm tired of wasting my breath, talking some sense into my sister, you go in for the kill!"

We high-five as if we just conjured up a master plan.

"All right, all right." Naya rolls her eyes. "Where'd you come from? Shouldn't you be somewhere boo'd up with your man?"

About a month ago, Bunny went out on a date with Miles, one of the truck drivers in charge of transporting our dismantled stage from city to city. What started out as 'a chance for a bitch to get wined and dined' quickly transformed into one of the cutest romances I'd ever seen, well outside of Naya and me, of course.

"Well, for your information." Bunny flips her hair, trying to conceal the giddy smile inflating her cheeks. "I *was* boo'd up with my man. We went to brunch earlier, but I came back to the arena early to grab my sneakers and stretch before rehearsal. So, let's use this time to head to the stage and workshop the choreography you're about to premier in this show, Naya."

Sinister grins cascade over me and Bunny's face as Naya reaches into her bunk and takes out her laptop.

"Fine. Let's see if I can even come up with anything."

* * *

"All right, let's run it from the top two more times," Naya announces through labored breaths.

A few stray curls have escaped her bun and lay across the back of her white tank top. Her arms glow as a thin layer of sweat highlights her muscles perfectly.

Before Naya yells 5, 6, 7, 8, a hint of nostalgia hits me, transporting me back to tour rehearsals. Back when naïve Khloe was brimming with stress and studying Naya in complete awe. A time when I couldn't decipher what was admiration, infatuation, or a mix of both. Long gone are the stolen glances and emotional spirals because I am sure of two things. One, I want Naya to stay in my life after the tour. I want to see where our relationship goes outside of the tour bubble. And two, I *need* to ensure that my home life in Los Angeles reflects that.

My limbs perform the steps, not like Naya taught it an hour ago, but like I've been performing it on this stage for months. All of us hit each line and body placement as if this piece were a part of the tour all along. That's how seamless Naya's choreography is. A divine mix of natural and groovy, yet fierce and powerful.

"Okay, ladies." Naya cuts off the music. "Grab some water, then I'll set the formations."

Moments later, we are back on the floor as Naya points out our positions. She softly chews on the inside of her cheek, that adorable expression that takes hold every time her creative brain fires away.

"Tiana and Bunny take front line and split center. Bunny, Khloe, and me will take the back line. Use the slide in the second eight count to move into a diagonal starting on stage right."

We follow the directions and adapt the choreography to travel.

"At the end of the third eight, everyone will face into Zion."

"What if he misses his mark?" I ask.

"He won't. Zion stops at this mark during this part of the song every night. He uses this moment to signal to his lighting director if he'll be stepping into the audience for the next song or staying on stage."

Of course, she noticed that.

She is practically made for this.

By the end of the second hour, our entire show is re-staged, rehearsed, and embellished with choreography by Nayara Alvarez.

"Thank you, ladies. You're all set to go to glam. If you have any questions, please hit me up at any time. I had my GoPro recording in the audience, so in a few minutes, you'll receive a video of the revised show in your emails. Just in case you wanna brush up on anything before tonight."

"Hey, that was amazing," I whisper to Naya after the ladies give their thanks and head toward the exit.

"Really? I hope the rehearsal didn't drag on."

"Naya, you created a whole new version of the show in just two hours, understanding the exact pace to move, so we weren't over-whelmed with new information. You're a fucking natural at this choreographer stuff."

"I can show you a good pace if you wanna sneak backstage real quick."

Her eyes flit over my frame, and I fight the urge to toss my shirt off right then and there.

"I'm serious, Naya. Have you ever considered pursuing chore-ography?"

"Sometimes..." Her jaw twitches. "The job is always way more than just choreography. It's about being vulnerable and putting my art out there, the steps swirling around my mind. Hiring dancers and cutting dancers at auditions is a responsibility that my secondhand embarrassment might not be able to handle. Don't even get me started on dealing with artists. We got lucky with Zion, but I've seen the other sides. You know Adam Lenard? Star Monroe's choreographer? Have you heard about the way Star Monroe speaks to him? Disrespectful isn't a good enough word to describe that mistreatment."

"I know you, baby. You'd nip that in the bud."

"You heard of Millan Ray? The famous pop artist? She only rehearses after midnight. Some woo-woo shit about the alignment of Venus."

"That's nothing a contract can't fix. A document with *your* working hours. She can get with it or get lost. I heard Paris Leon's choreographer has her list of preferred snacks and candles written in her rehearsal contracts."

"Yeah, but what about Gary Blake, the choreographer for Tony Ice? I heard he has Gary come to his house before every rehearsal to play basketball, and he's not the only artist to treat their choreographer like some strange hired best friend. Forget that. I don't want to be disrespected or be an unsaid babysitter because a lot of artists have the emotional intelligence of a toddler."

"Okay, I hear you." I cradle her face between my hands, stroking my thumbs back and forth. "I'm just saying you are freakishly talented and, with all that experience under your belt, overly prepared. Talent aside, you commanded rehearsal, free of ego and tyranny. BriAnn could never."

"Yeah." A soft smile curves in the corner of Naya's mouth.

"I'm not saying you have to decide now, but just know you could be the person to help change all of that. I'm pretty sure BriAnn isn't the only witch of a choreographer out there."

"She isn't. There are a few diamonds in the rough, but the majority are still a little... problematic."

"Well, before we go any further into this deep dive about your career, let's pause here for today. Live in the moment. Celebrate today, 'cause that choreography is bomb."

"Thank you, baby."

I pull Naya in until our lips touch. With each kiss, every electrifying pulse sparking between us, her hand draws along my back and waist, and I am reassured of how much I love this woman.

CHAPTER FIFTY-FOUR

"DID EVERYONE GET A SHOT?" Leah joins the group with her ginger shot raised to the ceiling.

"This stuff smells!" DayDay peers into his miniature cup with trepidation. "Y'all have to be some of the strangest but baddest bitches I've ever met."

Since Rae came down with the flu, we switched the shot of tequila for a ginger shot tonight.

"You'll feel better once that immune system is fighting whatever germ that has Rae hostage." Leah swirls her cup around. "To Naya. For not only re-staging the entire show but showcasing her soon-to-be award-winning choreography on the big stage!"

Leah's declaration sends a small wave of shock rippling through my body. She hadn't heard Khloe and I talking after rehearsal today, yet she *also* thinks choreography is a lane I am capable of.

"To Naya!"

The entire bus chirps in agreement. Everyone except Rae. In

hopes of avoiding the flu spreading, Zion had arranged for a personal car to transport Rae to the next city. After everyone takes their shot and the bus quiets down, Tiana and Leah cuddle under a blanket to watch some rom-com that premiered on Netflix. Bunny steps off the bus to spend the last moments before bus call talking to Miles. DayDay, still pissed at the group's healthy choice, pours himself a bottle of wine, plops down on the couch opposite from the ladies, and whips out his handheld game console.

"Come here." I interlace my fingers with Khloe. "There's something I want to show you."

I pass the bunks, leading her into the back lounge and shutting the door behind me.

"What do you wanna show me?" Khloe pleads. "The anticipation is killing me."

Without a word, I place my phone in her palm.

"Whose number is this? What do the…"

Her voice trails off as she absorbs the words on the screen.

551-231-0088: Hey, Naya. It's Zion. I got your number from Rae. I hope that is okay. If not, we can communicate through email if you'd like. I just wanted to say first off, I *loved* your choreography in the show tonight! During that part, I was so amazed that I nearly forgot the lyrics! I don't know what your plans are after the tour, but there's an up-and-coming rapper on my label that'll be starting tour rehearsals a month after Soakin' Wet Summer is done. I'd love to hire you to choregraph her tour.

"What?!" Khloe throws her arms up before they embrace me. She continues to shriek as her legs wrap around my hips. "A choreographer. For a tour! A whole tour, Naya! Congratulations, baby!"

"Thank you! I'm not sure what God's doing, but Ima just roll with it."

"Or you're gonna do more than roll with it."

She lowers herself back onto the floor, keeping me in her arms. I let my arms rest on her waist, my favorite place to be. Khloe swipes a stray curl from in front of my eyes.

"You're not only gonna roll with it, but you're also going to showcase your choreography across a national tour. Not one routine, multiple. You're going to create memorable, award-winning steps with a new artist that has none of the weird quirks the other ones got. And I know for a fact, you're going to, most importantly, provide a safe working environment free of unnecessary trauma and stress. Something all dancers deserve."

Though the tears don't come forward, they sting the backs of my eyes. I am overwhelmed. Overjoyed at the opportunity, the direction my career might shift in, and by this woman standing before me. This beautiful woman has not only grown to be sure of herself but is sure of me, too. Patient, tender, and wishes for the absolute best for me. The words fall from me before I can stop them, not that I would ever want to.

"I love you."

"Huh?" Khloe squeaks.

"I said, I love you, Khloe Thompson."

"Nayara Alvarez." She melts into me. "I love you. I've loved you for quite some time now. I love you, and I'm not sure what you want after the tour, but I don't want to be anywhere other than where I am now. In your arms, suspended in our own world while life fades to black around us."

"Oh, you thought this could end after tour?" I smirk, leaning in to kiss her before she can answer. "You can't get rid of me that easily."

Lips crashing, tongues dancing, our mouths and hands exploring each other hungrily. No matter how close we are, we still can't get enough. Khloe slides her hand up to the base of my neck, palming a fistful of my hair and yanking my head back. A moan shoots from my throat before I can control it. A sinister giggle curves the corner of her mouth as she yanks harder, leaning into my exposed neck, kissing, biting and licking. I gnaw on my bottom lip to avoid any more noises escaping from me, 'cause, at his rate, Khloe is about to have me interrupting everybody's movie in the front lounge.

She lightly trails her tongue from my collarbone to my earlobe, sending the sensation straight to the puddle forming between my legs.

"That's it," I hiss, flipping her around so her ass presses against my center just right.

She reaches for the table, to both steady herself and use it as a base to push press into me harder.

I grind against her, whispering in her ear, "I love how you think you run something, Khloe. But I run this. This is mine."

I slip my right hand under her tank top, seizing her pebbled nipple between my fingertips.

She draws a sharp breath through her teeth, relaxing her head on my shoulder and keeping the rhythm in her hips.

"And never forget," I say, using my free hand to press against her pussy. "*This* is all mine."

"Yes, baby!" she hisses.

"No, tell me. Who does she belong to?" I ask, massaging tiny circles into her.

Though her sweatpants are in the way, I can still feel her warmth heating my fingers.

"You!" Khloe's whisper intensifies.

"And what's my name?"

"Nayara."

I can hear the smile in her voice because she knows how I love to hear her say my name. In one swift movement, I move my hand, sliding under the waistband of her pants and underwear.

"Damn." My breath hitches the moment my fingers contact her heated slickness. With every tiny circle I massage into her swollen flesh and every stifled noise threatening to ring from Khloe's chest, electricity fires into the pit of my stomach. Desire striking my base and prickling through me. Khloe lurches her upper body off the table, allowing her back to rest against my chest and her head to fall over my shoulder.

"Please." One of her hands reaches for my neck and the other to my thigh.

"Please, what?" I press harder into her clit, sending small convulsions through her. "What do want, baby?"

"Fuck me. Please fu—Oh!"

Instead of letting her finish, I slide my middle finger into her, dipping in and out. Slow at first, then fast. I clasp my free hand over Khloe's mouth so her feral noises don't travel through the walls. Keeping a steady pace, I add my index finger to her pleasure. Her hips rock back and forth as she fucks my hand.

"That's it, baby," I breathe into her ear.

Increasing the speed of my fingers, I dip in and out of her, curving ever so slightly to her sacred spot. I remove my hand from her mouth and palm her breast, squeezing and flicking.

"Oh, shit." She digs her nails into me. "You feel so good, Naya."

"You feel amazing, baby. I can't wait to feel you after the tour too." With every word, my fingers push deeper. "I can't wait to feel you. Fuck you. Taste you. Again. And again. And ag—"

"Oh!" Khloe cries out.

Her body shudders as her walls clench around my fingers.

"Yes, Khloe. Come for me."

I hold her tighter, letting her sweet nectar run down to my wrist. After a moment, I slip my hand from her pants and take a taste for myself. The spasms simmer down, and her hands loosen their grip on my skin. The sounds of her panting breath and my soft kisses trailing her neck are the only sounds filling the back lounge.

"You said you wanted to get fucked on the bus, baby. And your wish is my command."

"What about you?" She turns to me.

"I'm fine, baby." My eyes dart around the room. "Plus, I think we've made enough noise on the bus tonight."

"The bus doesn't leave for another thirty minutes and there's a whole arena behind us." She cups my ass and kisses the side of my neck.

"Thirty minutes, you say?"

Khloe's hungry gaze sears into me as she licks her lips.

"I can be quick."

CHAPTER FIFTY-FIVE

MUFFLED Hip Hop music rattles the door once we exit the nightclub. The view at the back of the group grants me a front-row seat to everything. Leah and DayDay are attached at the hip with their elbows hooked. Leah's rosy cheeks and DayDay's slight sway are indicators of the 4 rounds of shots we'd had earlier.

Tiana is strutting at the front of the group as a man from the club, or as she refers to him, a stray, trails after her. Judging from his body language, he is spitting supreme game. Using his softer voice, peering down at her through suggestive, hooded eyes and raking his eyes over her every so often. Rae is still under the weather and quarantined, but I'm sure we'll plan one last group outing before the end of the tour.

"The Uber is just around this corner, y'all! Sorry, he said he had trouble finding the club!" Tiana calls back to us, then barely returns her attention to the stray. Out of all of us, Tiana's transformation is one of the most refreshing. A couple of weeks after her ex's back-stage debacle, Tiana left him for good, and I've never seen her so radiant. Long gone are the days of furrowed brows and text arguments. She's weightless, reclaiming her time. Sometimes, she might flirt with strays like the lanky man standing before her but is unwilling to pursue anything serious.

"Look at our girl, finally getting the tour life she deserves," Bunny says, hanging back to walk beside me. "That poor man doesn't even know Tiana is about to ghost him, though!"

"The *actual show* is Khloe." I gesture toward the front of the group. "Walking behind them, acting like she's minding her business, but ear hustling to the fullest degree."

"You know how protective she is over Tiana. May I remind you of..." She pretends to hold a chair over her head and slam it down on an invisible victim, causing hushed cackles to ripple through us.

"I think I know a thing or two about being overprotective... How are you and Miles?"

"Miles is just amazing, friend." Her eyes light up at the mention of his name. "Sweet, caring, patient and, most importantly, not married. Detective Spawling made sure of that."

"I still can't believe you hired a private detective to look into him!"

"Had to! I couldn't believe a fine man like that was single with only one kid out of wedlock, a kid who's about to be sixteen, so she's basically an adult. Good credit, fifteen years in the trucking industry, no arrest history. And he *owns* the trucking business, so he wasn't just yapping lies. Hell, I even checked out his parents. Educated, middle class and retired from the school system."

"Damn, do you have his social security number?" I nudge her arm.

"Nope, but..." Bunny's eyes fall to the floor. A somber expression takes hold of her smile.

"What, friend?"

"Miles has a lake house in Montana. He wants me to vacation there with him for a week after the tour. He wants to fly out his parents and daughter so I can meet them."

"And what's wrong with that? Bunny, that is beautiful. The man obviously adores you and wants to introduce you to his family."

"That's not too soon?"

My eyes travel back to the front of the group, at Khloe, trailing Tiana and the stray's heels. My eyes travel from her braids to the royal blue dress hugging her curves and down to the nude heels cradling her soft, pedicured feet.

"What's 'too soon' if you already know what you want?"

"It's not just that..." The tension in Bunny's words migrates to her tightly clasped hands. "He also offered to join him on his next tour. Travel the country with him for six months in the truck."

"And?!"

"And... I don't know. I'm just not used to this. He wants me around. He's already talking about building with me. Not in an over-bearing love-bombing type of way, but with reassurance, always ending with 'only if you're comfortable' and 'no pressure' or 'because I have a feeling you're gonna be in my life for a while.'"

"I know what you've been through, Bunny, but don't let that stand in the way of a good thing. I've seen the way he looks at you. That man is head over heels. I can't predict how it's gonna turn out, but you'll never know if you don't try." I reach for her hand, giving a gentle squeeze. "And what he doesn't know is that your best friend is crazy. If he fucks up, I'll be on the first flight out with a machete in hand."

"You are crazy, Naya. But I love yo crazy ass."

"I love you, too."

khloe

RESIDUAL WAVES of pleasure crackle through my core as Naya and I lay on our sides, tangled in each other. Our limbs woven together like a vine.

"I thought you'd want to go straight to sleep after getting up so early," Naya says, leaving a trail of light kisses from my collarbone to my neck and finally to my lips.

"I'm sorry. Did you hear how the bus driver barged into the bunk area, hollering at the top of his lungs this morning?"

"Did I?!" Naya puffs her chest, furrows her brows and, with her best deep voice, reenacts, "Gooooood morning! Rise and shine! Grab all the luggage and belongings you'll need for the day because you will not see this bus until check-out time tomorrow...blah blah blah."

"Hollerin' like he was in a stadium!"

"Well, I guess he has to after we accidentally left Tiana on the bus that one time."

I grimace, time-traveling back to my blunder. It was my job to make sure everyone was accounted for.

"I swear I did not see her! She was so balled up in her bunk, she looked like a big pillow!"

A heap of giggles burst from me and travel to Naya. I settle closer into her, laying my head on her bare chest, still warm from our previous *activities*.

"Yeah, after that brutal wake-up call, I didn't see myself going back to sleep anytime soon, so I decided to do..." I draw one circle around Naya's tender nipple, sending an aftershock through her body. "Something else."

"And what are you planning to do now? I hope it involves food 'cause between last night and this morning, you're depleting me of all nutrients."

A flashback of us in that pristine VIP room inside the arena floods my memories. Naya's body created a stunning shape as her back arched away from the couch. Her nails clawing into the side of the couch while she released into my mouth—

"There's a breakfast buffet downstairs. Wanna go check it out?"

I clear my throat, returning to the present.

We dress and head out the door in less than fifteen minutes. The elevator doors open, revealing a desolate lobby. Not a hotel guest in sight, just ambient music and one receptionist. As we step off and make a right toward the restaurant, I glance at my watch. I guess, when you've had a morning like Naya and me, you forget it's only 6:30 a.m.

"Table for two?" The host asks upon arrival.

"Yes plea—" Something catches my eye in the far corner over the host's right shoulder. Not something, but someone. Although her chair is faced away from us, I can recognize that olive green Essentials sweat suit set and those Gucci suitcases anywhere.

"Baby, look!" I tap Naya's arm. "It's Rae! Let's go check on her!"

"Ma'am, we're just gonna join our friend over there," Naya says, turning her attention back to the host.

"Sure, go ahead. A server will be by with some refreshments shortly."

"You don't think she's still contagious, right?" I ask Naya as we walk to the other end of the restaurant.

"I'm not sure. It has been four days since she received the diagnosis. Even if she is, the least we can do is check on her and move to another table if absolutely necessary."

"Okay!"

I don't even try to conceal the spring in my step. It hasn't been long at all, but these women have really grown to become my family on the road. I've really missed Rae these past few days. She's my after-show movie buddy and the resident dressing room DJ. As we finally round in front of the chair where her hoodie can no longer conceal her face, I open my arms out.

"Well, isn't it our favorite—Rae, what's wrong?" My words come to a screeching halt. Under the guise of that hoodie, Rae's face sits pale and swollen, almost as if she'd been crying for days. The exuberant Rae we'd both grown to know and love is hijacked by something else.

Naya immediately takes action, pulling up a chair right next to her. I position a chair on the other side, gently rubbing Rae's shoulder. Naya pries one of Rae's hands from her lap and takes it into hers.

"Sis, what's going on?"

Despite the action whirling around her, Rae's gaze locks on the table in front of her, a melancholic film over her eyes. Then, with no movement, not even a blink, tears fall from her eyes.

"You guys weren't supposed to see me," she mumbles with a hoarse voice. "Nobody was supposed to see me."

"What are you talking about, babe?" I ask.

"Yeah, what do you mean by that?"

Naya grabs a napkin to catch the tears leaking down Rae's face.

"I'm leaving the tour. For good."

"Why? There are only two weeks left. Our shows are practically flawless, and you are one of the most professional dancers I've ever worked with." Naya's choreographer voice takes over, business-oriented and logical. "There's no valid reason for them fire yo—"

"I'm pregnant."

The silence that drapes between the three of us is deafening. Naya's eyes glance up to me, then back to Rae, who still hasn't broken her gaze from the table.

"He wrote me a check and told me to get rid of it." Rae continues with an unsteady voice. "He said he was at the height of his career, plans on extending the tour, and he won't let a kid stop that."

From the corner of my eye, I catch Naya's expression matching my own. Bulging eyes and mouth slightly ajar. Stunned by the realization that has fallen before us. Rae is pregnant with *Zion's* baby.

"I thought he was gonna be happy, ecstatic even. We'd kept our relationship under wraps for privacy, but y'all don't understand. He said he loved me. He said I was the one and the only one. Us against the world. No matter what and now..."

Her words trail off, only to be replaced by soft sobs.

"Oh, honey." I rub her back while she's doubled over onto the table. "I am so sorry. That is a lot to deal with by yourself. You know, you could've told us. Any of us."

"Zion said if I told anybody, I'd regret it. You guys know this man has *connections* outside of the industry. Those aren't just conspiracies." My mind travels to some of the TikTok videos that have overtaken my feed since booking this tour. Multiple videos break down Zion's possible connections to gang activity, police corruption and even murder. All of which I considered just to be false accusations from self-proclaimed internet detectives. A chill runs up my spine at Rae's around-the-way confirmation.

"He's still allowing me to get my last paychecks, even though I am leaving early," Rae says through muffled tears. "As long as I go through with the procedure and sign the NDA."

"Sis, what do *you* want?" Naya lowers her tone, a serious air surrounding her words. "Do you want to keep this baby?"

Rae lifts her head like it weighs thirty pounds, peering into Naya's eyes with what seems like the last ounce of energy she has left.

"When I was nineteen, doctors said my chances of having children were rare because of the severity of my fibroids. Of course, I want this baby."

"Okay, so we have a few options. But first, we have to get out of this restaurant and to a more private space."

CHAPTER FIFTY-SEVEN

khloe

AS SOON AS we enter our hotel room, Naya collapses on the couch. I take off my purse, grab an overpriced water bottle from the mini-fridge, and sit alongside her.

"I can't believe you knew how to help Rae," I say after taking a long, well-needed sip. We'd left this room at 6:30 in the morning, and here we are now, returning five hours later. A lot of phone calls, sneaking around, and open web browsers later, Rae is on an international flight to Japan, where she'll stay with her grandmother and have her baby.

"I didn't know how to help." Naya exhales and throws her head back onto the couch, staring at the ceiling. "When I was a teen, my mom told me stories about how she helped one of my aunts escape her husband in Cuba. He was abusive and had his hands in the pockets of powerful men on the island. Thankfully, she was able to get my aunt on a boat to the Dominican Republic and later on a flight to Puerto Rico, where she settled."

"Oh, my goodness." My hand rests on my collarbone. "I can't imagine how scary that must've been for your mom."

"Scary isn't even the word. After helping my aunt escape, her husband and his men began surveilling my mom, convinced she had something to do with my aunt's disappearance. My mom only ever dreamed of leaving Cuba, but after the gang-stalking and death threats, she and my dad hopped on a raft at the first opportunity."

I sit in silence. Shock holding the words in my throat. Cognizant of the parallels between the women in Naya's family in Cuba, my family in North Carolina, and generations of black women all over. Her aunt's story reminds me of my grandmother's, who to this day, doesn't speak about her life before moving to North Carolina. We know she's originally from Mississippi and was previously married, but her life was so gruesome, she left in the middle of the night with nothing but a satchel and some money she'd been collecting for months.

"How'd you know what to do, though? The Wings Program? Knowing Japan was even an option?"

"The Wings Program is one of my favorite non-profits to donate to. I'd heard about them in college. A group dedicated to providing flights for women and children escaping domestic violence. It blew me away. I wasn't sure that Japan was an option, but I knew Rae is a first-generation American, so I figured the odds of her having family still in Japan were high."

"Okay, that makes sense, but going as far as splitting us up and assigning fake trips around the hotel to tip off security cameras? That's next level."

"Had to take extreme measures after Rae basically confirmed

Zion's connections. How could we have possibly aided her escape if you were at the hotel bar, and I was at the pool most of the day?"

"You know, if you weren't a legendary dancer and soon-to-be award-winning choreographer, you could easily have a thriving career as a detective. Lemme get some mini-fridge wine to celebrate."

I get up, grab the miniature wine, and begin screwing off the top.

"Detective, huh? You might be on to something…" Another feeling is sewn into her words. She pauses briefly, tension swallowing the space relief once occupied. "A career switch doesn't sound too bad 'cause-because I don't know how much longer I can do this shit."

Her voice cracks. When I turn around, tears are flying down her face. It doesn't seem real at first. My rock. My tranquil foundation buckling before my eyes. With every crack in her voice, pieces of my heart mirror the fracture. I rush to her side, embracing her. Wishing I can take away whatever pain this is.

"What do you mean, Naya? Can't do what?"

"This!" She throws her exhausted hands into the air. "It's never just about dance! The art! There's always shit! Shitty choreographers that are bullies. Shitty contracts we have to fight tooth and nail to amend. Regular shitty artists or supreme-level shitty, like impregnating a dancer and threatening her into abortion and silence. And that's just this tour, Khloe. Don't even get me started on the past tours. Sometimes I'm tired of it. Tired of all this shit."

Naya exhales, laying her head back on the couch's head and staring aimlessly at the ceiling.

"Baby."

I loop my arm into hers, unsure of what to say next. I chase all the options in my mind until Naya breaks the silence.

"We are overworked, underpaid, and the most stressed out, but we make the fucking shows. 90% of these artists can't entertain in a coffee shop by themselves, much less an arena."

"What about that alternative artist you toured with a couple of years ago? I heard she treats her dancers well."

"Bad Pink? She was the sweetest, always taking her dancers on all-expense paid trips in between shows, but to be honest, flights and free alcohol aren't enough. It's nowhere near enough when she cut a $250 million deal to stream our concert, an amount we never saw a cent of."

"What?!" I can't hide the disgust in my tone. "Y'all didn't get a buyout or anything?"

"Oh, she gave us *something*." Sarcasm drips on Naya's words. "She invited us to the premier. The expensive 'top of the line' premier, her manager ranted and raved about putting on. A fucking slap in the face to the measly $500 buyout we fought for, which they gladly declined. That's a fucking tax write-off for them."

"Damn. I had no idea, Naya."

"That's the thing. No one does. Dance careers look so flashy from the outside with the traveling and proximity to celebrities, but no one truly knows how hard this path can get."

Naya lays her head on my lap. Warm tears fall from her face and onto my legs. I stroke her hair, silently praying for this woman I care so deeply for. Pleading that God rids her of this angst.

"And you know what the worst part is?" She murmurs in between sniffles. "I have a bullshit degree that I pursued just to kill time before I moved to LA, and I haven't had a normal job in ten years. I'm unhireable and have no clear direction of where I would go next."

"Is being a choreographer really that bad of an option? I'm not trying to force it, Naya, but you're really a natural at it."

"Khloe." She says through a labored breath. "Dancers are at the bottom of the totem pole. The trash at the bottom of the trashcan. Choreographers are the trash bin holding the trash. One step above this insane life we choose. Nothing but glorified babysitters for the artists, emotional punching bags, and performance monkeys for camps that have unrealistic requests."

For the first time in our conversation, I don't rush to reply. I don't frantically search for the words to say. I welcome the silence, allowing it to take over the soundtrack of the drafty hotel room. Because now, I can't help but tip-toe into my own spiral. What life did *I* choose? This career is all shiny and brand new now, but will my fate be identical to Naya's in a couple of years? I already suffered at the hands of BriAnn during my introduction to the industry. What else will I have to navigate?

As a tornado of thoughts ravage my mind, my phone buzzes on the coffee table, catching my eyes. When I see that gut-wrenching text from Spam Likely drops down the screen, I turn away and squeeze my eyes tight, praying the message disappears, just like I have been for this entire tour. Maybe if I squeeze tighter, if I continue to focus on consoling the woman in my arms, my problems will all go away altogether

CHAPTER FIFTY-EIGHT

"ONE MORE SONG! ONE MORE SONG!" the audience chants.

I close my eyes, taking in the stage lights for the last time. I don't know what follows this tour, but stressing about that won't do me any good right now. After Khloe consoled me through my breakdown, I added career crisis to the list of topics I'd like to discuss in therapy.

The best I can do for now is to welcome the end of this journey with open arms. Be optimistic about what's coming, and celebrate one of the greatest blessings from the Soakin' Wet Summer Tour, my *girlfriend*. Khloe Thompson. Well, we haven't officially given it a title yet, but we did commit to seeing this relationship ride out after the tour.

"I'm so sorry..." Zion dips his head to the floor.

The audience buzzes in wonderment.

It took all last week for me to be able to look at him without snarling. He still ain't shit, but at least now I can end the tour without glaring at him every time he speaks.

"That was the last song in the last city of the Soakin' Wet Summer Tour, but guess what? If y'all come to the wrap party tonight, you'll get a sneak peek of my newest album, Love on the Road!"

The audience roars again, and that snarl nearly makes an appearance. From my peripheral, I see Khloe glance at me with the identical question looming in her head.

Does this album have anything to do with that fake love he cursed Rae with on tour?

"I love you guys from the bottom of my heart. I'll see you guys tonight at the wrap party!"

After the fourth house track, my legs are overheating from these leather pants I'd worn. Succumbing to the sweat attacking my body, I exit the dance floor and take a seat at the bar. Letting a cup of ice water cool my body temperature, I sit back and watch my tour family.

We'd spent the beginning of the party on the first floor in this massive club Zion rented. The DJ kept announcing that there was also a room upstairs, but everyone preferred to be sandwiched in the crowd observing Zion two-step in VIP. After an hour of being nudged around by fans trying to get a better view of Zion and hearing snippets of the album he most definitely wrote about Rae, we took *our* party upstairs. The same silver decorations, chandeliers, and pictures of Zion's past albums are on the walls but without the gawking fans.

Leah and Khloe hold each other's hands while they pretend to tango. Bunny and DayDay roll their hips down to the floor with the seriousness of a professional belly dancer. Tiana stands a couple of feet away from the crew, talking to one of the many strays that have approached her tonight. It's almost like men can smell that she's freshly single and they are willing to do anything just to talk to her, like cover the group's first and second rounds of shots—which I have no issue with whatsoever.

"Tired already?" Khloe appears at my side.

"A little..." I set my drink down and pull her into the space between my legs. "I'm taking a water break. Don't wanna be too tipsy when we get back to the hotel. I still have to pack for checkout tomorrow. You ready to go back to LA?"

A flash of emotion washes over her face. A feeling I can't exactly place. Then, just as quickly as it arrives, it vanishes, a sly smirk taking its place.

"I'm not ready to go home. Not until we break in my last hotel room on this tour."

Warmth ignites my core as my eyes rake over her body. Curves and dips are perfectly extenuated by a maroon dress that hugs her frame like glad wrap. Something I can't wait to rip off later. I let my hands round her ass while we share a kiss.

"Wanna get out of here?"

The door to Khloe's room barely closes before we are all over each other. A familiar dance I've grown to love. The rhythms between us never falter. My hands fumble with the zipper on the back of her dress. Flames engulf our bodies. Our hungry sounds fill the room. I can't believe how much I crave this woman. A drug I can never get enough of.

"Wait, baby." Khloe breaks her lips away with a gasp. "I danced a lot at the party. Let me go shower."

"Let's take *this* to the shower."

I claim her mouth again, gently pushing her further back into the room. That's when I see him. An unknown man dressed in all black sitting at the edge of the bed, with his eyes wide like saucers.

"How the fuck did you get in here?!" I yell, grabbing the vase from the coffee table and hurling it at the intruder's head.

A scream escapes from Khloe as he weaves his head out of the way and stands with his hands in surrender.

"You need to get the fuck out before we call the police!" I whip out my pocket knife, waving it in his direction.

"Naya, stop!" Khloe pleads, lowering my weapon. "It's okay."

My eyes dart to the head of the bed where something else catches my attention... Is that a fucking toddler? The tiny human lies sprawled out along the plush hotel pillows. Fast asleep, despite all the chaos.

"You know him?" I blink wildly. "What the fuck is he doing in your room? And why is there a child in here?"

And with her volume deflating to a whisper, Khloe's melancholy eyes bounce from the man, to the sleeping child, then back to me.

"He's my husband."

Book 2
The Lives We Run From
Coming Winter 2025
Chapter 1

BEFORE

Camera flashes twinkle from every which direction. This cap is sitting too tight on my braids and the the gown is irritating my legs, but I ignore it and broadcast my smile to the sea of people around us.

"Smile bigger sweetie!" Momma holds her camera with one hand and swipes a stray tear with the other. "I can't believe my baby graduated high school! Doesn't she look beautiful babe?"

Dad has kept his composure mostly, but when I grabbed my diploma and squinted into the audience, I could've sworn I saw tears streaming down his face. He'd never admit it though.

"She looks gorgeous. My little girl is all grown up."

"Alright, Alright!" Mike's mom hollers over the group. "Can y'all stop standing side by side like you're siblings! Michael Raymond the 3rd, you better hold Khloe like you love her!"

When Mike wraps a hand around my waist, drawing me in closer, the circus heightens. My little cousins draw their necks in disgust yelling ew! Mike's aunts and uncles hoot like he'd won a prize trophy.

Since we started dating, I've been accustomed to the microscope people put me and Mike's relationship under. Childhood church friends. Middle school crushes. And now High school sweethearts that have survived all 4 years without a single fight or break up. I'm used to our friends obsessing over our dynamic and labeling us "couple goals," because we rarely fight.

I know us. I'm used to us. Or I thought I did. Cause a few months before graduation everything changed.

"Khloe, honey!" Mike's mom waves her arm wildly as if she isn't a couple of feet away. "I think we've got enough pictures like this! Open your gown! Mike you too!"

We unzip our gowns, revealing my knee length, lacey white dress and mike's military uniform. All the graduates that have already committed to the service wear their uniform under their gown.

"What a good looking couple!" His family amps up.

"Yeah, they are going to have some beautiful children!"

"And that young lady's dress looks awfully similar to a wedding gown! Do I hear church bells in the distance?"

And *there* it is. The newest part of our relationship, the change looming over us since Mike's sudden decision to enroll in the service.

"Oh, hush!" Momma squeaks in the middle of the nonstop camera flashes. "They have plenty of time for that!"

"Of course they do," A voice calls out from behind us. We turn around to the sight of Sargent Lenard, the villain responsible for this circus. Before Mike met him, he'd planned to go to trade school. Open his own plumbing business and even had his eyes on an office suite down the road. That was before Sargent Ken Doll, with his perfect blue eyes and white American boy charm swooped in and ruined everything. I hold my breath, already aware of what's going to come from his stupid mouth and abnormally straight teeth. "They have time, yes. But, they've already been together four years now. The kids obviously like one another. Mike might as well lock things down before he gets deployed."

"Lock down? You make marriage sound like a prison!" Momma jokes, sensing my obvious discomfort. Sargent Lenard flashes his arrogant smile and continues.

"Never a prison! More like 'insurance.' A sure fire way to ensure that Mike and Khloe's lives are protected."

"But—" Momma starts.

"The little lady wants to go to college, right?" He uses the rhetorical question to interrupt her. "Military spouses are eligible for all kinds of benefits."

My neck swivels, desperately looking for someone, anyone to put an end to this shit show.

"That's amazing! The cost of tuition is only rising!" Mike's uncle adds.

"Not to mention the housing market! I wish I could purchase a home with military discounts!" My aunt blabs.

"If it's in God's will." The sound of my dad's voice troubles me the most, deflating any fight I had left. Momma drops her eyes to the floor and hooks her arm into my dad's elbow. As outspoken as she is, she's still a devout Christian woman that wouldn't dare challenge her husband in public.

* * *

I blink away the tears threatening to fall. My body is frozen, studying the stranger in the mirror staring back at me. The itchy up-do my mom considers classy and perfect for the occasion, instead of the Diana Ross unit I wanted. The uncomfortable heels already forming blisters on my ankle. The Cinderella-esque gown Mike's mom insisted I wear. "Only the best for a bride as beautiful as Khloe."

I love Micheal. His family may be pushy, but he's sweet and respectful. He is supportive of my dreams to become a nurse. He's easy-going, never raising his voice to me. Then there's his undeniable looks, wide muscular build, sharp jawline, pearly smile and smooth chocolate skin to seal the deal. I remember those first weeks of freshman year, every girl wanted a piece of Michael Raymond, top quarterback and honor roll student. He'd caught my eye a few times. His intriguing look made him look like he walked straight out of a sports magazine, but I never made a move. I was too shy. I kept to myself, my close group of friends and spent my lunch periods in the school library tearing through the historical romance section. That was until I ran into Mike, literally ran into him. Well, he ran into me. Tripped over me while I was balled up on the floor in front of a bookshelf tucked away in the back of the library.

"My bad!" His eyes twinkled as he helped me up from the floor.

"It's all good. I shouldn't have been sitting in the middle of the aisle like that. Why are you even here—?" The book in his hand catches my attention. A historical romance novel written by one of my favorite authors.

"Are you reading that?" I gesture to his hand.

"What?" His eyes dart around. "Oh, this? Naw, I'm returning it for my... sister."

"You sister, huh?" I smirk. "Well, returns are in the opposite direction from here."

"Yeah, yeah. I knew that." The next few days, I caught him in the library with same book and a different excuse. We'd talk a little here and there. By the end of the month, I learned Mike wasn't trying to return that book and he didn't have a sister. He was an avid historical romance reader, like me.

"Don't you go ruining that makeup!" Mike's mother barges in the dressing room. Don't worry, honey. I had the jitters on my wedding day too. That'll all go away once you say 'I do.' Promise."

"You're right Mrs. Raymond."

"Call me Momma Raymond, now. After today, you'll officially be my daughter. Alright! Ladies, put a pep in your step!" She addresses the bridesmaids in the room. A mix of family members I hadn't seen since I was little, and Mike's uppity cousins. "Go outside, find your groomsmen and line up! We are rolling in five minutes!"

The room vacates in seconds, leaving me alone with my thoughts and my silent mother in the corner of the room. She peers up at me through the mirror.

"Are you sure you want to do this?" She asks one last time.

Mike is a good man. A great man. His family has welcomed me with open arms. This relationship is good. Why wouldn't I wanna do this?

I inhale a shuddering breath and smile.

"Yes."

what happens next?

Pre-Order Book 2 of the Tour series on

EverythingYoe.com

acknowledgments

To my wife, Sheopatra, my first beta reader and greatest supporter. Thank you for holding me down throughout this entire process. Being my sound board, extra brain and grounding spirit when I'm overthinking. Anytime I'm unsure or not feeling the most confident, you're there to remind me of all the greatness I've achieved in this life and all the greatness that is yet to come. I love you with all of my heart.

To my chosen family, my sisters, THECouncil. Sheopatra, Storm, Crystal and Amari— the most animated beta readers I've ever met. With every twist and turn in the book, y'all were quick to text the group chat—like it was a soap opera lol. It was like being a book club but secretly knowing the ending. Amongst our busy lives and blossoming careers, y'all are always willing to take time for my art. I love y'all!

To all of beta readers and early readers, THANK YOU! After spending months alone with my manuscript, it's so refreshing to hear your thoughts! These pages are a mix of fiction and real-life experiences. To receive messages about the ways you all relate to this story makes my heart flutter. Out of all the books in the world, all of the authors out there, you chose to spend your time with my story and I do not take that lightly. Thank you!

Love,
Yoe Apolinario

Yoe Apolinario is a Tampa, Florida native who currently resides in Los Angeles, California. Most of her days are spent working as a professional movement artist, choreographing and dancing. During free time she's usually loving on her wife and pets, or reacquainting herself with one of her first loves, writing.

Keep up with me online!